US TWO

JANET HOGGARTH

Dear Alana
I hope you enjoy the book! Jenk x x x

B
Boldwood

First published in Great Britain in 2023 by Boldwood Books Ltd.

Copyright © Janet Hoggarth, 2023

Cover Design by Alice Moore Design

Cover Photography: Shutterstock and iStock

The moral right of Janet Hoggarth to be identified as the author of this work has been asserted in accordance with the Copyright, Designs and Patents Act 1988.

Every effort has been made to obtain the necessary permissions with reference to copyright material, both illustrative and quoted. We apologise for any omissions in this respect and will be pleased to make the appropriate acknowledgements in any future edition.

A CIP catalogue record for this book is available from the British Library.

Paperback ISBN 978-1-80162-745-0

Large Print ISBN 978-1-80162-746-7

Hardback ISBN 978-1-80162-743-6

Ebook ISBN 978-1-80162-748-1

Kindle ISBN 978-1-80162-747-4

Audio CD ISBN 978-1-80162-739-9

MP3 CD ISBN 978-1-80162-740-5

Digital audio download ISBN 978-1-80162-744-3

Boldwood Books Ltd
23 Bowerdean Street
London SW6 3TN
www.boldwoodbooks.com

To Neil for always supporting my writing. I really could not do it without you! All my love x

Give a woman a fish you feed her for a day. Teach a woman to fish and you feed her for a lifetime...

— OLD CHINESE PROVERB

PROLOGUE

THE LOST EMPORIUM

January 2019, Steyning

Nellie grinned optimistically at Cassie from inside the unkempt outbuilding, partly obscured behind her woeful stablemates – a Subbuteo football table missing half its players (a few headless cohorts held fast), and an exhausted-looking wine fridge. The poor fridge, obviously embarrassed at having fallen so far from grace, appeared to be incubating a Louis Pasteur experimental stab at a Frankenstein fungus. Cassie shivered – she detested mushrooms. How could you trust (let alone Put In Your Mouth) something that grew literally anywhere given the required length of time left undisturbed. She'd found some springing from Ant's neglected football boots in the porch once, their etiolated phallic heads wobbling as she flung the offending things into the front hedge.

Nellie's lights were on the fritz (or was that utterly fritzed?) – one was completely smashed while the other was cracked, reminiscent of a pair of unfortunate NHS spectacles crushed during a playground brawl. Her wipers were also suspended in animation across her mildewed windscreen. This potential purchase made Jeremy Clarkson's midlife crisis look like a sedate trolley dash at Lakeland.

'Mum, are you sure you want to buy it? It's a wreck.' Frank held his face in his hands and sighed.

'That's where you come in...'

'Oh no, I haven't the time to tinker with this.'

'I'm not asking you to do *all* of it. I'll do it.'

Frank's mirth burst its banks.

'I can do it!' she insisted.

'You gonna employ a spirit of a mechanic to help you?'

'Maybe...'

'Seriously, Mum, it's a bloody white elephant. I can see it's a bargain, but these things are money pits unless you refurb the whole thing at once.'

'She *is* a white elephant, except she's yellow and cream and she's called Nellie, so that's settled then.' Cassie wasn't budging.

Frank glanced sideways at his mum. She'd completely lost her pin on the map this time. They were all used to the crazy that had been emanating from her for the past few years. It was far too late to blame the menopause, that had already claimed her marriage (or was that Frank's dad's years of 'extracurricular' activities?). This was another level, suspended on a glittery rainbow bridge with the cumulation of crystals, the spirit guides and the aura cleansing. Not forgetting tarot cards, angel cards, crystal balls and pixie dust. Frank's latter teenage years had been accompanied by a constant stream of people shuffling into the front room after work seeking answers to life's big questions, and occasionally being told that they'd left their garage keys inside the freezer by some deceased relative whom they'd undoubtedly had a grudge against when they'd been alive. Once Cassie had started bringing in decent money, he'd helped her transform the lacklustre shed at the bottom of the garden into her 'office', and clients used the discreet side entrance next to the garage, bypassing the house entirely.

'I bought a Haynes manual on Amazon in preparation,' she reassured him. 'Leo told me to buy it.'

Frank smiled. He was used to Leo's patchy advice from beyond the veil.

'He said you'd help too.' Frank rolled his eyes. Leo had apparently wanted to be the next Jimi Hendrix before he'd died but now was like an annoying teacher at school who always forced you to volunteer for tray clearing in the dinner hall, or litter picking. He really hoped Leo didn't snoop around his flat. What if Frank was taking a shower? Doing a dump? Or, even worse, when Rachel came back after the Plough last Saturday and they'd attempted that gruelling position from *Plane Trains and Shagmobiles*. The windmill, or something? He'd ended up almost putting his back out...

'How did you even know it was here? No, don't tell me, Leo told you...'

Cassie laughed. 'How did you guess?'

With the help of Jezz, the verbose owner of The Lost Emporium, Frank hooked the camper onto the back of his tow truck, leaving the forlorn fridge and football table awaiting their forever homes. The upcycling business could be cruel, according to Jezz. One year the market would be raving about repurposed pallets, maximalism and wheelbarrow garden planters, as well as building frames out of anything, including old cutlery or setting objects, even false teeth, in resin, all for the ubiquitous gallery wall. Then before you knew it, the gallery wall was passé, undressed walls, minimalism and Scandi were back in and wheelbarrows as planters were in the doghouse. It was like the bleeding stock market.

As far as Frank could tell, VW camper vans had always been in vogue, but this yellow one appeared to be particularly buggered, the engine having been stripped out so the previous owners could employ the empty space as a champagne fridge, upgrading its kooky charm as a stationary outdoor room at their seaside bed and breakfast. Nellie had eventually wound her way to The Lost Emporium after the B&B went bust and the house clearance firm moved in like locusts. Thankfully she was rescued by Cassie, or was it Nellie who had really rescued her?

* * *

November 2021, Hailsham

Frank pulled up outside Cassie's Hobbit house. There was no room for him on the drive any more, not with Nellie monopolising all the space. His mum's small garage was barely big enough for a car, let alone the van. The chest freezer hogged the best part of it, crammed with an inordinate amount of food for an imminent apocalypse (no doubt predicted by Leo). Should there ever be a disastrous chicken Kiev shortage, Cassie was well placed to barter for steak and kidney pies or bread flour.

'So, when can you help me with Nellie's insides?' Cassie asked her son as she blew on her cup of tea. They were standing in the narrow galley kitchen, leaning against the rustic cabinets hand-painted in a warm peach tone that popped against the navy-blue walls, a packet of Hobnobs open between them, ready for dunking. 'I need to put a kitchen back in for the Big Trip, I found one on eBay that might be good? Looks like an original and the people said the fridge still works. I could put some disco lights in and have a bar too?'

'Mum, I haven't got any time at the mo. Can't you cope with the camping gas and the deck chairs for now? The bed's still pretty good. Most campsites have facilities...'

Cassie smiled at her only son; he was a decent lad and had worked hard getting his own garage up and running in just over a year. Cassie was used to her family rubbing up against her 'mad' notions. When she'd finally thrown in the teaching towel ten years ago to concentrate on using her 'gift', they'd all thought she was even more deranged than they had previously suspected. Though admittedly they'd eventually choked on their words like errant fish bones because leaving teaching had turned out to be a smart move...

Being a psychic was a bit like being an undertaker – ironically you had a job for life with a bottomless well of lost souls and friends and relatives desperate to reconnect with dead loved ones.

'Whatever makes you happy, doll. Teaching will always be there,' Ant, her husband and fellow teacher, had said at the time, his disingenuous support obvious from the outset. He'd clearly thought she would realise her idiotic mistake and come crawling back from underneath a pile of crystals and ask for her old job back. Not so. Cassie's psychic ability had propelled her towards this calling for years, but it was only once she'd gradually built her client base that she found the confidence to cut herself free from the day job. She had genuinely enjoyed teaching, but over the years it had become all about league tables. Individual pupils and their needs were steamrollered in favour of the homogenous achievement of some schools anointed with an academy status. It had become harder and harder to find everyday joy at Horsham High, newly transformed into one such Academy. Also, one couldn't really be a teacher *and* a renowned psychic – what if she could see future questions in the English GCSE paper? A conflict of interests...

Cassie loved her regular clients and the rapport they had built up, but she also looked forward to the thrill of psychic fairs: meeting new people, helping to solve riddles and offering solace and advice, relaying funny stories, hopefully making someone's day, rekindling hope or offering closure. Every day and every client was unique. She'd felt the need for a professional name to differentiate her from Cassie Higham, the teacher and Ant's wife. Cassandra Galaxy commanded respect and added a sprinkle of glamour, fancier than her prosaic married name. It wasn't until almost four years ago that Cassie cut her final tie to conformity and left Ant. To say he was surprised would be a lie – the ice had been so thin he'd been practically aquaplaning through married life. You can't play around behind someone like Cassie and hope to get away with it for ever. She had a whole battalion of sentries eager to dob him in.

In the end it wasn't Leo, or Precious, or the legion of others that raised the alarm. Cassie had always been well aware of Ant's extracurricular activities, and in a way, it suited her. She was stuck and she knew it, but she also believed an answer would present itself at the right time. As soon as Cassie reacquainted herself with Florence Villiers across a velvet cloth-covered Formica desk at New Moon Psychic Fair in Horsham Assembly Rooms, she knew this was the sign she had been waiting for.

Cassie's phone rang, jangling her away from the past. She answered it, motioning to Frank she wouldn't be a minute. Unfortunately, she was going to be more than a minute. It was the hospital. As the colour drained from her face, Frank would later wonder why his mum hadn't seen this coming...

1

AN INHERITANCE

March 2023, Felworth

Florence attempted to reread the letter. It was from a lawyers' office in Horsham informing her about an 'inheritance': a camper van bequeathed by a Ms Cassandra Galaxy, formerly Higham. She'd had an eccentric schoolteacher called Mrs Higham (surely not the same person?); she briefly tried to picture her, but her image remained indistinct like a character in a book, just an overwhelming essence of wild hair and gold hoop earrings. However, she fondly remembered Mrs Higham's termly treasure hunts, bite-sized treats dotted all over school making more of an impression than her face. Why would she leave Florence a camper van? Her mum, Edie, peered over her shoulder, snapping her back to the kitchen, her breath warming the back of her neck.

'Oi, privacy!'

'You forwent privacy when you never moved out,' Edie loftily retorted.

'At least have some boundaries.'

Edie laughed and started filling the kettle from the tap, sloshing it over the rim and into the sink, accidentally spraying her top. 'Better not let your dad see this wet T-shirt, might have a heart attack.'

Disgusted, Florence pulled a face. Why couldn't they tone it down; no one relishes the idea of their parents having sex. It was completely unnatural and set bile creeping up her throat. Sadly, poor Florence was subjected to more than the mere thought and occasional lewd comment – her parents were worse than politicians at a swingers party. She was forced to wear night-time ear plugs to block out the squeaking bed springs that mortifyingly leaked between the weak plasterboard walls and into her consciousness.

She forced herself to refocus on the letter; the first day's jet lag curiously spinning her out this time round. Maybe getting older made bouncing back a bit more arduous, though almost thirty-six was hardly prehistoric. Why did the name Cassandra Galaxy ring a bell? This was obviously one of those scams prompting you to ring the number provided while somehow the criminals hoovered out your bank account distracting you with chat about a camper van. Of all the things they were trying to scam her with, a bloody camper van. She could sell it, she supposed, if it was real, which it wasn't. She folded up the letter and rammed it on top of the bread bin along with all the other post that had piled up in the five months since she'd been in Sri Lanka. There were three other letters exactly the same, posted three weeks apart.

'You got quite a bit of post for someone who's only here for four months at a time tops,' Edie said, eyeing her daughter carefully. 'Those legal letters want replying to, they look real to me.'

'Did you read them?' Edie bit her lip the way people do when they've been sitting on a plump secret. Florence riffled through the envelopes and flicked out the other three, unearthing a tea-ringed one she had missed. On closer inspection she could see a faint rip where it must have been steamed open and glued back together. 'Mum!'

'I had to. What if you had an escalating fine or something?'

'But it's MY post. I've told you before not to open my post!'

'You left it here at your own risk...' Edie clicked the kettle and rummaged in the tea caddy for two tea bags, relieved they could talk about the letters. 'Tea?'

'Fucksake. Yes please.'

'You gonna ring the number then?'

'No.'

'But you've won a camper van! I know it's questionable but the least you could do is see if it's real?'

'I didn't "win" it, it's not a game show. And it isn't real. If it was, it would be here by now. They'd have found a way of delivering it if it was *that* urgent. Which it isn't because it doesn't exist. I bet that legal practice isn't even real.'

'It is. I googled it. And that Cassandra woman, you met her once. I took you to see her in Horsham, remember? A psychic, a year after—'

'OK,' Florence interjected. 'I remember, vaguely.'

'I wonder why she left you a camper van? Unless I mean, she must have known... Though you did run off before she could finish her reading. Did you talk about—?'

'Mum, no. *Please*...'

'Very odd though, no kids of her own? These vans are worth something if they're in good condition. I wonder what you said to her that made her remember you all these years later?'

'I don't know, Mum, it was so long ago ago...' But Florence could remember patches of conversation, and the gentle brush of

Cassandra's hand as she had offered a whisper of sympathy...
'What kind of person leaves a stranger a van in their will?'

'Might come in handy.'

'Why? According to Dad everyone always ends up selling
them. He used to say that about— Anyway, there's no way I'm
driving one again... I'm never here, as you pointed out.' She
screwed up her face, thinking. 'I suppose *you* could sell it for me if
I don't manage to while I'm away...'

'Yes, well, that's something your dad and I need to talk about
with you...'

At the mention of his name, Gareth cleared his throat. He delicately stepped into the kitchen, curious for a six-foot-four man
quite possibly one gene removed from a polar bear. Apparently,
when Dad was born, the doctors had declared him an albino.
Florence initially believed albinos had pink eyes, like those
rabbits, but that was a myth. Her dad had been bullied merci-
lessly at school and had prayed that when Edie fell pregnant that
whomever came out wouldn't be tarred with the same affliction.
Florence loved that her dad was distinctive in a pack of dads; she
could always spot him on Sports Day a shoulder above everyone
else, his gleaming thatch of angelic white hair the envy of all the
mums. Had he been lurking behind her the entire time? Florence
fidgeted, bookended between her parents as the kettle bubbled its
way to a watery climax. This felt suspiciously like an ambush.

'Florence, love, you know I'm retiring this year...' her dad said.
She nodded. 'Well, I want to sell the garage and begin my boat-
building course...'

'That sounds amazing, when does that start?'

He smiled, happy to talk about his new passion. 'Well, I'm—'

'No, Gareth, keep to the main point,' Edie butted in gently.

'Mum, let him speak!'

'Actually, we want to relocate,' her dad admitted.

'Oh, OK. When's this happening?'

'The house is on the market now,' Edie explained. 'Spring and summer are the best times to sell according to Alexa.' Her parents were influenced far too much by Alexa, their digital PA, an oddity in older people as far as Florence could tell. Alexa was the closest to a deity her parents had and they worshipped at her altar (next to the microwave) every day. Her mum even asked if she wanted a cup of tea each morning. 'Well, it's polite to ask, she does so much for us, and you know, when there's the rise of the machines, we want to make sure we're on the good list, so we don't get nuked, or whatever they decide to do...' Next they'd be asking Alexa what was the maximal position for multiple orgasms. Florence swallowed the fleck of sick in her throat.

'So, have you got a buyer?' Florence looked round the kitchen in faint disbelief. She was surprised anyone would want the place. Its three bedrooms pushed the boundaries of truth – her younger sister's bedroom was a walk-in coffin. Lennie's bed had been so miniscule she'd suffered curvature of the spine growing up. She rarely opened the door, the room was so Jenga'd up to the ceiling with the overflow from Florence's actual room next door. Goodness knows how they had shown prospective buyers around.

'We had a buyer but it fell through. No one since. The estate agent suggested putting your stuff into storage, make the house feel more of a possibility for a family.' Edie smiled encouragingly to Gareth.

'Storage costs a bomb though,' Florence griped.

'Yes, love, it does,' Gareth sympathised. 'Which is why we want you to pay for it. It's your stuff.'

'But I won't be able to afford to go away for ages if I'm paying you rent and food as well as storage. Can't we just ram it all in the garage until it's time to move? It'll fit in there with all the other crap, won't it?' Her dad shook his head, but Florence wasn't ready to throw in the towel. 'Where will you move to? Abroad?' she asked hopefully.

'OK, Florence, I think what your dad is trying to say is that we're moving to the seaside—' Florence executed a solo Mexican wave for one in appreciation. 'But we're downsizing.'

'Downsizing?'

'Yes. There won't be room for you.'

'But I'm never here.'

'All your stuff is.'

'Can't you just take it and put it in my room?'

'There won't be a "your" room,' Edie persisted.

'So where am I supposed to keep all my stuff when I'm away? Where will I stay when I come back? I can't stay with you?' Her mum and dad eyed each other over the top of her head like they used to during one of her epic childhood tantrums.

'We want to know that the house is just for us,' Edie asserted.

'So Lennie and I can't even visit?'

'Yes, of course you can visit. It just won't be your actual home any more.'

Florence sat down heavily on a kitchen chair and automatically rammed a digestive biscuit in her mouth from the open packet on the table. She had missed them in Sri Lanka.

'You're almost thirty-six, Flo,' Edie explained. 'It's about time you stood on your own two feet.'

'I do stand on my feet.' As if to make a point she jumped up, knocking the biscuits flying.

'You know what your mum means,' Good Cop said, bending over and rescuing the digestives. 'You need to finally fly the nest instead of being a boomerang kid. Set down some roots. Or stay abroad if that's what you want – get a job, permanently, or temp, do whatever, but find a base, somewhere that's yours. A house share? No one's dictating what you should do, just that we want to have our retirement on our terms, in our new home by the sea where you can visit us from your life, and maybe invite us to your house for dinner or whatever. Like a grown-up.'

'Yes, Dad, I get it. I just like living in the moment. Roots tie you down. Stop you seeing the world, expanding your mind.' Florence ignored the joint set of raised eyebrows.

'Well, whatever you decide, your stuff has to go in the next few days. I know it's short notice, but we have some viewings at the weekend, and your mum wants to get it all looking shipshape. I don't know why you have half of it anyway, if you're never going to set down any roots...'

But before Florence could slap down a snarky reply, the doorbell rang.

'Who the hell's that? We're not expecting anyone at this time of night! I never ordered anything off Alexa...' It was five in the afternoon. Florence rolled her eyes. Her mum hated surprises. She couldn't eat Revels in case she fell afoul of the sneaky orange one.

'I'll get it. Maybe it's Alexa come to finally meet her biggest clients. Better put the kettle back on!'

Florence approached the frosted glass panelled front door playing the usual game of guess the person. They were tall, probably a man she deduced heaving it open.

'Hello, I'm looking for Florence Villiers.' He'd raised his eyebrows in anticipation of it being her.

'Yeah? Who wants to know?'

'Oh, sorry, yes, I'm kind of here on behalf of Wentworth's Solicitors. I believe you've been sent letters about a camper van?'

'You're a solicitor?' Florence asked incredulously, appraising his attire: grease-stained jeans, heavy work boots, black bomber jacket and a monogrammed polo shirt sporting a frayed hem on one side. If she yanked it, would his entire top unravel from the bottom up like a roller blind?

'No, no, they asked me to attempt to deliver the van. There's no room to store it now Mum's house has sold.'

'*You*'re Cassandra's son?'

'Yes, Frank, how do you do?' He smiled at her, his eyes creasing in faint amusement.

Flo's parents joined her at the door on hearing voices.

'What's going on, Flo?' Gareth asked. 'This a friend of yours?'

'No, it's Cassandra's son delivering the camper van. It's real.'

'I know it's inconvenient, but the letters went unanswered,' Frank awkwardly explained. 'I was just moving the van anyway because the new people moved into Mum's house and you don't live that far from her... Thought I would just chance my arm; we had no telephone number for you.'

'Yes, we're ex-directory to avoid those call centre menaces. So sorry about your mum,' Edie said gravely. 'We met her once, years ago when—'

'Mum! I'm sure Frank doesn't want to hear about that.'

'No, I would. Mum never really let on why she wanted the van to go to you. She just kept saying you needed it, that Nellie would help in some way. Does any of that make sense to you?'

'No,' Florence replied, not convinced by his well-rehearsed reply. He knew all right.

'Oh, well one thing she did mention was that you used to be an ex-pupil of hers.'

'She *was* the same person!' Florence cried, emotively pressing her hand on her heart. 'Mrs Higham. She taught English; I used to love her. I'm so sorry, she was very special...' Frank nodded, pressing his lips together.

'I just remember her as Cassandra Galaxy, the psychic,' Edie said. 'She was ever so accurate. Told Jayne at work that she'd run into some money. She crashed into a Securicor van the next day while they were parked outside the bank collecting cash bags.'

'I can't believe she was also Cassandra Galaxy,' Florence reflected. 'She never mentioned she used to teach me when we saw her. Though it was a good fifteen years since I'd left school. I wouldn't have recognised her.' Especially because at the time she'd been unable to identify her own face in the mirror...

'Mum liked to keep her teaching career well and truly in the past,' Frank admitted. 'If you're not expecting it to be her then you wouldn't have realised they were the same person.'

'Am I allowed to say no to the... inheritance?' Florence asked cagily.

'Yes, of course,' Frank said, obviously expecting this kind of reaction, his face betraying nothing. 'I did say to Mum you might not want the van.'

'What did she say?' Edie asked, interested.

'Mum thought you'd accept and stick it out, not sell her. I wouldn't blame you if you did though...'

'Did she...?' Edie said eyeing Florence judiciously.

They all took a moment to reflect while Frank rooted around inside his jacket, extracting a letter.

'She wrote this to explain. I haven't read it, and she didn't want it posting. I was instructed to deliver it in person whatever happened with the van. She made a right meal of insisting that would make sense to you.' He handed it to Florence who turned it over in her palm, shaking her head at his enigmatic explanation. The weighty cream paper was obviously part of a fancy writing set. A wax seal embossed over the lip – a rococo heart cradling CG in a classical Roman style font – ensured its contents remained private.

'So this van, roadworthy, is it? Did you drive it here?' Gareth asked.

'Yes, it's parked on the road a few cars down. Hard to get parking round here, isn't it?'

'Tell me about it,' Gareth moaned. 'Ever since they built those luxury homes on the station car park everyone blocks the roads round here instead. They should introduce permits, but they won't...'

'Do you want to come and see Nellie?' Frank made a move to walk back down the garden path.

'It's not green, is it?' Florence wavered. He could keep his bloody van if it was. Maybe he could keep it anyway, she didn't need it in her life... Edie and Gareth exchanged anxious glances.

'No, Nellie's yellow, a split screen. She'd been off-road for ever until Mum found her. At least ten years, and before that, apparently, she'd been rescued from a wrecker's yard. She was born again when Mum bought her.' Frank's face clouded over as if recalling something meaningful before he wandered towards the gate, jangling the keys in his hand. 'She's not perfect, Mum ran out of money and time in the end, she's still got rust here and there and the inside needs a lot of work, but you can stay overnight in her; she's right-hand drive too.'

Buoyed up by the news the van was yellow, Flo decided to inspect her. They approached Nellie parked outside Mr Ogby's house, who would undoubtedly be twitching those curtains. Oh yes, there he was, rearranging something on his window ledge while justifying his self-imposed title: Neighbourhood Watch Leader. Florence wondered what the worst crime was he'd ever reported. He should look in the mirror, his lopsided toupee was a crime against hair. At least wear one with some silver flecked in it. What seventy-year-old had a full head of brown hair when the whole village knew he used to be ginger?

Florence released a sigh of relief, unaware she'd been holding her breath. Nellie's sparkling chrome bumper practically smiled at her and despite her palpable reservations, Florence smiled back. She would be able to get quite a bit of cash for her, fund her next trip, possibly Costa Rica, the pinnacle of her wish list, and maybe even pop anything left over in an ISA. She'd need the money one day, when she… Florence jumped as Frank slid open the side door, the recognisable sound threatening to spin her off her axis.

'Oh, she's a beauty!' Gareth exclaimed, stroking her left-wing mirror like it was a horse offering up its nose for a pat. The camper van's lemon-yellow and cream exterior glowed from an obvious polish, the cream dovetailing down the front of the van to kiss the bumper, slicing through the sharp yellow like cake frosting. Florence reticently poked her head inside the door to find homemade pink and yellow gingham curtains hanging alongside each window adding sweet-shop colour to the rudimentary interior. Sagging leather beige and brown striped back seats had been patched in places but Frank assured her they still managed to fold out into a small double bed, while the oak-effect laminate floor had peeled away from the edges. The original miniature kitchen had long been torn out, with the flooring running up the sides to insulate the interior held in place by new chrome trim which somehow further shamed the shabby laminate. There was space for another seat and folded on the floor were two bright orange and red striped camping chairs. Cassie had made matching gingham scatter cushions but they couldn't divert attention away from rust patches on the rear window frames and the undeniable fact that the interior needed ripping out.

'How's her engine? Anything we need to know about?' her dad asked, motioning to poke around in the boot. Frank opened it for him and her dad bent down to inspect.

'You could probably do with keeping an eye on her coolant. Her fan belt is also at the end of its life, but I have a spare ready

– you just need to get someone to fit it. I've been so busy with work and sorting out Mum's stuff that I've just not had time. Sorry.'

'Don't apologise,' Florence said, embarrassed. 'Are you sure your mum wouldn't want *you* to keep Nellie?'

Frank laughed. 'Mum knew that was the last thing I'd want. These camper vans can be temperamental unless everything's overhauled at once, which Mum didn't do.'

'You can say that again,' Gareth added. 'When Florence had one of these before, it was a bleeding nightmare. Though it wasn't in as good condition as Nellie...'

'Dad!' Florence hissed, a fierce flush exploding across her cheeks. Gareth clamped his lips together, shamefaced.

Frank was either oblivious to the tension, or had decided to ignore it. 'You used to have a VW van?' he asked in surprise.

Florence hesitated while her parents studied the floor. 'Yes, and no. It wasn't technically mine, it was... a friend's.'

'Oh, OK. So you're familiar with them?' Florence nodded. 'Do you want to have a go?'

Florence almost backed into her dad. 'No, I'm good thanks.'

'Do you have somewhere to keep her?'

Florence shook her head. Their small drive was already taken up by two cars. She felt like she was adopting a cat knowing she was severely allergic. She wouldn't have her for long though if she found the right website, maybe eBay? She would start searching later.

Florence eyed Frank. 'Sorry I never replied to the letters. I've been away for five months, got back last night. I've only just opened all my post. I thought the letters were a hoax. How did the solicitors know where to find me?'

'They're lawyers – they have special powers...' He smirked at her. 'As does—*did* Mum...'

'The electoral roll probably,' Edie enlightened them. 'You're still registered here.'

'If you have any issues, or you need to ask me anything, here's my number.' He handed Florence a white card embossed with his business logo and all the various social media outlets, the garage landline, as well as a mobile number and email address. 'I'll register Nellie in your name online, if you can just email me all your details. She has a full tank of petrol. There's a camping stove in the cupboard under the bed too if you're feeling adventurous.'

'Do you at least want to come in for a cuppa before you go?' Edie asked. 'I might have a panettone left over from Christmas we could open?' She looked hopeful. 'An early Easter treat?' Like Christ's rebirth would swing it.

He appeared to be thoughtfully considering it, am-dramming it up. It was just for show because he replied, 'That's very kind, Mrs Villiers, but I need to get back. My train's in ten minutes and I don't want to miss it.'

'Let us get you an Uber home,' Gareth said, like the silver-tongued host he pictured himself as. Florence didn't even think her dad had ever uttered the word 'Uber' in his life. In fact, she remembered from last time she was home, Uber didn't exist in Felworth. There was the station, which in itself was curious because Felworth only had the two pubs and the two convenience shops, a church, plus the undertaker's. Why did it need a station? Felworth wasn't exactly a bubbling hub of activity with a generous population. But the station had set itself up as a crucial selling point, actually listed as a bonus to country life in her parents' house's particulars on Rightmove, as Florence would later discover. Apart from the station and three buses a day, Greyhound cabs near Hailsham was the best travel option or dodgy Saul whose Datsun Sunny was always parked up behind the Hope and Anchor. However, it was always debatable whether he was scraping just under the legal limit to drive. The only way you could tell was to ask him to breathe on you, but no one wanted that, so people just tended to risk their lives, or walk the three million miles to civilisation after the buses and trains had stopped running. All this passed through Flo's mind before anyone spoke.

'I'm OK getting the train,' Frank insisted. 'Thanks though.'

'It feels wrong just waving you off. Let me at least give you a lift to the station,' Edie offered.

'I'll walk. It's fine. Please, don't worry about me. I need some fresh air and it's a lovely evening.' It wasn't. It looked like the sky was about to vomit forth hail and brimstone, but they all pretended it was like a storybook evening with swallows zooming round the sun-dappled sky like harmless kamikazes.

'Right you are,' Gareth said. 'Thank you for dropping by. And Florence will email you everything, won't you, Flo?' Flo was busy staring at the van, wondering how the hell everything had just turned upside down in less than half an hour. When she failed to agree, her dad barked her name. 'Florence!'

'What?' Gareth nodded towards Frank who was trying hard to restrain a smile threatening to overtake his mouth.

'You'll email Frank your particulars...'

'Yes, thanks. I will. Thank you so much for this. I really am so sorry about your mum. She was a brilliant teacher. I hated the English syllabus but she actually made it fun. I remember her raging on about all the white old men that we had to read in order to pass our exams and she would get us interested in other books by women and black writers. She made reading accessible to those who didn't connect.'

'That's lovely to hear, thank you. I'll await your email...' Frank waved them goodbye and headed off in the direction of the station. They stood watching, and when he took a wrong turn at the fork down the bottom, Gareth shouted: 'It's right!' He corrected himself then was gone.

'You gonna open the letter?' Edie asked, peering at it in Florence's hand.

'Not in front of you. Good job it has a seal,' Florence scoffed. 'No breaking and entering!'

Upstairs behind the closed bedroom door, Florence slid a biro in the corner of the envelope and stabbed at it to get some purchase before it yielded; the paper was deluxe quality. No wonder posh people used special letter knives. She unfolded it then rubbed it flat on the floor where she sat, back propped against her bed.

Dear Florence

You probably won't remember me – you were otherwise distracted by recent events, but you made quite an impression on me. I taught you English at Horsham High a long time ago – Mrs Higham. You and your friend Rowena were quite the double act. Your friendship reminded me so much of one special friend from my past. Tracey and I did everything together just like you and Rowena. I don't know if you can recall, but I was called Cassandra Galaxy at that psychic fair you visited with your mum. It had been quite a few years since I had last seen you, but I remembered your face, and of course, my guide told me who you were. I had unconsciously been carrying the weight of my own grief for years when I bumped into you again. I lost touch with Tracey and I don't think I ever truly recovered. Seeing you again rekindled memories of when a man had also wedged himself between us, just like you and Rowena, splitting us apart. I can still recall the weight of your grief for the man and for Rowena. The tarot cards and my guide predicted you were about to embark on a lengthy journey before finally realising your truth. This substantially mirrored my own life – I had also been running from my past, of who I really was. The awakening was profound on my part.

I felt compelled to leave you my camper van as my final act. I won't explain my illness, it's boring, and yes, I should have seen it coming. However, this is where the van comes in – my guides told me the van would be the key to a new door for you after I had finished with it. If I can do one thing before I pass, it is to hand back the gift you unwittingly gave me when I saw you in Horsham – transformation. I left my husband in the weeks after I saw you. The fallout was awful and moving on from that took some time, financially and emotionally. You see, I'd wanted to find Tracey, apologise, but only once I was in the right place. I wanted to do it in person during a silver-haired gap year, travelling the country in Nellie. Sadly, the gap year never happened, I became too ill. I wasn't sure what I was going to say to her turning up after all these years. We had studied together at teacher training college in Altrincham many moons ago, and those days had been some of the happiest of my life, when I had been truly myself. I let it all go to fit myself into the square peg I wasn't built for. These days things would probably be different.

Anyway, enough of my waffle. I hope Nellie brings you the joy she brought me – she saved me during my divorce. I used to drive to the sea to sit with an early morning coffee and watch the sun rise, keep things in perspective, look at something bigger than the problem. Try that, try anything to get back behind the wheel, find that inner and outer freedom again. Running serves a purpose for a while then eventually everything catches up with you. I don't think Nellie was ever meant to be solely for me, please give her a chance, she has a way of *opening people up. Be well, stay curious and more than anything, always be yourself.*

'Because everyone else is taken,' Florence muttered, Rowena's laughing face flashing across the back of her mind like a slap. It had been one of her favourite sayings.

With fondest regards.
    Cassie. x

Florence lay the letter on her outstretched legs. The words hadn't really sunk in because she was trying so hard to remember exactly what Cassie had said at the time. She was still flabbergasted that she had also been her school English teacher and that she hadn't even noticed. How had she not noticed? *Because the mind sees what it wants to.*

* * *

Hey, Flo. You back now? I got news. Wanna hook up?

Yep, your place?

No. The Hope? Need a pint.

'Mum, Dad, I'm going out.'

'We haven't talked about you moving your stuff yet,' Gareth reminded Flo as she jumped down from the kitchen stool where she'd been absently peering through the hatch watching *The One Show*. A childhood memory intercepted her. Lennie pretending to be a customer in their café while she 'cooked' cold baked beans in the kitchen, shoving them through the hatch to the waitress, usually Rowena from next door, occasionally Nana...

'I'll sort everything tomorrow, I promise,' she called through the hatch. 'Nellie can take everything to charity or storage...'

Both her parents whipped their heads away from the TV. 'Are you sure that's wise, love?' her mum said frowning. 'I don't want you jumping into something that might overwhelm you. Driving Nellie might, you know...'

'You just said I had to stand on my own two feet!' she retorted. 'And clearing out my crap means I have to take the stuff somewhere.'

'Pile it up and I can take it to the tip in my van,' her dad said.

'Dad!'

Edie hit her husband at the same time. 'Gareth, it's not going to the tip! Flo just needs to go through it. She might want to keep some of it...'

Florence grabbed her puffa jacket from the wooden coat stand next to the front door and stepped out into the cold night air before her dad could offer a clumsy apology.

Years had passed (which now felt like centuries) since she'd looked at that stuff her parents wanted in storage. Maybe Dad was right, why was she holding on to it? Anyway, she could forget about everything for a few hours. Have uncomplicated sex with Tariq; friends with benefits. *School* friends with benefits – she and Tariq had history as far back as Maths club. They'd both been struggling in Year Ten and Mr Fentiman had suggested extra lessons at lunch. She'd expressed surprise at Tariq's attendance. He shot her down of course: 'That's racist – assuming all Asian kids are good at maths.' She'd stuttered that it wasn't what she meant when it clearly had been. He forgave her when she offered him a whole packet of banana Hubba Bubba and let him copy her homework. They remained friends after school and one bodged attempt at uni, but then lost touch. He was now a heating engineer for British Gas, but before that had been a private detective for his uncle. 'Bloody hell, Flo, it wasn't like that!' he'd laughed when she'd asked if he'd ever discovered a dead body when tracking a missing person or cracked a cold case that had stumped the police. 'It was all benefit fraudsters and divorcees trying to uncover hidden assets. I got sick of sitting in fields or crouching in bushes with a long lens camera waiting for the subject to appear and give the game away. Being a gas engineer is more reliable, and I was always good at tinkering with machinery and whatnot.' Tariq found odd pockets of time in between shifts when he could squeeze in a quickie and he owned his own flat, which was handy – Florence couldn't very well bring him back home.

She arrived at the pub and spotted him at a table by the fruit machines wearing a black baseball cap pulled right over his face.

'Hey.' She bent down to kiss him, but he threw his arms up to stop her.

'Sorry, just don't want anyone seeing.'

'God! OK. We can leave and go back to yours if you want?'

'No, sit down.' She did as she was told. He glanced at her from under his cap and looked away immediately. He had a remaining half a pint and he suddenly necked it. 'How was Sri Lanka? Did you have a great time?'

'I did, but what's going on?!'

Curiously Tariq appeared to be wrestling with an invisible opponent. He wasn't a complicated man, his emotions and thoughts usually drifted just below the surface and he toed the line in almost every aspect of his life. The only thing that felt vaguely rebellious was drinking pints and the occasional tot of Baileys. Being Muslim went hand in hand with being teetotal, or so his parents thought. Flo suspected she was also a secret, but was OK with that. As long as they were both single, they had agreed to free flow. Their clandestine arrangement had been ticking over for around two years, ever since he'd pitched up at her parents' to fix the boiler when she just happened to be home from her travels. He'd uncharacteristically flirted when her mum had left the kitchen and Flo had boldly asked him for a drink, their schooldays acting as a safety blanket.

'Look, I didn't want to text you while you were away...' Tariq squirmed. 'I've met someone.'

Florence wished she had gone to the bar and bought herself a red wine.

'Oh, I'm so happy for you. What's she like?' She wasn't happy at all, she was raging. She'd been looking forward to a proper shag, it had been a while.

'She's, er, same age as me, an accountant. Aunty set me up.'

'Set you up? I thought you never wanted one of those set-up arrangements.'

He shrugged. 'This is different. It's serious.'

'Oh.'

'Actually, sorry, I'm engaged.'

Florence jumped up. 'Do you want a drink? I'm getting one.'

'Did you hear me?'

'Yes, I'm processing. Drink?'

'Pint. Thanks.'

Hands shaking, Flo strode to the bar avoiding full eye contact with Scott, the barman, who still hadn't made it to the University of Leeds by the look of it, ordered a shot of tequila, a large Shiraz and a pint. This day was rapidly going downhill and she'd only been back in the UK twenty-seven hours. She necked the tequila before sitting opposite Tariq.

'Can I be bridesmaid?'

2

GLAD TO BE HOME

'I still can't believe they're just upping and pissing off to the seaside?' Lennie spat down the phone. 'Like they don't have a care in the world.'

'They don't, Lennie. Dad's retiring and Mum's reducing her hours until she retires.'

'But what about babysitting the grandkids when we're at work. What about feeding the cat when I'm on holiday? Who's gonna do all that?'

'Stop being dramatic, you don't even have any kids or a cat!'

'But I will, one day. And I'm gonna be screwed cos no one will be there to look after them.'

'You will, it's your job!'

'What? Twenty-four seven? No breaks?'

Sometimes Florence found it tricky to differentiate between Lennie role-playing for kicks or if that was how her brain actually functioned. 'Them's the rules. Why do you think I don't have any dependents?'

'FFS.' Lennie was fond of acronyms and abbreviations. Flo

wondered what she did with all the spare time she saved utilising them. Maybe that was the secret to how she managed to shoehorn Instagram into every corner of her life in a mediocre attempt at becoming some kind of influencer. Lennie inhaled hard on her vape down the phone, probably coconut and vanilla flavour wafting over her tongue. Vaping seemed as pointless as potpourri to Florence, the sickly smell reminding her of cheap Impulse body spray without the fey promise of day-long freshness. Florence shook her head at her younger sister's pathological self-absorption. Lennie was the axis that they all revolved around, according to Lennie. Especially now she was engaged. 'How'll Mum help with the wedding if she's living miles away? How'll she do all the MOB (mother of the bride) shit?'

'Lennie! She'll probably move nearer to you in Lancing . Anyway, you're not getting married for two years. Put a sock in it.'

'Sorry, yes, you were saying, Tariq's getting married?' That was the thing with Lennie, you could tell her to shut it and she obeyed. However, if anyone took a pop at her favourite people, their God better have mercy on their soul. Lennie was as loyal as a pit bull, ripping would-be offenders inside out with her verbal jousting, leaving them flayed open scraping their splattered ego off the floor.

Florence had walked back from the Hope an hour after she'd met Tariq, ringing Lennie at the same time. There seemed no point lingering if sex was out of the question. It was also rather dispiriting with Tariq eyeballing the door every five seconds terri-fied Shani, his accountant fiancée, was about to find him out.

'Do you still want to be friends now the benefits part's redun-dant?' Florence had asked earlier in the pub. 'Are you allowed?'

'I can do whatever I want!' Tariq had blustered overconfi-dently, cracking his knuckles. 'Be happy for me, Flo. I've wanted this for ages. Family, kids, house, a little dog... It's my dream.'

'Why didn't you ever say?'

'Because I knew it wasn't yours. We didn't have those sorts of conversations, did we?'

'I might want those things, one day.' He shook his head and smiled, boldly grabbing her hand briefly, before fear got the better of him. 'I *am* happy for you, I said I was, didn't I?' Maybe it was for the best. She hoped they would at least remain meme pals. He was the only person apart from Lennie who communicated mostly in memes mined from Instagram. Almost any situation or emotion on the planet could be encapsulated in a meme. Florence was a huge fan of the medieval ones – people being brutally beheaded in a marketing meeting, or women violently knifing a well-deserving victim. A picture tells a thousand words, or two hundred and eighty characters if you were on Twitter... Florence was better on her own anyway.

'And you're OK with the marriage thing?' Lennie probed further as Flo reached the station, just round the corner from home.

'Yeah, I'll get over it.' Florence sighed down the phone, still slightly miffed. 'He's getting married in September.'

'FFS, that's quick! How can you plan something so soon? I've broken out in hives thinking about it.' Lennie had a PhD in procrastination. Legend told that the doctor had resorted to a Ventouse delivery with Lennie and that the subsequent birth had ended up a bloodbath version of the 'Hokey Cokey', Lennie unable to agree if she wanted to stay in, or come out, in out, in out, shake it all about. Asking her to decide about anything (chocolate or mint choc chip ice cream, Lurpak or own brand butter) was like waiting for a prevaricating chess master to slide a rook into checkmate. When visiting a restaurant, it was impera-tive that Lennie chose her meal at least a whole week before on the website, and selected a backup option should it be 'off' that night, plus a double backup, just in case. She was barred from deviating.

'Not everyone's like you,' Florence conceded. 'I think they just want to get married and start life. Apparently time is ticking and Shani's ovaries are limping towards some kind of baby apocalypse.' Florence wondered what was happening to *her* ovaries. She envisaged two prunes suspended inside her, squeezing out the occasional egg of dubious quality, teetering on the brink of retirement. It was ridiculous that women had to heft a womb, ovaries and fallopian tubes around inside them until they died, unless they had a hysterectomy. What happened to internal organs when they weren't required any more? Could they just opt to shrivel up, become absorbed by the liver or the pancreas? *Come over here, ovaries, this part of the abdominal cavity is particularly fleshy, lots of nice pillowy tissue to bed down on, have a good old snooze.*

If Lennie had a degree in dithering, Florence had a masters in elaborate internal dialogue. She specialised in off the wall purple sky thinking that would have been more admissible in the head of someone tripping their tits off in a shaman's hut. There had only ever been two people in the entire world that appreciated her same skewed take on life, one of them had ghosted her and the other one was AWOL.

Night had now properly fallen and the stars were masked by a bank of invisible cloud. Florence had reached Nellie parked under a streetlight and bid Lennie goodbye, never once mentioning she had just inherited a camper van. At a supposedly grown-up thirty-three, Lennie could still not be trusted to play by the rules and therefore might bring up the past. The sisters remained in regular contact, but they weren't best friends. Florence loved Lennie, it was expected as her older sister, but their time together sometimes felt like an uphill hike. Si deserved an MBE, like those saintly community leaders who've sacrificed so much time for a cause close to their heart. Her parents had breathed a united sigh of relief when Si had proposed – an alternate ending would have meant the whole dating debacle subsuming everyone's lives once more. No one wanted that... If anyone, apart from Tariq, was a prime candidate for an arranged marriage, it was Lennie. Yet Simon loved her in spite of her peccadillos. Or maybe because of them.

Florence peered through Nellie's gleaming windows, the streetlight casting an amber glow over the steering wheel. Some minor pimping was required inside before she listed it for sale. She'd googled VW split screen prices earlier and had promptly choked on her tea until it had squirted out of her nostrils while she spat the mouthful back in the mug. A VW in tip-top condition could sell for up to a hundred and thirty thousand pounds! That was a life-changing amount of cash. Of course those vans had the classic roof extensions, a full working kitchen, tasteful leather interior with flash trim, a new chassis and spotless brand new engine as well as walnut dashboards and only four thousand miles on the clock. One fancy van had a wine fridge, disco lights and a bar. Poor Nellie was rather scruffy by comparison. She looked at other 1964 VWs in a relatively similar condition and they ranged from fifteen to thirty thousand pounds. Dad would know how much to list her for, or he could find out – he knew so many car people.

As much as Florence had loved her old schoolteacher, Florence refused to buy into her self-proclaimed clairvoyance. Mrs Higham could have heard all about Florence's life via another source. These days, very little was off grid unless you deliberately scorned a digital footprint. How had her mum got sucked into believing? Psychics and mediums were no more real to her than religion. If you couldn't smell it, taste it, feel or see it, it wasn't tangible according to Florence. When you died, that was it, end of. *Aha, but what if it wasn't the end? Energy has to go somewhere – that's simple science...* The problem with Florence's brain was that a debate was never off the agenda because squatting inside her head was her diametric opposite, her devil's advocate.

She left Nellie and headed to her parents' house. That boxy, terraced fifties modern semi was the one constant in her life. She and Lennie had enjoyed a happy childhood inside those four walls with two parents who had loved them and each other, which in itself was a rarity – a fair few of her friends' parents' marriages had since collapsed. Next door, Ro's mum and dad had separated just after she'd turned twelve, leaving Denise heartbroken and Ro balancing on the edge of rebellion, swilling with teenage hormones and brewing hostility towards all men. She'd thought about Rowena twice in less than five hours. She *never* thought about her when she was travelling, too many bright shiny things to engage with.

Florence turned the key in the front door and walked into the hallway hoping to watch some inane telly before bed. That was one of the few things she missed – crap telly, and decent tea bags, though that hadn't been that problem in Sri Lanka, tea capital of the world. Freshly brewed leaf tea was a luxury now she was home; Tetley had been ruined for eternity. She swung open the door to the front room where her parents were engaged in what could only be described as a quickie on the sofa.

'Argh! Get a room!' Florence swiftly retreated, changing direction towards the kitchen. Spotting the open red wine on the counter, she reached in the cupboard above for a glass, choosing a sturdy tumbler for posterity's sake – every bodega in Rio used them, easier to keep upright if a fight broke out. She glugged down several mouthfuls of Tesco's finest whatever, trying to eradicate the image of her half-naked mum straddling her dad (who still had the remote control in his right hand), his jeans bunched round his ankles.

'Hello, love, we weren't expecting you back so soon. You usually stay over with Tariq. I assumed that's who you were meeting...'

'I was, but decided to come back early.' She glared at her mum, willing her to address the scene she'd just been subjected to.

'Everything OK? Tariq still working for British Gas? I bet he missed you.'

'No, he didn't miss me,' Florence said evenly. 'He's getting married.'

'Oh. Are you OK about that?'

'Why wouldn't I be? I'm not his girlfriend.' Edie looked at her as if awaiting more information. 'She's called Shani, she's an accountant. Apparently his aunty set them up.'

'Oh, that's nice. Shame for you, mind. Do you want a cup of tea? I'm making one for your dad...'

Florence shook her head. 'I'm going to the conservatory.' She swiped the wine bottle at the same time. 'You and Dad can have the front room.'

'Don't you want to come and watch telly with us? Thought we could start a new box set now you're back.'

'No, Mum. I'm a bit traumatised. Don't want to revisit the scene of the crime. Your top's on inside out...'

'Flo—' But Florence climbed down from her high horse and swept out of the room. She skimmed her hands along the bookcases her dad had built beneath the conservatory windows, a slim spine out of place in a protective plastic cover amongst her mum's hoard of chunky Black Lace racy sex novels. Edie didn't need to read Black Lace – she was living it. Florence reached down and slipped out the book: *Of Mice and Men* – her old school copy.

Inside on the library record page she'd scrawled *FloRo 4 ever* in
pencil. She smiled as nostalgia flooded her veins. Their portman-
teau, FloRo, had felt so cool at the time. She could barely recall
the plot from *Of Mice and Men* but Mrs Higham's face finally
sharpened into focus, Rowena's having never faded...

3

FLORO

April 2002, Horsham High

Sleep beckoned from beyond *Of Mice and Men*. Florence was supposed to have read it over the Easter holidays, but of course she hadn't. She'd attempted a few times but couldn't get past the opening pages. She actually enjoyed reading and writing but the authors they covered were predominantly dead which equalled boring in most cases.

Ro kicked Florence under the desk.

'What?' she hissed while Mrs Higham was explaining the four main themes woven through the book's narrative.

'You were snoring!'

Florence pinched the skin on her arm to wake herself up.

'So who can tell me what the final theme is?' Mrs Higham asked the class of tranquillised teenagers. Her gold hoop earrings had tangled themselves in her curly hair and a chunky clear crystal wand on a gold chain had wedged itself in her cleavage.

Flo wondered how old she was, at least forty, too ancient for hoop earrings! The whole class gazed anywhere other than at her, dreading being singled out. Florence concentrated on her furry camo pencil case from WHSmith; the zip had permanently chewed into fuzz, snarling up halfway so things incessantly fell out. Florence resented spending money on a new one; that was tantamount to coughing up for sanitary pads or cotton wool, boring necessities foreshadowing grown-up life. So instead she had safety pinned it shut like a stapled gaping wound. Her pencil sharpener was always going AWOL.

'Florence? Any ideas?' Mrs Higham had her speared under a lepidopterist's pin. She picked at the pencil case zip and pursed her lips before looking up. 'Anything?'

'No, Miss.' They always called her Miss despite her married status.

'OK... Can you tell me what the previous three themes were?' How was deciphering the premises in *Of Mice and Men* ever going to help in the real world? What about budgeting for gas bills, or what to do if you needed an abortion? Life skills that actually mattered, as well as making a basic mac and cheese and what combination of drugs cured a hangover.

'Sorry, Miss. I haven't got a clue. I wish I did, but I don't.'

'Everyone, stand up now!' Mrs Higham's voice skimmed the top of their heads. She clapped her hands intimating urgency. When no one moved, all caught in the spotlight, she clapped again. 'Now, people. Get some blood flowing. Wake up!' Florence sighed and scraped her chair back on the floor, setting off a chain reaction. Soon everyone stood behind their desks, scratching armpits, picking undies out of bum cracks, and generally behaving like bears waking from deep hibernation. Florence stifled a yawn. She stared at Mrs Higham who seemed to be listening to something somewhere else, before nodding.

'Right, we're all going to form a rough circle. Louis come here.' She stationed Louis Jenkins from the front row next to her and everyone else shuffled into a wobbly oval in between the desks. 'Closer to each other if you can, I know it's hard with the desks in the way. Move chairs if you have to. Now turn to the person on your right, who will turn their back to you, then we're going to patter our hands on that person's back like this...' She turned to Louis and started gently slapping his back like she was giving a particularly lame massage. Soon the whole room was filled with the noise of torrential rainfall in a lush forest. People started laughing, but Florence rather liked its soothing rhythm. 'Work in a pattern, draw circles with the pattering!' Miss instructed. No back was left untouched, not even Mrs Higham's. The people who no one talked to were having their backs attended to by someone they knew by sight, but not by touch. Laya Tozer was patting Florence's shoulders, which Florence found unworldly. Laya was from the Sporto Crowd, and wouldn't normally waste energy looking down from Mount Olympus on Florence and her pitiful ilk. Years later, she heard Laya had suffered a teenage eating disorder and despised her legs so much she spent five grand getting the 'fat' sucked out of them.

'Stop!' Miss shouted this time to be heard above the din. The pattering petered out like a passing storm cloud. 'Thank you, everyone. Sit down.'

As Florence sat down, Ro caught her attention, flaring her nostrils and her eyes at the same time. 'Heavens to Murgatroyd,' she hissed under her breath. 'She's only gone and lost the plot.'

'I understand why you're disengaged with this book. I'm not a fan of teaching old white men's stories. The English syllabus hasn't changed since I was your age, and I studied this very same text. I feel your pain.' A few conspiratorial sniggers wafted across the room. 'However, loneliness is something that's universal, cross cultural, and that's the final theme we'll discuss for this book. All you need to do is take notes, listen to me and my vast wisdom giving you all the answers you will need in exams, and then you can forget all about *Of Mice and Men*, until your kids are doing GCSEs.' More laughter, and screeching from Daniel Benn that there was no way he was EVER having kids. Mrs Higham held her hand up as if pressing down the volume. 'But what would be the point of that? Ticking boxes? Books are supposed to open a window onto a different way of seeing, a fresh viewpoint or a way of connecting with the world, describing comparable experiences so you see yourself in the text, thus feel less alone. Reading something that speaks directly to you, that reflects you and who you are is important. How is a long dead white American middle-class man going to connect to you here in this classroom? He isn't, but the themes will. I wanted you to experience togetherness just now, when I made you pat each other's back. You were connected. But imagine if there was no connection, no one to pat your back – you might feel left out. Loneliness is the final theme. I know all this feels arbitrary, but one day, maybe you'll look back on today when you see someone who might need their back patting. Books can bring joy and offer experience far beyond the narrowness of these walls.' A few heads started nodding. 'I've a treat for you once we get through this, we're going to read a book called *The Outsiders*, and watch the film too. It was one of Tom Cruise's first roles, I think you might enjoy it...' Amid the excited chatter Florence smiled at Ro, who grabbed her hand. She whispered to her: 'I'll always pat your back.'

* * *

March 2023, Felworth

. . .

Florence jumped, the clashing rain on the glass roof shooing away 2002. She'd wanted to be an English teacher just like Mrs Higham. She'd particularly enjoyed the termly treasure hunts with clues linked to books they had read in class, or stories she knew they loved, ones recommended by her or titles in the current zeitgeist. *Harry Potter* always featured heavily. Mrs Higham squirrelled sweets and pound shop tat around the school grounds while waiting at each checkpoint, a member of class carefully bestowed with the mantle of quiz master, would mark the literary multiple choice questions, and hand out the clues for the next destination. Everyone took turns at manning the Checkpoint Charlies, and were rewarded handsomely with chocolate. Even at lofty fifteen, the children eagerly anticipated these treasure hunts, the most disengaged pupils who firmly believed learning was parallel to pissing into the wind were often the ones most anxious for victory. Her heuristic way of teaching offered everyone (not just book smart kids) some autonomy over their own future. They attained top drawer exam results while discovering dormant aspects of themselves, swimming out into the world with those gifts permanently under their belts. Mrs Higham alone had been the instigator of Florence's reading obsession.

Edie tentatively poked her head in the conservatory, her top now the right way round. Her parents were opening a family bag of Doritos and Edie wondered if Florence wanted a bowl, but soon levered herself onto the arm of the opposite sofa.

'Listen, love, I know selling the house feels very sudden, but it isn't to us. We've been mulling it over for ages. We've lived here for thirty-six years – I was pregnant with you when we moved in. Your dad's kept on top of repairs, but it needs an overhaul now. The amount of money it would take for a facelift is the price it would cost to move to the sea. We've no room for all your baggage... Oh, love, I'm sorry.' Her mum leaped up from the sofa arm as Flo's face crumpled, smothering her in a hug, her familiar Dior lingering on her neck. 'Now I feel awful...'

Florence shook her head. 'No, Mum. You're right.' She furiously rubbed her nose. 'I'm sorry I've taken the whole storage thing for granted. I can't think about what's in Lennie's cupboard. It's about time I went through it all, I'll do it tomorrow, I promise, I can chuck it all in Nellie. Tariq getting married, you moving – they're all signs that I'm stuck. The only thing that instigates change is boarding a plane and heading somewhere new...'

'At least wait till I get back from work. You shouldn't drive Nellie on your own for the first time.'

'Mum, I *have* to do it on my own. It'll be OK, it's not *the* van. It's *a* van. They're different. Anyway, I'm going to sell Nellie. She's my ticket to Costa Rica, I can finally go, do it properly!'

Her mum raised her eyebrows. 'I'm sure Cassie didn't gift it to you so you could sell it straight away. It was her dying wish, Flo.'

'And my wish is to sell her. If she was such a psychic, she should have known that...'

'That van's important,' Edie continued. 'I can feel it. You're meant to keep her...'

'We'll see...'

4

I'M NEVER GETTING MARRIED

Dear Florence

Thanks for your email. I've informed the DVLA that you are now the new owner of Nellie. They will send through the log book paperwork. I forgot to mention the other day that Mum left the protective cover for the van folded inside one of the cupboards under the back seat. I would put it over her if you're not able to off-road her in a garage. It also keeps her safe from prying eyes. Please get in touch if you ever need to ask anything about her. Good luck – I hope she brings you the happiness she brought Mum. She managed to fit the engine pretty much on her own, with maybe a bit of help, and do some welding to the underneath. She was determined to put some of herself into the van!

All the best

Frank Higham

Florence stared at the glowing screen on her phone, eyes throbbing from lack of sleep. Reading emails in the dark wouldn't nudge her back to the land of nod. It was four in the morning and she was still breathing in Sri Lanka time. Omesh, her designated butler and expert sommelier, would be setting the table on her veranda now, breakfast for one facing the Indian Ocean (or to be a complete pedant, the Laccadive Sea). In Apa Villa, a tiny chic boutique hotel in Thalpe, Florence had quickly become accustomed to Omesh's convivial morning chats as he'd served her breakfast – hoppers (a substantial rice-flour and coconut pancake bowl, served with eggs and fresh chillies) or exotic fruit platters adorned with sides of impossibly crispy bacon, silken omelettes and caramel-infused locally sourced coffee.

Florence's tummy rumbled and she pushed back the duvet, swinging her feet over the edge of the bed and planting them on the thin beige carpet, her shoulders automatically hunching against the nip in the air. She rummaged in her drawers, finding her fleecy tracksuit bottoms and comfy grey hoodie, before heading downstairs. There might be some past their sell-by date bagels in the bread bin if she was lucky. The heating wouldn't kick in until six thirty and Florence knew better than to override it. Her dad was a polar bear by nature too; he preferred the cold and ruled the thermostat with an iron paw.

After tea and a disappointingly stale bagel not even salvageable by toasting, Flo ventured outside into the crisp, blustery morning protected by her cosy puffa and Edie's Ugg boots. As she strode towards Nellie, fingering the keys in her pocket, the road partially lit by cascading amber halos from intermittent streetlights, she glanced at Mr Ogby's front windows. The curtains were drawn, the house cloaked in darkness, but she'd wager he had sensors in the bushes, ready to spring into life, warning him about movement in the road outside. Flo reached Nellie and stroked her nose, unable to deny she was gloriously beautiful. A light went on in the Wickhams' next door to her parents'. They'd bought the house after Denise, Rowena's mum, sold up a few years previously. They'd recently had another baby, Florence could hear them crying, the party wall was so thin... Sudden memories surfaced of screaming fights tearing through her house as Rowena's parents ripped verbal chunks out of each other in their back bedroom under the impression no one could hear. No wonder things had turned out this way... *What way, Florence?* She shook her head, she didn't need reminding, but her brain had other ideas.

* * *

December 1999, Felworth

Denise was sobbing into a glass of wine when Florence and Ro pushed open the kitchen door after school. They were chattering away about the school Millennium party. Apparently everyone was supposed to dress up as somebody or something from the outgoing century.

'Where you gonna get a Tinky Winky costume from?' Florence asked Ro as they burst into the kitchen initially oblivious of Denise sitting at the table, tears rinsing off her mascara, black rivulets coursing down her cheeks. Florence noticed before Ro who had automatically dived into the snack cupboard above the toaster to grab two bags of Mini Cheddars and two small cartons of apple juice. As Ro slammed the cupboard shut, just managing to prevent a Hula Hoop avalanche from tipping out of the split selection bag, she realised Florence was staring at her with her lips clamped shut and her eyes stretched wide like saucers. She clocked the half-empty bottle of Blossom Hill before noticing her mum slumped against the wall, a ring of crumpled tissues scattered around the chair legs.

'Mum! What's happened!'

Denise tried to speak but all she could muster was a strangulated gurgle culminating in 'Daaaaaaaaaaaaaad.'

Florence jumped to. 'Shall I go and get Mum?' Rowena nodded frantically.

Florence's mum was a nurse at the local GPs', therefore supposed to be filled to the brim with compassion and medical knowledge. Of course she was extremely well informed on an array of issues, her specialist subject being: how to spot fake illness, while having zero sympathy for moaners or hypochondriacs (which made up 80 per cent of the patients at Daisy Bank Practice, according to her). By the time Florence, Lennie and Edie arrived, the mystery of Denise's unravelling had been revealed. Denise was now smoking a constant chain of menthol cigarettes, lighting one from the end of another before the previous one had even burned halfway. This slowed down the telling of the story, but gave her time to catch her breath (before she scorched it away and tarred her lungs like the flat roof on the extension). Rowena sat in shock, shovelling a second bag of (Flo's) Mini Cheddars into her mouth on autopilot. Her eyes had glazed over as she absorbed the information in its second telling, coughing occasionally from the smog emanating from her mum.

'He just left. Said he didn't love me any more, that he hadn't for years, he'd just been treading water till *she* could get out of her situation.' Denise inhaled deeply, reaching into the almost empty cigarette packet for the next in line.

'I'm sorry, Denise, that's so awful. Just before Christmas too. What timing. Did you have any idea?' Edie asked, wafting smoke away from her face.

'We'd been fighting, I thought he was seeing someone again, like the last time...' Florence glanced over at Rowena. She felt so sad for her. What must it feel like to have your dad just up and leave? She couldn't imagine her bear of a dad ever doing that. He and her mum still declared their love for each other about twenty times a day. Admittedly, it made her want to chunder, but she would rather have vom-worthy loved-up parents than soap opera ones like this. 'He kept insisting there was no one; I didn't believe him. Maybe someone from work – I kept on at him, but he was adamant. Now I know he was telling the truth about it not being someone from work. I don't know what's worse, him leaving, or Tammy being the one he left me for.'

'Tammy? Your best friend, Tammy?' Edie almost shouted. Florence knew Tammy – Ro called her Aunty Tammy. They all used to go camping, her husband and their two kids, Isabelle and Alex. 'Bloody hell, Den, that's appalling! So he's shacked up with her and the kids? What about Tom?'

'She asked Tom to leave. He refused, so she moved into some flat, oh, argh, ogh God. Sorrrrrrrrry...' Denise dissolved into a puddle, her dual aspect cigarettes, one lit one awaiting a flame, dropped onto the kitchen table, Edie sweeping in to stub out the lit one in the ashtray before hugging Denise tightly and fiercely nodding her head in the direction of the living room at Florence, code for get Ro and Lennie out of here.

'I'm sorry about your dad,' Florence said to Rowena as they sat in the festival of beige living room, CBBC on the TV occupying Lennie, her eyes glued to the screen, shovelling her after-school Hula Hoops into her gaping mouth.

'Thanks,' Ro said impassively. 'I knew he'd leave. They'd been rowing every night for weeks. I used to hide in my room with my head under a pillow.' Florence had consistently asked Ro if she was OK, they could all hear the rows, but she'd refused to talk.

'When will you see him?'

Ro shrugged defiantly, her heart fossilising.

'Mum said he'd be in touch. But I don't want to see him.' Ro's eyes flashed dangerously. 'Fucker.'

Florence gasped and Lennie snapped her head away from the television.

'You said the F word! I'm telling.'

'Lennie, it was an emergency. Shut up!' Florence ordered as Lennie started to unfurl her body from the cross-legged slouch she'd slumped in, coat still on. Fuck was reserved for really, really dire situations, of which this was one. So it was OK. But Florence had only ever said it quietly to herself. She knew Ro said it, because Ro was a rebel. But the word still felt too illicit for every day usage outside of whispering to oneself, or Ro muttering it in retaliation about French tests or Maths home-work. This was the first time it had been used against a person, to her knowledge.

Lennie slowly sat back down and returned her attention to the TV, one ear listening out for more evidence to stack up against her older sister.

'I can't believe Mum's best friend stole Dad. That's like the biggest worstest thing ever. Best friends aren't supposed to do that. Men though, they do all kinds of rubbish stuff,' Rowena spat rancorously. 'It's not like this is the first time Dad's left.'

Florence almost pointed out not all men were like her dad, but knew better than that. Ro had cried nonstop at school the last time her dad had left and Denise had had to come and collect her from the nurses' office. Florence had fretted for the remainder of the day, terrified that Denise was going to leave too, spiriting Rowena away for ever. But this time things were different. Andy wouldn't be coming back.

'Yeah, can you imagine one of us doing that? Stealing a

husband? Like for real!' Florence couldn't imagine how you would find yourself even wanting to do something remotely like that.

'I know. For actual real, you stealing my husband!' Rowena echoed. 'It would have to be *me* stealing yours because there's no way I'm ever getting married. Especially after this.'

'Then I'm not getting married either,' Florence announced in solidarity, not really sure what she was signing herself up for.

'I am!' Lennie piped up. 'And he's going to be rich!'

'Why can't *you* be the rich one?' Rowena asked.

'I will be too. We're going to live in a castle. And you're not allowed to visit.'

* * *

March 2023, Felworth

The light went off in the Wickhams' and Florence unlocked the van. The sliding whoosh as it opened disturbed her once more but she briskly elbowed her unease away. *Not today, Satan.* Stooping, she crept into the van, and using her phone as a torch sought out the cupboards under the back seat, opening them until she found Nellie's silver cover crumpled up behind the gas stove. She drew it out like a magician with a string of handkerchiefs until it billowed around her. She thought she may as well have a go at fitting it now instead of later, it couldn't be that hard, and after several false starts, she worked out the zips, the angles and the front from the back, yanking the cover over the van leaving the main flap open. Before she fastened up Nellie properly, she sat inside the darkened van, the flap rustling with the occasional gust of wind, her torch beaming into all the nooks and crannies, casting sharp shadows behind her. That was when she noticed an envelope on the laminate floor. Sudden knocking on the side of the van startled her; she grabbed the letter and shoved it in her coat pocket.

'Hello?' a voice called. 'Everything OK...?'

5

MR OGBY

Mr Ogby. Florence rolled her eyes, contemplating what offence she had committed at this time of the morning. When she poked her head out of the flap, she noticed his toupee was crooked, the shiny pink bald part of his head exposed above his left ear like a billiard ball.

'Yes, Mr Ogby, I'm just zipping the van up to protect her from the weather.' Not that she needed to explain, she hadn't broken any law. What was he doing up so early anyway? She shined her torch away from his face. His perfectly ironed navy chinos looked like they had been stored in a Corby trouser press, and his maroon crew-necked jumper revealed a stiff pale blue collar poking out like a funnel holding up his head. He was remarkably rakish for a widower. Florence imagined her dad turning feral if her mum left, or died before him. He'd embrace full polar bear, white beard out of control and hair sprouting from every orifice, clothes melded to his hirsute body.

'Good, good. I heard some noise, I was just checking it was you. I saw you had a new van. Didn't want anyone vandalising it or stealing it. Thought I'd get dressed and come out and see for myself.' Vandalism was rife in Felworth. Old Mrs Richards at number twelve was known for denting cars with her Zimmer frame if you didn't give way to her at a junction.

Florence briefly glanced at his face. His John Lennon specs had slid down his bony nose revealing crêpey mauve half-moons beneath each watery grey eye. Had he always been as nosy? Mrs Ogby had died when Florence had just turned thirty. She had been quite chatty, and Florence recalled her handing orange ice pops over the fence when she, Ro and Lennie had been playing in the back garden on a particularly hot summer afternoon. Ever since her death Mr Ogby had thrown himself into being the road busybody famous for his never-ending curtain twitching. She recalled the funeral cortege outside the house – black horses with the equally black plumage stamping their hooves, impatient to get the show on the road. His two grown-up sons who lived in London had come down with their partners. Apparently they barely managed to squeeze in visits, according to Mum. 'Busy lives. Kids, jobs, you know how it is. That'll be you one day,' she'd said, her tongue firmly in her cheek. Florence was never having children and her jobs were a means to an end.

'No need to worry, Mr Ogby. It's all good out here. It's very early, don't you want to go back to bed?'

'Bob.' Florence looked at him nonplussed. 'Call me Bob. Mr Ogby makes me feel even older than I already am.'

'I've always called you Mr Ogby.'

'I know, but you're not a child any more, Florence.' Those words inexplicably brought tears to her eyes and she had to hurry them away with the back of her hand, pretending to be tired herself, faking a yawn. She curbed the desire to reach out and straighten his toupee.

'No point going back to bed, I don't sleep so well these days,'

Mr Ogby said quietly. Florence almost asked if that was because of the spyware control panel she imagined he had in his bedroom.

'I'm sorry to hear that.' This was the longest she had ever talked to Mr Ogby in her life. 'Do you want to come in and see the van?' His face momentarily lit up like a Christmas tree before fading.

'That would be lovely, but I can see you're busy. Maybe another time when you're out here tinkering.' Florence nodded before scrambling out of the van and locked the door, then proceeded to zip Nellie into her cover while Mr Ogby watched.

'Right, I'm going inside,' she said decisively. 'Hope you manage to get some sleep.' He nodded and walked back up his pristine path before turning.

'I'll keep an eye on the van if you like, while it's out here. Must be worth something.'

'Thank you, Mr—Bob.' He smiled weakly at her then headed inside. She caught him rearranging his toupee in the hallway mirror just before shutting the front door.

Her house was still asleep when Florence stole back inside. She perched at the kitchen hatch, placing the battered slim cream envelope on the counter – it was the same as the one Frank had hand delivered earlier. 'Tracey Parker' was inscribed across the top stating her address as Berkhamsted School in Hertfordshire, the matching purple wax seal keeping its secrets safe. Florence sniffed the envelope. She sniffed everything, like a dog checking out potential friend or foe – it was neither, just carried a faint smell of indiscriminate incense. Along with music and sound, taste and smell felt like intangible keys that unlocked the secrets to her dormant database, anchoring her in memories interred from the past, or recent experiences still clinging to her skin like rainwater. Florence imagined some of her memories swirling like sinners from the fourth upper circle of hell in Dante's *Inferno*, eagerly awaiting liberation, crashing into her present intent on wreaking havoc. On those occasions she would shut them down before they could escape.

'Tracey Parker, Tracey Parker...?' She ran upstairs and skimmed through her own letter, finding 'Tracey' at first glance, before bringing it back down to the kitchen. How had it ended up wrapped in Nellie's protector? It wasn't a coincidence. Had Frank put it there? Why would he do that? Maybe Cassie had meant to deliver the letter, leaving it in the van then got too sick at the last minute. But surely she would have just posted it, though to be honest, Mum was always complaining about letters getting lost and parcels turning up three months after they'd been posted. There had been an article about it on the BBC website while she'd been away, whole streets not receiving post for six months. But that had been before Christmas, things would have improved by now, surely? Florence could just post the letter, there was a post box stationed right outside on the opposite side of the road. You couldn't get a taxi for love nor money in Felworth, but you could send a letter to anywhere in the world without getting out of your pyjamas. She googled Tracey Parker at Berkhamsted School, just to make sure, and came across a recent local newspaper article about her forthcoming retirement after a successful twenty-five-year tenure.

Florence jumped up and rifled through The Really Useful Drawer beneath the microwave, chock-full of elastic bands, random envelopes, paper clips, pen lids separated from their pens, a dog-eared notepad, loose batteries, ancient money-off vouchers and plasters. Right at the back she found a book of four second class stamps with only one remaining. It was a sign, not that she believed in such nonsense. She slapped on the stamp. 'Bingo!' She strode into the hallway where her parents' wedding present, an original 1980s wooden steel pendulum clock, informed her it was five fifty-five. The clock was in fact six minutes fast. Her dad reset it every time the clocks changed but by the time it was due another spring forward or fall back, it had eaten into the correct time, useful if you were perennially late.

Florence jammed her feet back into her mum's Uggs, and opened the front door. She marched down the path, dawn sneaking up behind the trees, and pushed open the garden gate, looking both ways before crossing the road. An old-fashioned post box with a narrow mouth stood on the kerb outside the new people's house. Florence still hadn't made their acquaintance, a man and a woman (thirty-somethings), no kids, just a black dog. They had moved in over two years ago, but remained the new people as far as the rest of the road was concerned. Florence stared at the tight postal slot and rested the letter on its lip. *Just post it.* She pushed it halfway in, the open maw ready to swallow on the final push. This was most likely the important letter Cassandra Galaxy never got round to delivering, full of apologies, asking to say goodbye in person so she could enjoy peace in her final resting place. What if it got lost in the sorting office like so many other letters had? What if she never opened it, just like Rowena had done with all Flo's letters...? What if...? *Just post it.* Mrs Higham's face flashed in front of her eyes. Not an indistinguishable Cassandra Galaxy but her teacher who had inspired a whole classroom of cynical children to achieve full marks on *Of Mice and Men* in their exams. 'Goddamit!' She snatched the letter from the unreliable jaws of the Royal Mail and dashed back over the road without looking, swearing the entire time until she shut the door behind her, heading to the kettle to make tea and mull this over.

Sipping her tea, she stared idly at the kitchen blind before a radical thought popped like a water balloon above her head. 'Wow, Cassie was good,' she whispered to the bread bin as she tapped the letter on the worktop, the thought crystallising. Florence brought Tracey's letter straight up to her face. 'Are you a clue I have to deliver in person?' Hadn't Frank mentioned something about his mum insisting he hand deliver Florence's letter? Was that Cassie's way of planting the seed? Flo paused, letting the improbable notion sink in then shook her head. No, Cassie just wanted this letter safely delivered because she'd been unable to do the job herself; there was no treasure hunt. What would be the point of that? She already had Nellie, the so-called treasure. This final road trip would be grateful repayment for Nellie's endowment, it was the least she could do. Cassie had cited a gift of transformation in her letter, asking Florence to give Nellie a chance. Well, she *was* giving her a chance, then she was going to sell her, and disappear to Costa Rica – that would certainly be a transformative experience! Florence had been putting off Costa Rica until she could afford to explore for at least six months, a year would be a dream, and thanks to Cassie's generosity that was now on the cards. There was nothing keeping her here if she didn't have to return to work. Florence laughed at her ridiculous treasure hunt assumption. Cassie had had enough to deal with without constructing a cross-country wild goose chase. With a plan brewing, she decided to search for campsites in the Berkhamsted area, but first she had to excavate her past belongings and get rid of those boxes...

6

ROWENA

Rowena leaned against the sink in her compact kitchen and idly stared out of the window into the miniscule back garden. The Lilliputian lawn acted as a convenient landing strip for the native sparrows and blue tits residing in the beech hedge camouflaging the ugly right-hand fence panels. The lean-to shed and adjacent water butt disguised most of the rear fence panels, leaving just the left ones fully exposed awaiting the advent of sapphire delphiniums and blue and white agapanthus, if the army of rapacious slugs didn't devour the delphiniums first. However, this spring Rowena was armed with copper rings and pellets and if those failed to protect the budding delphiniums, she'd stand guard and hurl the offending slugs and snails over the fence where they could take their chances on the road.

As small as the place was, Rowena loved that the two-up two-down and everything in it was hers, the unstable years of house shares far behind her. She watered her windowsill ferns then made a gallant attempt at slurping her tea. It still resembled how she imagined pond water would taste if she scooped up a mugful and drank it. This was a huge inconvenience because tea was one of her favourite tipples of all time after red wine, champagne and most vodka cocktails. Plain water didn't scrape into the top five. Gin was also conspicuously absent from this list ever since the infamous Gordon's gin factory incident.

In the summer break before Rowena's third year of her psychology degree, she'd lodged in Basildon for two months with her mum's cousin, Claire, sleeping in her daughter Sam's creaky single bed while she was away with her boyfriend travelling round Europe (Transylvania, looking for vampires). Sam's brother, Ben, was in the room next to Rowena and barely opened his door the entire two months. At fifteen, he was a gangly monosyllabic ball of hormones, and whenever he happened to venture downstairs foraging for yet more snacks, a whiff of sweaty socks and another more deeply upsetting musty odour wafted onto the hall landing. Rowena tried not to think about it too much. There were perks to being an only child. Despite the free accommodation in a black-walled room plastered with Marilyn Manson posters, a black duvet-covered bed with matching bat-patterned cushions, unsettling pictures of skulls and a general atmosphere of imminent death hanging in the air, Rowena quite enjoyed living in a different house without her stepdad doing her head in.

Cousin Claire worked as the HR manager for the Gordon's gin factory and secured Ro a summer job on the production line. What Claire had failed to express was that the entire team on said production line was made up of residents on day release from the local old people's home, with a handful of token students dotted in between. Ro helmed the mini gin bottle conveyor belt to check that all the bottles were upright as they approached the machine wrapping the duty label on the top, known as the top strapping machine. The bottles occasionally toppled over and Ro had to right them to avoid a pile-up. On this particular day, a mini bottle tumbled approaching the machine, so Ro leaned over, like she had done a few times before, and flicked it with her index finger. However, in a million to one sliding doors moment, her finger got sucked into the top strapping machine. Ro screamed, frantically gesturing with her left arm, *not waving but drowning*, yelling until her lungs burned, to no avail – no one stopped the machine. Mathew, the other student stationed near her end of the conveyor belt, was on a tea break, leaving behind pensioners, Joan and Mabel. Both were hard of hearing and slow on their feet, and by the time anyone had pieced together what was happening, Rowena's finger would have been chewed to a pulp. She took matters into her own hands and yanked her digit out, blood exploding all over her and the gin bottles à la *Texas Chainsaw Massacre*, her finger a mangled mess. That afternoon as she sat shivering with shock in considerable pain in A and E next to a man with his severed thumb in a Sports Direct mug full of ice (thank heavens to Murgatroyd, her index finger was still attached, just), she realised her ambitions of being a world class guitar player, or tiddlywinks champion were dashed. Nose picking too would have to be middle fingered, but that felt wrong, like she was stuffing a sausage up her nostril, unable to navigate a satisfactory scrape around.

As well as her wages at the end of the summer season, Ro received two grand compensation which she put towards her final year, but she was off gin for life. Writing was something she had taken for granted before that summer, immediately after it required much concentration to hold her pen in a way that didn't offend her withered finger. As winter approached, she found herself forced to wrap the unfortunate member (scarred and forever stunted in comparison to the remaining fingers) in a hankie when studying in Leeds University library to protect it from the cold. This was until her nana knitted a set of finger warmers – eerily similar to those joke willy warmers bought for stag dos and Secret Santas, but a smidgen smaller – to stave off the chills. But what had turned out to be even more absurd was the occasional throbbing, or buzzing, or tingling she experienced in the shrunken finger when something wasn't right. Like third eye intuition or a gut feeling alerting her to remain vigilant until whatever it was had revealed itself. More often than not it was something as innocuous as stay in and watch TV rather than trek three hours by bus to a lame party in the hills, or don't accept a date with the knuckle-dragging Neanderthal. Rowena sometimes ignored this inside track and whenever she did, it had been to her detriment.

Rowena smiled to herself as she tipped her pond tea down the sink, and wondered where those shrivelled finger warmers were. She hadn't popped one on for aeons, not having sat in a draughty library since. Her assaulted finger was still stubby but the lividity had faded over time along with some memories from her past. Ro was an only child and felt the full force of her role within her relationship with her parents. Her dad was finally on his own after decades of a yoyo relationship with Tammy (or That Fucking Tammy, as she had been known by both Ro and her mum). Rowena still couldn't reconcile this fresh version of her dad, Andy, with the man who'd masqueraded as her father up until the past few years. He'd joined a men's group in Brighton, where they sat around in a circle and discussed what was going on with them, what they'd suffered in childhood (no sun block application and a few clips round the ear according to her dad), what they'd learned, taking responsibility for their mistakes, and were allowed to hug in a safe environment. Her dad had taken to wearing prayer beads round his neck and linen trousers with flip-flops, even in the winter. He holidayed in Goa and attended yoga retreats all over the country and sometimes abroad. He even meditated, for fuck's sake. He was still a carpenter, but as he liked to inform Rowena, 'Jesus was a carpenter'. She deleted the daily words of wisdom, abandoned Instagram when he tried to befriend her as some kind of reinvented bumper sticker guru, like he was the first person on earth to discover that 'letting go of the outcome' was a path to contentment. It was embarrassing but at least he made an effort to keep up their relationship. And the new aura did suit him, his crinkly face had taken on a calm glow, his salt and pepper hair now shaved like a monk (mostly to disguise the widow's peak ziplining to the back of his skull). Ro found it hard to believe what he had been like before he received his epiphany (or rather, when he was forced to realise he was a bit of a tosser after Tammy finally left him). However, he had taken it upon himself to rehash the past, and not just his own. Soon after he joined the men's group, he began dropping insightful snippets into conversations whenever they met after work, or in a local pub for a drink.

'So, we've been talking about allowing the past to hold you to ransom this week at The Group,' he'd said one Friday last November when he'd met her for an early evening pint after school. Whenever her dad mentioned The Group, Rowena capitalised the lead consonants in her mind; he spoke with such reverence she felt it only appropriate. She sipped her Merlot in the Cinque Ports and eyed him with amusement, wondering what on earth he was going to spit out. 'It made me think of you.' *Oh God...*

'Why?' She knew why though and wished she'd kept her mouth shut and changed the subject. She shuffled her bum on the creaking green leather Chesterfield sofa opposite her dad in his armchair. He placed his pint on the small dark wood table between them and picked up the deli-grade packet of posh cheese and onion crisps that was mostly filled with air.

'You and Florence.' He crunched what must have been the giant alpha crisp of the packet, a few golden flakes fluttering down onto his jumper. Rowena stared at him, her mouth half open, eyebrows raised in a 'really?' expression. 'Rowena, you've never met anyone you've had that bond with since all that business. Do you not think it's time to let it go?'

'I have let it go, Dad.'

'Have you though?' He licked his fingers. 'Wouldn't reconnecting with her be healing?'

'Have you heard yourself?'

He held up his hands. 'I know, I get it. It's just that doing all this work on myself makes me want to extend the privilege to you.' Rowena rolled her eyes and put her wine next to his beer on the table, one leg bolstered up with folded beer mats to mitigate the wobble. The wooden floors were all a bit wonky in the Cinque Ports. Or maybe it was the ghost who constantly tripped up patrons and tipped chairs. This traditional drinking den was apparently haunted.

'Dad, why would I reconnect with Florence? I don't need to know about her life with Clinton, they're probably married now – good luck to them, and I mean that. Being married isn't the contented endgame everyone thinks it's going to be.' She shot him a hard stare and he had the grace to look shamefaced. 'I'm fine as I am. I genuinely wish them well. That part of my life is done, I moved on pretty sharpish after I realised it was me who'd elevated everything into a place it didn't belong, and never had – it was embarrassing. She probably doesn't want anything to do with me, who could blame her. Honestly, I'm not that person any more.'

Her dad reached over and squeezed her hand. 'I know, love. You've done really well. I just remember how close you two were, that's all. And you don't seem to have found that connection with anyone since FloRo. You were quite a team.'

The tingling rattled Rowena and she pinched her nose to staunch tears from forming. What was wrong with her? Crying had become a habit recently, not like her at all; she was known as the Ice Queen at school, not by her pupils though. Her dad pretended not to notice and nosedived into his pint like old times, blocking out emotions, but unlike the past it was for Rowena's benefit, not his own.

'Tell me about this bloke you're seeing,' he said instead, changing tack. 'You're keen, aren't you? Few months now, isn't it?'

Rowena's eyes lit up. 'Yeah, it's going OK. He's the first man I've liked for a while.'

'I'll have to meet him.'

'I don't think we're at that stage yet...' Rowena recalled the last time she'd seen Nate, he'd been naked, pulling on his Calvins before heading off to an important meeting. He lived in France mostly, something to do with tax breaks and the bank he worked for, so she snatched time with him when he could. The sex was proper boneshaking amazing. She'd even howled last week, totally forgetting that Nate was there at all. It was slightly mortifying, especially when a gaggle of neighbours nudged each other on Tuesday dragging out the bins in their little housing complex. The walls were notably vellum thin.

'Whenever you're ready. It would be nice to give him the once-over.' He smiled, his lupine face appearing momentarily menacing until he started laughing. 'Don't worry, I'll never mention it again! How's your mum?'

That was a good question and one she always answered with the same words.

'Mum's great. Happy as ever...'

Her mum *was* blissfully happy, so much so she barely communicated with Rowena, wrapped up in her life with Suleyman, her second husband. She'd met him about two years after Ro's dad shamelessly absconded with Tammy. He moved in quite soon after, was younger than her mum, no kids, didn't want any kids (lucky because Rowena's biggest fear was their house being usurped by a screaming baby). He was OK. Bit of a drip. Worked in IT, he'd visited Denise's work to fix some bug at the care home and the rest they say, is history – a tale Denise liked to rehash after a bottle of Mateus Rosé, drunk in a completely un-ironic fashion. They'd moved to Deal after all the 'hoo-hah' next door. Rowena had been glad at the time. She no longer lived at home, but it made visiting much easier, no more SAS-style running up the garden path under the cover of darkness avoiding Edie or Gareth and the bald pity in their eyes. But after time had passed, she felt Deal was a bit too far, especially now. Her parents had unwittingly switched ranking in her life based on their proximity and effort made. Her mum's steady retreat and her dad's rekindling coincided at a particularly pivotal moment.

Still standing at the sink, Rowena abandoned thoughts of tea altogether, when a text pinged on her phone. Her dad.

How are you feeling today? I hope you're taking a break from lesson prep. Those kids are lucky to have you. Enjoy the Easter hols, Ro. You need to rest.

Rowena replied one handed whilst eating a Jammy Dodger, her latest craving crowded in amongst ready salted crisps, plain white toast, scones with sun dried tomatoes and feta cheese, ketchup-smothered boiled egg sandwiches, Coco Pops and pretty much any food group not listed as a green vegetable. The Jammy Dodger crumbs dropped all over her phone. She would have to get better at multitasking...

All good. Only been sick once today. I think the baby's started kicking.

7

JUST DRIVE

The house was silent, Florence's parents were at work; the ticking of the hallway clock just audible above her thumping heart. She stared despondently at the boxes stacked up in Lennie's dusty cupboard of a room. Seven years since they'd been hastily packed there. Seven years since her life had intractably switched direction without her consent. Florence chose the smallish box on top of the left tower, lifting it down and laying it gently on the floor. She sliced a kitchen knife down the centre of the brown parcel tape and tenderly peeled the flaps apart, open heart surgery, her hands shaking.

'Come on, Flo,' she chivvied herself.

The slanted edges of a few photo frames greeted her. Oh shit. Oh no. She still hadn't looked at the pictures her dad had whipped off her phone and securely stored in the cloud – how was she supposed to face physical versions? She hastily refolded up the gaping wound and set the box aside. She'd realised this act would stir up things she'd worked so hard to suppress, but hadn't really prepared herself. What had her therapist said? Allow it all?

Surely not *all*? What if she just allowed a few slippery buggers through and the really ugly ones could remain stapled to the base of her memory bank, where they'd lived for the last seven years. She sighed, bringing down another medium-sized box from around the side of the bed, which had been buried under bin bags. Once open she could safely see it was full of kitchen things: her IKEA roasting trays, the stylish UFO-shaped colander, all the utensils that used to live in the cute jar she'd picked up in that boho shop in Brighton. She steamed ahead unpicking the second tower until a whole box full of gift-wrapped presents knocked her off course. Florence gasped and slammed the flaps shut. She wasn't sure what every single package was, but she remembered the round one. A Frisbee for the dog they were going to adopt...

* * *

December 2015, Brighton

'He's so cute, look at him! He needs us,' Florence cried, pointing at the screen on her laptop. Clinton smiled indulgently at her, dimples puncturing his smooth brown cheeks. His smile never failed to flip her inside out. 'He's called Sailor. Hello, Sailor!' She giggled at her own lame joke. Clinton slipped his arms around her waist from behind and nuzzled her neck. They both stared at Sailor, a grizzled blue brindle Staffordshire bull terrier with rascally eyes. He needed a forever home, but the Dogs Trust website was flooded with dogs needing forever homes. How did anyone choose one over another?

'So far, that's the eleventh doggo you want to adopt,' Clinton chuckled. 'We can't afford all of them. They cost a bomb, you know. Two at the most I would say. Insurance—'

'But you'd get discounted care at work!' Florence interrupted. 'Marianna would treat them for free, I know she would. And you know a lot.'

'I'm a veterinary nurse, not the actual vet,' Clinton reminded her. 'I think we should stop looking, we've enough dogs to consider. With choice comes pain, remember? Are you sure you can work from home for a bit when we get one?'

'Phyliss said so. Customer care's all done by phone and email anyway. I can be anywhere.' Phyliss, her immediate boss, lived with her ageing mum (who loved sherry and old school wrestling) in Portslade. She had three grown-up children and Florence fancied she had a rotation of married lovers that visited bringing offerings of chocolates and took her to the cinema to watch black and white films. Phyliss appeared to hail from the post-war under-stated glamorous era: she wore court shoes, twinsets and carried matching patent handbags coordinating with her outfits and care-fully curated nails. She could only be in her late fifties, but her otherness set her apart from the vanilla workforce. Florence liked her enormously and decided she definitely enjoyed a racy sex life – why else the constant dressing up? Either that or she was a muse for an artist and posed naked every weekend in a garret in Kemp-town. Florence enjoyed cooking up a convincing backstory, it kept life interesting.

Florence found it faintly ridiculous that she had ended up working in Customer Care for Brighton and Hove council. The job was only ever meant to be a cash injection while she contem-plated her options after graduating two years previously with a two one in English, dropping out of her initial teaching degree after a corrosive break-up ripped her tender soul to shreds, heartbreak consuming her like a flesh-eating virus. She'd truly believed she and Toby would be together for ever (well maybe until they were twenty-five which had seemed like eternity at a callow eighteen). She'd fallen hard for him, her first ever love, and locked herself in her childhood bedroom for ten days during reading week, refusing to return to Leeds for the exams, unable to breathe without crying let alone focus on essay questions. Neither her parents nor her snarky sister could persuade her not to allow this shard of glass to determine her future. However, it was Rowena's daily phone calls that eventually penetrated her misery, with Florence reluctantly dragging herself back for the exams. As she ran to and from the sports hall for the three major exams, head down in case Toby should appear, Florence latched on to the idea that perhaps he'd died in order to shut down whispers about Lola, a girl from another halls. The dead can't date... This mode of thinking shepherded her through the worst of the week until it was time to move all her stuff into the new five-bedroomed brownstone house in Headingly she would be sharing with Rowena, Taylor, Liv and Becky. Once home for the summer, the whispers about Lola increased in volume so Rowena hauled her off to Corfu with the earnings of Flo's dog walking job for a last-minute getaway the month before they all had to return to uni. While in sunny Corfu bathing in the Ionian Sea, the sensation of something bigger than her solidified her liquid centre and the gouging pain lessened its chokehold. Ro returned home, while Florence remained, the sunshine her new friend, and found a job working in Niko's beachside bar. She needed to boost her measly bank balance, and reassured Ro she would follow her back in time for the beginning of their new term. She was still there at the end of September after an email landed in her inbox, informing her she would need to repeat most of her first year alongside starting year two – she had failed all her end of year exams...

Florence, feeling stupid and also not fully sutured back together, flew home, her heart encased in a protective shell of defiance. She was dropping out. Her parents reiterated that the loan would still have to be paid back, that if she worked hard the dean would overlook the missed first month, why make life even more difficult for herself? But Florence only considered the now, which if she had been living like a mindfulness guru, would have been exemplary. Bumping into Toby around campus with Lola was a bridge too far, especially after he'd rehashed the hackneyed phrase seemingly every boy of every sexual persuasion had burned into their brains from birth: *it's not you, it's me, I'm not ready for a serious relationship, blah blah blah...* Paradoxically he'd then proceeded to glue himself to Lola with her perfect blonde hair, pouty lips, delicate hands and feet and fake beauty mark that she painted on daily on her right cheek. Ro promised Florence that she would get over it one day, and look back on this and laugh.

'Laugh? How will I laugh? He ruined my first year of Leeds. You're in a different year and I'm repeating, we're not FloRo any more...'

'We stopped being FloRo the minute you put Toby before yourself or your mates,' Rowena said judiciously down the phone. Ro was already living in Leeds in the house they were supposed to be sharing. Florence was furious because Rowena was right...

'So which dog are we going for?' Clinton asked, bringing her back to their task that evening.

'Sailor! We can go away in the van, take him for seaside walks, go camping. He'll love it!' But when they enquired, Sailor had already been adopted. Operation Pets at Home was suspended pending further notice while they reconsidered. They already had Clinton's guinea pigs, Bramble (black with a white patch on her eye) and Toffee (caramel brown apart from a black patch on her right eye) to care for. Florence had been surprised at how attached she'd become to the furry balls of fuzz. They recognised her voice and squeaked greetings to her from their hutch in the living room underneath the bay window while she and Clinton cooked dinner.

Florence loved their flat, tucked down the side of Brunswick Square, near the promenade on the second floor of a vertiginous white pebble-dashed Victorian building. Their bedroom Juliet balcony overlooked the backyard of a chip shop, but if you stood on a stool and stretched, you could catch a splinter of sea trapped between the casino and the arcade. When they'd moved in, Clinton had gifted her a canvas of Cuckmere Haven painted by a local artist in bold blocks of Fauvist pinks, blues and greens. Printed over the top in handwritten script, the poem she'd recited the night they'd met in Volks while completely annihilated, *Nothing Gold Can Stay*. Florence had screeched when she'd opened it, bowled over by the gesture, insisting on hanging it opposite their bed so it greeted them every morning on waking.

The dog search eventually resumed consuming Florence until she brushed herself into a corner, failing to notice Clinton's gradual retreat. She only surfaced after she asked him what beers he wanted for his thirtieth birthday party in December because she'd seen a crate on offer in Aldi and maybe they should start stockpiling – it was only August! 'I don't want a party, Flo!' he'd shouted uncharacteristically. 'How many times have I told you?' When she burst into tears he sucked his beautiful lips into a grim straight line, inhaling through his nose. She'd been hiding behind the dog-quest façade, using it as a shield against the pit of snakes in her belly. She recalled Toby before he dumped her, his vacant eyes, his lack of enthusiasm for any physical touching, not just sex, hand holding and feet rubbing – he'd been cutting the ties gradually, his wandering eye already hitched to another wagon. He'd also feigned exhaustion as an excuse for not seeing her.

'I'm sorry... I'm tired. Let's do something, just you and me? We can go away in the van, sit by the sea, have some drinks, watch a sunset. The usual spot?' Florence nodded, but they never did make it to their special place.

* * *

March 2023, Felworth

Florence slipped the key into Nellie's ignition and turned it over. She started first time but the noise of the engine wrong-footed her, so she immediately turned it off, gripping the steering wheel, tears spurting from her eyes.

'Flo, you can do this. You have to do this...' She looked up from studying her hands to find Mr Ogby staring at her from his doorstep, a troubled expression upon his face. She waved to reassure him all was OK, but he took it as an invite to approach her, wearing his navy house slippers. She hastily brushed her cheeks with her hands and prepared a smile. Mr Ogby, Bob, peered through the driver's window. She wound it down and it comically jammed halfway.

'Where are you off to?'

'I need to take boxes to the charity shop, and book storage for the rest of my stuff I'm keeping. Mum and Dad are moving.'

'I saw the house on Rightmove. I like to check, see what's going on, being head of Neighbourhood Watch and everything.'

Florence fixed her face into a kind of interested half smile.

'I better get on, just wanted to see if this worked before I piled all my stuff inside,' Florence said in her faux jolly hockey sticks voice, not fooling Mr Ogby in the slightest.

'Will you be OK, driving this thing on your own?' Florence swallowed against the lump in her throat. She focused on Bob's toupee which was actually straight, his tufty strawberry blond eyebrows betraying him. She nodded. 'You know you can store anything in my garage if you want. It's full of the kids' junk they don't want any more, adding to it won't make a jot of difference. Haven't put the car in there for years.'

A treacherous tear sneaked over the rim of Florence's eyelid and she furiously blinked before another followed, then another.

'This the first time you've driven in a van since...?' Bob asked quietly, briefly flicking his eyes away. Florence could only nod. 'Do you want me to come with you, take her for a spin around the block?'

'Yes please,' she croaked.

'I'll just lock up.' Florence leaned over and opened the passenger door as Bob nipped up his path to switch off all electrical appliances, unplug the Sky Box, check the gas and other safety precautions she imagined him engaging in before leaving his home.

He folded himself into the passenger seat, patting his toupee to make sure it was present and correct, and Florence turned the key. Nellie burst into life and this time she didn't cry. She revved the engine, floored the clutch, slid the gear stick into first, checked her mirror, indicated, checked again, then guided the engine to the biting point before accelerating at the same time as turning the wheel. She pulled out then instantly stalled.

'Sorry.'

'Don't apologise.'

She began again, juddering off, the engine screeching – it had been years since she'd driven a van, or a car for that matter. 'Where shall we go?'

'Just drive. I haven't got to be anywhere.' So she did. 'Are you OK?' Bob asked as they turned right at the Felworth crossroads near the Donkey's Tail pub.

Florence was sure she'd spotted Tariq's van zoom along the Horsham road ahead of her. 'I am actually. I think the thought was worse than the deed itself. I'm just going to pop to the station and back. Then I need to pack in all the boxes for St Catherine's charity shop.'

'St Catherine's...' Bob mused. 'That's where Judy ended up.'

'Oh, I'm sorry, I didn't realise.'

'Been six years next month. Feels like yesterday sometimes.'

Please don't talk about your wife. Please, please, Florence silently implored, ignominious about her reluctance to witness others' loss.

'She'd like that you're donating to it.' Bob's face cracked into a nostalgic smile, pouring balm on her brittle conscience. 'How many boxes do you want to put in my garage?'

An hour later, sweaty Florence had twisted her hair into a ponytail using the emergency hairband permanently shackled to her wrist. She was certain she would be buried with one in case the need arose to tie back her hair on the journey to the underworld. She wiped her top lip – one could fill various boxes with indeterminate crap and force gullible twats to carry them from one room to another up and down stairs while army major types screamed orders at them until they passed out. Boxercise. Maybe it was already a thing.

'Why don't you throw them out?' Florence asked looking at Mr Ogby's sons' twelve dusty boxes of university and teenage crap next to her own more modest eight boxes (four of them rammed with books). 'Surely they don't need any of that now?'

'It gives them an excuse to visit,' Bob said wistfully. Florence's cheeks flushed. Was this the only carrot Bob could dangle? What about filial duty, love? What about an elderly man whose only close relationship appeared to be with his chestnut-coloured toupee, and even that was built on a bed of lies.

'You can come and get your stuff any time. Just knock,' Bob said handing Florence a cup of tea when what she really needed was a glass of water.

'Won't it be weird for you storing all my stuff after Mum and Dad move away?'

Bob shrugged. 'They won't be leaving for a while yet. Anyway, you might find somewhere of your own and need it all back sooner than you think.' Florence shook her head. 'Then why are *you* keeping it?'

'It gives me an excuse to visit.' She laughed.

Before she left, Mr Ogby suggested she park Nellie permanently on his drive instead of on the road after she'd returned from St Catherine's to find her space occupied by a green Volkswagen Passat. 'Makes no difference to me, there's room for the car and the van.' Florence had wanted to hug him, but was concerned she might dislodge his toupee and she wasn't sure she could handle something as intimate as that with a septuagenarian she had only very recently started 'hanging out' with. What did that say about the state of her if Bob was actually the mainstay in her reduced friendship circle? And was it even a circle? A more accurate description would be triangle. Maybe she could count Tariq and Shani as two separate people or would Tariq now fall off the edge of the triangle, officially coupled up as he was? She was curious to meet Shani, but she suspected Tariq would prefer to hold off that rendezvous for eternity.

'Oh, how do you know my husband?' Flo imagined Shani kicking off the conversation.

'We were at school together. Mates really. Oh and I sucked him off in his Ford Transit Connect in the lay-by outside Felworth. The one with the cherry stand in the summer. And pretty much everywhere else, including the house you now live in.'

Florence hoped he'd bought a new mattress...

'Mr—Bob, have you ever been to Berkhamsted?'

8

BUN IN THE OVEN

Rowena fingered the shiny torn-off printouts in her hand. Four monochrome scans of life thriving in her womb. She'd called her mum while her dad had strolled off to retrieve the car, intentionally parked miles away, the hospital car park perennially full no matter what time of night or day you arrived.

'I'm sorry I couldn't get the time off work, love. You should have given me more notice.' Six weeks wasn't enough of a warning at Eagle's Rest nursing home. Denise appeared to live there when she wasn't tending to Suleyman's needs, or so it seemed to Rowena. Her mum inhaled on a cigarette, her lunch break feast. Denise believed in a healthy diet of cigarettes and coffee (if it had been good enough for all the nineties super models, it was good enough for her) – it kept her requisitely slim but had fractured her impermeable dark skin, furrows now entrenched round her frayed lips and creases radiating like starbursts from her eyes, the smoke kippering her from the inside out. Suleyman knew better than to beg her to quit. 'I'll get fat, then you'll leave.' That was her only answer and it didn't matter how many reassurances he dealt.

Rowena patted her own expanding belly hidden beneath her

ASOS classic black winter coat, unconcerned about her journey towards swollen ankles, stretch marks and chafing thighs. This was a predicament she'd not expected to find herself in. Children had never featured in her future at all. They were ever present at work, being a Psychology teacher at Seaford Head – she couldn't really avoid them. But these were teenagers, not babies, amorphous and helpless poised at life's promising starting line, relying on parents or carers to coax them towards the people they would eventually flourish into. Teenagers tenderly straddled the cusp of adulthood. They were mostly fully formed at sixth form, their wingspan large enough to fly and face the vagaries of experience: loss, love, adventure, boredom and everything in between.

'All's healthy, the baby's doing well,' Rowena reported to her mum.

'And how are you doing?' Denise asked. 'I remember still puking my guts up at twenty weeks. Gawd, I never wanted to do it again.' Her mum always succeeded in grasping the central role; it was a special talent she had. Rowena sighed.

'I sometimes throw up, but it's eased off now. I don't look pregnant really, school don't know.'

'I never looked pregnant until I was about to squeeze you out. Could have worn a string bikini and got away with it.'

Yes, yes, from all those cigarettes you smoked, keeping me small and asthmatic, Rowena wanted to bring up, but didn't.

'Any news from Nate? Is he going to support you?'

Rowena stifled a laugh. Support her? He'd vanished like an explorer sucked into the unyielding rainforest by the Green Goddess. His profile hadn't resurfaced on Bumble, Hinge or Tinder. Not the one he'd pinioned her with anyway. He may well be called something else now, Freddy or Anthony, scrolling the Tinder shallows for easy prey. Quite possibly he had his own account on Tik Fucking Tok, Dr Misogyny, doling out top tips on how to screw women over. Tosser.

* * *

When she'd realised she was pregnant, Rowena had been shocked, but astonishingly not horrified. She readily jumped into a future untethered by reservations and fear of rejection where Nate decided to settle down and stop travelling so much. She currently only saw him once or twice a week when he stayed with his mum in Shoreham while he commuted into London for meetings in head office. Last month they'd had a sex-fuelled weekend away in a country hotel then the rest of the time he lived in Paris. She allowed herself to dream of finding somewhere local big enough for all three of them... She had no idea why she felt safe to fantasise or accept that someone had potential longevity, or indeed, the heart not to hurt her. With hindsight she realised it was probably her hormones protecting the multiplying cells inside her. Mother nature was a powerful force. Something Nate had pontificated on before consummation, when they'd been 'dating', comparing his love of gardening with wanting a genuine connection during sex.

'Gardening with gloves on is like having sex using a condom. You need to feel the earth and mother nature with your fingers.' Rowena had protested that she didn't want to take the pill, she had historically used condoms, or withdrawal when in a longer relationship, but that hadn't been for some time now. In the end she compromised with a sexual health test and a diaphragm, the friendly nurse at Morley Street clinic demonstrating how to insert it inside a dummy vagina. As she had perched on the edge of the moulded navy plastic seat, Rowena couldn't help wonder what it must be like to work in a factory where they made medical models. Who did they model the vaginas and penises on? And can you imagine putting Vagina Model on your dating profile? Or even worse, Fake Vagina Creator! It threw up too many unsavoury scenarios in one's head that Rowena missed the initial demonstration by Dianka, the nurse, and so she had to repeat it. 'Don't forget, if you can't feel your cervix through the diaphragm, you have it in wrong. It's like touching the end of your nose…'

Balanced on the loo seat, peering at the sixth positive pregnancy test in her bathroom, Rowena had snorted – why couldn't men take a fucking pill? One had been in development for as long as she could remember, but back in the Swinging Sixties, they had just blindly handed out the contraceptive pill to women world over, apart from the steadfast Catholic enclaves and countries not rich enough to line the pockets of Big Pharma. The medical profession hadn't seemed too concerned about side effects, about bloating, sore breasts, mental health issues, fertility issues, cancer. *Take this and shut up, love, be grateful you won't get pregnant.* But the male pill had been tested, retested, checked for undue side effects – and it still wasn't available! God forbid they discover it forces them to go off sex entirely, or put on two stone in a month.

Telling Nate she was pregnant had been like skydiving while he clipped the strings with hedge trimmers. He'd breezed into the hallway after work completely unaware of Rowena's latent anxiety, all hulking masculinity and brooding sexual tension, his dark hair freshly cut, perfectly contoured to the nape of his sexy biteable neck.

'I was in a meeting with Deutsch Bank and all I could think about was taking you from behind on the sofa right there.' He eyed it lasciviously through the half-open living-room door, marking his territory. He leaned in to kiss Rowena, pulling her to him so she couldn't help but feel his rock-hard erection pressing into her belly. Rowena sucked her stomach away, her desire dampened by her recent discovery.

'Listen, Nate, can we talk?'

'Can we just get cheeky first? I know it's presumptuous, but you really are the most beautiful creature I've ever had the luck of encountering,' he implored. 'Not dumping me, are you?' Nate brought up the subject of rejection regularly. It had endeared him to Rowena because she was obviously an expert on the matter having pre-emptively dumped many poor souls before they could do the same to her. Well, somebody had to have her back... Conversely, there weren't any plans for binning Nate, and if this reveal went well, then who knew what was going to happen for them both? Maybe instead of the south coast, she could join him in France and teach at a TEFL school? She was definitely qualified. *If* she decided to keep the baby, that was.

'No, I'm not dumping you,' she laughed, kissing his cheek, expensive woody bergamot cologne tickling the back of her throat. Usually his smell would fire off frantic alerts to her nether regions. Instead it constricted her intestines, forcing bile up her throat. She smiled against the nausea. 'Come and sit down, I just need to tell you something.' His features contorted for a millisecond as he fought to control what was undoubtedly fear and let her lead him to the sofa, which only moments ago had been the principal prop in his sexual fantasy. 'I did a pregnancy test, actually six, yesterday. They're all positive...'

The cartoon *Road Runner* popped into Rowena's head as she watched Nate absorb the news. His eyes shifted focus, hardened, and the person couched beneath the man she thought she knew skulked from the shadows. He let out a lugubrious sigh.

'I'm married with two kids, I can't have any more.' Followed by, 'I'm sorry, Ro, I was going to tell you if this got complicated with feelings or whatever... I think you're going to have to get rid of it. I can't support you. This was only ever supposed to be a bit of fun. You knew that, didn't you?'

Rowena had thankfully done a solid job of constructing her stockades and her hefty drawbridge spontaneously drew itself up...

'Why did you make all that shit up about falling "in like" with me when you were living a double life? About always being so busy with work, living in France. God I'm a fuckwit...'

'All that's true! I do live in France. My family lives there. I totally fell for you. I didn't mean to, I've been trying to hold back. You cast a spell on me.'

Nate suddenly sounded like one of her pupils at Seaford. 'The dog ate my homework, Miss. I promise, I'm not lying!' No, that was an insult to the kids at school. She hoped they knew better than this. His batting eyelashes flapped uselessly, their charm fruitless.

'Then why the actual fuck are you on Tinder?'

'Everyone is. I get lonely over here.' Nate sulked like the entitled brat he was.

'Buy a sodding hamster.'

He had the temerity to smirk.

Oh, why hadn't she seen it? She'd evidently been blinded by his flouncy Oxbridge name and the firestorm sex. It hadn't been like her to swipe right on such an obvious posh boy. The usual suspects on Tinder and Hinge typically erred on the side of average or crouched behind profile pictures scanned from a hard copy photo taken in the early noughties. Bumble occasionally coughed up a few surprises, but nothing like Nathaniel. To be fair, he hadn't really promised her anything, he'd just omitted telling the truth. Mendacious little shit.

'Get out.' He remained seated. 'Are you deaf now as well as a total knob, get out!' The rage billowed Rowena's sails, swelling her chest, granting her the strength to follow the courage of her convictions as her psychic finger began tingling in solidarity.

He stood, and shook his head. 'What are you going to do about the...?'

'None of your fucking business.'

'You know I can't support you, my hands are tied... How about you give me your bank account deets, I can forward you some money to sort this out?'

'I don't want anything from you, you twat.' Rowena longed for a witness to observe this craven insouciance. 'I don't ever want to see you again. Your poor wife and kids.' For a moment it appeared a retaliation was on the cards, but he thought better of it, faced with SS Rowena. 'Is your name even Nathaniel Lightfoot?'

Nate hesitated, a lie so tantalisingly palpable Rowena could almost taste it.

'No.' The truth at least closed the circle. He walked towards the front door and opened it, stepping out into the dusky evening. 'I'm sorry, Rowena. You really do deserve better than this. I couldn't really believe my luck when someone as gorgeous as you was willing to accept scraps from the table.' She slammed the door in his face.

Afterwards, Rowena had sat in the dark at her small IKEA table half folded flat against the wall, clawing back some space in her neat square kitchen. Thunderstruck by the last hour, she couldn't even dredge up a self-pity parade. She felt rinsed through with shame that she'd been taken in by such a charlatan. The story required a ruthless edit; it showed weakness and Rowena was hailed as a tower of strength by those who knew her. She was one of those people who gathered an eclectic mix of characters from the four corners of her life, investing time and effort into new friendships, keeping all plates spinning with birthday cards and meaningful check-in texts. When Florence had flown the nest leaving a vacancy for superior BFF and soulmate, uni friends, Ebi and Mya, had both jostled for position. Should Rowena ever get married, they hypothesised they would now be the bridesmaids. But Rowena was never getting married, or having children – on those points she had been very clear.

What Rowena needed from her virtual Rolodex of connections was someone who could help shape a decision for her. Right now. She flicked through some likely candidates:

Ollie from her very first marketing job at a Brighton tech start-up (which they both hated and used to bitch about in the stationery cupboard while filching biros and Post-it notes). But Ollie was ill equipped, recently married to husband Arnie, now living his best life in Jersey. They were clueless about kids, about how your body traitorously flooded your bloodstream with feel-good hormones so you questioned the pillars upon which you had built your entire life. Not all of her friends had families, yet.

Terry-Anne had just come out of the closet they had all suspected she'd been skulking in for over ten years, and was dealing with her own dramatic life change. Ro's other friends were either single like her, or struggling to get pregnant (Mya, leaving her out of the question), or were perpetually exhausted by babies and never had any time (Ebi). Rowena was doubtful she would get a measured answer from anyone. She didn't want to involve her mum because her whole war cry had been Your Dad Left Me a Single Parent! That picture would not be rosy. What was she seeking? Validation either way? For the first time in years, Florence had intruded into her thoughts. No! Rowena didn't want her thrown into the mix along with everything else. She put her head in her hands as one final person, obvious really, floated on a wave of incredulity into her mind's eye. She picked up her phone.

'Dad, hi, have you got a minute...?'

* * *

Rowena carefully slipped the scans into her coat pocket before replying to her mum.

'Not heard a squeak from Nate, which suits me fine. He probably thinks I've had an abortion.'

'Don't you at least want to know if he'll cough up something along the way? Babies are hard work and expensive, Rowena.'

'No, Mum, I don't want anything to do with him. It's just me and Squodge from now – we're going to be a party of two.'

9

DELIVERY FOR MS PARKER

The van was partly shrouded by two baronial sycamore trees tucked just off the single file road near Friston Forest. It was a spot Clinton and Florence were convinced only they knew about. The odds were, locals appreciated it too, but no one ever parked here when man-made spaces were plentiful elsewhere. They'd chosen this spot because they could stay overnight without being hassled by villagers or drunks on their way back from the pub. Florence always enjoyed the verdant walk down towards the River Cuckmere, eventually winding their way to the shingle beach and the titanic chalk sentinels of the Seven Sisters iconic cliffs. But as soon as you gazed towards the horizon, across the English Channel, the fine pencil line of France invisible except on a magnificently clear day, the cliffs were immediately dwarfed in the face of infinite opposition.

Clinton hadn't answered any of Florence's texts, or picked up the phone. She wrung her hands, sweat oiling her palms. As she reached the tailgate, Florence fully expected the green van to pull out through the bushes and head towards West Dean, having caught her approach in the poky rear-view mirror...

Florence jumped awake, sweat pooled on her chest like the River Cuckmere, snaking its way towards open water. Her T-shirt clung to her skin underneath her navy Gap hoodie, irritating the fading scars hatched into her back and hips; she resisted the urge to gouge at them with her fingernails. Sometimes she forgot they were there, unintentionally exposing them by wearing a shorter vest top or low-riding jeans. One morning at Apa Villa when the monkeys were eyeing up her mango artistically fanned out across her breakfast plate, she'd tied her sarong a tad too loose in her rush to greet Omesh. His was the only decent conversation she would have all day, apart from basic chat with the tuk-tuk drivers. Omesh had already arrived radiating his usual cheerfulness, setting down her pot of coffee next to the mango. He would soon be back with her hoppers. Florence had greeted him and reached over to pour some coffee, her sarong slipping below her hips. She always asked if he wanted one too, and he refused as usual. This time, instead of leaving with his tray, he hovered. Florence glanced at him, his face had split into an uneasy frown. 'Are you OK?' she had enquired. But Omesh lowered his voice.

'I should ask if you are, Ms Villiers.'

'I'm great, honestly!'

He nodded and slid the tray under his armpit and wandered back through the frangipani trees to collect her pan-fresh hoppers, the vanilla nectar wallowing on the breeze. When she returned from her sun-baked day on the beach, skin bristling with salt and sand, a little jar of coconut oil and a silver tin of beautiful coconut sweets crowned with crystallised pineapple pieces awaited on her shaded porch table. There was a note delicately scribed upon one of the villa's pale blue postcards found in reception:

Dear Ms Villiers, please accept these gifts. The coconut oil is to soothe your skin and the sweets are to soothe your soul. Regards, Omesh

She had thanked him the next day but the note was never mentioned, Omesh respecting her privacy. However, each day when she returned from her sightseeing, a new flavour of sweet appeared for her to sample. On the day she left, he'd pressed a fresh tin into her hand and wished her well. 'Don't forget about us!' Florence's eyes pricked at the memory. The sweets were long gone, munched on the homeward journey.

She peeled off her damp layers, grateful she had spare clothes with her, which was a luxury compared to her adventures abroad. She didn't want to drop by Tracey Parker's posh school a dishevelled mess. This time she was travelling in style, Nellie cocooning her from the drizzle spatter on the front windscreen. The pink and yellow gingham curtains granted immediate privacy from prying eyes, but she was the sole pitch today, maybe some sheep in the neighbouring field would appreciate a floor show when she got dressed. There were no electric hook-ups on Manor View Farm, just outside Berkhamsted, and she'd peed in a washing up bowl in the night and placed it carefully on the driver's seat, ready to pour away come morning. The farmhouse and Portaloos were a brief trudge across open grass, freshly cut in preparation for her visit. She felt honoured.

* * *

'Hi there, I have a delivery for Ms Parker.' The efficient-looking middle-aged woman seated behind the imperious walnut desk flicked her eyes up and around Florence in a subtle once-over. Florence wondered if she was the same person she had spoken to on the phone two days ago when she'd spun an elaborate lie about dropping off Ms Parker's retirement gift. After he'd worked out the quickest route for Flo, Bob had sensibly suggested she check Tracey would be in before she arrived unannounced. The woman certainly matched with the mundane backstory she had dreamt up while talking to her. Florence had discerned by the tone of her voice that she was the kind of person who would have matching floral tea towels and oven gloves, and swapped them at Christmastime for festive ones to complement the Christmas doormat that lived in the cupboard under the stairs for eleven months of the year. She'd love to know how many of these backstories ever hit the mark. She'd decided on day two in Apa Villa that Omesh had really been a spy for the Sri Lankan government and was so deep undercover that he had forgotten his real job, family and former life in order to fully embrace his role as a butler. He was infiltrating illegal ivory trading, according to Florence, which of course was plausible.

'You can leave it here, I'll make sure she gets it,' Tea Towel lady said in an efficient clipped cadence. Florence withdrew the envelope from her bag, but kept tight hold of it, letting go felt wrong.

'I know this sounds crazy, but I'd like to hand deliver it to her myself, if you don't mind.'

The woman stood up; Florence didn't know why she bothered, she barely reached the top of the desk. A small office behind Tea Towel lady was home to two more nondescript women sat at computers busily typing. The sun must have come out because light streamed in from the vestry-style leaded windows, crowning Tea Towel lady with Christ-like light. Florence had to avert her eyes; it was blinding.

'You're right, it does sound crazy.' Tea Towel held out her hand for the letter resting her open palm on the desk. Florence gently shook her head. 'I promise that Ms Parker will get the letter.' She spoke to Florence like she was a small child refusing to share her toys.

'I really need to give it to her.' A UPS courier had entered the mix, sneaking up behind Florence without her realising.

'I'm collecting something to go to Oxford.' He chewed gum and hid behind aviators like he was starring in an indie film all about his life.

'Stay right there,' Tea Towel lady said, waggling her index finger at Florence. 'I'll be right back.' Rude UPS guy didn't alter his dead ahead stare and chomped like his life depended on it. There was no barrier holding Florence back from entering the bowels of Berkhamsted School. Rude UPS guy didn't give a shit what she did; it was now or never. She peered through the back office doorway; Tea Towel had shimmied past a desk and was bending down to retrieve the Oxford package. Florence walked towards a dark wood-panelled corridor straight ahead, the strip of wall above painted an accurate shade of Farrow & Ball Armpit Stain. She turned left, taking a gamble that Ms Parker's office would be in that direction. She believed that most head teachers' offices were near reception and quite often on the left. There was no supporting data, Florence was simply operating on a hunch. The first door was a single toilet, the one after a broom cupboard, then third time lucky, she found a not quite closed slate grey door marked with an understated gold plaque, 'Ms Parker' embossed on it in black.

'Excuse me! Miss!?' Tea Towel called from her desk, not yet following in hot pursuit. 'Come back!' Like that ever worked on anyone, apart from possibly a well-trained dog. Florence imagined Tea Towel vaulting the desk, her athletic prowess not in question being official gatekeeper. She heard some shuffling and click-clacking of heels on polished herringbone oak floor. Here she came...

Florence knocked on Ms Parker's door before pushing it open, poking her head round before steaming in, just in case she caught her in a secret self-ritual (nose-picking, looking at porn, scrolling Tinder, watching her dog cam...). The office was empty. She had time to step in, quietly close the door and take a minute before Tea Towel found her. She'd come this far and having crossed all the frontiers, was almost inured against forthcoming consequences, certain her little excursion wasn't a prison-able offence.

Ms Parker's impressive office boasted a generous bay window with slate grey panelling beneath, while heavy burgundy damask curtains framed the view of the red-bricked chapel and green velvet lawn outside. Florence found the dour chapel to be an ugly hulk of a building encroaching on the surrounding area. Why couldn't the Gothic-obsessed Victorians have been more graceful like Sri Lankan Buddhists? At least Ms Parker had opted for vermillion Chinois wallpaper on the chimney breast, hummingbirds swooping across the top of the mantelpiece and behind the enormous gilt mirror, while above the panelling, dusky pale pink graced the other walls. Just as Florence finished admiring Tracey's taste (the navy velvet sofa and old-fashioned double writing desk an elegant touch), Tea Towel knocked on the door.

'Is everything OK in there, Ms Parker?'

Florence decided to try the sofa, like Goldilocks; it was just right. She stroked its pile, the shade darkening as she brushed it with her fingers. She picked up a glossy school brochure from the glass coffee table in front of her when Tea Towel entered smoothing her blonde hair as she did so. Florence discerned she wasn't a natural blonde by the blanket coverage of bleach and severe lack of undertones.

'I think you need to leave. We do have a security guard. All I have to do is call him.'

'Do you know how long Ms Parker will be?' Florence asked

innocently. She could just leave the letter on the desk, but something was feeding her deliberate obtuseness, as if Cassandra Galaxy herself were whispering directly into her ear, which was, of course, utter bollocks.

'Right, that's it, I'm calling Tony.' She strode over to the writing desk, picked up the landline phone and stabbed a few digits into the keypad. Florence suddenly fretted she'd taken it too far when a tall woman in a grey pinstriped trouser suit breezed into the room. Ms Parker had arrived.

'What's going on, Gwen?' Ms Parker's face flicked between Gwen Tea Towel and Flo. She cut an arresting sight with Afro hair cropped close to her skull like a salt and pepper swimming cap, red-framed cats-eye glasses accentuating piercing green eyes that undoubtedly shot fear into the hearts of misbehaving kids and adults alike.

'I'm just calling Tony to help me with this... intruder.' Wow, Florence had been elevated to the canon. She slowly stood up so as not to startle anyone.

'Hello, Ms Parker. I'm sorry I barged into your office, but I have a letter I need to hand deliver.'

Ms Parker's shoulders broadened and she breathed deeply as if allowing undisclosed information to come forth.

'See, give her the letter and go,' Gwen barked, superiority flooding her veins. She replaced the receiver in the cradle, the threat of Tony no longer required.

'What's your name?' Ms Parker asked, completely ignoring Gwen.

'Florence Villiers.'

Ms Parker's resounding 'Ahhhh,' was imbued with a quiet knowledge.

'Come on, let's go,' Gwen ordered, not party to the abstruse exchange. Florence remained perfectly still. 'Missy, time to leave or I *will* call Tony.'

Ms Parker shook herself and turned to Gwen. 'It's OK, Gwen. I've been expecting Ms Villiers.'

'But—she—'

'It's fine.' She glanced at Florence and ushered her to sit on the sofa where she joined her. 'She's going to stay for a bit.'

Gwen's features briefly twisted into a scowl before she nodded, defeated.

Florence waited for Gwen to close the door before she spoke. 'Have you really been expecting me?'

'Yes.'

'So you knew I was bringing you a letter?'

'I believe the letter is for you?' Ms Parker's eyes twinkled.

Florence brought the envelope up to her face. 'No, it has your name on the front.'

'My name was bait to get you to come here.' She looked meaningfully at her Apple watch. 'I've a meeting in about ten minutes, are you free later, about six?'

'I am free, yes.' Florence hesitated, irritation snipping at the base of her throat. 'Should I open the letter here or later, or on my own?'

'I think that's something only you can decide.' She smiled. 'I would offer you a hot drink but I don't think you'd have time to finish it.'

Florence put the letter back in her bag. There wasn't enough time to begin a proper conversation without being cut short, yet Florence wanted to fire questions at Tracey.

'Where shall I meet you later?' she finally conceded.

'There's a nice pub on the canal called the Rising Sun. We could meet there for dinner if you like, my treat?'

'That would be lovely, thank you.'

'And, Florence? Sorry about Gwen – she can be a bit of a jobsworth, but she's got my back. Runs everything like clockwork. I loved your tenacity. Cassie said you wouldn't give in.'

'You spoke to her?' Tracey tapped the side of her nose. 'Six at the Rising Sun. I'll be sat at the back avoiding any parents.'

10

THE TREASURE HUNT

Dear Florence

So sorry to engage in subterfuge and force you to drive Nellie all the way to Berkhamsted. Either that is exactly what has happened, or you have ripped this letter open and are reading it at home. But I believe that you will follow the treasure hunt in the right order, exactly like you used to at school. I loved putting all the clues together, creating riddles from the books we were studying. I guess you're wondering what on earth is the point to all this. Tracey will explain our story when you see her properly. I primed her you may visit, within a suggested time frame. I thought you might try to deliver this before she retires. I must confess, I haven't worked this all out on my own, I have guides that point me in the right direction. And they laid down a pathway of action, and now you're on it, with any luck. See you at the next stop.

With love

Cassie x

Florence tore open the letter outside the school gates. Her hunch had been correct, this *was* a flaming treasure hunt. Had Cassie really believed she could 'transform' Flo's life with a few woo woo letters and some chocolate mini eggs? Anger swelled in her chest and she bitterly screwed up the paper, squashing it into a hard tight ball. Fuck's sake, they weren't at school now! She should just piss off back to Felworth, scrub up Nellie and ring that valuer her dad had mentioned, Winston someone, see how much money she had to play with. Florence stormed back towards the high street in the direction of Waitrose car park where Nellie awaited, her crème pâtissière and lemon mousse paint job clearly distinguishing her from the pole to pole metallic grey and blue four-by-fours she was fenced in amongst. Ten minutes into her hostile retreat, Florence stumbled to a halt outside a charming gift shop, her rage having blown itself out. She could hardly stand Tracey up in the pub; that was rude. She could leave a message with Gwen the Tea Towel, say she wasn't coming. As Florence battled with her conscience, she glanced in the gift shop window, the lively display of kitsch knick-knacks and eclectic homewares momentarily pausing her internal dialogue, her eyes alighting on a familiar recherché glass utensil jar, catching her by surprise. It was the same ornate glass fish-shaped one, the utensils intended to poke out the top of the creature's mouth. She had bought it in one of those achingly cool shops in Brighton Lanes, a housewarming present for her and Clinton. She'd been so excited carrying it home to show him. They'd not bought much stuff for the flat because it came furnished and what essentials were missing were either passed down from parents or found cheaply on Facebook Marketplace. The fish utensil jar came with no enchanting anecdote attached, no scratches or chips, it was up to them to inflict wear and tear, welcoming it into their new life.

Roaring sea beat in Florence's ears, swaying her gently on the spot. She lifted one foot then the other and stepped towards the shop door, pushing it open. She located the storage jar flanked by brightly coloured glass candlesticks, patterned sushi bowls, distressed hurricane lanterns and various aspirational homewares on a prominent display table helming the front of the shop. She picked it up, exactly like that time when she'd bought it eight years ago on her lunch break. She'd walked home from work with a bounce in her gait; Clinton would love it. He loved anything to do with animals. This whole nesting phenomena had been completely novel to Florence. She and Rowena had discussed getting a flat together, but with Ro's paltry junior marketing executive wages, and Florence having only just graduated, they'd realised that moving into a flat share with lots of randoms was their best option. They had originally considered living at home until they had gathered enough money, but Florence had presaged they'd never leave if they did that, and they'd still be living next door to each other with their parents until they were thirty...

After her abrupt ejection from FloRo's convenient house share in Kemptown, Florence had soon found herself in the Brunswick Square flat with the promise of a dog to join the incumbent guinea pigs, and her first adult relationship with Clinton Siems that betrothed a viable future, despite its contentious inception. She had moved up a couple of pay grades since starting out in Customer Care at Brighton and Hove Council, consequently a one-bedroomed flat was within their reach. No more housemates queuing for the bathroom. No arguments or passive aggressive barbed comments about bins, dirty plates, unwelcome overnight guests, or who moved my cheese? Everything within the flat was theirs. If they wanted to indulge in sofa sex halfway through *Gogglebox*, they could. A few teething problems were inevitable. Florence's irritation at scrabbling through the middle drawer every time she was cooking drove Clinton to distraction. All the utensils rolled around like loose change in the bottom of a bag, some of them tangling up in the hand whisks – 'They do it on purpose!' Florence would screech. She was predictably more tetchy just before her period, but Clinton wisely refrained from asking what time of the month it was. He didn't want to find himself stabbed with a truculent fish slice. Instead he upcycled an old plant pot and decanted the most useful utensils into it. It wasn't perfect and didn't go with the budget baroque cum mid-century modern vibe Florence was hankering after on Pinterest, but they both agreed it was handy to be able to grab exactly what you needed.

Florence held the utensil jar up to her face in the little shop in Berkhamsted.

'Can I help you?' a voice asked behind her. The jar slipped slightly in her hand, but Florence recovered and turned to see who had spoken.

'Oh sorry, no, I was just looking.'

'It's just that you looked like you'd seen a ghost, that's all.' The woman smiled. 'If you want to ask me anything please do. That jar also comes in blue glass as well as clear.'

'Thank you.'

There was a coffee shop next door and Florence ventured in, abandoning the fish jar. As she leaned back in the window seat, observing mothers with buggies and recalcitrant toddlers dragging their heels, she couldn't flush the utensil jar from her thoughts. The unfortunate jar had only lasted a year. Clinton had been so chuffed when she'd brought it home, and had laughed at her discriminately selecting the most photogenic utensils for their Instagram debut. But a year later, the jar shattered in a supernova explosion on the kitchen floor, utensils flung around, car crash victims awaiting paramedics. It had been her fault, she hadn't understood, and his frustration had triggered a white rage...

Tears cramped the base of her throat. Florence abhorred public crying and tried her best to nip it in the bud with the espresso she'd ordered, necking it in one before biting into the cheese toasty. She wasn't hungry, but Florence adhered to the belief that one didn't have to be hungry in order to eat. The savoury, crunchy, fried bread edifice of gooey West Country cheddar was exactly what was required to ground herself in reality. Whenever she wandered dangerously off-piste inside her own head on her overseas adventures, food always plugged her into the present moment. Nothing could compare biting into a recondite culinary delight, whether it be from a ramshackle roadside stall or a top class restaurant boasting a panoramic view of Christ the Redeemer.

Florence made up her mind. She would meet Tracey, tell her she wanted no part of whatever this was and then drive directly to Felworth. She felt she owed Tracey some kind of explanation. She paid for her lunch and popped back into the shop next door.

'Hello, please could I buy the utensil jar in blue?' She walked outside, swinging the bag, not quite bouncing, but with a subtle spring in her step. Lennie's birthday was approaching and if she didn't like it (Lennie was a prolific re-gifter) Florence could always store it in Mr Ogby's garage along with the rest of her life until she eventually got round to reclaiming it. Her phone pinged. Tariq. It could only mean one thing, meme o'clock. Sylvester Stallone as Rocky prepping for the fight of his life lifting weights and running in sweats: *introverts preparing to make a phone call*. She snorted, relieved he'd not relinquished his duty of care in supplying comic relief. She forwarded it to Lennie.

Florence eventually found the Rising Sun at seven minutes past six after trudging the wrong way down the towpath. Laughable as it was, she continued to struggle with Google Maps and surrendered to patronising satnav even for a straightforward trek. How anything had ever been discovered before Google Maps, let alone longitude and latitude, was an alchemic mystery to her. A few customers were sitting outside luxuriating in the last dregs of the sunlight before the drop in temperature. The pub was adjacent to the canal towpath settled behind a lock, much like a Constable painting, one of which undoubtedly hung above the traditional mantelpiece inside. Florence had visions of old men, sheep dogs and open fires as she approached the cosy bar. It was definitely a place to quietly sup a pint of draught ale rather than giggle over cocktail happy hour. Florence couldn't remember when she had last hung out in an old man boozer with a gaggle of friends over a few bottles of wine.

Ms Parker was as good as her word and had tucked herself away at the back near the toilets. She waved her over and Florence edged past a ubiquitous old man nursing a pint of Guinness. Tracey made to stand up, but Florence motioned for her to sit back down.

'What can I get you?' she asked Florence, her face more relaxed than earlier work mode.

'Nothing, I'm not staying, I just wanted to let you know I'm going to head back now...'

Tracey frowned. 'Is it something I said?'

'No, you haven't done anything. I just want to go home.'

'I'm sorry to hear that. Are you sure I can't buy you dinner before you go, it'll take you a long time, won't it? Better than eating motorway trash?'

'No, I'd just rather leave. Sorry.' Florence remained standing.

'Please, Florence. Stay for dinner. The quesadillas here are amazing...' Florence dithered; she *was* hungry. 'I promised Cassie

I would play my part. If you want to ignore everything after, fair enough, I'll have done what I was asked to do.'

Florence slowly sat down. 'OK, but I'm not up for any weird psychic stuff or ghosts sending messages from beyond the grave.'

'Do I look like I can raise the dead?' Tracey smirked, still in her sober suit and as far removed from a peddler of woo woo as could be. Florence shook her head. 'Good, right what would you like – here's the menu.'

When Florence had settled on the vegetarian quesadillas, Tracey smoothly opened up proceedings as if chairing a job interview.

'Cassie was your teacher at school? I imagine she was very good.'

'She was. I never liked school that much but we all looked forward to her lessons because she managed to bring some kind of relevance to our own lives, with the treasure hunts and what-not. She was the reason I decided to train to be a teacher...'

'Oh, you're a teacher too?' Tracey smiled encouragingly.

'I dropped out after the first year.' Florence jumped in with a quick denial. 'Stupid really, I regretted it later on.'

'It's never too late if you want to teach.' Florence gave her best non-committal shrug. 'This country's in desperate need of good teachers; it's in crisis. Though way too much needs to change...' Tracey shook her head sadly.

'So why am I here, what made you agree to this... "treasure hunt"?' Florence asked cagily. So far there had been no treasure.

'Cassie's diagnosis shocked her into finally getting in touch. She'd been thinking about it ever since she'd left Ant, but it never felt the right time. I'd not seen her since graduation day over forty years ago.'

'Not one word?' Tracey shook her head. Despite her cynicism, Florence was intrigued. 'How did the reunion come about?'

'She'd written a letter with her contact details inside, said she would love to reconnect, if I had time in the next month. I'm not on social media, but she asked some old college friends where I worked. I did sit on the letter for a few days, then emailed her. She drove up in Nellie the following week, stayed the night on a campsite in Tring near where we live. I had no idea she was ill when she turned up. She'd aged like all of us, but not dramatically, nothing that would cause concern.'

'Wasn't it awkward?'

'At first, maybe, so much time had passed, but as soon as we started chatting, the years melted away. The original fall out felt irrelevant. Age and experience taught me she had just chased what she'd thought she wanted, what society had expected.'

'And what was that?'

'A conventional family. To blend in. Not having to hide who she was from her pupils, herself, her parents.' Tracey's eyes softened remembering her friend.

'*Was* she hiding?' Florence realised she had no idea what Tracey was intimating.

Tracey took a sip of wine and met Florence's eyes above the stubby brass tea light holder. 'I believe she was... Cassie and I were more than just friends.'

'Oh, I see.'

'She broke my heart, disappeared with Ant instead of moving in with me after graduation.'

'Oh wow, you were a serious item.'

'She was my first love,' Tracey said wistfully, as if she were back in the Farmer's Arms at the beginning of the first year where she'd first stumbled across Cassie. 'I know this might appear unconnected, but Cassie wanted me to tell you our story... When you appeared at the psychic fair it became a pivotal moment. She felt like she had properly graduated from schoolteacher to professional clairvoyant after you didn't recognise her. She was living her dream, shedding the past – with one last tie to cut – Ant. At the same time she could see all the things you had been through, and it reflected her own unfinished business. Not precisely, but enough for Cassie's third eye to get involved! She presented a good enough case for my participation, said it would really help you see past blocks, possibly move you forward, if you understand what I mean?'

'Not really.' A wasp of annoyance buzzed at the back of Flo's throat. 'Whatever you think my "situation" is, it's nothing like this. I don't need anyone telling me what I should be doing with my life. My life is fine as it is. I'm... managing OK.' She shifted in her seat, squirming to the edge of the chair. She still had her coat on, prepared to take flight, as always.

'I'm not here to tell you what to do with your life, that's up to you.'

Tracey reached down for her bag on the floor, a sturdy battered brown leather knapsack that was at odds with her sleek pinstripes, yet somehow offset the look perfectly. She drew out another thin envelope, the same as the one Florence had hand delivered only hours before, sliding it towards her across the table.

'I'm not saying what she saw was real, or that spirits or ghosts or whoever they may or may not be have any answers, but she felt these things deeply enough to drag herself off her impending death bed and come here, settle her debt with me, leading by example. Would she be lying if she said you had been running from something?' Florence stared straight ahead, unmoving. She was right back at school again, not having revised for a test. 'It's up to you what you do with this envelope. Open it, don't open it, burn it. That's the power of the envelope, it keeps information safe until you're ready to read it.'

The urge to hear the rest of Cassie's story outweighed Flo's impulse to escape back to Nellie. 'How did Ant persuade her? What happened?'

Tracey tapped her fingers on the table between them and cleared her throat. 'I was a member of the Gay and Lesbian Student Alliance at Altrincham, and Cassie was always helping out. We were on the same course so we naturally gravitated towards each other. She was very popular with everyone, so I obviously thought I never stood a chance. I'd only recently come out to myself, so the idea of being with her was... revolutionary.'

'Was Cassie a lesbian?' What alternate universe was this where Florence openly discussed the sexuality of her deceased former English teacher?

Tracey fondly recalled the 1979 second year Halloween disco in the college bar. Cassie had dressed up as a 'pimpkin', half pimp, half pumpkin (orange face paint, fake fur coat and hideous suit procured from Oxfam, her purple shirt stuffed with a cushion). Tracey's bat costume was more conservative, having created wings from bin bags and borrowing a dance major's black unitard. The last days of disco reigned alongside Two Tone but punk hijacked the dance floor. Tracey wasn't a fan of punk, preferring ska, but the white middle class Arts Major DJ controlled the dance floor. Cassie was pogoing to the Sex Pistols when she tripped on someone's feet, grabbing hold of a ghost, pulling off their disguise and face planting on the beer-splattered floor. Tracey had scraped her up and gathered some ice from the bar, wrapping it in one of her wings, dabbing Cassie's bashed nose. They ended up outside getting some fresh air, Cassie's head starting to sting.

'Do you need to go and lie down?' Tracey had asked, concerned about the red mark on her chin as she dabbed that too.

'No, I just need...' Instead of finishing her sentence, Cassie lunged at Tracey, planting her mouth on top of hers, her tongue quicksilvering seeking Tracey's own. Tracey jumped back. As much as this had been her cloistered fantasy for an entire year, she understood her responsibilities.

'Cassie, you're drunk. I don't think you want to do this.'

'I do want to. I'm no more drunk than you.'

'You'd an extra pint of snakebite so I'd say you are... You don't mean it.'

'How do you know what I mean?' Cassie reproached.

'I don't know. But I live in this world, and this feels like you're being a tourist.'

'That's insulting.'

'Sorry...' Tracey scuttled back to her corner, fear overriding her desire. 'I don't want to "start" something, and then you waltz off, ignore me, pretend it never happened.'

'I'm not a man!' They both started laughing. 'Give me a chance, Trace. It might be fun. Stop being so serious!' Tracey knew she erred on the side of solemnity. She viewed partying as an obligatory part of student life rather than something to be wildly relished. She preferred learning, being part of an intimate group, helping out at GLSA events, supporting fellow members. In that respect, Cassie was a total paradox: a social live wire, practically ethereal with her crystals and her bizarre intuition, gut instincts supplanting cold hard facts. Tracey didn't have a third eye to consult on the matters of the heart, so leaned over and kissed Cassie gingerly on the lips.

'Let's take it slow...' And that was that.

'Cassie was Cassie, she didn't have a label,' Tracey attempted to best illustrate her lost love. 'All the boys were enthralled by her, she was constantly outwitting hulking rugby types trying to pin her down. Ant was part of that dubious gang. But Cassie just wanted fun, to be a free spirit, no strings, though when we finally got together we were properly committed, but only in private.

Publicly we weren't officially an item, just "friends". We never held hands, kissed, that kind of thing. She claimed she was scared of the latent homophobia, of her parents finding out. Don't get me wrong, so was I, but at college I was truly myself. I think her real concern was shame about how she felt... Plenty of people conducted relationships in the shadows fearful of familial recrimination or getting beaten up – they were different times. I was so proud of "us", of being seen with her; I wanted to shout it from the rooftops, but she wouldn't let me. I was so head over heels that I would have streaked across the quad if she'd asked me.' Florence smiled. 'Despite all the cloak and dagger, we had a ball, flying to Greece in the holidays, picking apples in France another summer, then the final year arrived...' Tracey's eyes dimmed. 'Ant had always liked Cassie, but he also fancied everyone with a pulse and made it his task to win her round, save her from the lesbians, like some kind of trophy to be won on the pitch. He pursued her hard, used all his charm – there was no denying he was fun, likeable and represented a more conformist life. Eventually she wavered.'

Tracey paused to sip her wine just as their food arrived, the steam wafting off the molten cheese fogging up her glasses. Flo shrugged off her coat and cut into hers, watching the cheese ooze out onto her plate, sliced mushrooms and half-moon courgettes trapped inside its lava flow wilting the lambs lettuce salad. Tracey carved up her quesadilla and wisely waited for it to cool before trying it.

'We had both applied to schools near each other in Birmingham post graduation. But I'd been so focused on us getting into adjacent schools that I'd failed to notice Ant slipping in the back door, feeding her lines about marriage, about kids... Kids weren't on my agenda – I knew she wanted them, that she was bound by convention more than I was, but I naively thought she would get over it when what we had was so good. We were very young, too young to be making such huge decisions that would change the rest of our lives. But we started to fight about how everything was so serious all the time, and that was when Ant swooped in with his charm and his "let's have fun". He'd secured a job down on the south coast, filled her head with tales of the seaside, of beach walks, of parties, of you're only young once. He was like a dog with a bone but Cassie couldn't see that. She was amazing at helping other people work out their problems, brilliant listener, fantastic friend, kind, everything you could wish for, but when it came to her own life, she couldn't offer herself any advice. It was as if that third eye blocked up with sludge whenever she faced a personal crisis.' Tracey shrugged sadly. 'It turned out she was seeing Ant behind my back and I made her choose; she chose him.'

'That must have been painful,' Florence empathised, scooping up a mouthful of quesadilla with her fork, burning her tongue in the process.

'It was at the time, but you move on. I ended up meeting my wife soon after, so it's all good.' She smiled reassuringly at Florence.

'How did you feel when you saw Cassie again?'

'I wasn't angry or upset if that's what's worrying you. I think she'd overblown how the fall out had affected me. But I hadn't let it; I had a life to lead. Cassie's clairvoyance helped people with personal difficulties, with grief, but also shone a light on events in her own past that she'd not dealt with. It was a way of tying up loose ends before she passed. But it was also a clue on the road to helping you...'

Florence sighed. She didn't need any help. 'Did you see her again?'

'No, I so wished I had. We kept in contact afterwards and I was supposed to visit but she died suddenly. I went to the funeral, it was lovely. Ant was there of course. I said hello, water under the bridge and everything.'

'It wasn't awkward?'

'No, he actually apologised, perhaps realising he'd deterred her from her true north, but then she wouldn't have had Frank. I'm not saying Cassie and I would have made it – we were extremely immature, but possibly his arrogance and manipulation swayed her from following a different path, one more in line with who she was...' Tracey's green eyes shimmered beneath the weight of reminiscence. 'He was hit pretty hard by her death, even if he did have someone else waiting in the wings.'

The door to the pub swung open as a group of young women all wearing smart work clothes barrelled in, laughing and talking loudly about an unfortunate character named Will. They let the door slam behind them as the queen bee of the group ascertained what colour wine they were drinking and instructed the rest to rearrange tables and chairs as Will's justified desecration continued. Florence smiled to herself, poor Will's ears must be burning...

'Do you know what's in the letter?' she asked absently, still staring at the girls positioning tables in a rough circle.

'No. My role was to simply deliver it and to tell you our story.' Tracey followed the direction of Florence's gaze. 'It's easier to ignore a letter than someone revealing their truth, the parallels might resonate, nudge you into action...'

Florence drifted off, longing to pour a glass of red and sit amongst the cluster of uncomplicated girls now neatly huddled in the opposite corner. She wasn't bothered about hurling insults at useless Will (who she had now overheard was yet another serial shagger with a proclivity for dick pics), she would have been content just allowing the boisterous female banter to caress her, transporting her back to another lifetime where most weekends began in a similar vein...

'Are you OK, Florence?' Tracey asked concerned, as Florence reluctantly wrenched her eyes back to their table and half-eaten dinner.

Florence forced a smile. 'I'm fine, thank you. And I do appreciate all the effort you've gone to. I'm not completely blind, I see what Cassie was getting at, but I...' She shrugged, closing her eyes, suddenly swamped by memories she'd effectively ring-fenced for years. 'I need to go. Thank you for the dinner. I'm sorry...' She grabbed her coat and glanced at Tracey who nodded.

'Take care of yourself, Florence.'

As Florence shot towards the door pushing out into the crisp night air, Tracey sighed, picked up her glass of wine and drained it. 'I tried Cass, I tried...'

Later that evening the dark deterring her, Florence decided to stay another night at Manor Farm, at ten pounds a day she couldn't really complain. She lay protected under Nellie's roof inside her sleeping bag, wrapped in Dunelm furry blankets like a bear awaiting spring. She slid her finger under the envelope flap and opened Tracey's letter, pulling out an artist's postcard of the Seven Sisters cliffs painted in bright pinks and blues from the aspect of famous Seaford Head Nature Reserve. Ice cracked upwards from her toes until her fingers numbed with disbelief. She turned it over. It was blank apart from two sets of carefully written decimal numbers.

50.7722549

0.1136139

11

CAT'S OUT THE BAG

Rowena reread the text, the tip of the all-seeing finger burning hot with indignation. She'd blocked Nate's number, but retained it in her contacts. She wasn't sure why – she had no intention of telling him anything about the baby, and he'd made it perfectly clear that he'd wanted nothing to do with raising the child or helping out financially. She suspected this was one of his many burner phones he used for dalliances.

Ro, it's me. I feel so bad about running off like that. I know it's been months since we've seen each other. I just want to know what you've decided about the situation. Are you OK? X

Nathaniel (not his real name) was a man of moderate gestures: flowers, decent champagne (nothing below twenty-five quid a bottle), maybe a weekend away in a five star country house hotel staying in an entry level room overlooking the fire escape, certainly not a suite with its own roof terrace and a view of the rolling hills. If he genuinely was concerned for Rowena, a medi-ocre present from Amazon or Moonpig would have materialised by now. This text spoke of a man on the ropes, scared shitless in case his wildly sewn progeny was on its way, about to slice through the epidermis of his perfect life, exposing the fatty tissue riddled with deceit. Nathaniel was obviously hoping that the burgeoning embryo had been dislodged having had no time to develop arms and legs and a heart – something he'd clearly been born without.

Rowena's thumb hovered over 'delete', ready to eradicate the unknown number and block it. What if he kept texting her from different numbers? Better that she tell him what he wanted to hear, *then* block him. He would never try and find her after that; he'd just be so relieved his wife and kids (if indeed they even existed) weren't ever going to file for divorce (thus bleeding him dry) and that he could safely prey on the next woman. Maybe this time he would brave a vasectomy. Or catch chlamydia.

Please don't contact me again. I had an abortion, so your dirty little secret is safe. Have a nice life.

Rowena pressed 'send' and didn't immediately block the number. She wanted to make sure he received the message. She awaited the typing speech bubble, but it didn't appear. She had a tonne of marking to finish – five books, it may as well be twenty. She desperately wanted a glass of wine, but the nanny state had decreed that was against the rules. Obviously she didn't adhere to the nil by mouth, wasn't swayed by the tiny encircled cheery pregnant woman knocking back a glass of wine, a theatrical slash slicing her swollen belly in half. The warning was obsolete really. If you were pregnant, half the time you felt too sick to drink, and if you were an alcoholic, nothing was going to dissuade you from downing a bottle of wine or gin. She always felt so judged at the Co-op self-checkout when she was IDed. 'It's not for me,' she'd lately started bleating if her protruding tummy had sneaked into view. She usually only braved the shops if she was wearing a massive coat, her bump buried under myriad layers. She'd noticed that strangers, especially elderly people, felt it was their civic duty to comment on her body. 'How pregnant are you, love?' one old man had asked recently when she'd held the door open for him and his wife leaving the dry cleaner's. 'None of your business' almost dropped off her tongue, but 'Actually, I'm not pregnant,' got there first. The man's face froze, his wife grabbed his arm and dragged him towards to the café next door, as he tried to dig himself out of the hole with 'I'm so sorry, I just thought, but you look...' Ingrid behind the counter raised her eyebrows.

'What?!' Ro had complained, her fuckwit level tolerance at an all-time low.

'That was a bit mean,' Ingrid chastised.

'He shouldn't have said anything!'

'He was just trying to be nice.'

'How is telling someone they look pregnant *ever* being nice? What if I wasn't pregnant?'

'But you are.' Ingrid pursed her luscious red lips.

Rowena presumed Ingrid didn't subscribe to her school of thought, and probably still told little girls they looked pretty, and asked who was their favourite Disney princess. Rowena had fought many battles with her mum about that line of questioning.

'Mum, we don't ask girls shit like that any more. You ask what they like doing, what's their favourite book, pizza topping, literally anything that doesn't make them feel it's about how they look and reinforce the whole patriarchal Disney princess stereotype.'

'They like being told they're pretty!' Denise cried at the same time checking her reflection in the charity shop window.

'How do you know what they like? You're just thinking about

yourself. They might be gagging for someone to ask them what's the point of fractions or whether they've tried coding.'

'Everyone likes to be told they're pretty, Rowena, even you!' Her mum had sniffed and teased her hair from out underneath her scarf.

'Not if that's the only thing anyone can think of to say. You don't tell boys they're pretty.'

'I'd say they were a handsome young man and I liked his outfit.' Rowena had slapped her forehead and continued walking ahead. The constant commenting on people's weight was another bug bear. Imagine you've won the Booker Prize but all the prize-giver could mention was haven't you lost weight, you look great. It made Rowena want to raze the Disney empire to the ground.

Rowena poured herself a small glass of Rioja and placed it out of reach on the kitchen counter like a dangling carrot. She was mindful of what she drank and one was enough or it triggered a headache. But she'd need a treat after the marking. Coming up for air an hour and a half later, marking complete, she reached for her phone and the wine. There was a reply.

Thanks for letting me know. It would be good to meet up when you're ready. I miss you.

Rowena crushed the impulse to fire off a chain of expletives that would have terrified hairs into existence on Nate's waxed chest. Instead she deleted and blocked his number. She was telling work about her pregnancy tomorrow; she'd run out of baggy tops that foiled her secret. Mya, Ebi and Oli knew, but no one at school. It had been tricky to disguise the puking at first but luckily, concentrating in class somehow distracted her. She'd leaned over and hurled into her wastepaper bin the minute the kids had left for lunch a few times. The perennial snacking was troublesome – she had to constantly eat without anyone noticing. She'd lost count of the amount of times she submerged beneath the desk to shovel in some emergency Cadbury's buttons.

The one good thing about her job was she would have the school holidays off and the nearby nursery was apparently decent according to Ofsted. Thankfully the waiting list wasn't horrific. Her dad had also dropped a surprise.

'Rowena, I'd like to make up for all the crappy parenting over the years. I have some money set aside for you. It'll be useful for nursery fees, plus I can help out on Fridays. Carl said he'll cover.' Rowena had ended up asking him to repeat it all because the shock almost rendered her deaf. Her dad was offering to be daddy day care!

The following morning after Nate's texts, she found herself sitting outside Mrs Wilson's office, Sunni, her PA, inspecting her from her desk by the window, her cheese plant reaching for the light, almost tipping over in its eagerness to achieve maximum photosynthesis. Maybe it suffered performance anxiety living in the head teacher's waiting room. Just before Mrs Wilson called her in, she was suddenly thrown back in time to September 2002, anticipating an absolute roasting from Mr Greave for skiving off final period with Florence to go and meet the Sugababes signing CDs in HMV Brighton.

'I'd do it again,' Florence had whispered to her before they were summoned. 'It was brill.' They'd fist bumped and faced the howling music together, two weeks of litter picking and detention after school a small price to pay for touching Mutya's hand.

How bizarre that it was Flo who had originally wanted to be a teacher and here Ro was, half-baked dreams of working in marketing ground into the cheap nylon carpet of that shitty start-up when she finally grasped it was the last thing she wanted. After her old boss had asked her to babysit a Year Nine work experience girl from the local school, Rowena subsequently realised what she had enjoyed most about work that week was showing Talia the ropes, explaining, and watching her confidence expand. Marketing could shove its seven Ps up its shallow arse. Teaching was relentless, the pay was OK, the lesson plans strenuous yet formulaic, the marking so boring, yet she loved her kids, something she could never have predicted. She'd circumspectly digested all the teaching horror stories before applying to train on the job in Bexhill, and it had initially been less gardening theory on tending fertile minds and more like mass-produced growbag boot camp with added terror and weedkiller. But she mostly took it in her stride, confident she could surmount the stress and constant firefighting. Nothing was as bad as the tinpot dictator CEO of a local bakery chain aiming for a slice of Greggs pie screaming at her in a meeting that her campaign to increase footfall was absolute shite and she couldn't market her way out of a sausage roll. She wouldn't have minded but she had only been incubating the role until her boss employed an account manager. Thankfully, the eventual move from Bexhill to Seaford Head was the right fit. It helped that she mostly taught sixth form, that the twelve kids this year (average class size for Psychology was fifteen) chose to be there, and actually buckled down. The sixth form operated separately from a smaller satellite building situated diagonally across the road from the main school. The kids automatically matured once they were no longer swimming amongst a sea of minnows, the atmosphere toeing the line of a university *salle d'attente*. It was generally calm apart from the ubiquitous teenage girl screeching.

The school was plagued by the same funding issues, lack of textbooks, constant Ofsted scrutiny, dwindling stationery supplies and regular staffing shortages as every other state school in the country, but somehow, Seaford managed to style it out more than most due to solid management and a ferociously competent PTA. They still had children walking through the doors on an empty stomach in ill-fitting uniform with holes in their shoes, but the surrounding area cradled the school with frequent fund raisers and a breakfast club subsidised by a consortium of local businesses. Rowena felt she and her baby were in the right place to shoulder this journey alone. The community spirit thrived as more and more young people moved into the area perpetuating the inflow of children. Rowena was riding the wave of Seaford's arrival as the most up and coming East Sussex neighbourhood.

No one had been more surprised than she was by the whole quixotic career plan switcheroo. Naturally, Florence had encouraged her at the time. 'You make me want to try teaching again.' But she never did, and then they lost touch before she even started. Sitting on the moulded plastic chair under Sunni's inquisitive gaze, Rowena wondered what Florence was doing with her life now. There had been a time when she couldn't even formulate the letters of her name, let alone sound them out like a child learning phonics. She eventually filled the empty space around the loss with new experiences, none of them referencing Flo, learning on the job proving to be a powerful mistress of mindfulness. However, just because she had moved on didn't automatically mean Rowena wanted to reawaken the dragon. How do you snap back from screaming 'You're dead to me!' at your best friend, the keeper of your darkest hours and childhood milestones?

FloRo had been one of those intense friendships that burnt bright then imploded like a star. That was the story Rowena sold herself. What if Florence and Clinton had branched out with a family? How did that make her feel, now she was pregnant herself? She allowed herself to imagine them with three kids, all born so close together creating a triumvirate of chaotic mess: no sleep, no sex, no life – well, she was in charge of this reality, why make it a doddle for them? They would be sinking under a menagerie of pets too, Clinton would have seen to that. She ventured into a fantasy where she bumped into them in a park, Rowena with her baby Elissa (she was convinced she was carrying a girl, though for now the epithet Squodge sufficed), they with three boisterous boys tearing round, terrorising everyone. It was uncomfortable and they were gratifyingly creased like a well-thumbed copy of *Vogue*, their undying love dimmed from constant caregiving and a dearth of intimacy. Rowena had swirled with a mix of relief and smugness that she had held on to her sanity while Florence's had slipped its moorings after baby number three. Eat sleep baby repeat. She waved them goodbye, leaving them to wonder about her life, not letting any details slip.

'Rowena, do you want to come in?' Mrs Wilson said, her head poking round the edge of her door. She smiled professionally, her eyes engaged elsewhere...

Now Rowena was officially out of the pregnancy closet, she could safely wear more comfortable maternity clothes. Mrs Wilson had said all the right things, adhered to the Burgundy Book and Florence could work to almost the end of term. She would be there for exams, which was important to her and the kids, and then she could have some time at home to nest before the arrival. But as she left school that evening floating on a cloud of optimism, the early evening sun toasting her shoulders, she glimpsed the flash of a familiar car as she reached the pavement in front of the sixth form building. She craned her neck to peer over the passing DPD van, just to be sure. She didn't know the registration, but the Audi driving towards the town centre was the same Atoll blue as Nate's company car. She remembered the name of the colour because Nate had only just taken delivery of it a week before they started dating and he'd had to proudly wait for that particular tone because it was limited, dull car detail that he wrongly thought she might be impressed by. Why hadn't she run a mile, that was surely a red flag? Had he been parked up waiting for her to leave? She wrapped her winter coat around her thickening waist and headed in the direction of home, a flicker of unease tampering with her otherwise jaunty demeanour.

12

A THORN BETWEEN TWO ROSES

Florence awoke in a sweat, the sun boiling her eyes in their
sockets through the windscreen, slowly poaching them like eggs
in a pan. It was nine in the morning and the temperature in the
van had warmed up considerably since last night when she had
tossed and turned inside her mound of bedding trying not to
piece together the day's events. She tore off her beanie and
pushed back the duvet, wriggling out of the sleeping bag more
slug than butterfly. Florence was in virgin territory. The past, the
present and the future had all fused together inside her head in
one giant conflagration. Of course she could see the parallels of
her story with Cassie's and Tracey's. She was pretty sure she was
supposed to be Cassie's avatar in her story, with Tracey taking on
Rowena's mantle. Rowena and Florence had never been lovers
though. But the ending of female friendship had the wily ability
to fracture more lives than the break-up of romantic bonds.
Women's friendships quite often outlived marriages, partnerships,
holiday romances, fleeting friends with benefits ad infinitum.
They were fostered upon shared experiences sometimes created
out of necessity or happenstance. A web of links could be traced

back to how one became friends, nubile roots snaking their way through education, holidays, neighbourhoods, work, friends of friends, family ties, children, hobbies or perhaps just random encounters at a bus stop in 2005 while off your nut after all the clubs had shut.

Florence reached for the postcard she'd let flutter onto the floor beside the bed. She reread the meaningless decimal numbers hoping that by continuously staring at them she would suddenly decipher their mystery. Cassie wasn't even alive to ask for a hint of what direction she'd need to forge. The whole point was she had to work it out herself. In a flash of mercurial brilliance she copied and pasted the numbers into her phone's browser but Google just spat out 'did not match any documents', whatever that meant. Were they mathematical answers to something? Or the components of a puzzle? She added them together and this time Google tricked her with links to polarised-neutron diffraction study and exchange rates of the Japanese yen versus the Brazilian real. The total was inconsequential, but the picture on the front of the postcard was not. Cassandra Galaxy must have had to sacrifice a lamb in order to procure such intimate data from the spirit world. Cuckmere Haven had been *their* place. She had fully expected Clinton to get down on a bended knee one day and ask for her hand in marriage while simultaneously being battered by the wind scuttering along the cliffs of the Seven Sisters. 'You should go for a walk up there, reclaim it,' her mum had said a year on from Clinton leaving. 'Why would I ever need to go there again?' she'd almost shouted back.

Florence found her constant trips abroad a welcome break from society's pressure to 'meet someone else'. She wasn't immune from wanting to have the occasional uncomplicated shag, and bumping into Tariq had saved her from dipping her toe into dating apps. Her parents had been visibly relieved when she'd started seeing him – not realising the terms of their mutual agreement. Electronic dating in the twenty-twenties had mutated into a full-time job and one that Florence had no inclination for. The sheer amount of effort subsumed daily just to find someone you quite liked the look of, let alone spin plates of all the other dates, while keeping on top of beauty admin, life admin, self-care admin, family admin, and your actual job, no wonder birth rates had bellyflopped in recent years. No bad thing with global warming, but still, where was the romance, the fun and frivolity? Florence still idealised that meeting a partner should be organic (not that she imagined herself ready to play that game again): eyes meeting unexpectedly across a crowded bar, the fortuitous touching of fingertips over the photocopier at work, tripping over running in the park, crashing trollies in the frozen veg aisle at Aldi, falling hook, line and sinker for the new love of your BFF.

'No!' Florence yelled at Nellie's windscreen. 'I don't want to go there.' Ignoring her, a memory powered through her defences, stripping her bare and forcing itself into her head. 'It wasn't like that!' Florence buried her head under the duvet and waited for the storm to pass...

* * *

April 2015, Kemptown

'He keeps looking at me,' Rowena breathed heavily in Florence's ear. 'Did you see?' But Florence's pickled eyes could only focus upon a halo of lights. Afterwards her brain would shut down, the whole evening a surreal loosely stitched chain of hazy flashbacks all recounted from Rowena's point of view during a post-mortem the following morning accompanied by pounding heads and theatrical groaning at totally mortifying antics. It was Florence's twenty-eighth birthday and she, Rowena, Terry-Anne (sporting box fresh neon pink hair), Mo and Ollie had initiated celebrations on Brighton seafront, crawling through insalubrious joints, a whirlwind of cackling, before careering into the Volks Tavern nearer home for the final leg of revelries. Florence subsequently woke face down on her crumpled bed, fully clothed in her finest granny chic charity shop dress, biker boots, one still on, one somewhere under the bed, her beige mac balled up on the floor, the arms yanked inside out protruding like insect legs. Someone had used her mouth as an ashtray. Florence didn't really smoke, she loftily thought of herself as a social smoker, scabbing cigarettes off willing donors or men hoping to trade the favour for something else. No such thing as a free lunch. *Why, God? Why?*

Desperate for a wee, she slowly eased herself into a sitting position, head swooshing. Her bed was marooned in a sea of chaos – drawers spewing garments onto the ocean floor, her clothes rail bending under the impossible weight of a multitude of hangers. Mismatched shoes bobbed like boats upon the choppy T-shirt waves, creased blouses and bunched-up jeans discarded before she'd left yesterday lunchtime. Florence kicked the lone boot off into the mêlée and opened her bedroom door, the stench from her feet making her gag. The house was still, though the aroma of toast hung in the air, signs that someone had made it downstairs alive. She knocked on the bathroom door before pushing it, the bolt still hanging like a limp leg pierced in place by one lone screw. It had been that way for a year. Why bother fixing it when you could just knock? Florence couldn't recall how she'd got home, or if she'd snogged anyone. She pulled down her tights and knickers, levering herself onto the seat before letting go, the sweet relief just about the only good thing she had going for herself right then. As she was squeezing out the last drops, the bathroom door flung open and a man jumped back in shock as if interrupting a crime scene.

'God, I'm so sorry, I thought it was empty!' He gripped the door handle, knuckles straining against his dark skin. Hungover though she was, Florence could be side swept by a particularly impressive pair of delicately boned hands. They must belong to a surgeon or a musician... She liked the idea of musician and granted him a tortured artist backstory as she gawped at his perfectly aquiline features framed by copious wild, just-fell-out-of-bed black hair. Standard Florence behaviour that she was weeing right in front of him, her ankles fettered by her tights like a prisoner in transit, while at that precise moment her stomach decided on violently evacuating itself. Remaining seated (what other choice did she have?), she twisted, leaned over and spectacularly chundered into the bath, splattering red wine, carrots (*why, God, why?*), pizza and what tasted like half masticated Marmite toast. She immediately felt warm hands graze the back of her neck and gently clasp her hair as she heaved round two, chunks of peppers and onions delightfully shooting out of her nose like ping-pong balls, stripping her nasal lining at the same time. Panting, she rested her chin on the rim of the bath, awaiting further assault.

'You OK? All done?' the man asked, his voice calm and reassuring.

'I think so... No.' She retched up one last streak of bile. 'Now I am.' He let go of her hair and handed her some torn-off loo roll. Florence gratefully wiped her mouth, spitting into the bath, why bother with niceties, he'd seen it all now.

'Better out than in,' he said chirpily. 'Do you want me to get you a glass of water?'

'Do you mind?'

"Course not. The glasses are in the kitchen?'

'Cupboard next to the fridge.'

The minute he left, Florence wiped, yanked up her knickers, blasted and poked the puke down the plug, rinsed her mouth, spitting out the foulness, swilled with Ro's tooth-whitening mouthwash, splashed her face with water, hastily scrubbing the flaked mascara and eyeliner with a wet tissue, dragged her fingers through her matted hair and pinched her pallid cheeks. Why she was bothering was a mystery even to her, but it made her feel better so that when he materialised with the glass of water she wore her shame well instead of it wearing her.

'Thank you.' She gulped the water, then gradually slowed to a sip, wary of shocking her innards. He made no move to leave the bathroom and she wondered how long she could realistically keep him here. She perched on the side of the bath in what she hoped was an invitingly sexy manner, but after he'd witnessed both gates of hell emancipating the souls of the damned, all she could hope for was that she didn't look like a complete twat.

'How was your birthday?' he asked brightly. Had he not drunk at all?

'How did you know it was my birthday?'

'You told the whole club. You made me buy FloRo drinks at the bar.'

'Oh God, was I awful?' Florence never knew what tricks Bad Florence got up to when she blacked out. It wasn't a common occurrence, but none the less, she always wondered how she operated in that shadow world where an entity that looked like her, and sounded like her, existed without boundaries or care for others' opinions, and was utterly free, if quite annoying and rude on occasions.

'No, don't worry, you were amusing.'

'Did we...?'

'No!' He shot his hand out as if stopping oncoming traffic. Below her raging hangover, Florence felt acute disappointment in both the facts and his reaction to them. 'Sorry if you got the wrong idea. Nothing happened between us. I wanted to make sure you got back OK. Your friends had left and you and Ro were insisting on walking home on your own. It was three in the morning and I just wanted you to be safe.'

'Where did you sleep?' Before the man could reply, a voice rumbled from the hallway.

'So that's where you are. I thought you'd done a runner,' Rowena purred, standing in the doorway, her fake furry throw wrapped round her body, a fifties movie siren, hair perfectly tousled in matching his and her post-coital bedheads. All she was missing was a half-smoked cigarette dangling from her hand.

'I was just getting Florence here some water.'

'Aren't you the gentleman?' Florence's heart plunged into her ribs. Rowena was flirting with him. They must have...

'Sorry, thank you for helping me out,' Florence blustered, not daring to look at him, scared of flying too close to the sun. Though it may have already been too late. She picked herself up and squeezed past them both.

'No worries. I hope you feel better soon. Happy birthday again.'

Florence fell into bed and forced the handsome stranger out of her head. But it was hard when he was in the room across the narrow hallway. She put her earphones in and listened to a chill-out Spotify playlist, riding the waves of biliousness until she heard the front door slam. A minute later, Ro knocked on her door.

'Can I come in?' She barged in without waiting for an answer, wearing a retro Siouxsie and the Banshees T-shirt teamed with men's stripy boxers. Ro could wear anything and pull it off even when dressed as Tinky Winky.

'I'm in love!' she wildly declared.

'Already?!' Ro never spoke about men like this. They were routinely given the side eye and cold shoulder. 'It's only been five minutes.'

'Oi! Don't piss on my bonfire! I never like anyone.' She settled on the edge of the bed.

'I know, that's what I mean. Why's he special?'

'Er, did you just see him?'

'Yes, he's fit. But that can't be everything.' Florence could hear irritation in her voice.

'Of course not! He's just so lovely. He walked us home, though you won't remember any of it. He practically carried you up the hill like a sack of potatoes. Then he force-fed you Marmite toast and pints of water.'

'What's his name?'

'Clinton, he's a veterinary nurse. Obsessed with animals.'

'Did anything happen?'

Rowena paused, preparing an answer. 'I wish I could say yes. We talked for ages then we just kind of passed out on the bed next to each other. When I woke up, he was gone, and I felt so upset, but he'd found you in the loo.' She shot Florence a wide smile, flashing her impossibly white teeth. 'He's so kind.'

'You don't really know him though. He could be a Netflix true crime axe murderer.'

'Hey! He isn't. He had ample opportunity to kill us both *and* Terry-Anne.'

'You seeing him again?'

'He's got my number. I mentioned about maybe midweek drinks. He said he was keen. Said you should come too, maybe he could bring his flatmate.'

'A double date? No way!'

'Please! I really like him.' Rowena thrust her hands in prayer position against her chest and tilted her head, wheeling out her best puppy dog impression. 'I'll never ask you to do anything like this again. Ever.'

'Fine,' Florence grumbled, a flame of unbearably dark longing flickering in her insides.

Consequently the following Wednesday Florence found herself abandoning finishing her to-do list for the next day in favour of jumping on an earlier bus so she could inhale dinner in order to spend as much time as possible perfecting her make-up and tonging her hair in replica of the wavy mid-length style she'd scrolled to on Pinterest at lunchtime. Florence placed agreeing to play the sacrificial lamb of dating, the wing woman, in the same category as scraping dog shit out of the grooves in your trainers with a toothpick. Florence's duties as wing woman (categorically similar to bridesmaid without obligatory salmon-pink meringue dress, earpiece and clipboard) had now extended to making them both dinner (reliable after-school pesto pasta) and forcing Rowena to actually eat it in case she drank too much red wine, thus alleviating the end of evening carrot-splatter hair. It was exhausting!

'Can you do my back?' Rowena begged, wrapped in her dressing gown as she prodded her pasta with a fork, not even managing half a bowl, a waft of wet Weetabix in the air. Florence never understood her obsession with fake tan – Rowena had amazing caramel skin, her granny hailed from Mauritius so she'd handed down perfect colouring. All Ro focused on was that her legs didn't match her face. 'They're a different shade, Flo! Look, LOOK!' And she'd shove a calf in her face to hammer home the exact reason why she spent a fortune on St Tropez. 'It's all very well being fucking brown, but when your face is ten shades darker than the rest of you, you feel like a zebra.'

'He won't even see your back!' Florence said. 'It's just a drink!'

'You don't know that. It might turn into something else... Please??' Florence huffed. 'Please, please, please – I'll love you for ever...?'

'OK, OK! Get the facecloth and hot water, and cotton wool!'

Rowena abandoned her dinner and raced round the house gathering the required paraphernalia for blackhead popping. Florence usually relished this simian-like nit-picking; the black-heads had a tendency to propagate into full-blown spots across Rowena's back if left to their own devices. With Terry-Anne assisting the harvest as chief hot cloth wetter, they managed to clear all potential zits with very little squeezing, satisfaction all round. By the time they were ready to leave the house, Florence was desperate to curl up on the sofa and watch *EastEnders*. As Terry-Anne settled in for the night with her phone in one hand and the remote in the other, her pink hair fading fast, Flo couldn't help feeling a twinge of envy.

'Knock 'em dead, girls!' Terry-Anne called from her cosy nest. 'You both look fab!'

'Honestly, do I look OK?' Rowena asked while picking knickers out of her bum crack as they walked to the bus stop at the end of the road, the streetlights' amber glow defusing the effect of her baby pink high-necked blouse.

'You look beautiful, and I'm not even having to lie. Clinton won't be able to take his eyes off you.' As much as that were true, it still pained Florence to say it. She'd had two sex dreams about Clinton that week already. In both dreams he'd offered her a cup of tea after he'd made her cry out mid orgasm, then asked what biscuits she'd like to dunk. Florence reasoned that perhaps it was just because he'd held her hair while she was puking. That somehow his actions had fused an invisible bond between them, like survivors of a horrific natural disaster, forever melded by their harrowing experience. Florence trusted the feeling was fleeting and when she saw him, she'd be able to appreciate Clinton's pulchritude and leave it at that.

To her knowledge, FloRo had never ever fancied the same man. Florence certainly hadn't hankered after any of the self-determined bad boys that Ro occasionally dragged back, and eventually got bored of. Her own misanthropic view of relationships always poured poison on any stunts they could pull. Rowena's heart remained open for sexual liaisons, but attachment was an unknown concept. As soon as a particular type of man discovered this, it was as if she'd lit an invisible touch paper awakening his ardent desire to win her over. Rowena had been forced to block countless men on social media and her phone. But this was different. Rowena had never 'liked' anyone before. After a bus ride where Ro's left leg ceaselessly jittered, Florence was glad to get off and walk to the pub, not used to this epicene version of her best friend.

'I feel sick,' Rowena hissed as they reached the Sidewinder pub. 'What's wrong with me? The finger's not playing ball either, no tingling tonight. It always tingles if I'm on a date...'

'You actually like someone and you can't control the outcome.' Florence bit her lip, the words overriding her usual anodyne response to harsh realities. Ro abruptly grabbed her arm just as they were about to swing through the pub door.

'What's that supposed to mean? You think I'm a control freak?!'

Florence sighed, buying some time, burying her own emotions about that evening.

'Sorry, that came out wrong.' She turned to face Ro, whose nostrils were flaring, a dangerous precursor to the latent rage always simmering whenever relationships, marriage and her father were discussed in detail. 'What I meant to say was you never like anyone, and this time you do, and you're not used to feeling out of control about it. It's a new experience for you.' A bead of sweat pearled in her right armpit and trickled down her side. Ro eyed her implacably for a split second, then nodded.

'Yes, that sounds about right.'

Florence breathed out slowly.

'Come on, let's do this!' Ro cried, linking her arm through Flo's and they strode through the door together. Florence cast her gaze across the pub just as Clinton looked up from his friend where they sat in the centre of the room on a table for four. Florence involuntarily tensed her stomach, the air woofing out of her lungs, a prize fighter crumpling in the ring. Their eyes locked through the asymmetric spaces between bodies and chairs, and he bestowed upon her a smile redolent of a thrilled dog greeting its owner. The pit of Florence's stomach melted into a woozy mess. He waved, so utterly delighted that he'd spotted her. Rowena latched on to Florence's gaze, following it and waved enthusiastically.

'He's seen me. Argh.' She turned to Florence, who hastily rearranged her features. Was she trying too hard not to look invested? Florence clutched Ro's hand.

'Breathe and be yourself...' Florence whispered.

'Everyone else is taken! Yes, yes, I know!' They squeezed through the narrow avenues between tables to reach the boys. Clinton stood, he was so much taller than Florence had remembered.

'FloRo, this is Eliot.' His friend turned as Clinton sat down. He was white bread handsome with his tasteful untucked navy shirt, but Florence already knew she wasn't interested. She forced herself to sit on the chair opposite Rowena and role play.

'Drinks, what's everyone having?' she asked spotting their empty pint glasses.

'Let me get these,' Eliot offered and started scraping his chair back.

'No, I'll get them. Honestly, it's OK. Pints of what?'

Florence jumped up before he could beat her to the bar, took the orders and weaved her way next to the glass collecting area, historically the best place to get noticed. It was a busy evening and the dissonance of conversation competed with the singer songwriter playlist piped through the hidden speakers. There were only two people behind the bar that evening and Florence relaxed her shoulders, staring ahead at the array of bottles awaiting her turn.

'Hey.' Clinton abruptly crowded her space, filling it with his aftershave, a sensual wood spice mix that tugged at every string in her bow.

'Hey. Have you changed your mind? You want a nice Pinot Grigio instead of a Long Man?'

'Just seeing if you wanted any help.'

'I need to get served first...' Florence's head filled with air.

'Thanks for coming this evening. I wasn't sure you would.'

'Well, Rowena kind of forced me, to be honest. But I'm happy to hang out. Who's your friend?'

'I was going to introduce you properly before I got the drinks, but you ran off first. Eliot and I were at uni together.'

'He's a vet too?'

'You don't remember anything, do you?' He laughed at her, eyes twinkling, mocking her.

'About what?'

'The other night. We had a whole conversation. I'm not a vet. I'm a veterinary nurse.'

'Oh yeah, I think Rowena mentioned it, though I can't really remember?'

'Take notes next time.' He shifted closer to her as someone else squeezed themselves against the bar in an attempt to gain the attention of the harried barmen. Clinton's breath warmed the side of her face triggering an uncontrollable wave of prickling down her spine and across her scalp.

'OK, tell me what I missed then.' Florence turned back to check on Rowena who was laughing at something Eliot had just said, his arms gesticulating enthusiastically.

'They're fine. Don't worry about them.' Clinton touched her elbow with his own and grinned. Florence was momentarily confused. 'You missed my life story...'

'Oh, I'm sure Rowena remembers it.'

'She wasn't there at that point, she was dancing. Anyway, a business degree wasn't for me.'

'You did a business degree? How does that translate into being a veterinary nurse?'

'It doesn't. I realised when I was trapped in a McJob selling advertising space that I really wanted to be a vet. Had always loved animals, but I'm not scientific enough and also had massive debt from the other degree. So I looked into being a nurse and you can train on the job. So I did.'

'I was supposed to—'

'To be a teacher. Yeah, I know. It's not too late.'

'Did *you* take notes?'

He laughed. 'You told me all about your favourite teacher, Mrs Higham, and I looked up the poem when I got home. I like it.'

The floor fell from Florence's stomach. '"Nothing Gold Can Stay"?' she whispered.

'Yes.' Everything dawned at once. '"Nature's first green is gold"—'

'I think you should sit down.' She was in need of a glass of water.

'You don't like the poem?' He affected a crestfallen expression.

'I love the poem.'

'You don't like me?' He smirked, smugly.

'I *can't* like you, don't you see? You're on a date with Rowena.'

'I am?' His entire face shot into his hairline.

'Yes.' Florence hissed so hard that spittle flew from her mouth and splattered the bar top. She wiped it away with her sleeve.

'Oh. I was under the impression this wasn't any kind of date. We were just hanging out.'

'OK, that's better.' Florence's relief was short lived.

'But you're the reason I'm here in the first place. Not Rowena.'

Florence shook her head vehemently until her brain hurt. 'No. No, no, no, no! You stayed the night in her room.'

'I didn't. I lay next to her on the bed when we were chatting because there was nowhere else to sit, then she fell asleep and I went downstairs onto the sofa until I found you in the loo.'

'Why did you stay the night?'

'Why do you think?'

Florence groaned and lay her forehead on her arms on top of the bar. 'But you were in her room after I went back to bed.'

'Yes, to grill her about you. I could hardly ask you for your number after all the puking – it would have looked weird... If she took it the wrong way, that's not my problem.'

'But it's *my* problem.'

'Hey, look at me.'

'No. I don't even remember meeting you, apart from when you watched me puke and wee.'

'We're off to a good start then. No boundaries and you can come and watch me wee in a mo when I go to the loo, then we're equal!' Florence laughed in spite of herself and lifted her head.

Clinton's head tilted to one side. 'I asked her if you *both* wanted to go out for a drink when she originally suggested just the two of us. I was only interested in meeting you. I can tell her and then you've done nothing wrong. It's all me. If you want to see where this'll go, that is. Do you want to see?'

'No. I can't. I'm really sorry. You don't know her. This would… cause ructions.'

'Surely she'll understand?'

'She won't. Can't you just like her a bit, then see how it goes? She's very hot.'

'She is, but I like *you*. I liked the poem in the club – so unexpected! No one's ever recited poetry to me before. I could feel what it meant to you.'

'I'm sorry, I can't.' The barman caught her eye and Florence gratefully waved him over and placed her order. She turned back to Clinton. 'Let's sit down, act like nothing's happened, and then you can see how you feel. I can't do this, so chat to Ro, make an effort, and then we go our separate ways.'

'If that's what you want.'

'It is.' She handed him the two pints, picked up the bottle of house red and two glasses and they solemnly made their way back to the table. This was all her fault. If only she'd not drunk so much, then she would have been conscious. But Ro had seen him first, declared him with her flag. No man was worth *that* potential aggro.

13

CRACK THE CODE

Florence hummed the *EastEnders* theme tune as she gunned down the M23, the sun ushering her back to the south coast in a bombastic seaside lifestyle advert. Every tree, every hedgerow, every single patch of sky fervently frothed, nature's cinematographer accelerating pantone saturation levels. She half anticipated sheep in the conveyor belt fields to spontaneously burst into song, line dancing their way to the water troughs. What would they sing? As she tried on songs for size ('Sheep Caroline', 'Sheep Home Alabama'), Florence pondered the last forty-eight hours. She was loath to immediately return home. Cassie's clue hadn't joined any dots; she remained stumped at the first round. Actually, second round if she counted the hand-delivery of Tracey's letter to herself. Unless the clue was Cuckmere Haven as the postcard so brazenly declared? But the area was vast. Surely Cassie wouldn't wave her off into the eye of the hurricane? Whatever, she was ignoring the whole thing. It was time to sign on to TempsRUs as soon as she could, start the ball rolling, list Nellie too...

'When will you stop running, Flo?' her dad had asked when

she'd returned from Greece, the final pit stop on her tour of southern Europe the previous summer.

'I'm not running.'

'Don't you get sick of packing up, returning, McJobbing, then running away again? Don't you ever just want to be at home for more than a few months? Set down some roots, reconnect with friends?'

'Dad, I never had a gap year, I never worked abroad, I didn't do any of those things because of messing up my first degree – there was just no way I could afford it. I'm making the most of this now.' *Was that the truth, though...?*

'What happens when you're too old to do it?' Her dad wasn't prone to disquisitions, or leaking emotions, and at the time Florence had believed that her mum had put him up to it.

'How is anyone ever too old to live their life how they want to live it?' Flo bit back.

Unwavering, her dad stuck to the script, watching her reaction, gauging the impact of his next bullet.

'Don't you think it's been long enough now? Time's passed, you're a different person, Rowena will be different too – it might be good for you to reconnect, ground you a bit. It's such a shame—'

Florence had blazed out of the kitchen and stomped up to her room, echoes of every teenage storm gathering pace as she slammed the door. At thirty-five, she'd felt ridiculous, because part of her, well almost all of her, had known her dad was right. He'd been right about the intervention too...

Florence stopped humming, took her right hand off the steering wheel and gently stroked her left side. She couldn't feel the scars under her denim shirt, but they were there, like stars in daylight. A faint echo of the pain that could occasionally flare up like a problematic wisdom tooth, threatening to pound the stuffing out of her...

The first time she'd cut herself she'd only meant to relieve the torment that jabbed its barbed fingers into every joint, every tender molecule of her being. At the time it made total sense that outplaying the pain would somehow negate everything, like anaesthetising with alcohol or drugs. However, she associated drinking with fun, with partying, with sitting in the camper van enveloped in matching Dunelm furry throws clinking chunky tumblers of cheap red wine as the sun surrendered to the gnarled branches of Friston Forest. Back at home, once more ensconced in her childhood bedroom on compassionate leave from work, her brain scarified, the harsh world around her lit by overly bright splashes of colour, lights flashing menacingly (the Christmas tree had felt sinister while ordinary objects changed colour like a bad acid trip), she'd contemplated a razor blade. Squeamish was Florence's middle name. As a child the words lungs, pulse and veins could spin her into an uncontrollable fit of Victorian-like collapse, a mere blood spot away from full-on fainting. She'd need to cut where she couldn't see. With this in mind, Flo only grazed her skin, like slicing through tape on an Amazon parcel, the sting focusing her into the present, away from the past, from Clinton. She breathed freely, her lungs loosely expanding, like she'd been given a shot of adrenaline. She finally inhabited her body, no longer looking from the outside in, a stranger in a strange land. The buzz lasted a minute, maybe more, then it evaporated leaving Florence stranded with her corrosive feelings in her bedroom, unprepared without any tissues to mop up her blood. Shame crept over her. No, she wouldn't try that again...

But she did, each time the feelings reached fever pitch, when she couldn't tolerate any more wacky *Alice in Wonderland* trips, and longed for the world to fade back to 'normal', where she lived in her body, instead of floating above it like a disconnected balloon. The wounds were literally bleeding into parts of her body in public view. By the time her parents sat her down in the kitchen, her lower back and thighs were a Jackson Pollock of lesions. At thirty, Florence felt herded into a corner by good intentions backed by little understanding. Having lost a lot of friends when she'd settled down with Clinton, she'd been left with workmates, who were lovely, if peripheral, and her family. Her dyadic days were finished, costing her two life partners. There was no one like Ollie, Terry-Anne, Mo – they chose Rowena because she would have roasted them otherwise. Terry-Anne lived with her, she had no choice. Self-laceration had quickly become a way of coping, an addiction, she'd even inured herself against the gore. But her parent's intervention had shocked her, ripping off the blinkers.

'Love, you can't carry on like this. You need help. Grief is so profound, everyone deals with it differently, but you've had a double dose. It's no wonder you've got yourself in such a state.' Florence had wept, tears of shame, fear for the future, of never being able to simply exist without her anxiety throwing her to the dogs. She was lost both literally and figuratively.

'Just tell Ro what happened,' her mum chanted almost daily. 'She'll be here in a flash.' The energy and effort it took to make it through a whole day was Herculean. Florence couldn't deal with Ro too, and let her slip through her fingers; FloRo was no more. Florence felt safer on her own...

Eventually therapy had blunted abandonment's edges, her therapist giving a title to her acid trips and out-of-body experiences: Florence was experiencing derealisation and depersonalisation triggered by trauma and grief. She was relieved to know she wasn't that special. She'd genuinely believed she had lost her mind. However, naming the beast wasn't an insurance policy against her brain unexpectedly fomenting such witchery. What had been the real turning point was when her nana had died – ironic. She'd left Florence and Lennie a small lump sum of cash in her will. It had been her mum's idea to visit somewhere bigger than her, not to run but to be with herself, hopefully without her brain sparking another bugged out trip, just maybe she could put a pin in everything. Almost two years after Clinton left her, Florence travelled alone to Thailand initially for two weeks, but ended up resigning from her job at Brighton and Hove Council before trekking over the border to Vietnam, inadvertently crossing the threshold into her new nomadic life. As it turned out grief's strongest gift was the art of not giving a fuck. It was easy to materialise a visa, everything was now online, only a click away. Life was fleeting, and too brief to stay in your narrow lane, something that Florence felt as deeply as the incisions scored into her body. Lying on a sunbed in a deserted out-of-season MerPerle Hon Tam resort, the stars gently pressing into her eyeballs, their brilliance almost necessitating sunglasses, she finally felt a disconnection from the anxiety of the world feeling 'too much, too bright, too loud', almost as if she had bundled up the past and set it in a box for later. And so began her journey forward, one exotic escape at a time, taking her further and further away from the box. Until now.

Cassie's words wound their way into her thoughts, about taking Nellie down to the sea to watch the sun rise. It was too late for that, but they could certainly head to the coast before returning to Felworth, she could do whatever she wanted, Nellie was hers to do with as she saw fit. Florence drove straight to Worthing beach and parked next to a pop-up coffee shack on the promenade. Worthing was a safe place – no previous associations, just the sea, the beach, the sky. She sat in contented silence in Nellie's driving seat sipping her steaming latte from the shack, the coffee scalding her tongue while a westerly wind battered Nellie's sides. As the first few splatters of the incoming rain shower hit the roof and the windscreen, Florence was overcome with a feeling of complete stillness. Prickles surged from the base of her neck to the crown of her head, as if someone was hovering close behind her. Florence held her breath, waiting for the sensation to stop, but it didn't. The rain pattered on the roof and the prickles spread across her entire skull, her hair endeavouring to stand to attention, like she had her hands on the spherical Van De Graaff generator in a Physics lesson, the whole class laughing at her.

'Cassie?' Florence whispered reverently before scolding herself. 'Flo, you idiot.' She whipped her head around and of course no one was there. But that didn't stop her from feeling uneasy. At four thirty Flo turned Nellie into her parents' road, and drove up Mr Ogby's driveway. Before the engine had even stopped, he appeared on his front doorstep, toupee all present and correct, mug of tea in hand.

'Did you deliver the letter OK?' he called as soon as she opened Nellie's door.

'Yes, but it wasn't for Tracey.'

'Who was it for then?' He'd abandoned the doorstep and strode over surprisingly sharpish, tea slopping over the rim of his mug and dripping onto his pristine pressed grey trousers, troubling Florence somewhat.

'It was for me.' Florence reached over and yanked her rucksack towards her from the front seat.

Mr Ogby screwed up his eyes, balling them into the centre of his face like a puzzled mouse. 'That make no sense.'

'Everything about this adventure is a bit cuckoo,' Florence agreed.

'Do you want a cup of tea? I just boiled the kettle.'

It had been years since Florence had ventured inside Mr Ogby's house. She'd been a child, his wife had been alive and the boys had still lived there. He'd asked her parents to keep an eye on the place when they went on holiday after there had been a few break-ins in the area. He wondered if they could close and open the curtains, switch lights on and off, simulate the family's existence. The house had been much neater than her own home, which was worn around the edges like frayed sleeves on a favourite cardigan. Her mum had longingly stroked the plush grey velvet sofa and matching armchairs, the cushions perky and overstuffed, unlike their own defeatedly saggy red corduroy sofa with the tea stains and constant pebbledash of biscuit crumbs. It had only been retired a few years previously and her mum had retrieved five pounds in small change secreted in the cracks down the back as well as a diamanté earring and one blue trainer sock. Florence had found the Ogbys' glass coffee table particularly exotic. She'd nosed round everything, especially the two boys' bedrooms. They had been teenagers at the time, a whole different species. She remembered the *Sports Illustrated* calendar pinned on one of the walls. An impressive congregation of boobs, Pamela Anderson pouting, breasts bursting in all directions like skin-covered helium balloons...

She followed Mr Ogby into the kitchen, the opposite layout of her parents' house.

'Milk?' He flicked the kettle again. There wasn't a utensil out of place, a speck of dust or a ring mark on any of the shiny white counters or glistening hob. A blue glass vase of daffodils sat splendidly in the centre of the round kitchen table covered with a red and white gingham cloth. Florence admired the fact that Mr Ogby still took massive pride in his house. It felt like a home, which threw Florence off guard, the tiniest of aches pinching deep in her belly.

'Yes please. Are you sure you don't mind me leaving the van on your drive?'

'Not at all, there's enough room. Been a while since we had two cars.' Florence's tummy twitched at the utterance of 'we'. He motioned for her to sit at the table.

'And the journey was OK?' He poured milk into the tea, spilling a small drop which he hurried away with a sponge. 'Nellie didn't protest?'

'She was as a good as gold.' He nodded and handed over the mug and a floral china plate with two custard creams impeccably chevroned a centimetre apart.

'If the letter was for you, why did you have to drive all the way over to Berkhamsted?'

'Because it's a treasure hunt, of some description,' Florence explained.

'From the lady who left you the van?'

Taking Mr Ogby's presence as an unorthodox confessional box, she unburdened herself. She confided in him about Cassandra Galaxy, about her fractured relationship with Tracey; about Mrs Higham being her and Rowena's beloved teacher; about how she used to set eagerly anticipated treasure hunts; about how she had met her at a psychic fair yet not recognised her; about Cassie connecting her own situation with Tracey to FloRo's demise without going into any of the details; about how this treasure hunt was supposed to be a parting gift to help Florence reconcile the past, the intricate machinations still lost on her. Throughout, Mr Ogby listened intently, sipping his tea every now and then, dunking his custard creams, until one half broke off, dissolving beneath the surface. He remained silently engaged until she lifted her mug to her lips.

'Do you have the postcard?' Florence slurped her tea then reached into her bag and drew out the card. He turned it over reading the back. 'It's a map reference. This number is the longitude and this is the latitude – if you type it into Maps it'll show you where.'

Florence momentarily floated above the table, to a different time, to the white cliffs where the wind whistled across the flat plain guiding the serpentine water out towards the English Channel. She dug her nails into her arm to bring her back to the present.

'Do you want me to give it a go?' Mr Ogby asked kindly.

Seven years since she'd last been there, if it was the place she was expecting, had instinctively known from the minute she opened the envelope. Florence's eyes wandered through the doorway and into the hall beyond where photo frames stood to attention along the narrow wooden shelf above the radiator. Her eyes landed on a picture of Mrs Ogby proudly standing next to one of her sons in a mortar board and gown. Which one, Flo couldn't be sure – they both looked the same to her.

'No, it's OK...'

'Are you sure you don't want me to check?'

'No. Actually, I better go, said I'd make dinner.' She stuffed the postcard back in her rucksack. 'Thanks for the tea.'

'What will you do about the rest of the hunt?' Mr Ogby asked her retreating back, his interest piqued.

Florence shrugged. 'I'll look up the coordinates tomorrow,' she lied as she closed the front door behind her.

14

LET DOWN GENTLY

Rowena's neat bump itched at night interrupting her sleep, as if an army of busy ants scurried beneath her overstretched skin. Towards mid-April, once Rowena had officially announced her pregnancy at school, her mum had begun driving over from Deal on her weekend day off, Nana Mode finally rumbling into action. She'd gallantly taken up vaping too. 'Less poisonous around the baby.' She'd not cared a jot about smoking when Rowena had been little. Ro could still remember car journeys where she precariously hung her head out of the Vauxhall's window to avoid her mum's second-hand smoke, narrowly avoiding decapitation by overtaking motorbikes.

'I got you some raspberry leaf tea – it's supposed to prepare your womb for an easier labour.'

'Thanks, I think.' Labour was still a nebulous construct in Rowena's mind, the latest blockbuster film she would eventually watch when it landed on Netflix. She understood her baby had to squeeze its way out of a constricted opening and that it would hurt. When she'd pressed Ebi for her take on childbirth, she'd been let down gently.

'Do you want the truth or the fairy tale?' she'd said jiggling baby Leon on her hip while spoon-feeding Bella in her food-splattered IKEA high chair. Rowena had offered to feed Bella, but that had resulted in screaming and a firm zipped lip against homemade fish pie, and Leon refused to be put down without affecting the same hysteria. Ebi needed a third arm to sip her glass of Merlot – at least Ro could help in that respect and held it up to her lips.

'The truth?' Rowena winced.

Ebi regarded her with pity as she scraped white sauce off Bella's chin.

'I'll give you the fairy tale... It hurts like hell. And then when you think it can't hurt any more, it does. Then afterwards you wee yourself all the time.'

'Jeez, what's the truth?' Rowena groaned.

'That it's all worth it in the end. Look at me, living the dream.' Rowena had almost choked her with the Merlot.

As Rowena's mum bustled around the kitchen pulling together a lunch of one low fat cheese slice chopped up into a bag of salad for her (*no dressing, got to keep the chubby wolf from the door, Rowena!*), and a toasted tuna melt sandwich for her daughter, Ro was ready to confess about the Audi she'd spotted numerous times around Seaford. The car had the same registration, since squirrelled away on her phone notes like Miss Marple. Then two days ago she had become aware of it hovering just up ahead as she walked back from school. The maddening thing was she had no real idea if it was Nate, or whatever his name was, because she had never taken any interest in his car in the first place. The initial incident had flagged up recognition, but that might have been because it was a comparable car, not the exact one. Creeping paranoia since accompanied her whenever she left the house, throwing constant glances over her shoulder and making sure her coat covered her bump at all costs. She wouldn't be able to hide it for ever. But her mum threw something else in the path of her Nathaniel worries.

'Do you want me at the birth?' Denise asked wide-eyed and keen.

'I don't know, Mum. I haven't made up my mind.' The Krakatoa of lies, of course. She needed to build herself up to letting her mum down gently otherwise there would be a scene, where Denise placed herself front and centre. The entire reason behind not having her at the birth in the first place. Rowena had thought about asking a friend, but who? There wasn't anyone that would easily stomach such an infliction of pressure. 'Do you want to hold my hand while I poo a watermelon?' In the past if someone had ever been stupid enough to ask her, she would have booked root canal that day. There had only ever been one person that came close to fulfilling birth partner in lieu of the father...

* * *

April 2015, Kemptown

Everyone else was up and awake; Rowena could hear the pipes clanging in protest as hot water bolted through them. She lay in bed, still gloriously cloaked in the previous evening's closing kiss, while wondering what had happened with Florence and Eliot. They had wandered off after closing time, Eliot insisting on walking Flo to the bus stop while she and Clinton went in search of a late-night hole in the wall for a nightcap. They only had one drink, Clinton declaring an early start, but they managed to chat squeezed in the back of the grimy bar, him drinking a ginger ale and she an amaretto, art students sneaking cheap vodka from their bags into Cokes bought at the bar. No one noticed it was so busy.

'Tell me about FloRo,' he'd asked. 'How long have you two been friends?'

'For ever! We grew up next door to each other, I told you that the other night.'

'Oh yes. And you've never fallen out?' he probed.

'Well, we've had spats, nothing serious. Sisterly squabbles...'

'Ever fallen out about a man?' he pressed further.

'No! We never fancy the same person – I think that helps.'

'What would happen if you did?' Clinton's eyes had watched her carefully.

'I don't know because it's never happened.'

'What if you fancied her boyfriend?' he asked gamely.

'She doesn't have one!'

'Hypothetical boyfriend.'

Rowena had routinely chewed her nails while considering an answer. 'I'd never tell her. I guess I'd just have to get over it.'

'What if he fancied you?' Clinton carried on.

'Well, then he'd be a sleaze!' She narrowed her eyes, suspicion swimming into view. 'Why are you asking me all this?'

'No reason. I find girls' close friendships fascinating. I think because I grew up with a brother.' He smiled, dispersing concerns as easily as a child charging through a flock of pigeons. A faint throbbing in her telltale finger went ignored.

By the time they left, the rain had established itself and Clinton chivalrously shielded her with his denim jacket. There was no offer of come back to mine, no talk of a second date, but Rowena didn't believe this was the end, he already felt like a friend. Was there a chance this evening marked a beginning? She'd decided on a taxi home and as they waited for it huddled together, the rain trying its hardest to penetrate their denim canopy, Clinton leaned over and sought her lips with his. It wasn't a passionate snog, but a gentle testing of the water. Rowena responded enthusiastically, her legs barely withstanding the shot of electricity warming her groin.

'You're a sweet girl.' Her chest momentarily filled with concrete; there was a 'but'.

'That doesn't sound good.' She giggled nervously as the lone taxi silently pulled up to the kerb beside them, its lights pooling on the slick pavement.

Clinton's eyebrows yoked together in contemplation. 'I don't know what to do.'

'About what?'

He shrugged as if hoping she had an answer, then shook his head. 'Nothing's straightforward, is it?'

'I don't know what you mean.' Clinton's rhetoric puzzled her.

'Shall we have another date?' he finally asked.

'Yes. I think that's a great idea!' A church choir rang out inside her head. 'Text me. I'm free Saturday but not Friday. Oh, Sunday's a good day too.'

'I've no idea what I'm doing. I'll let you know.' He chastely kissed her cheek and sent her on her way.

The next morning, as Rowena waited for the bathroom, she checked her phone to see if he'd texted. Nothing since he'd politely messaged last night just as she'd climbed into bed after their date. She reread it once more.

Hope you got home OK.

Florence was already downstairs eating Marmite toast leaning against the oven reading *The Goldfinch* when Ro reached the kitchen gliding on a golden future where she said 'we' instead of 'I'.

'Are you OK?' Florence checked, concern clumsily etched across her face.

'Never better!' Rowena could have cartwheeled all the way to work.

'Oh.' She pulled her best clownish arched eyebrow expression.

'Are *you* OK?' Rowena asked.

'Yeah, why wouldn't I be?'

'Because things didn't pan out with Eliot?' Florence laughed drolly. 'What? He was cute! Admit it!'

'Yes, but I'm not interested.' She flicked the last of her crumbs into the sink and ran the tap, rinsing her plate at the same time. 'So what happened with Clinton?'

'We kissed.' Florence inhaled sharply, the news catching her ribs. 'Don't be so shocked. I actually like him. It's a good thing, remember!'

'Wow, that's great.'

'You don't sound convinced.' Rowena sniffed.

'I am, really, I am,' Flo assured her.

'I know, I get it. My track record isn't reliable, but that's cos I'm not bothered about the whole settling down thing. Never have been. But this feels... different. It's like being with you, except I don't want to rip your clothes off and shag you senseless.'

'Nice. Thanks for that grotesque image. I'll take it with me to work.'

'Sorry. It's that I can imagine making dinner with him, or introducing him to my parents. Those other blokes, not so much. They were just...'

They both lapsed into silence, reliving the parade of dance floor Lotharios Rowena occasionally allowed to grace her bed.

Not that any of them were murderers or domestic abusers, just odd, or behaved with such indifference that Rowena may as well have been single, which did in fact suit her perfectly. If Rowena could have chosen anyone as a favourite, it would have been Fred the groundkeeper for his spectacular exit. Ro had been dating him (drunk dialling) on and off for a few months – usually her limit – when they went on a night out, hooking up with Terry-Anne and Flo at a bar in town. Things got very messy, very quickly – all Ro's blokes flirted with a variation of self-medication. Florence said she wouldn't have diagnosed any of them as fully fledged, card-carrying addicts, but the line was just a footfall away. This particular evening, Ro and Fred had been on a bar crawl, culminating in an ironic dance-off in Pryzm. Florence was sober compared to Rowena who had matched Fred drink for drink. The DJ dropped a unifying party banger, something with a cheesy chorus that must have triggered Fred's rugby-playing days of old. He sprung into Freddie Mercury mode, prancing round their closely guarded patch of dance floor, chanting the words like a whirling acolyte, sweat flying from his glistening forehead. One minute Fred sported an impressive mouth of gleaming white teeth, but in the crack of a whip during a rousing choral solo, he snapped his head forward managing to spit an entire row of gnashers onto the dance floor where Terry-Anne inadvertently punted them with her wedges into the mosh pit. They were consumed by the horde of stamping feet, never to be found. To this day, Rowena often thought about the rats that presumably prowled the edges of the empty dance floor before the nightly clean-up officially started. She liked to imagine a rodent lording it with a fine set of teeth, the envy of all its ratty friends. That night, the discrepancies quickly fell into place. Fred had never stayed the night, always sneaking off as soon as he'd whipped his undies back on, and she'd never been invited to his flat. Maybe he'd not wanted her to find his secret stash of Steradent. He'd played rugby in his youth and lost the top teeth in a tackle that had verged on illegal. She binned him pretty soon afterwards, not able to get her head around a man with no top teeth, but mostly because what was the point if she didn't really like him? The set of teeth was the pediment in the tumbling house of cards.

'Wow, the parents! Serious! All after one date?' Florence eventually asked in the kitchen.

'Well, technically a date and a half, if you count the night we chatted for ages.' Rowena realised she was singing into the wind with such weak evidence, but it was testament to her strength of feeling. 'Anyway, don't worry, I still wouldn't let him stand goal end at the birth, you know that place is specially reserved for you.'

Florence burst out laughing. 'I thought you weren't ever getting married or having kids,' she reminded her.

'Things change...' Rowena smirked, only half joking. 'I have a second date lined up, so let's see when we get round to marriage and babies. Got to reach fourth date nirvana first!'

After a second date where they had dinner in Terre Terre, a vegetarian restaurant in the Lanes (Clinton's vegetarianism, proving his absolute commitment to animals), Rowena had found herself clinging to the idea of how well they physically suited each other. Their union would produce such beautiful children. Ro realised she'd loosened a few bricks in her self-constructed stockade and instead of her inner being drowning in anticipated terror, she boldly embraced it. So what if she had feelings? They couldn't kill you. She'd been OK after her dad had left. Eventually. After she'd actively loathed him for years (it took up so much energy!), and vowed never to speak to him again. After she'd returned all his letters unopened. After she'd helped herself to all the negative abusive words flung around the house by her mother and built herself a protective fort against it ever happening again.

But her dad never gave up being her dad. He refused to stop ringing, writing, turning up with birthday presents (that she accepted – they were expensive!), or sending her texts when she had a phone (she didn't block him, he'd paid for the mobile contract). Ultimately, she allowed him back in. Life was better with him in it, especially now her mum was miles away and Suleyman had usurped her. Rowena had drawn the line at playing happy families with Tammy, Isabelle and Alex. She was civil, and that was all that was required. What Rowena couldn't know sat in Terre Terre covertly adoring Clinton every time he sipped his glass of Rioja, was that when Tammy left her dad in 2021, their parental relationship would further flourish, and all the bad blood, anger, disillusionment would mature into a stable adult relationship, a phoenix from the flames of a toxic pyre. But all that was yet to come, as Rowena absently imagined just for a millisecond introducing Clinton to her father.

'Is your mum local?' she asked him, picturing a joint dinner with both families flanking them. *Rowena! Get a grip.*

'She lives in Horsham...' and so Clinton revealed a snapshot of his childhood, both parents absent in their own world of work, brought up by his gran and a rotating door of au pairs. His father, an ENT surgeon, distant and cutting (the irony) and his mother, chief exams officer for Christ's Hospital private school. His brother managed to live up to their exacting standards and was a doctor, ticking the glittering boxes. Clinton did not.

'I think it's great that you're a veterinary nurse. You have to do what makes you happy. We only get one life,' Rowena said meaningfully.

When they walked towards the Pump House, Rowena itched to hold his hand and brushed against it as it swung in time while Clinton walked, keeping his stride shallow to allow for hers. He didn't take the bait. Rowena ignored the prescient gnawing in her stomach, as for her finger, it was practically numb, irked at being snubbed. They took a table near the bar and he ordered ginger ale instead of red wine for himself. She ploughed into conversations following slim openings offered earlier.

'Do you like poetry?' Clinton asked in the middle of an amiable chat about music festivals and long drop toilets.

'What kind of poetry?'

'Any kind. Name your favourite poet.' This was not an exchange Rowena was used to on a date. When she usually faced the name your favourite category, it was ordinarily a cocktail, holiday destination or sexual position (just before they tried it).

'Shakespeare?' Truth was, Ro wasn't a massive fan of poetry. She'd endured it at school and Mrs Higham had introduced them to some off-syllabus stuff, and she'd enjoyed it, but not enough to pursue it away from timetables and homework. Not for pleasure. Clinton nodded.

'Who's yours?' she asked, keen to keep the conversation flowing.

'Don't worry... You ready? I need to go, I've doggo surgery in the morning.' Rowena still had half a glass of wine and inhaled it. She didn't feel the effects until she reached fresh air. 'Is North Street best for your bus?' She nodded. 'Good, me too, I'll wait then catch mine.' Something had shifted. He was smiling, being gentle-manly, in that respect the same. But the axis had enigmatically tilted, the evening having brusquely drawn to a close when Ro's dates would usually start revving their engines. As they reached her bus stop, Ro boldly took his hand. He didn't protest, but there wasn't an expected bolt of electricity either.

'I've had a lovely evening,' he said before leaning in to brush her cheek with his lips, then stood back and almost appraised her. She looked her best that evening; her hair had respected the rules and hadn't frizzed in the damp (slicked down with an alchemic assortment of products acting like curtain weights). Clinton appeared to be having some kind of internal discussion she wasn't privy to. She waited, smiling, she had some pride – he could ask for the next date, her eagerness under wraps.

'My bus is about to turn up,' she said glancing at her phone – *one minute away.* 'Thanks for a great time.' Where was the voracious snogging, shots at the bar, the tumbling into a bush, almost having sex in an alleyway? In the past those incidents had construed a great time. Maybe she was finally adulting; Clinton felt the right person to try it with.

Clinton snapped to and hugged her, giving her an extra squeeze. 'Hey, I'll text you in the week.'

'No worries. If you're busy, just let me know.' He waited for the bus to pull up, neither of them filling the silence with meaningless niceties. Normally that would have forced Rowena to spout absolute garbage just to allay her fear of the void, but Clinton's calmness deemed it unnecessary. As the doors opened, she stood on tiptoe and grabbed the back of his head, planting an open-mouthed kiss on his startled lips. He responded and all her pent-up passion flowed as she amorously pressed her chest against his, then nibbled his lips as she withdrew. 'Bye!!!' She glanced over her shoulder at Clinton's open mouth as the doors shut, his brain leaping to catch up with the ambush.

'So you've finally got a third date?' Florence asked five days later, a tad incredulously, Rowena thought. Clinton texted when they were making dinner with Terry-Anne in the kitchen – pasta twists and Aldi own brand sauce, midweek end of month scraping the barrel food. Terry-Anne had some dramatically floppy courgettes that were on their last legs rammed at the back of her shelf in the fridge and Florence had donated half an aubergine that looked like it had returned from trench warfare. Rowena was currently attempting to slice away all the suspect brown spongy flesh with the expertise of a field surgeon. Salt in the wounds would revive it...

'Don't sound so surprised. I haven't fucked it up yet,' Rowena objected, brandishing the knife.

'Bit of a record for you,' Terry-Anne remarked, hacking the lame courgettes into chunks. 'Well done.'

'Thanks, slag.' Ro smirked.

'When's the date?' Florence asked regarding Rowena's knife skills.

'Tomorrow.'

'Bit last minute, isn't it? What if you were busy?' Florence protested.

'I'm not though, am I?'

'Yeah,' Terry-Anne agreed. 'He's had all week to arrange it.'

'What is this? Pick on Rowena night? He's been busy. Maybe he had a late opening? Being a veterinary nurse is stressful.'

'Just saying,' Terry-Anne judiciously replied. 'Prime date nights are usually Saturday or Fridays.'

'I know that, I'm not stupid.'

'Sorry, hun,' Terry-Anne replied. 'Just looking out for you. I know you like him. Don't want to see you get hurt.'

'I've been fine so far. I think he's just shy...' Florence made an indiscriminate sound. 'Spit it out!' Rowena didn't appreciate the passive aggressive atmosphere. 'Do you not like him or something?'

'No. It's nothing. Sorry,' Flo blustered.

'It must be something. You've been weird since I started seeing him.'

'I haven't. Just be careful...'

'What's that supposed to mean?' Rowena quizzed her.

'Same as Terry-Anne. I'm pleased you like him and a third date is good. Thursdays are the new Fridays.'

'Thank you, yes they are!' Rowena said in relief.

Regardless of her housemates' concerns, Rowena had been disappointed with the Thursday evening date, and its eleventh hour offering. As she walked to Clinton, pulling her coat closed against the sea breeze whipping through the Lanes, the jitters gripped her innards. Every seagull seemed hell-bent on squawking a prophetic 'No, no, no!', swooping so close Rowena fancied she felt feathers brush her scalp. She spied him through the glass before he spotted her, sat at a table near the entrance of the Pump House. Psychic finger tingled sounding the oncoming death knell. She pushed the door and he met her gaze, smiling, jumping up at the same time.

'Red wine?'

'Yes please.' Drinking on an empty stomach, Rowena, she chastised herself. Well, it was an emergency if she was to believe the soothsaying seagulls. She slipped into the seat opposite, her palms damp, and shrugged her winter coat off her shoulders, draping it round the back of the chair. The pub had yet to fill up with pre-weekend office workers celebrating the imminent two days' freedom.

'Here you go.' Rowena took a gulp of wine. Not being in control was Rowena's driving fear; her wheels were about to spin off.

'So, how have you been?' she asked, waiting for the wine to work its magic.

'Busy. Couple of poor cats got run over yesterday. Didn't make it. It's always sad...' Clinton's face clouded over, as if paying respect to the departed felines. 'Look, I need to talk to you...'

Rowena's heart double beat in her chest, invisible fingers flicking it. *She* was the one who doled out the endings...

'I really like you, but there's someone else,' Clinton tried to explain.

'You have a girlfriend? Oh for fu—'

'No! I'm single.' Clinton was visibly upset. 'I would never do that.'

'How are you single if there's someone else?' Rowena felt sleight of hand was at play.

'Sorry, I like someone else more. But I'm not seeing her,' he clarified.

'Does she know you like her?' Rowena snatched the role of agony aunt.

'Kind of, but not how much,' Clinton admitted. 'It'll probably never go anywhere or even happen. I really thought you and I could date, but it feels unfair.'

'So I'm sloppy seconds?' Rage bubbled, ready to fly, tears threatened.

'No! Jeez, I knew this wouldn't go well.'

'Sorry I'm not making it easy for you.' Rowena drained her wine, the alcohol not even battering the sides, adrenaline overriding it. She sniffed hard against the lump in her throat, determined not to relinquish this small corner of control.

'Look, I'm just trying to do the right thing. It feels wrong dating you when I'm still hung up on someone,' Clinton defended himself. 'You're hot, funny, and if I'd not met this other girl first...'

'You're not making this any better.' Rowena sighed heavily. 'I don't know why you bothered if that's how you felt in the first place.'

'Because I wanted to see if we had a spark. I also didn't want to give you a crap excuse. You deserved to know this isn't about you.'

'Well, it is about me, because if I was better than this other "Susan", then we'd be dating, and you'd have forgotten about her.'

'It's not about better. You're great, you really are. It's just my heart's elsewhere and won't be distracted.' He scratched his head. 'I wanted it to work...'

'You've not even snogged this woman?' He shook his head. 'So what the fuck are you playing at? What if she's crap? What if she can't talk about long drop toilets and burping the alphabet?'

'Then I'll give you a ring.' Rowena laughed despite facing the gallows. 'Look, Ro, I mean it, I am proper sorry. I'm not a dick. At least I don't think I am. This may have been the dickiest thing I've done and I shouldn't have led you on.'

Rowena believed him. He was so cute, and the fact he'd not tried to shag her and get away with it spoke volumes. Somehow, it did help that he wasn't being a vile twat.

'This is unprecedented,' she admitted. 'I'm usually the one issuing marching orders.'

'Would it make you feel better if you binned me?' Clinton fought a smile.

'Don't push your luck.' She ran her finger round the delicate rim of her wine glass making it sing. 'She like poetry, this Susan?'

'Oh God. Yes. That was shit, sorry.' Clinton covered his face with his hands.

'Who is she?'

'You don't know her. Anyway, it'll be a miracle if it happens. But I need to sit it out until I let her go. And I can't do that with you there.'

'You want some advice?' He nodded, wincing. 'Just tell her exactly how you feel, what you've given up. It's like you need to know so you can move on. Unless you try, it will always be hanging over you.'

'Thank you, Ro. That's why you're so cool. You've got your head screwed on the right way round. You sure you don't fancy Eliot? He thinks you're hot!' Rowena punched him playfully on the arm. 'Too soon?'

'Way too soon.'

'Do you want another drink?'

She wavered. 'Actually, no. I'm going to go.' She reached round grabbing her coat and thrust her arms inside.

'I can walk you to the bus stop,' he offered courteously.

'You finish your pint, I'll be OK on my own. I do it every day.'

Clinton stood up and Rowena stretched over, pecking him on the cheek as she did. Even his smell was addictive.

'Thank you, Rowena, for being so understanding.'

'If you change your mind, you've got my number. But I'll have met someone else and won't remember who you are in two weeks.'

Rowena spun round, waving as she walked off through the door, not looking back. *His loss.* But by the time she turned the key in the front door, the fight had dissolved, while dejection remained. The rarity of unearthing someone that she liked properly wasn't lost on her. Tears pricked the corners of her eyes and she furiously wiped them away.

'I hope fucking Susan knows what she's got,' she raged at the microwave.

She sequestered a tin of baked beans and a fork, stomping upstairs with the dregs of a bottle of wine to sit in her room and binge *Sex and the City* on her laptop. She pretended she was asleep when the other two arrived home at ten-ish, voices bellowing from after-work drinks. She'd tell them in the morning, but right then, she needed to wallow, get the tears over with. Rowena had an image to upkeep.

15

LENNIE SPOTS A FAMILIAR FACE

Lennie scrutinised the ingredients list on the back of the crisp packet as she sat on an empty promenade bench awaiting Florence's arrival. The crisps claimed to be vegan, but one couldn't rely on their infallibility. There was every chance they had been packaged in an environment where milk particles carelessly flew around like dust motes, ready to land in the flavouring pot, disguised as innocuous onion powder. If she was going to be vegan, she was going to be vegan one hundred and ten per cent. Of course, people with a life-threatening dairy allergy, which Lennie did not have, reserved the right to be so particular. It was necessary to stay alive and avoid an EpiPen being rammed below your sternum in the middle of Greggs. Lennie occasionally wished she did suffer something *almost* as bad as a life-threatening allergy – any severe health battle was good for the Gram, it made influencing much easier because you automatically had an authentic audience ready to connect with your hashtags. Being glamorous helped hugely alongside the deadly threat of miscreant peanuts or mozzarella balls. It was head and shoulders above having a terminal disease, no one wanted that. However, there were thousands of influencers with gigantic followings in that realm too, though admittedly, even in Lennie's follower-chasing eyes, their influencing was for the betterment others: check your boobs, your poo, your prostate – something Lennie found so utterly gross. She couldn't even fart in front of anyone, so drew the line at wishing illness upon herself in the pursuit of online success. She had *some* scruples.

Lennie was a living and breathing Instagram addict and Si had bought her a neon pink T-shirt that read 'For the Gram'. He'd hunted it down on Instagram, naturally. What Lennie really wanted, apart from the perfect house, wedding, life, was to be an influencer. But that goal was evading her. How could one be an influencer with three thousand and eighty-two followers? She had achieved a lot to get that many with the pretty lame horse content she posted. The trouble with Lennie's profile was one would assume that she had shares in the VIP area of an edgy London club, lived mostly on holiday, was constantly winning at life and not assistant managing a Brighton call centre for Saga Insurance. What she did do was go clubbing about twice a year, took along four different outfits with bling accessories (tags still intact ready to return after one use), changed in the toilets and created about twenty different posts in one night, role-playing her heart out while Si stood at the bar, waiting to drive her back to Lancing. 'It'll pay off, babe,' was what she told him. Saint Si knew it wouldn't, but he loved Lennie so stomached it. It was only twice a year...

Lennie's side hustle remained covertly in the wings – she didn't want to lose her actual job because until she made the big time, attracting sponsorship deals (wishful thinking), she had to keep the cash flowing. She used a generic Instagram handle (Bright-ongrrrl89), only ever revealed a third of her face, or forced Si to shoot from behind, and she never posted anything damning or controversial. Apart from the time she fabricated having a

Westie called Mr Popples to cash in on the Dogs of Instagram tidal wave. It didn't work out – her obsession with dust, mess, dented cushions and smeared glass would have overthrown the dog in the first week, had he been real... Hashtag blessed was bandied about like wedding confetti, and if Lennie was completely honest (a rarity) fundamentally, she rather enjoyed being the assistant manager of a call centre, and the relative anonymity of Instagram gave her a buzz, so that she could fake her life, create her own upstaged reality and see where it took her, a bit like orchestrating your own theatrical fairy tale where you call the shots and play every part to see how many likes you can garner (all pictures taken from above – no double chins!). Who wouldn't want to do that?

The crisps passed the test and Lennie popped one in her mouth watching day trippers wander past munching hot dogs carrying animal helium balloons while clouds scurried across the sun driving down the air temperature, the occasional easterly gust nipping at her ankles. She'd already posted a story about #home-madelunch when two people tried to steal Flo's seat. She tersely told them it was reserved for her sister. Florence was supposed to meet her for lunch, but she was already late. She'd just recently managed to secure a job round the corner from the Saga offices, temping for Si's recruitment company. Mainly general admin duties, filling in for the young office assistant who'd had a skiing accident and was now in traction at Brighton General Hospital after being flown home from Val-D'Isere. Lucky for Florence! Lennie had last seen her sister on Easter Sunday ten days before. She and Simon had met Flo and her mum and dad at the Park View in Worthing for lunch. The vegan roast dinner had been a generous affair (no choice tempered all the stress), but Lennie wouldn't have picked it if she'd not been vegan. Truthfully, Lennie missed chicken more than fish, and the smell of Florence's garlic and rosemary stuffed poussin was almost too much to bear. Lennie wanted to whip the bird from her plate and rip off the crispy, pancetta-wrapped skin and crunch it between her teeth, salivating as the salty goodness exploded across her tongue, knowing that she still had a juicy carcass to polish off. She'd prodded her grey lump of garlic and sage marinated roast Chikun and had sighed. No matter how much she drowned the processed soya bean, pea protein, alfalfa joint with gravy from the dainty brass jug, it never managed to live up to its misleading soubriquet. She snapped the required photos of her Easter lunch, from about ten different angles, then Si took a dozen of her, knife and fork in hand, thrilled in her virtuousness while everyone around her devoured animal flesh, content with their choices. Hashtagsavetheplanet, hashtagveganfood, hashtagmeatismurder, hashtagnoanimalsonmyplate. Being an outlier was a sacrifice...

Florence had briefly mentioned a trip in Nellie to Berkhamsted at the lunch, but before she'd finished the tale, their food arrived with great fanfare from the attentive waiting staff, a bottle of their finest cava produced in an ice bucket, a treat from Simon. 'Yes, it's vegan,' he hissed before Lennie could get a word out.

'Here's to Lennie and Simon finding a wedding venue, to us finding a new house and selling the old one, and to Florence...' An excruciating pause; it was a minefield proposing anything for Florence, but Gareth found his footing. 'To Florence enjoying her job enough so she stays longer than four months.' Everyone cheered, including Florence, the culmination of her first adventure in Nellie remaining undisclosed. Apparently Nellie was now listed on a specialist camper van website for eighteen grand. Why had Mrs Higham left it to *her*? Lennie could have used that amount of cash for her dream wedding...

'Sorry I'm late.' Flo slumped down next to her sister on the bench clutching an M&S prawn sandwich and box of grapes, jolting Lennie back to the present. Florence shielded her eyes from the glare off the sea. 'Shoulda brought shades.'

'How's work?' Lennie asked through a mouthful of crisps. She'd prepared her standard inoffensive puy lentil salad and brought it to work in a takeaway container.

She'd previously made a yellow lentil dahl that she'd spotted on Instagram at the very beginning of her vegan journey. Everyone referred to her veganism as a phase, enraging her. 'Why can't you admit I'm a vegan?!' she'd snarked at Simon when he'd dared to ask how long the 'phase' would last. Simon had apologised and kept quiet, not commenting on the occasional sausage roll wrappers he'd noticed stuffed inside Lennie's car door pocket. The yellow dahl had been touted as low calorie, high protein and packed full of nutrition. The bubbling hadn't started until she'd been on the phone for an hour and her toilet break was way behind her. Halfway through a call with a woman about a car insurance policy involving eye tests, she felt her stomach strain against her skirt waistband like an unruly presence had brewed itself into life inside her bowels, and was seeking the easiest exit. Lennie had clamped her knees shut as if preventing her backside from exploding and sucked in her pelvic floor at the same time. The churning pain was unlike anything she'd experienced as an adult. There had been an incident aged fourteen on a school Geography trip when she'd held in roiling flatulence all the way from the Devil's Dyke. She'd lasted until the road outside school when the driver hit a speed bump at an unfortunate angle, jolting Lennie in her seat. Lennie had begged her parents to move schools afterwards but they, of course, were not sympathetic. 'Farting is a bodily function!' her mum had said in her best nurse's voice. Lennie had to endure weeks of torture concluding in a whoopee cushion hidden under her school cardigan at the beginning of tutor group. Thankfully Cordelia

Franks vomited in the middle of French two weeks later so she was saved...

Back to the Saga call centre and Lennie had spun into a panic. Vanessa was chatting to a customer on her left and Lawrence was busy to her right. She could hardly just get up and leave. What to do...?

'Mrs Cartwright, can I please ring you back. I'm so incredibly sorry, I've just been called away. Yes, I have your number. I'll be no longer than ten minutes...' Lennie threw down her headset and barely made it to the ladies' in time.

Meanwhile Florence eagerly ripped open her prawn sandwich, flying in the face of potential harassment from circling gulls. 'Yeah, work's fine. I don't see much of Simon. He's always in meetings with clients.' She bit into it hungrily, chewing with the intensity of a fallen carb dodger. Lennie eyed Florence's lunch longingly. She quite fancied a prawn sandwich right now. Fish not so much, but prawns were succulent and they didn't try to choke you with their devious little bones. She screwed up her crisp packet, shoved it in her bag and took out her takeaway container and fork.

'Oooh, lentils. You're so good. You'll be getting all these brownie points, I don't know who from, but I'm sure someone's noticing. At least the seagulls won't want yours.'

'You never said what happened when you gave the letter to Mrs Higham's friend.' Lennie had also been taught by Mrs Higham, and had liked her. She wasn't as clever as Florence, but Mrs Higham had allowed Lennie to forge her own relationship with reading and English without the shadow of Florence darkening her experience. She enjoyed the subject while it was a requirement, but as soon as she could, she dropped it. Wasting money on further education wasn't part of Lennie's life plan, cerebral gymnastics was not her arena. She wanted to work, save for a house and become a grown-up as quickly as possible, something she'd been striving towards from about the age of ten. She joined an insurance apprentice scheme after A levels, and found being paid to turn up to work a great performance enhancer. They should have been bankrolled at school – she would have aced it then. She didn't normally handle the phones, but two people were long term sick and the line manager was constantly weeing – she was about to go on maternity leave, so for now, Lennie was a hand on a deck, or ears in a headset.

'No I didn't...' Florence absently mumbled between bites, a prawn escaping onto her lap, a glob of mayonnaise staining her pink maxi skirt. Gulls screeched menacingly above.

'So? What was she like?' Lennie asked interestedly.

'Nice...' Florence stared out to sea.

'And...?'

'I gave Tracey the letter, and it... wasn't for her.'

'Who was it for?' Lennie forked lentils into her mouth and chewed at speed.

'Me. Mrs High—Cassie had written it to me.' Florence remained gazing into the distance.

'Like the other letter, that came with Nellie?' Florence had eventually told Lennie everything. Who else did she have to talk to, now Tariq had dropped off the scene?

'Yes, but different...' She glanced at Lennie, frowning. 'This is one of those treasure hunts, like we did at school.'

'Oh, God, I remember! We all used to love them... She actually said it was a treasure hunt?'

Florence nodded silently. The tide was turning on the shingle high up on the beach, the deflation and acceleration of the waves just about audible above the drone of traffic as it shushed upon the shore. Lennie understood enough about her sister to realise that this might be one of those situations when allowing conversation to worm its way through self-erected obstacles was crucial. So she said nothing, plunged her fork into her lentil salad and scooped up another mouthful. As soon as she'd started chewing her third forkful, Florence cracked. 'Tracey had a letter for me, from Cassie too...' Lennie nodded encouragingly, unsure whether that was an invitation to start digging. So she gulped another mouthful and chewed thoughtfully while Florence opened her grapes. Lennie checked her phone – she only had fifteen minutes before she needed to head back. She had a meeting with People Operations regarding the new working hours before jumping back on the lines. They were trialling a four-day week. How? – they hadn't enough staff to cover the shortfall. All well and good telling people they can opt for four days, but someone had to pick up the tab. The office didn't shut down. Lennie impatiently raced through her salad, scraped the last lentil onto her fork by cornering it against the side, then snapped on the lid before ramming the tray in her bag. Florence was still picking off individual grapes.

'Oh FFS, spit it out.' Lennie's true form hustled her short-lived imperturbability out of the way. She scrabbled around in her back pocket for her vape, inhaling deeply. Mmmm...

'What?!' Florence gawped.

'What did the letter from Tracey actually say? I have to go soon. You were late and you obviously need to talk about it or you wouldn't have mentioned anything. I've played by the rules so far, so come on, get on with it.'

Momentarily stunned, Florence stumbled, but recovered enough to blurt out what she was skirting round. 'I opened the letter when I was back in the van. It was two rows of decimal numbers.'

'What did they mean? A code of some sort?' Lennie asked impatiently.

'They were a map reference. Mr Ogby worked it out.'

'OMG. Is he your new BFF now? He knew before you told Mum and Dad?'

Florence hesitated. 'I haven't told them.'

'So you went to the treasure hunt destination with Mr Ogby?' Florence shook her head. 'By yourself?'

'No. I've not been at all.' Florence turned to look at her now, her face slipping into neutral.

'But you've known where this place is for three weeks, the next stop on the map, and you've not gone?'

'Yep.'

'Why?'

'Why do you think?' Florence snapped.

'Where is it?'

'Where do *you* suppose it is?'

'I haven't got a fucking clue.'

'Then you don't get to know.' She stood up. 'I'm going. I need to buy tampons.'

'You're just going to leave? Not tell me? That's a bit shit.'

'It's not about you, Lennie. This is about me. Bye, I'll see you next week.'

Lennie shook her head in exasperation as Florence stalked off to Boots up through the Lanes then back to work. Lennie had no insight into the contents of the other letters, Florence had barely revealed what the first one had said. The map reference could be anywhere in the entire country...

Lennie swung her bag onto her shoulder, dusting off a few loose lentils from her lap, the gulls wouldn't thank her for the scraps. She turned towards the crossing near the shopping centre, meaning to head up West Street when she spotted her. Rowena. It was definitely her, striding along the opposite side of the road away from the shopping centre, her hair bouncing in that enviable way, full of vitality, evoking a glossy show pony. Lennie had always coveted her hair, even as a little girl. She wore an enveloping winter coat, strange for this weather; it was quite warm today. Lennie almost crossed the road to catch her, but something pulled her back from the kerb, her hand hovering over the button. *Decimal numbers.* She sucked on her vape, the coconut and vanilla gently warming the back of her throat. *A place that elicited such a strong reaction...* Lennie fancied she heard a rushing sound as realisation hit her square in the head. God, she was a turd sometimes. What game was Cassie playing? No matter, Lennie fully believed that this entire charade was leading to a conclusion they had all wished for Florence for years. Beyond her better judgement, she trusted Mrs Higham. Everything she had ever initiated at school had been for the acceleration of her pupils' education and personal development. Why would this treasure hunt be any different? And people thought vaping was bad for you – she always had her biggest cognitive breakthroughs while partaking of the vape!

Lennie watched Rowena turn into Ship Street, possibly heading for the car park, swinging a Hennes bag in time with her gait. An elderly gentleman pressed the button and the green man appeared. Lennie crossed in a daze, allowing the woman in front of her to press the next button at the halfway point as she pulled her phone out of her pocket and texted Florence.

I'm really sorry. I've just realised where the clue is. If you want me to come with you, I can.

Thank you. I don't want to go there.

It might help you open up. Move forward. Talk about it.

The green man beeped again, safety first. Lennie waited until she had crossed before checking the reply.

Nothing will help.

There's probably another clue there. Don't you want to see what it is?

After the apparent sign from the universe (Lennie wholly believed in signs, psychics, horoscopes) she began to tap out that perhaps the following clue would be the whereabouts of Rowena, something she KNEW would help her sister. The fact no one was allowed to even talk about her, let alone mention Clinton's name in case Florence... *in case Florence what*? She had no idea any more because everyone was too scared to mention either of them, not that they needed to. It was just so unhealthy! Lennie understood her own culpabilities with decision-making, Instagram obsession and revulsion at mess, but she wasn't running away from any of it. In fact, she wholeheartedly embraced her eccentricities. She deleted the message, what was the point? Florence needed a rocket up her arse to finish this. Lennie knew what she had to do.

16

THE STALKER

Jammy Dodgers. She needed Jammy Dodgers. Rowena was so confident of the biscuit aisle's location, she could have navigated it blindfolded. She shuffled towards it like a sniffer dog in a cocaine-seeking frenzy. *What the fuck!* They'd moved it. In its place were rows and rows of tinned soup. She burst into tears, angry yet, at the same time, sheepish that while people were being slaughtered for living on the wrong side of a border, she was experiencing a tectonic meltdown about raspberry jam centred biscuits.

'Are you OK, love?' an elderly woman asked. She was proudly wearing a badge that read 'Ask me for help' – she obviously worked at Sainsbury's.

'I think so. Sorry. Do you know where the biscuit aisle's gone?' Rowena wiped her eyes with her fingers. The woman eyed her with compassion, clocking her rotund belly poking out from her open coat.

'I told them not to move everything about, but no one listens to me. You're the tenth person today that's got upset because they couldn't find what they wanted. Here, follow me.' Despite her age, the woman was spritely and Rowena had to almost run to keep up. She dashed down the aisle adjacent to pastas and rice, revealing the biscuits with a flourish, still housed opposite the tea and coffee, but now at the other end of the shop. 'They wanted to move stuff around after the Easter eggs disappeared. Bad move, I think... Biscuits are necessary in these uncertain times, don't you agree?'

'Yes!' Rowena cried a bit too loud. 'I don't know how I would get through the day without them. They stop me feeling sick, and they're a treat. Though to be honest I'm eating them as meals mostly. Green veg tastes ick.'

'Well, when you get to my age, everything's a treat. Since Owen, my husband, passed last year, I've stopped proper cooking. I get a good discount here and I eat what I want. Spent my whole life avoiding this and that trying to be healthy. Makes no difference – we're all going to die, just extends it by a few years, and you can't always guarantee those years'll be worth it.' In response to Rowena's hastily raised eyebrows, she softened. 'Sorry, I know that sounds doom and gloom. I just meant have what you want, live life, eat the biscuits. Baby will always be OK. We all smoked, ate whatever we wanted, apart from liver, and our kids are all OK. Enjoy yourself while you can.'

A busy mother and two kids scooted by with a trolley-full of pizzas, a huge sack of bargain pasta, fruit and veg rammed in the front section, a value chicken sitting proud in the baby seat like a fleshy headless Buddha. What meals would she and Squodge eat together when the time came?

'How long were you married?' Rowena asked, now irrationally in love with the woman, wanting to whisk her home and install her in Squodge's room as a live-in nana. Her hair was a wreath of lilac candyfloss, the roots darker than the sugary tips, making her age hard to pin down.

'Fifty-five years. Not all of them great, mind you, and when the kids were little, he was a bugger, off gambling and stuff, but we got through it. I often thought life would be easier without him then. But now he's gone, I miss him. You got a husband?'

'No, I'm doing this on my own.'

'Good for you. Honestly, I think that's the best way, you and the baby, no one else interfering or getting in the way...' Rowena nodded in agreement. 'Look, you go and get your biscuits, I need to go on my break. Hope it all goes OK.'

'Thank you. Do you mind if I ask your name?'

'Marylin.'

'I'm Rowena, nice to meet you, Marylin. I'm always in here so see you again, hopefully!'

'Yes, love, ta-ra!' Marylin toddled off towards the chocolates.

Rowena smiled to herself. She hadn't heard anyone say 'ta-ra' for years. Not since she and Florence used to say it to each other as children playing 'old lady' cafés in Florence's living room. Rowena reached for the Jammy Dodgers and suddenly recalled that they used to serve them in their café. How could she have forgotten that? And those other biscuits with the jam and cream filling. What had they called the café? Lennie and Ro used to take turns at being the waitress and best customer while Florence 'cooked' in the kitchen, pushing the cold baked beans and other delectable dishes through the hatch. They had proper waitress notebooks for tearing off the order so she could slam it on the wide shelf and yell 'Cook!' through the hatch.

Rowena slid four packets of Jammy Dodgers off the shelf into her waiting basket. *What was the name of their café?* It was bugging her now. She stood perfectly still, as if awaiting the answer to drop from Sainsbury's cavernous ceiling. Why did Florence keep elbowing her way into her thoughts? Was it because she was pregnant? She had been closely re-examining her childhood archive for clues about how not to parent recently. Unfortunately, most of her life had been bilaterally linked with Florence's like a set of conjoined twins, it was impossible to slip a knife in between and separate them. Most significant memories showcased Florence as a supporting character in every narrative: her dad leaving her mum for Tammy; the time she fell off her scooter and broke her wrist – Florence had been on her BMX and they had been racing to see who could beat the other to the T-junction at the top of the road (Florence had won); every Halloween she and Florence always dressed up as witches, forcing poor Lennie into being their cat and knocked on all the doors in their road up until they were about thirteen; her first kiss with that mingdog, Archie, at Florence's fourteenth birthday disco (she could still feel his tongue on a spin cycle); when she lost her virginity aged fifteen and three-quarters to Kyle (why oh why?) and the only person she told was Florence who immediately made her do a pregnancy test, even though it was too early to tell (thankfully she hadn't been with child); when she failed her maths GCSE by three points and Florence patiently explained past papers to her before the October resit; when she drove Florence into Brighton the day she passed her driving test to buy ice creams and to swim in the sea, but they'd forgotten their bikinis so swam in their underwear turning it see-through; when they'd got matching tattoos on their bums: FLORO inside a heart, but Florence had screamed in pain and had almost been left with FL until Rowena made her clench her hand throughout and ended up with a dead arm and nail marks that lasted until pub closing time; when she lived in a flat share with Terry-Anne in Kemptown and Florence moved in – they had the time of their life, until they hadn't...

Rowena swiped a packet of Jam Sandwich biscuits for old times' sake and stalked to the self-checkout. Terry-Anne was coming for dinner at the weekend to introduce her new girlfriend. She'd not seen her since the pregnancy announcement. Terry-

Anne was not only a lesbian, but also a vegan melt. What on earth could she make? Cold baked beans and Jammy Dodgers? They were vegan... As she scanned her biscuit haul, she became aware of a familiar face in the toilet paper aisle. Clinton, surely not; his vet practice was in Brighton. He and Florence wouldn't live all the way over here unless they had kids. Hordes of families had moved to Seaford, rebranded as the affordable Brighton where you can park outside your house (no one had been able to do that in Brighton since the late eighties), and house prices were more in line with the national average. Sadly there was no pier, but there was also a distinct lack of tourists and the beach was often relatively empty, even in high summer. Sunbathing on Brighton seafront was like participating in a Guinness World Record attempt for the largest game of sardines.

'Clinton' distractedly wandered off towards the magazines, and Rowena craned her neck. His hair looked tidier and he may have put on a tiny bit of weight... She lost all concentration, testing the impatient checkout.

'Please scan the next item or finish and pay.'

'Fuck's sake,' she mumbled under her breath, glowering into the anti-theft screen in front of her. She scanned the rest as if competing in an Olympic event and shovelled them all in her rucksack before hesitantly making her way towards the magazine aisle. She'd just remembered she needed to buy a copy of *Mother and Baby*, wasn't that the original idea before Jammy Dodgers subsumed her...?

With a tempest raging in her chest, she struggled to stifle a disquieting memory as she rounded the corner housing the greetings cards. She'd crossed this threshold before, furtively pursuing Clinton in a shop. Only that time she'd known for certain it had been him.

* * *

July 2015, Brighton

Rowena hadn't meant to go into *that* Boots. She'd intended to pop into the one nearer home, but she wasn't bothered about rushing back. Terry-Anne was out with uni friends and Florence was at work drinks, even though she didn't have any real workmates. Florence had been socialising heaps recently. She had also disappeared off for a weekend with 'friends'. Not that she required a release form from Rowena, but a whole congregation of newly acquired 'friends' suddenly seemed to have crawled out of the woodwork in the last month. Ro had yet to meet any of them.

'I reckon she's seeing someone,' Terry-Anne had declared a few nights ago after Florence had rolled home at four in the morning, sober.

'She usually tells me everything,' Rowena had said, wounded.

'Maybe it's someone we wouldn't approve of or he's married, or has a girlfriend – he could be from work.' Terry-Anne paused *Unforgotten* while they debated.

'I guess,' Rowena had limply agreed. 'I still think she would tell me. I'd tell her.'

'Deffo married or attached then,' Terry-Anne surmised. 'Have you asked her?'

'No. Because she's never shut me out before. I feel like she'll tell me when she's ready. I don't want to make her feel awkward.' None the less, it was strange.

'Have you noticed how she's lost a bit of weight too? I mean, she was never a chub at all, but she's a bloody skinny minny now. That always happens when you meet someone significant. You can't eat, can't sleep – then throw into the mix they're married with kids. Total Jane Austen wasting disease.' Terry-Anne sniffed imperiously, obviously pleased with her literary analogy.

Rowena was averse to the idea of Florence getting mixed up with a married dude. She'd not forgotten the broken mess left behind after that dick at uni ditched her, robbing the joy from the exhilarating starting line of adult life. She'd only ever really had one proper boyfriend since that episode, but hadn't let herself get too attached, the memory of the suffering and her subsequent downfall the principal deterrent.

'I don't need a boyfriend, I have you!' she always used to joke after the occasional one-night stand, brushing off the obvious ignominy at breakfast as soon as the man had sneaked past them all and out of the front door. She wasn't built for temporary flings either. She habitually chose people unworthy to make it easier to disengage. And if someone half decent did pursue her, she sabotaged with every reason under the sun so that he never became a contender. *His eyes were too close together; he limped* (he did not); *he sniffed too much; he lives too far away* (Worthing is not too far away); *his shoes squeak; I don't like his jeans; his mum voted Tory; he's vegan* (fair dos); *I reckon he claps when a plane lands...*

'OK, I'll ask her on Friday,' Rowena sighed, hoping the guy wasn't married. That would be a tricky conversation... 'We're going to the pub then. You've got me worried now. I think you might be right...'

Walking into Boots two days before her FloRo date, Rowena marched towards the make-up wipe aisle – the definition of insanity! There were so many brands of make-up wipes. She swore allegiance to no particular one and scanned the shelves for the offers, grabbing two Garnier packets – BOGOFs. A persuasive face pack caught her in its tractor beam and she had to divert her eyes. The trouble with shopping in the big Boots was its legion of temptations burning holes in your purse. As she turned away from the face packs she caught a glimpse of a striking side profile prompting her heart to burst in her ribcage. His cheekbones still sent shock waves towards her groin.

Clinton walked towards the checkout with a basket. It had been nearly four months since she'd last seen him but he still occupied her daydreams which troubled her. Naturally she'd had a mini fling and a completely unfortunate one-night stand with a man from the Coalition bar involving some confusion leaving the bathroom and an attempt to get in bed with Terry-Anne. She'd been a good sport about it, thankfully. Clinton strolled ahead of her to the row of self-checkouts and while he was finishing she turned her back, grabbed her receipt and caught him shooting through the door with his rucksack full of deodorant and hair stuff. Not that she had been spying. Her finger pulsed and she shook it. *I'm not following him – I've got to go this way to the bus stop...* They cruised through the Lanes and out onto the blustery seafront, Rowena hanging back. *No, this was weird*. She was about to turn round when he started waving at someone. Rowena made a snap internal inquiry, did she want to know who he was meeting? Maybe it was the girl he'd been hung up about. She should at least compare notes.

She walked slowly, deliberately out of step with him, eyes cast down to the chewing gum pocked pavement. In her periphery she noticed him wave again and this time she looked directly towards the recipient, her pupils dilating double time as she involuntarily choked, a cyclone rushing up her throat...

* * *

April 2023, Newhaven

. . .

Rowena caught her ankle on the edge of the magazine stand, knocking a few copies of the *Radio Times* onto the floor. She glanced towards Clinton and he turned from leafing through *Livingetc*, and immediately picked up the magazines. It wasn't him; he was too short. His face only bore a suggestion of resemblance; how had she thought they looked alike at all?

'Thank you, I'm so clumsy,' she gushed.

'No worries.' He smiled and walked off through the shop. Unusually deflated, she abandoned all thoughts of *Mother and Baby* and headed towards the exit. Just as she reached the plastic bag recycling, Nate walked through the entrance on a cloud of debonair pomposity, his eyes gunning for hers.

'Fancy bumping into you here.'

17

FIGHT OR FLIGHT, AGAIN

'What are *you* doing here?' Florence asked, opening the door to Lennie. 'Someone's coming to look at Nellie in fifteen minutes.' It was early Saturday and she'd not even made her second cup of tea, her brain lingering in limbo. Florence was *not* a morning person. Sunbeams struggled to penetrate the dense weeping willow in the front garden, their stippled light cascading across the tufted lawn – it needed cutting. Her dad had asked her to do it after Nellie's viewing but she had to work her way up to it. Just the thought of unhooking the Flymo from above the deck chairs while trying not to clip the paint pots made her chest cave. She had accidentally knocked over a tin of Courgette Flower emulsion the last time she'd cut the lawn, the lid not at all secure within its calcified crust, ruining her trainers and the shed floor.

'Just popping in,' Lennie said in the voice she reserved for Instagram reels.

'You never "pop" in anywhere...'

'You gonna let me in?'

'Sure.' Florence stepped aside allowing Lennie into the hallway. Her parents were suspiciously absent. Usually when guests arrived they were like expectant terriers crowding the narrow hallway. They'd been in the house pottering upstairs literally seconds before the door went, they would have heard it was Lennie. Their indifference was a little disconcerting.

'Tea?' Florence asked, heading into the kitchen, misgivings trailing behind.

'Great, thanks.' Lennie perched on the nearest bar stool and watched Florence make the drinks.

'So, what's going on?' Florence probed warily, handing her sister a mug of tea with 'Save the NHS' across it.

'Nothing. I'm just in the area and thought I'd swing by...' Lennie kept her eyes trained on her tea as she sipped it, even though it was in close competition with the surface of the sun.

'Where's Si?' Florence asked.

'Playing golf with Gaz and Motto.'

'I don't know where Mum and Dad are. They were here a second ago.' Lennie shrugged. 'Is everything OK? You and Si haven't fallen out?'

'We're all good...'

Florence stared at her sister, but she wouldn't meet her eyes.

'Is this about the other day?' Lennie's eyes flicked up as she feigned bewilderment. 'Our text conversation, about the map coordinates?'

'Ohhh, thaaaat.' Lennie's teeth clenched when she sounded the T.

'Lennie! You're shit at whatever you're trying to do. Just tell me why you're here!'

Lennie sighed, carefully placing her tea on the counter and gnawed her thumbnail before speaking.

'Fine, yes, I'm here about the other day,' she relented.

'I knew it. Why didn't you just say?'

'Because you're such a slippery fish,' she retorted. 'I need to take you out; we're going on a little drive.'

'No! I could tell you were up to something. You can't leave the house to go to the bloody corner shop without working out a timetable of events.'

'Funny... You better get your trainers on if we're going out.' Lennie eyed Flo's bare feet.

'I'm not coming.' Florence's heart picked up pace to a brisk trot, her fingers beginning to throb. 'This guy's coming to see the van with his wife, they'll be here soon.'

'We can go straight after, so you haven't time to think.' Florence fiercely shook her head. 'I really think you should,' Lennie said firmly. 'That's where the next clue is. Don't you want to find it?'

'You go without me if you're that concerned.' Florence's petulance could outshine Lennie's on occasion.

'I think you're missing the point. Remember at school, Mrs Higham always pushed us to do better, *be* better than we thought we could?' Florence nodded truculently. 'She made us look at the world outside of the classroom, outside of the shitty GCSE syllabus. It was the only way I was ever going to get through fucking *Of Mice and Men*. But she never made us do something we really couldn't do, did she?' Florence's hostile glare could have stripped paint. 'Did she, Florence?' Florence shook her head slowly. 'I'll be with you every step of the way. You just need to be present, that's all. I'm sure Cassie will be there too, supporting you.'

'I don't believe in all that psychic claptrap.' Florence stalked into the hallway, abandoning her tea, she didn't want to be a shaking mess when the guy arrived. She wanted him to take Nellie for the asking price so she could get out of here, back on the road, delve into another adventure where she was in control...

'Where are you going?' Lennie asked, instantly suspicious.

'I need to get my trainers... that bloke'll be here in a minute.'

Gareth and Edie suddenly appeared from nowhere like extras in a stilted comedy of errors.

'Hello, love. You OK?' her mum asked, her face set in an anxious question mark.

'I'm fine.' Florence made a move to go upstairs.

'All ready for Nellie's big sell?' her dad interrupted. 'Still think you should keep her, she'll go up in value if you sort her interior.'

'I can go to Costa Rica sooner if I sell her, get out of everyone's hair.'

'Oh, love, we like having you here,' Edie protested. 'I thought you were staying until the move at least...'

But Florence mounted the stairs, ignoring her, hovering once she reached the landing then pretended to shut her door. She had no intention of going with Lennie.

'How was it?' Dad asked quietly, presumably to Lennie. 'She seemed OK.'

'Yeah, well done, love. That can't have been easy. She'll thank you for it in the end.'

A furnace blasted at the base of Florence's skull, rage tearing through her chest as she charged into her bedroom straight towards the window, briefly peering into the garden. Jabbing her feet into her trainers she grabbed a hoodie and her rucksack, throwing in Nellie's keys, her phone and purse before standing on her desk chair. She turned the handle on the right UPVC window, then clambered onto the narrow inner ledge. Balancing, she estimated the drop being three metres tops. She could make that distance if she landed correctly. A clean getaway relied upon her family waiting in the hallway or they would see her land in the garden. With hesitation being the death of triumph, Flo drew in a massive breath, threw down her bag and hoodie then, before she could analyse her actions, slid her legs over the ledge and launched herself towards the grass. She landed squarely on her feet, the shock shooting tremors up her shins and jarring her back. When movie villains escaped out of first storey windows mid-chase, they always sprung off into the night. Her body felt like it had been split apart and tacked back together inside out. She hobbled off down the driveway...

Crouching behind the bay tree bordering their other neighbours, the Wickhams, Flo wondered how to reach Mr Ogby's without being seen when the sheer ridiculousness caught up with her. What *was* she doing? Jumping out of windows like a rebellious teenager desperate to make a forbidden all-night party. She was thirty-six! All this ludicrous activity just to avoid minor conflict with her family. Evidently it was more than that; she'd managed to evade an anxiety-induced derealisation bad trip since following her inner wayfaring lodestar across the world. But confrontation also happened to be Florence's Achilles heel, she'd prefer to swallow warm sick than face it. Florence was the kind of person who dreaded picking up the phone, even from a known caller, and God forbid an unrecognisable number, that would be googled rather than answered. Throwing caution to the wind, she stiffly marched down the pavement in full view of the house. She opened Mr Ogby's gate and pushed it aside to make way for her exit just as a Volvo estate nipped into a rare space two cars down. Predictably, the front door opened to the tune of sliding bolts and three different locks turning one after the other, a symphonic sweet release from the nightly barricade.

'Hello, Florence. Are the people here?' Bob called.

'I don't know, Mr—Bob. I'm just taking her out for a quick spin. It's an emergency.'

He hovered on his front step clad in his pressed navy trousers and a crisp dog-toothed blue and white short-sleeved shirt, appropriate for the fair weather. It was already eighteen degrees according to Florence's phone, and it was only nine in the morning. An April heatwave was on the cards.

'You've decided to keep her?' He smiled broadly, hoping he was right. He'd already tried to dissuade her from selling: 'Florence, vans like Nellie don't come along very often. She'll bring you so much joy. Why don't you give her a chance?' He'd echoed the exact words in Cassie's original letter, a 'sign' by any other name. But Florence was adamant now, what would she need a van for when Costa Rica beckoned? No more wild goose chases...

'No, Nellie's still for sale but I just need to go somewhere... Can you intercept the Harrises for me before they ring our doorbell? They'll be here in a minute. Tell them I'll call later, this can't wait, so sorry!'

'Right you are. Is that them now?' Florence looked right behind her at a couple unstrapping a baby from the back of the Volvo. She couldn't face them, she just wanted to escape anywhere, it didn't matter where. Panic nipped at her heels as she opened Nellie's door and jumped in the driving seat. With shaking hands, she turned over the engine and Nellie coughed into life. Reversing out of the drive required another set of eyes to avoid a potential collision, but Flo was ready to take what was coming; she didn't need anyone else. As she checked the distance between her and the gate post she glanced up and caught her puzzled family watching from their doorway. Guilt washed over her, maybe she should stop, talk, listen. But when she reversed into the road on a wing and a prayer, an oncoming car forced her hand, preventing any kind of recrimination or apologies from either side. Florence floored Nellie and drove off without a backward glance, missing the baffled Harris family staring at their prospective van disappearing in the opposite direction.

Turning right at the top of the road she headed towards the

coast, snapping down the sun visor, following signs for the A26. The monotony of driving lulled her brain, allowing Rowena to creep into her head once more, filling the space Cassie had chiselled out. She'd dreamt about Rowena last night, but had immediately blocked all recollection of it. Instead she wondered if Rowena knew that she had been single for years, that the hair shirt she wore itched so badly she needed to strip herself naked and burn it on a bonfire along with the past. Knowing what she knew now, would Flo change anything? Boyfriends, husbands, partners, they come and go, like prime ministers or skinny jeans, but the stable brickwork, the steadfast tree with the connective roots was always friendship. It remained when other relationships curdled. Would she trade those eighteen months for a lifetime of unfailing friendship?

18

COMMON DOG AND BIDET GIRL

May 2015, Kemptown

'Florence!' A lone seagull screeched mournfully from a chimney above drowning out Clinton's voice. Oblivious, Florence marched towards the bus stop on her way to meet Rowena and Terry-Anne after work. The light evenings were blooming incrementally later making drinks in town feel like the first flush of summer. She'd enjoyed a day off in lieu and had been tidying her room as well as the rest of the house. The girls had a monthly cleaner as part of the tenancy agreement, but her hoovering was cursory at best, the dust balls under the TV cabinet were beginning to form their own solar systems. 'Florence!' This time she heard and turned finding Clinton waving, briskly striding towards her from further up the hill, the sun illuminating him with an outlandishly celestial aura.

'Hello,' Florence croaked, her lungs constricting. When Rowena had revealed he was hung up on another girl, Florence had sheepishly made the overriding assumption that she was that girl, based purely on their previous chat... The realisation had filled her with prohibitive joy.

Clinton was wearing his vaguely medical work uniform, a purple emblem of a cat and a dog cupped by a pair of hands stitched on his blue shirt pocket.

A witty repartee evaded her as he approached. 'What are you doing out here? Is the vets' over this way?'

'No, I was dropping a cat back to its elderly owner. He'd come in for a scale and polish.' When Florence looked nonplussed, he elaborated by pointing to his mouth. 'Teeth.'

'That's very kind of you.'

'All part of the service.' They stood awkwardly, she shielding her eyes from the glaring sun, their former conversation wedged between them like a nightclub bouncer. 'How have you been?'

'Yeah, fine, fine. You?' Florence chewed the inside of her mouth.

'Good.' He smiled. 'How's Rowena?'

'She's great. Dating someone else now.' She disclosed the latter merely as an act of solidarity towards Rowena; she would want him to know she'd moved on. However, Rowena was as familiar to Florence as every imperfection on her own face, so she was under the reliable impression that she *hadn't* moved on yet, she'd just papered over the unforeseen hurt with sex. She would move on eventually, but Rowena had unreservedly opened herself up allowing Clinton unsanctioned access few had been permitted.

'Oh, glad she's OK. How about you?' he probed.

'What about me?' Florence checked her phone, it having buzzed in her back pocket. 'Sorry.' She read the Three Witches WhatsApp group message from Rowena.

Running late, be there at sevenish. Soz.

Terry-Anne was typing but Flo feigned reading until it appeared so she didn't have to stare at Clinton. His presence was enough to melt her sanity.

Shall we meet at 7.30 then? I just need to finish off a few bits.

They all agreed the new time and Florence replaced her phone.

'Everything OK?' She nodded. 'I meant are *you* dating anyone?'

'God no.' Florence baulked.

'OK. I was only asking. I'm not your mum.'

'Sorry, I just get sick of answering questions about my non-existent love life.' Her neck burned from recklessly disclosing intimate details.

Clinton looked at his watch. 'OK, it's after six, I've clocked off now.' He clapped his hands together. 'I've the van with me and need to drop it back, do you want a lift into town? I'm assuming you're going that way?' *Well, it would be rude to say no...*

* * *

'So you're not an admirer of fan fiction?' Clinton asked in all seriousness.

'No, it's always shit, so badly written. That's what those awful *Fifty Shades* were. I couldn't get past the first page.'

'You bought it? Lined whatshername's pockets?' He was laughing at her as he drove round the Level, the traffic crawling behind lorries and impatient drivers honking when there was no hope of moving any quicker. A vague warm animal aroma emanated from the caged space in the rear. Florence was reminded of the sloth house in Drusillas Park – her mum used to take her and Lennie during the school holidays when they were young. They'd loved the sloths and the giant ant eaters – a strange hybrid of a badger and a baby elephant.

'No way. I went into Waterstones and read it. Try before you buy,' she replied loftily. 'Totally crap. It was so prosaic, like no one had set a red pen to it.'

'Oohhh, big words!'

She had been concerned that her evident passion for him would seep out of her pores rendering her mute, but they hadn't stopped talking, conversations crashing into each other in their eagerness for airtime. Sidetracked by their lively discussion, her stomach had ceased to churn as they chatted about books, music, TV, films and animals.

'What animal would you be if you could do it for one day?' Clinton asked as they crept round the Level.

'A bird, so I could fly. Does that count as an animal?' Florence asked hopefully.

'Yes! It's a creature. I'd be a dog. I love them. I'd want to run up and down the beach chasing balls and running in the sea.'

'Of all the animals in the world you'd be a dog? Not a tiger, or a deer, or an antelope? Just a common dog?' Florence mocked him.

'Yes, just a common dog. I'm not allowed pets at my house share, so I could be a dog for a day instead. I've managed to sneak in two guinea pigs though, Bramble and Toffee. I have to hide them at work when we have a house inspection.'

Florence found that adorable. Clinton pulled into a crowded side road, every space occupied apart from a meagre gap that would require a tin opener to get out of.

'You'll never fit into that,' Florence kindly informed him as he optimistically lined up the van.

'Yeah? How much do you bet?'

'A glass of wine.' Florence's heart skipped.

'I'd prefer a pint after this.' He winked.

'OK, a pint then. But I want wine when you lose.' Florence's mouth instantly parched as he reversed slowly, expertly turning the wheel, no parking sensors easing the tricky manoeuvring. 'I could get out and guide you?' she offered.

'Nah, I'm good. Look, we're in!' He swivelled his head to face her, beaming. 'I believe you have a debt to settle.'

Florence rolled her eyes melodramatically and sighed. 'If I have to.' She steered him towards the Bath Arms, a small pub tucked away near Brighton Pavilion. She wasn't hiding from anyone, she just felt it was in their best interests not to bump into any mutual acquaintances.

'There you go, well done on defeating an awkward parking space.' She placed his pint of Adnams on the table, condensation streaming down the sides, before perching on a stool. He slipped a beer mat underneath it before lifting it up to clink her wine glass.

'Cheers! What *are* we cheersing?'

'Your parking prowess?' she suggested.

'How about friends reunited.' Florence grinned and clinked again. 'How long do we have?'

'Before what?'

'You turn into a pumpkin. I'm assuming you're meeting friends. I know it can't be a boyfriend.' His eyes teased her.

'An hour.'

'OK, we can cover a lot in an hour.' With the timer on, they sprinted through favourite authors, veganism versus vegetarianism, and the best holiday destinations, whilst managing another hurried drink before the hands reached midnight.

'Can you stay for one more?' Clinton asked optimistically.

'No. I'm meeting Rowena.'

He nodded, understanding immediately. 'Can I at least have your number?'

Florence hesitated. Here was a man who had laughed until he cried about the time she washed her face in the bidet on the French school trip because she'd thought it was a special hand basin, totally unaware her roommate had been weeing in it daily thinking the genuine toilet was for number twos. The hour in the pub had felt like ten minutes spent with Rowena and Terry-Anne giggling over bottles of Merlot on a Friday evening.

'Is that a good idea?' she said regretfully.

'I think it's a brilliant idea.'

'Of course you do. You won't be the one impacted if anyone finds out about this little jaunt.'

'I've never been accused of being on a jaunt before.' His eyes twinkled mischievously. 'When can we have another one?'

'I don't think we can.' Florence apologetically informed him.

'Would Rowena *really* be that upset?'

'Yes. She'll see it as a massive betrayal.'

'But she's seeing someone else now. You told me.'

'That means nothing. She'll dump him in a week. You're the only man I've ever seen her like in a meaningful way. She has a complicated history with male role models...'

'What if we're just friends? You're free to date other people, like we're on Tinder. In fact, let's say we're each other's Tinder custodian.' He looked rather pleased with himself. 'We report back on all the other people we're seeing when we meet for a platonic drink, award them marks out of ten, make sure we're not dating absolute twats.'

'What if I don't want to date anyone? Do you? Are you dating anyone else?' She'd been too scared to ask earlier, not sure she was ready to accept an affirmative, even though this frisson was cursed.

'I'm not dating anyone else.'

Her heart soared as a message pinged in her back pocket.

I'm here. Where are you two bitches?

'I have to leave. Rowena's already at the pub.'

'So this is it? I might see you again when I'm delivering cats to their owners? Or on a night out when I can't even talk to you in case someone has a strop?' Clinton pulled a sad face.

'OK, fine, you can have my number.' She read it out. He sent her a smiley face and she saved his details as Common Dog. He laughed, her moniker of Bidet Girl complementing that perfectly. They both jumped up at the same time with Florence leaning over to kiss his cheek. He brazenly moved his head while she inadvertently brushed his lips so he pressed them gently against hers, a glimmer of unspoken passion reignited before he withdrew, leaving her desperate for a full snog, caught between her priggish conscience and what felt like the rest of her life.

'Er, bye,' she mumbled.

'Bye.' His eyes drooped. 'I'll give you a head start so no one sees us together.'

Florence ventured out of the flock-walled pub and into the brilliant sunshine beyond, treading carefully for her insides were scrambled. What had she walked away from? Before she'd even finished texting the girls, her phone pinged.

What was your favourite childhood food? I thought I'd compile your dating profile for you, save you some time...

By the time the Mesmerist swam into view less than five minutes later, she had narrowly avoided dog poo twice, and had actually careered into a lamppost because her eyes had been glued to her phone the entire time replying to Clinton's texts. Her heart had been cruelly whipped into a stiff piqued meringue. She was just behind Terry-Anne and hastily rearranged her expression as she sat down at their table, ready to start the evening, her mind lingering in the Bath Arms.

'What's up?' Rowena asked, narrowing her eyes. 'You're away with the fairies.'

'Nothing, I'm fine.' Rowena let it go and they managed to have a fun evening dancing and knocking back shots of tequila.

When Flo awoke the following morning, the reality of no fresh texts crushed her, spinning her hangover into class A territory, almost as bad as when she had first met Clinton... And so her week stretched out, every day a little less flattened at the radio silence until Wednesday evening, when he finally texted.

Are you still alive?

Yes of course I am! Why?

Oh, her heart sang like a rousing dawn chorus.

You haven't texted.

Neither have you.

Are we still friends?

Yes!

Friends text don't they. It's not banned.

I thought you were texting me.

I wasn't aware this was the Victorian era. You text me.

Florence giggled, wishing she could stow away in her room and play text tennis all night. Instead she had to subtly reply while she and Rowena watched *Sex and the City*.

'Who is he?' Rowena asked, clearly agitated at Flo's distraction.

'It isn't a he. Friend from work.' Rowena sighed and turned back to the TV. By Friday Clinton and Florence must have exchanged a million texts until Clinton curtailed their volume.

I think we should have a friend drink. Are you free tomorrow?

She wasn't. She had promised Rowena she would accompany her to Deal to visit her mum.

Sunday?

Yes. I will be back after three.

They were to meet in Brighton at the Bath Arms like before.

'Are you sure you haven't met someone? You seem... different,' Rowena pressed.

'I swear I am not shagging anyone,' Florence replied truthfully.

'That wasn't what I asked...' But Florence didn't elaborate and as hard as she tried to be present and focused on her weekend in Deal, her mind kept latching on to an idea of what this thing was with Clinton, or rather what it wasn't. She needed to discuss it with a friend, with Rowena, seek her advice, but of course that was preposterous, like asking Marie Antoinette to sharpen the guillotine.

Florence pondered the feasibility of continuing in the friend zone until Rowena was utterly done with thinking of Clinton as a prospective partner. Maybe if she got engaged to someone else, though there was slim chance of that, Flo could die waiting. Instead she decided to put out feelers while they were having dinner in Deal.

'I saw Clinton last week.'

Mid mouthful of red Thai prawn curry, Rowena widened her eyes as if she'd just chewed a lethal ghost chilli. Bolting her food like a dog necking a tasty treat, she shook her head at the revelation.

'What?!' Rowena squeaked. 'Why didn't you say?'

'Because I didn't think you cared,' Florence boldly answered. 'You're seeing Lance.'

'Meh... Did you say hello? Where did you see him?'

'In the Lanes on the way to meet you.'

'That's why you were so weird when you turned up!' Florence nodded, it was after all, not a lie. 'How did he seem? What did he say? Is he seeing that girl he was hung up about?'

'I have no idea. I didn't ask him.'

'You should have!'

'I just said hi and nothing much else. Oh, I told him you were with someone else.'

'Good, thanks!' Rowena fist bumped her. 'How did he seem when you told him that?'

'Normal. Sorry...'

'Oh well, his loss.' Rowena resumed eating.

'So you're over him?' Florence asked warily.

'Yeah, 'course!'

'You wouldn't kill anyone who was casually dating him?'

'Depends who it was.'

Florence had her answer.

'You OK? You look funny.'

'All good.' Florence was left with only one option. 'Here's to no more crap blokes.'

'I'll drink to that!'

* * *

'So you're dumping me without going out with me at all, even as friends?' Clinton leaned back in his chair in the Bath Arms an incredulous look planted upon his face.

'She will literally kill me. I had a verbal warning.'

'You told her we were in touch, as friends?'

'Not as such, no. I said I'd bumped into you...' Then she relayed the conversation word for word.

'I think she'd be OK with it in the end.'

'Clinton, I'm not willing to ruin a lifetime's friendship over one man. She made it pretty clear.'

'But what if we're kismet?' he said almost sincerely.

'I don't believe in fate, in any of that bollocks.'

'Neither do I. I was just seeing if you did.' He smirked. 'But seriously, you don't know what it would be like. We could do a test drive, like when you buy a car.'

'That would be just as bad.'

'Not if we both decided we actually didn't like each other, that we, you know, weren't compatible.' Florence could feel her defences slipping. 'That poem you recited hit the right note. "Nothing Gold Can Stay": life's too short. Just because someone else had notions and the other person had none at all. I have no feelings for Rowena, nothing – I like her as a person, she's great, but no romantic spark exists for me. I tried hard because you asked me to. Everything in that messed-up situation was about *you*.' He jabbed his hands through his thick hair, scratching his scalp at the same time. 'I get it though, she's your best friend. But she's manipulating you.'

'She isn't!' Florence couldn't stomach anyone tarnishing Rowena's name. 'She doesn't even know about this.' She waved her hands in the air like their mutual attraction was a fly dismissible with the flick of a wrist. Clinton reached over for his pint and sipped it, keeping his eyes on Florence. 'I just don't think I can put her through this.'

'OK. Fair enough.'

Florence drank her wine in silence. Why did she feel like something monumental had ended?

'Answer me this then, don't overthink it, say the first thing that comes into your head.' Florence looked up, into his open and honest face, his kind eyes guiding her out of the slump. 'What is it *you* want?'

Without hesitation, without embarrassment, without her scolding conscience clipping her wings, Florence firmly stated her heart's desire.

'You.'

19

FANCY SEEING YOU HERE

Florence essentially let Nellie follow her nose and so far she'd plumped to tootle down the back route in the direction of historic market town, Lewes. Florence adored Lewes, an antiquated shopping destination (with a castle!) that hadn't surrendered its heart to the towering pillars of retail. Its main artery boasted plenty of independent traders and cafés, offering a less formulaic trip than a cookie cutter out-of-town shopping behemoth. More Diagon Alley than Westfield. The only issue was parking and traffic with it being a significantly warm Saturday; teenagers and tourists would be out in force swamping the pavements dawdling in quadrille formations. The sun had warmed Nellie's insides, and Flo had to wind the window down, hard going without power steering.

However, Nellie made no indication of turning towards Lewes and bombed straight over the Brian the Snail roundabout by the Cuilfail tunnel, past the ridiculously brutalist central ammonite sculpture that had probably caused more accidents than texting whilst driving. Florence believed art was there to be leisurely contemplated, not thrown at you head on like sculpture flash cards while trying to navigate a hectic roundabout. Through the tunnel they drove, with Florence frantically winding up the window against the smell of the fumes. Safely out the other side, Nellie dithered between the A27 and the A26. Instinctively, Nellie kept her nose to the ground and carried on along the A26 towards the sleepy coastal town of Seaford. The tarmac carved through the bucolic landscape, various trees still in the process of unfurling, hedgerows flickering with tender foliage not yet scorched by pollution or the elements. Florence's armpits prickled with fresh sweat. She didn't feel fully prepared to drive down towards the Seven Sisters and deliberated stopping so she could go a for a wee. Thankfully her pelvic floor hadn't been terrorised by childbirth; she'd stupidly needed one before she jumped out of the window.

Florence couldn't recall her last visit to Seaford, possibly with Clinton picking up camping supplies at the giant Sainsbury's just outside the town. It wasn't a place she would ordinarily visit, Felworth leaning more towards Brighton. This stretch of East Sussex coast was synonymous with retirement homes and elderly residents, especially Eastbourne, the next town along.

Clinton. She had assimilated his continuing absence now. The agony of losing him had burrowed so deep she could scarcely feel its raw urgency on a daily level after toiling so hard at filling the gaping void with distraction. The loss was reminiscent of an infinitesimal splinter embedded in her skin, invisible unless prodded by a memory or meaningful happenstance, then it throbbed, threatening to totally engulf her unless she ran in the opposite direction. It was in her dreams where the grief arose, blistering and untamed like the day it had grabbed her by the throat. The nightmares didn't always seek her out when she was travelling, they preferred to haunt her as soon as she set foot on British soil. A dream last night about Rowena hadn't been a nightmare as such, more like a revisiting of the past but with a different ending. Florence wound down the window again, steering single-handedly and posed the question once more: would she change the past if she could?

* * *

May 2015, Brighton

'Well, I think we can safely say we're compatible,' Clinton laughed, leaning on his side, supporting his head with one hand. Florence ran her hand over his hairless chest, wondering if he waxed it or if he'd won a genetic lottery. She wasn't a fan of hirsute bodies, they always made her think of Tom Selleck in *Friends*, and that killed it for her.

'Yes, we're in trouble now.' She lay her head on the crushed blue pillow and stared at the high ceiling in Clinton's inadvertently minimalist bedroom. After fearlessly snogging in the pub, Clinton had promised her that no one was home in his Hove house share. 'There's only two of them and Lennon's on holiday till next weekend and Pete's at his girlfriend's. We'll have the place to ourselves.' On the walk back, they stopped in every dark corner to deliciously kiss. The anticipation overthrew Florence's rationale and by the time they stumbled in the door, Clinton calling out hello just in case, they were ripping off each other's clothes at the foot of the stairs. Clinton produced a condom from his jeans pocket as Florence unbuttoned them, yanking them down in one triumphant swoop.

'I hope you've got more than one,' she breathed, wishing she'd raided the bathroom cabinet at home.

'Here, the sofa or upstairs?'

'Sofa.'

The curtains were drawn wide but a solid privet hedge offered some protection from prying eyes, unless someone actually knocked on the door while making a concerted effort to peer in, they were safe. Florence was so far gone, she would have had sex in front of an audience; she'd never experienced this kind of animalistic passion before. There was an audience of sorts – Clinton's guinea pigs nestled in their cage by the French doors at the back of the room. But Florence didn't know about their presence until afterwards. Past sexual encounters had always been fuelled by alcohol or half-heartedly succumbed to because it was what one did in a relationship, wasn't it? Not that she'd ever been forced, she'd just not connected with herself, or anyone else in this way before. Foreplay usually exploded into a desperate need to reach the hallowed finish line with Florence often finding the act of having sex more of a detached bathetic experience.

Clinton fell apart as soon as he entered her, unable to hold himself together. He buried his face in her neck. 'That's never happened before,' he groaned, mortified.

'Don't worry about it. We can have another go in a bit.' Even the bite-sized length of time was enough for Florence to discern that the next attempt was going to be the shag of her life.

'I can finish you off,' he offered. 'I have a few tricks left up my sleeve.'

'I can wait...' He kissed her and Florence didn't have to wait very long at all...

They made it up the stairs for the third and fourth times, old pros by then, instinctively knowing what buttons to press and when to hold back. Florence found it surreal, like they had been born purely to have limb-trembling sex in some kind of procreation miracle. Nothing else in her life felt as certain as that fact.

'I can't ever go back to having vanilla sex with mere mortals now,' she said. 'I'm done for.'

The shadows on the walls had lengthened and Clinton flicked on his bedside lamp. It was almost eight thirty and Florence was supposed to be joining a house Netflix night. Her phone had been pinging in her bag. She crawled out of bed, partially wrapping the duvet around her midriff, and pulled her bag towards her by the strap. She had three messages from Ro and one from Terry-Anne, asking her what time she would be back and should they make her food?

'They're going to kill me,' she muttered trying to marshal her feelings, guilt gnawing away in her empty stomach. The need to self-flagellate, rid herself of the shame, subsumed her. She pinched her leg as hard as she could.

'Did you tell them you were meeting a man?'

'No, of course not! I said I was meeting a friend. I should go back.' He smiled resignedly. 'Sorry.'

'No, you have to do what you have to do, don't apologise.'

'So what are we going to do?' Florence reached around under the duvet trying to locate her knickers, betrayal lingering like a bad smell.

'Well, you know my stance, the ball is entirely in your court.' He shucked his T-shirt over his head.

'Maybe we could keep this quiet, see how we get on,' Florence suggested. 'You never know, you might get sick of me and it will run itself out. Rowena will never need to know.'

'I don't think that's going to happen.' He smiled at her ingenuousness. 'But if you feel like that's how it will end, then you carry on. I know how I feel.'

'But how do you know how you feel?'

'I just do. I don't think I'm going to get bored of you any time soon.'

Florence sighed. She also thoroughly believed she would never tire of Clinton. They were doomed...

* * *

Over the ensuing months, Florence tried very hard to contain her feelings. When she was at home with the girls, she felt like a voile curtain had drawn itself between them. She couldn't let anything slip, not one word, not one clue, until she was sure it was the right time. She lived in a state of heightened anxiety at being caught in the act, which was why she and Clinton took a few weekends away in cheap hotels, just to spend time together without constantly looking over their shoulders. It was on one of those weekends in Hastings that Clinton finally fast-tracked their clandestine love affair. They'd just taken a postprandial stroll hand in hand down the beach when they'd stopped to admire the view of the old town behind them, the ancient cliffs rising above, the funicular railway shuttling passengers up towards the castle ruins where William the Conqueror had once appraised his new kingdom.

'I know I'm in love with you,' Clinton said, squeezing her hand. 'I've never felt like this before.' Florence thought her heart would fly out through her mouth and flutter away with the gulls.

'I love you too. I have done for ages but I've been too scared to tell you.'

Clinton lifted her chin with his hand and kissed her on the lips.

'This isn't fizzling out then, hey? About time you told Rowena?'

'Not yet.' Florence bit her lip. 'It's only been a few months.'

'How long do we have to wait until the mythical right time? She might be mad forever which is insane. I only kissed her once.

There's nothing for her to hang her feelings on. It was all one-sided.'

'I know. Please just give it a bit longer. Can I wait until she starts her new job? She hates work at the moment, she's just got a few more weeks left, then she starts on that school direct thingy, where she trains on the job to be a teacher. I think it'll be the making of her; I can't upset that.'

'OK, OK, I'm sorry.' He held his hands up. 'I'm just fed up of sneaking around. I want us to be able to be ourselves, to do what we want. We've done nothing wrong.'

Florence agreed, but Clinton's declaration of love buoyed up her determination to act decorously. They weren't merely shagging, though that was what they spent most of their time doing, snatching every breath they could in his bedroom when they could be sure they were alone. This was probably 'it' for Florence: her cinematic big love. The timing was spot on; she was twenty-eight and ready to take the next step in whatever non-existent life plan she had tacked up at the back of her brain. Retraining to be a teacher was also not written down on that plan, but that field would have to remain temporarily fallow or she would look like Rowena's clone: stealing her boyfriend and then copying her career. However, when the truth detonated, it was swift and sharp, no time for a candid explanation in the face of unadulterated fury.

One evening Clinton had promised to meet Florence on the seafront before they walked back towards Hove, the opposite direction to Rowena and Terry-Anne. They never held hands out in public, or kissed, you never knew who was taking notes. Florence was waiting by a crossing, intending to press the button as soon as he appeared. He'd texted he was two minutes away. She spotted him waving and saluted him back, her chest expanding to accommodate the rush of feelings that arose every time she saw him.

'Hey, you ready to taste the culinary delight that is a tofu stir-fry? I've got the ingredients in here.' He patted his rucksack. Before Florence's brain could engage, Rowena hurtled towards them seemingly out of nowhere.

'What are you two doing? This isn't what it looks like, is it?' Her voice was shot through with pleading and barely contained rage while her eyes flashed between Florence's bloodless face and Clinton who seemed slightly startled, but otherwise unperturbed.

'Hello, Rowena,' Clinton said calmly. 'How are you?'

'Confused. What's going on?' she asked. 'You two friends all of a sudden? That's a bit weird, isn't it?'

Confounded beyond speech, Florence could only silently blink whilst hastily cobbling together a conceivably tall story, as useless as bringing a paper straw to a knife fight.

'We're a bit more than friends.' Clinton jumped in front of her while Florence implored him with her eyes.

'What?! *You* and *her*?! You're together?!' Neither of them said a word. People were queueing at the crossing, trying not to stare at the distressed woman with the wild hair gesticulating at the striking young man.

'Shall we take this somewhere else?' Clinton eventually suggested, Florence still overthrown by the histrionics.

'Where do you suggest?' Rowena spat at him, ignoring Florence. 'The pub where we went on our first date?'

'Ro, don't,' Florence mumbled. 'It's not like that.'

'Oh, you're just fuck buddies? He's hung up on someone, Flo, he'll bin you off like he did me.' Florence squirmed. 'Oh. Oh oho ho, nooooo!' Rowena's face lit up like a whirling Catherine wheel, short-lived delight snapping from her lips at discovering the Holy Grail of humiliation. '*You!* You're the girl. Oh my fucking God, this has been going on for months!'

'It hasn't!' Florence finally turned up the volume. 'This is new. I turned him down so many times.'

'Yeah, looks like it! Well done, you!' Rowena started clapping.

'Hang on!' Clinton interrupted. 'We've done nothing wrong. We had one date. One! I admit, I liked Florence before that date, but she had already turned me down. She wanted me to date *you*.'

'Oh this gets better and better. I was the pity date. The way in to meet Florence. In through the back door!'

'No!' Florence cried. 'Please can we go somewhere more private to talk?'

'Absolutely not! I don't want to talk to you. What about mates before dates, Florence? What about that?'

'I'm sorry, Ro. I was going to tell you eventually, once we were more established. Nothing happened at all until very recently. I didn't choose this.'

'Well, it looks like you have. I'm going. Don't bother coming home. Ever.'

'You can't throw Florence out of the house!' Clinton snapped, clearly exasperated at the drastic direction the encounter was heading. 'You have to move past this.'

Rowena gulped down some air and wiped her face with her hands, leaving them momentarily covering her eyes. 'Don't tell me how to feel,' she hissed between her fingers. When she moved her hands, something had shifted. Her anger had evaporated leaving tears in its wake. Rowena never cried. Florence stepped towards her, intending to offer a hug, but Rowena flicked up her palms in defence.

'Don't. I need to leave.' She turned away from them and trudged in the direction of the Lanes.

'Rowena!' Florence hitched her bag further up her shoulder. 'I should follow her.'

'I think she needs to be on her own,' Clinton said reasonably. 'Now is not the time.'

'But she's so upset.'

'Yeah, I can see that, but you going home with her won't remedy that. She needs time to let it sink in and then I think you'll find she'll realise she's being a bit ridiculous. Yeah, be a bit upset, whatever, but attaching this amount of grief to such a non-situation between me and her is pure drama.'

'I don't think this is about you and her. I think it's about her and me...'

* * *

April 2023, Newhaven

Florence turned into the spacious Sainsbury's car park in Newhaven, just outside Seaford, Nellie slipping into a space near the middle. She checked her phone – four missed calls from Lennie and her parents. A text from her mum. She shoved the phone back in her bag without reading the message and headed inside straight to the bakery where she chose a cinnamon whirl and a cheese and olive bread roll to go with a massive bottle of water. After the self-checkout she found the toilets. Staring into space as she dried her hands, she decided she would 'allow' Nellie to take her to the cliffs. After all she and Clinton had lived in Brighton and she hadn't blackballed that; it was more about what the cliffs represented. At the end of the day, they were just cliffs, like Brighton was just a city (or was it a town? She was never quite sure), and she could do with a walk to loosen up her jarred back after her Jason Statham getaway. She laughed to herself about her dramatic antics and wiped her hands on her shorts. Leaving the toilets, she swung her rucksack up onto her shoulder and hesitated on the threshold trying to remember the direction of the exit. Spotting the sign she lock-stepped towards it, the water sloshing on her back.

Having made the decision to face the Seven Sisters, Florence felt a tingly warmth seep into her head and down towards her heart. It was the right thing to do. The larger scar on her back tingled so she stopped to give it a good scratch beneath the rucksack. That was when Rowena walked past her in a massive coat. Florence's breath stalled like she'd been shoved into an ice bath, ears ringing. A very handsome man joined Rowena from outside, greeting her, all smiles. Florence presumed he must be her husband or partner. He certainly looked the part, well groomed, tall, caramel blond hair, broad shoulders, the kind of man who was born with the inherent knowledge he was destined to rule from the pinnacle of the feudal pyramid. But Rowena stalked away from him; Flo couldn't hear their conversation, her ears were still buzzing, but the husband trailed after her. Florence took a breath, she'd been holding it for a whole minute. She sensed they'd had a row. Florence impulsively walked after them, keeping a safe distance like a tracker in the jungle stalking wild animals in their natural habitat not Sainsbury's car park. She crouched behind a Skoda after she'd determined Rowena's car, the boxy red Polo. Her partner wouldn't let her close the car door once she was sat in the driving seat. She heard a few words carried on the warm breeze: 'Lie to me... Owe you anything... My wife...'

Rowena eventually managed to pull the door closed and reversed out of the space, joining the maze of roads leading towards the exit. Florence ran pell-mell to reach Nellie, fumbling her keys out of her pocket. She slammed them into the lock, throwing her bag onto the passenger seat and jumped in. She craned her neck to see if she could spot the red Polo. She found it winding its way past the small zebra crossing, joining a queue to get out onto the inner ring road before entry onto the main drag towards Seaford. Nellie burst into life and Florence scooted round the car park seeking the best route. She ended up in the queue five cars behind Rowena. She was certain her heart had stopped but it was just beating so fast she could barely feel the continuous tempo. Impatiently she tapped out a rhythm on the steering wheel. Rowena turned out, heading for Seaford and Florence didn't let her out of her sight, dipping in and out of view as she maintained her distance behind the car in front. Now would not be the time to run into the back of someone.

As soon as she hit the main road, Florence brought Nellie up above the thirty miles an hour speed limit. 'Where are you, Rowena?' She spotted her turning left past the station. Flo hadn't prepared a likely outcome in her head should she ever bump into Rowena, her last words thrown at her in their final showdown at the house in Kemptown still sharply etched into her psyche eight years later. 'Don't you ever, EVER, contact me. You're worse than Fucking Tammy. At least Fucking Tammy didn't know how this was going to make me feel. You did, you were there; you promised you'd never do this, we made a pact, and now you're dead to me.' After she'd haphazardly packed up her dad's van with all her stuff, Terry-Anne had hugged her in the hallway.

'Stay in touch. This will all blow over, I'll talk to her. I'd no idea she could be such a drama queen. She only kissed him, right?' Florence had nodded, but the waters ran deeper than the kiss. Terry-Anne didn't understand Flo's lifelong promise, forged when they were twelve, to uphold friendship above all else, above betrayal. Terry-Anne and Flo did meet up, but it became as furtive and sneaky as when she'd first met Clinton, so ultimately Florence stopped trying to juggle something that was never going to outlive Rowena's stubbornness. Florence had Clinton, a new life on the horizon and eventually a flat to make a home once his previous tenancy ran its course. She would just have to concentrate on that instead.

Florence had blocked out all eventuality of an accidental meeting suspecting Rowena had most possibly moved away like Denise. She'd dropped off the face of the earth, all initial unopened letters returned after texts and emails had unquestionably been blocked making this unprecedented sighting as exceptional as a dodo. While Rowena pootled in her Polo, Florence trailed her, turning right into a rabbit run of large houses, some of them so grand they could have confidently graced the aspirational cover of *House Beautiful* magazine. Rowena led her through Seaford's hinterland and then hovered outside a set of impressive wrought-iron gates, behind which a modern development was tucked away. The gates juddered open and Rowena inched through them. Florence parked Nellie behind a white Honda Civic ten metres away from the gatepost and jumped out. She could have easily slipped in before the gates closed, but she was unsure how she would escape and what she wanted to achieve. Just before the gates met, a moment of insanity threw her towards them but she missed the gap by centimetres. She stared into the complex and watched Rowena park in front of a small fake Tudor house with an identical black door to all the others. Florence noted the number: six, the development was called Beach View, although the sea was at least three roads away. Maybe you could see if from a bedroom. Florence left before Rowena got out of the car.

'Where next, Nellie?' she asked exhaustedly. The cliffs were only fifteen minutes away.

20

NATE'S A JAKE

Rowena marched as fast as her belly would allow to Sainsbury's exit, her omniscient finger guiding the way.

'Ro, hang on. Do you want to grab a coffee?' Nate and his alias chased after her. He'd changed his hair – blond with brown undertones and cleverly woven honey highlights replaced the chestnut locks Rowena had plunged her fingers into during sex. She preferred darker-haired men. He could be a cash-strapped soap star advertising teeth whitening products with that freshly dyed mane.

'Go away,' she hissed at him, the automatic doors parting like the red sea. She walked quickly towards her car parked in a spot some distance from everyone else. Now she wished she had parked within sight of at least one other. She clicked the button two metres away, its lights flashing like a homing beacon.

'I just want to talk,' Nate puffed, jogging to keep up.

She reached the car at the same time he did.

'Please leave me alone. I'm not interested in talking to you.' She opened her car door and eased herself into the seat. As she pulled the door he seized it. 'I'll scream if you don't let go.' Her hands shook so she placed them on her bump, protecting it. His grip remained on the door. 'I mean it.'

'No you don't. Part of you wants to know what I have to say.' Bollocks, he was right. She stared at the steering wheel refusing to look up at him. 'Why did you lie to me?'

'My body, my right to do with it how I please.'

'I asked why you lied,' he said rationally. 'I totally understand your reproductive rights.'

'I don't owe you anything.'

'You do if I fight you for access.' Rowena's head snapped up. 'Thought that'd make you listen.' His floppy fringe hung over one eye and he ruffled it out of the way with a sweep of his hand. His humourless face chilled her heart. His presence suddenly felt very menacing.

'You don't want anything to do with the baby. You said so yourself.'

'I changed my mind,' he replied evenly.

'Too late, I don't want anything to do with you, and neither does my baby.'

'Our baby.'

'What about your wife?' Rowena changed tack. 'You said it'd ruin everything. Best to stay away, don't you think?'

'Don't worry about my wife.' He smiled animatedly, revealing all his perfectly straight teeth like a horse on show. He loosened his hold for one second and Rowena snatched the door handle, slamming it shut and started the car. The engine revved as she crunched into reverse, eager to escape. He couldn't just barge back in like this and demand to be involved, could he? She almost knocked over an old man on the zebra crossing outside the entrance. As she turned right towards Seaford Town, she burst into tears. Why hadn't he just left her alone and gone back to his wife and kids in France? Why the sudden interest? She drove home in an absolute daze, checking her rear-view mirror every two seconds. She had no idea what her rights were, she needed to look them up the minute she got home.

As soon as she was inside her front door, she drew the blinds, switched on the side lamps and retrieved her laptop from her desk in the hallway. She peered out from the living room window, past the gates to the road beyond. No one was loitering, and there was nothing he could do anyway, she was safe as long as she was inside her house, locked in the complex. After logging on to her laptop she typed in what rights does the father have towards his unborn child. Google shot out streams of information. Rowena waded through them until she found a reputable website. Reading with relief she discovered that he had no rights at all and couldn't even contact her. It was only after the birth that things got trickier when he could apply through court for a paternity test, but it was lengthy and costly. Contesting custody was way down the line after that. Well, she would worry about that then.

Rowena attempted Netflix that evening, not engaging with the limp crime box set she'd been recommended by Geography teacher, Phil. It wouldn't have mattered if the show featured a naked Channing Tatum offering to break the fourth wall and burst through the screen to shag Ro senseless, she would have remained numb, scrolling fluffy animal memes on her phone or staring into space. The episode in Sainsbury's car park had rattled her, brought into sharp focus how much she did not want to share the parenting of Squodge. She wanted to do this her way, not have Squodge spirited away to another life every other weekend, or every other week like some custody deals she'd witnessed at work. What was the point of her heroically coping on her own for the first two trimesters only for Fuck Features to swoop in and win father of the year treating Squodge to Centre Parcs, buying them all the flash gadgets Rowena was intending to outlaw because she bore constant witness to the damage endless screen time was inflicting on future generations. Huge swathes of kids struggled with concentration, with social skills; God knew what the younger ones coming up the ranks would suffer having been plugged in since birth. At least her current sixth formers had experienced some early life without the perpetual bombardment and sensory overload. Most kids these days didn't know how to fill a minute of solitude without doomscrolling social media, or filming every waking moment editing life down into bite-sized content for the Devil's broadcaster: TikTok. No wonder social anxiety, self-harm and depression were prevalent amongst young people. Rowena had deleted Facebook, Instagram, Twitter, even LinkedIn, some years previously. It had been a no-brainer cutting out the incessant urge to compare one's lowly existence against the scrolling conveyor belt of cherry-picked unblemished lives. It was bad enough swiping through dating apps. As for *Love Island* – she refused to watch it. Two sixth form girls had arrived at school during the last series, their lips infected from dodgy filler injections. She'd had to march them to A and E, knowing full well they would not heed it as a gentle warning and would be filling their faces full of poison as soon as they could. She was all for your body your choice, but tampering with eternal youth at eighteen? She wanted to protect Squodge from it all, and she could only do that if she had full control!

She would have to knock the Jammy Dodgers on the head before Squodge started solids, parenting by example, naturally. Her own childhood had been far from ideal, Edie, Florence's mum had stood in countless times when Denise had slipped off the deep end about her dad playing behind her back, or forgetting (five times) that she needed a packed lunch for a school trip because she'd been traumatised by one thing or another. Rowena now understood this was not entirely her mum's fault, rather her parents' union bred toxicity and it was unintentionally handed down to her. In the end Edie used to prepare two packed lunches for Florence to be on the safe side.

Rowena shook her head, why this ceaseless bathing in the past? Breaking contact with Florence had meant snapping her bond with her parents too, and Lennie, her brittle little sister whom she had adored, much to Flo's chagrin. They had once felt like family and when she periodically thought about them, her shoulders drooped. Of course she could visit, but that felt... wrong, especially after all this time. She would never forget Gareth's face as he loaded up his van, the hazards flashing, outside the house in Kemptown, Terry-Anne running back and forth with bin bags. She could feel disappointment wafting off him. That solitary fact almost made her run out to prevent Florence leaving. But her pride had already cemented, stupefying her with its arbitrary rules and regulations, unyielding to anything supported by the mantra: she betrayed you. Rowena harboured a soft spot for Florence's dad. He'd been kind and always listened whenever she spoke, unlike her own dad who'd been permanently preoccupied. She wondered what Edie and Gareth were doing now. If they were grandparents, playing with Clinton and Florence's adorable children. They would be the best grandparents in the world. She had a sneaky suspicion her own father was going to somehow challenge that crown, which was the biggest surprise of them all. Rowena smiled, switched off the TV and heaved herself off the sofa. Bedtime. She had to be on form to face lunch with her mum tomorrow, pizza in Seaford Town, though her mum would probably just order a salad (no dressing, juice of Satan, Rowena) and steal a slice of Rowena's pizza, which always irritated her. *Just get a whole one, eat one slice and take the rest home for Suleyman.* Apparently the calories didn't count if you ate the food from another's plate...

'Why don't you want him to be a part of everything?' Denise asked at lunch the next day in Vicini Vicini, a ten minute walk from the house, not quite understanding Rowena's stance. She reached over and, as anticipated, wiggled a slice of vegetarian pizza off her daughter's plate, surreptitiously gliding it onto her own, her face poker straight, her hand working autonomously. Rowena wanted to stab it with her fork, but instead overlooked the transgression.

'He's a snake. I don't trust him.' Surely her mum would understand? 'He has another family – said he's married, though who knows. How can he be involved?'

'But he's the baby's father. Does he have rights?' Denise nibbled the pizza like it was a Ryvita. 'At least your father paid his way.'

'Mum! Whose side are you on?' Rowena cried incredulously.

'My grandchild's! Though I won't be advertising I'm a grandmother. The baby can call me Denise.' Rowena shook her head in disbelief. *Welcome to my childhood, Squodge.* Ageing was an eternal battle Denise had been fighting since she'd discovered her withered elbows could somehow betray her. One of Rowena's earliest memories was of her mum watching TV with two squeezed lemon halves gaffer-taped to her elbows, the acid apparently eating away all traces of a life well leaned on. 'But seriously, Ro, I don't think you realise what an undertaking this is going to be. You're on your own, I live miles away, having someone to help will be important. What if you have a C-section? Who will look after you and the baby? I can come for a week, work have allowed it, but I can't come for six.'

Rowena bit her lip. She may as well say it. 'Dad said he would take time off.'

Denise's eyebrows merged with her hairline, her mouth forming a perfect O.

'You OK?' she asked as her mum coughed herself into speaking.

'Yes, just surprised, that's all.' Denise smoothed her hair. 'He said he'd help if you're having a C-section?'

'He said he'd help full stop. You see, I'm not alone. Dad will be around.'

Denise appeared to have trouble swallowing.

'I'm pleased for you, Ro,' she managed to spit out eventually. 'Glad he's stepped up. The baby needs a male role model in its life. You had a rough ride with your dad, but thankfully Suleyman oiled the brakes.' Rowena suppressed a laugh. Suleyman was hardly her idea of a male role model. Nothing wrong with him, but he was her mother's cheerleader, he'd barely noticed Rowena's existence. 'At least your dad has carried out some improvements, worked on his faults. Good job you had one parent with their eye on the ball.'

'Yes, Mum.'

April rumbled into May and Rowena's ankles gently swelled like pink grapefruits. Every day something else niggled inside her. Her back felt like it was filled with liquid rubber – one wrong move and a disc could pop out of place. Meanwhile her fingers had begun amassing all the excess water from her ankles and feet like ancillary storage tanks. She was reduced to wearing flip-flops to school; all her sandals and shoes pinched her feet and she couldn't actually reach to prise them off.

'Miss, what happens if you go into labour during school time?' Gabriel, one of her favourite pupils, asked during form time. She had been reduced to sitting with her feet resting on a stool or she would have ballooned by lunch, her knees drowning in a sea of flesh: punishing cankle-isation, something she wished she could remedy with a safety pin before they morphed into thankles.

'Then you, Gabriel, will be in charge of ringing for an ambulance.'

'But we're not allowed to use our phones during school time.' He grinned.

'I think I would make an exception for that occasion.'

Every morning when she left Beach View, and every evening when she walked out of the school gates, Rowena checked and double checked in case Nate was watching. Why she thought he had time to sack off his life-consuming job and spend valuable hours staking out her work and home, was ludicrous. But her withered finger was buzzing, implying heed all gut feelings, mindful of the outlandish fear which involved him kidnapping her until she gave birth, eventually stealing the baby. Maybe she had been overdosing on too many sickly dark true crime box sets. His motive for contacting her was so muddy she couldn't begin to understand, especially with another family waiting in the wings. *What if the family never existed in the first place?* Conceivable. It still didn't factor in his motive though, unless it was genuinely powered by his paternal instinct. Unlikely...

Rowena whipped her head around before keying in the code for the side gate, wondering how long she would have to keep up this charade. As she turned the key in her front door and pushed it open, something scraped along the doormat. Rowena moved it with her flip-flop – a letter addressed to her. She bent awkwardly to pick it up and brought it with her to the kitchen. As she waited for the kettle to boil for her thrilling drink of hot water (tea was still offensive), she opened the formal-looking envelope.

Dear Ms Beard

 We are writing to you to inform you that our client, Jake Belfield, will be seeking shared custody and parental responsibility of your future child should he be proven to be the child's father, which he will aim to ascertain through the courts via a DNA test. He has instructed us to steer him through the legal process and potential court proceedings should you deny him access to your unborn child.

We will be in contact after the birth in the eventuality of the situation remaining unresolved.

Yours sincerely

Stephanie Chapman

Rowena sat stunned at the kitchen table, the kettle boiling itself into a frenzy. She reread the letter five times, scrutinising the address of the legal firm, Chapman and Leman, based in Ashford, Kent. The letter appeared genuine, the thick cream paper watermarked and the headlining address professionally printed in a glossy dark grey classic font. She rang the number and was redirected to a fielding system offering various options to leave messages for particular departments and direct lines to press should you have the correct three-digit number. She did not, but also the practice was probably about to shut now. They couldn't tell her anything about Jake Belfield: client confidentiality. Everything in the letter was upheld by the website she had read very thoroughly last weekend. Obtaining visiting rights and custody was hard going if the mother opposed it, but not impossible. And refusing him would mean a costly court case unless she could find a pro-bono lawyer willing to represent her. Nate had shed his skin, revealing Jake who surely had adequate funds for this pointless exercise.

Rowena screamed at the wall. This was not how it was supposed to turn out. She unblocked Jake's main number on her phone and stared at a blank text box. The urge to fire back utter contempt was onerous to restrain.

'Count to five, Rowena. It's what you would tell the kids.' She breathed five deep breaths, the train currently steaming through her ribcage gradually abating. She rang her dad.

'You have two choices, Rowena,' he rationalised. 'You can go crazy, ringing or texting him and feeding the drama that he's creating, or think. What's his incentive here apart from being in the baby's life? Is there another aim and what do you think it is? Did you have any reason to suspect anything else when you were dating?'

'No. I really liked him, but he couldn't get out of the house quick enough when I said I was pregnant, brought his wife and kids into the equation.'

'And you took that at face value?' her dad, the expert, asked.

'Yes. He was using a fake name on the dating apps, obviously to keep incognito. I don't know, there are so many awful people out there... I find it hard to really know if someone is real or not.'

Her dad sighed down the phone before replying. 'I don't know how to respond other than I used to behave like that and I'm so very sorry.' He paused, Rowena screwing up her face at the discomfort. 'Bloody good job there wasn't Tinder back in the day!' He chuckled to himself before realising his error, his tone turning serious. 'It's all driven by fear. There are genuine people out there wishing to make an honest connection other than just, you know, the physical side of things. It just takes time to find them. Maybe they have to find themselves first...' When her dad had smashed out of his echo chamber, he'd really trampled it into the ground.

'Thanks, Dad. So what should I do?'

'Ignore him. If he really, really wants to be in this baby's life, make him prove it. At the moment, it's all hot air.' He cleared his throat. 'Is he definitely the child's father?'

'Yes! I didn't have two on the go at the same time.' Rowena refrained from adding, *like you*.

'That wasn't a judgement, Rowena. But you could say you were with someone else and they're the father. He has a lot of paper-work to sift through to prove anything.

'Anyone can get a solicitor's letter, one of his mates probably wrote it for free. If he's willing to go that far, maybe he *is* real, and has had a change of heart. He could be thinking this is his chance to do the decent thing. He should have gone about it better though. This is all guns blazing without chatting.'

'I wouldn't talk to him,' Rowena reluctantly admitted. 'I told him I wanted nothing to do with him, and drove off. I really don't want to share Squodge... I thought he had a family!'

'Maybe he does, and maybe he's going to juggle everything – some people can.' He coughed, his shame creeping into Rowena's ear. 'Sometimes the abstract notion of a child is easier to ignore than the reality of knowing for certain there's one of your children roaming out in the world and you've never met them. It might be a practical way for you to afford this on your own. You just never know, it might work out for the best. Hard to see now, though, but sometimes these situations can turn out better then we think.'

Before bed, Rowena had started reinstating all her social media platforms for stalking purposes, but stalled halfway. She'd only be feeding the drama in a different guise. Instead she filed Jake's letter in the clear plastic folder with her maternity notes that she permanently carried. Some of what her dad had said made sense... However, she didn't want Jake anywhere near Squodge, no matter how much he tried to prove he was worthy. The finger had spoken – it had ceaselessly throbbed since the letter's arrival.

With only eight weeks until her due date, she'd signed up for single mums birthing classes in Brighton as nothing existed locally. Ebi had emailed her some information on doulas – birth partners, who also helped afterwards once the baby had arrived. Rowena had baulked at the price, everything was expensive enough on one wage, but she wasn't keen to give birth alone. She had a little while to decide.

Exhausted from the letter's upheaval, Rowena abandoned the day and climbed into bed at eight in the evening. As she switched her phone to silent, a text popped up from an unknown number.

Evening Rowena, you should have my legal letter by now. I hope we can come to some arrangement that suits us both, I genuinely don't mean to cause you any distress. Let me know when is a good time to meet up.

21

FLO TO THE RESCUE

Florence was in no mood for whatever was waiting at home after returning from her rash window getaway. Her family needed to keep their beaks out of her life. No one lectured Lennie on how to be a grown up, to relinquish her ridiculous dreams of influencing an entire generation of gawkers in the metaverse before she lost her actual real world job. They let her string her own bow. She regretted telling Lennie about Cassie's ridiculous treasure hunt.

'I don't mean that, Nellie. It's not ridiculous. I just don't like being told what to do, by anybody.' She patted Nellie's dashboard affectionately.

Five hours later, standing in the hallway listening for movement, she shut the front door quietly behind her, not wanting to publicise her return yet mindful of the genuine possibility she might intrude on a bold re-enactment of the lesser known positions in the *Kama Sutra*. Frantic scrambling in the kitchen as the kettle switched itself off.

'Hello, Flo. Bit drastic, don't you think, jumping out of the bedroom window?' Her dad raised his eyebrows, arms folded across his chest, holding himself in. His flies were undone.

'Yep, I know. But you guys were ganging up on me. Again.'

'Florence, no one was ganging up on you.' Gareth's face scrunched in preparation for the challenging conversation. Florence's mum appeared behind him holding two mugs of tea, one of which she handed to Gareth. Florence could see a pair of knickers poking out of her shorts pocket...

'Are you OK, Flo? You could have really hurt yourself. Honestly!' she said trying to make light of it.

'I'm totally fine. Look, still in working order.' She pulled a party twirl to diffuse the tension.

'What were you so against that you had to jump out of a first-storey window?' her dad asked.

Florence cut her glance between her parents. 'I'm not ready to open the door to the past. If I do it'll be on my terms, not because someone thinks it'll make a difference... How exactly is it going to help?'

'Look, Flo, we're only worried. Everything's up in the air with the house move, we just don't want *you* feeling up in the air. You've still never talked about it. Maybe Cassie's right, reconnecting with Rowena would—'

'I actually walked to the Seven Sisters earlier,' Florence interjected, hoping to shut them up.

'Oh wow, Florence, that's amazing. Well done,' her dad said, clearly relieved. 'How was it?'

'Good. Quite windy.'

'That's not what I meant.'

'I know...' She sat down at the hatch, seeing herself aged eight passing cold baked beans through to Rowena the waitress, who sucked on a pencil pretending it was a cigarette, drawing it out of her mouth to tap imaginary ash onto the carpet. 'I felt OK. I parked at South Hill Barn, got a coffee from the guy at the exhibition space, walked down to the beach and along to the bottom of the cliffs and back.'

'No flashbacks?' her mum asked in her nurse voice. 'Or anything else?' Her mum had always found it hard to acknowledge Flo's acid trip symptoms almost taking it personally that she couldn't 'fix' her.

'No, nothing. Just the sea, the sun and the wind. Small steps, I'm taking small steps. I know you're worried, but walking along the beach helped. It was... normal.'

'Oh, Florence, that sounds so promising.' She allowed her mum to squeeze her hand before she shot her eyes towards her dad, who discreetly nodded. 'Look, love, we've been meaning to tell you... We've got a buyer for the house and if everything works out, we'll be moving out of here mid-August.'

'Have you found somewhere?' Florence hid behind an implacable façade as she hastily calculated how soon she could sell Nellie so she'd have enough cash to sort visas and fly straight to Costa Rica. She'd ring the Harris family in a bit, apologise profusely for her disappearing act...

'Yes, we made an offer earlier on a small house in Shoreham-by-Sea quite near the beach,' Edie answered guardedly.

'OK, thanks for telling me.'

'Sorry, I know it's all so last minute, but it does give you time to plan. You can stay with us temporarily if you need to post move, no rush.' Florence's mum smiled hopefully. 'But if not, I'm sure Lennie would love to help you out.'

They both knew that was a lie...

After grovelling to Mr Harris about her unforeseen emergency she rearranged the visit for the following Saturday. Nellie had since accrued three more interested parties, but Flo felt she owed Mr Harris first dibs. As the days flew towards the weekend, Florence found herself inordinately preoccupied with her sighting of Rowena but felt at a loss how to approach the situation. Nerves ate away at her rendering her jittery, replaying Rowena's last words to her over and over again. Would she still wish Florence was dead? She had managed to keep the hate alive for her dad well beyond its sell-by date... While Friday evening loomed, the only thought Florence could entertain was taking Nellie out at the same time the next morning and retracing her exact steps to the beach. It had proven to be therapeutic, had it not? Mr Harris wasn't due until midday...

Saturday morning Mr Ogby (in never seen before scruffs) was already in the garden weeding like a demon. He remarkably didn't look up from where he was kneeling when she opened the gate.

'Bob!' He jumped. 'Are you OK?'

He turned round, flustered. 'Yes, good, good, thank you.'

'Are you sure? You don't seem it.'

He put his trowel down and slowly stood up, dusting his knees off.

'James has set me up with someone.' James was his eldest son.

'Oh wow. He didn't sign you up for Tinder, did he?'

'No!' Mr Ogby looked horrified. 'Do they let people my age on Tinder?'

'I think anyone of any age is allowed. Not that I've ever been on a dating app.'

'How do you meet anyone then? *Have* you met anyone?' What a preposterous conversation to have. With Mr Ogby of all people. 'Sorry, you don't have to answer that.'

'I haven't met anyone, no. I'm still single.' Tariq briefly skittered across the back of her mind. No, he was all done and dusted now.

'That's been longer than me, hasn't it?'

Florence half smiled. 'The year before you, yes.' Silence descended, filled with twittering birdsong and the distant rumble of a tractor. 'So what about this date?' Florence jogged him back on track. 'Who is she? And when is it?'

'It's today. Later on. That's why I'm weeding. The garden's a state.' It wasn't. It looked as immaculate as everything else in Mr Ogby's life.

'She's coming here? That's the number one no-no dating rule, Bob!'

'We've already chatted on the phone. She suggested it. She's divorced... the mum of one of James' old school friends.'

'Do you like her?'

'Well, we got on well. I don't really remember her from when the kids were at school – Judy dealt with all that. But she says she remembers me picking the kids up from her house several times. I can't even remember doing that. All such a long time ago...'

'I hope you have a lovely date. You never know, it might be the beginning of a beautiful friendship.'

'Thank you.' He smiled sadly. 'The last date I went on was with Judy. Everything's so different now...'

'Just be yourself, Bob.' Florence wanted to suggest ditching the toupee, but didn't have the nerve.

'I know, I know,' he laughed. 'Everyone else is taken!'

As Flo climbed into Nellie, a text pinged: Tariq. Bold typeface meme: *Don't let anyone with bad eyebrows tell you shit about life.* Flo snorted and almost forwarded it to Lennie, but braked in time. She'd assume it was a pop at her. Lennie could be a tad heavy-handed with her brow micro-filling pen...

Florence would later thank Bob for delaying her chatting. Because if she hadn't been late, she mightn't have got stuck behind the lorry, hemmed in between the hedge and the double white lines, missing her cue...

'Come on, come on, why so slow?' she muttered under her breath through the Brian the Snail tunnel. The lorry was carrying what looked like bricks under a tarp. Florence hated being the first vehicle trapped behind a notorious moving roadblock. It always placed you under so much pressure, hyper aware of the line of dissent behind desperate for you to make the move and overtake. But Nellie didn't have the necessary revs to power through; Flo could almost feel the silent cursing aimed at her lack of gambling against the oncoming traffic. Surely if traffic was careering down the opposite lane she was safe from scrutiny. Apparently not. As soon as the white lines split, the Mercedes behind her pulled out and overtook, evidently expecting her to fall back and leave a space in case an advancing car appeared over the brow of the hill.

'You absolute twat!' she screamed when exactly that happened, slamming on her brakes, hoping the next car in the raging convoy wasn't tailgating her. With no more near misses she arrived at the big Sainsbury's in Newhaven just outside Seaford slightly frazzled and bought a medicinal pizza roll as well as a cinnamon whirl from the bakery. On red alert she scanned the aisles; Rowena wasn't here. Florence had discerned that the quickest way to reach South Hill Barn car park near the Seven Sisters was cutting through the labyrinth of Seaford backroads rather than a more circuitous route of the A259. Setting off from Sainsbury's she followed the way Rowena had unwittingly led her last week, left instead of right after the station, slowly trundling through the manifold rows of Edwardian and pre-war houses conjugated in a surprisingly pleasing arrangement. Florence found herself crawling in the direction of Chyngton Road leading to the car park when she suddenly recognised where she was and turned down Rowena's road; Beach View was on the left. Florence almost choked on the last bite of pizza roll when she spotted Rowena on the pavement a few metres from the main gate, chatting with a tall blond man, possibly the one from the supermarket, her eyes screwed into an irate knot. On second viewing, Florence clocked her swollen belly. *Why hadn't she noticed that last week?*

Florence impetuously swerved into a space two cars from where they were talking and wound down both windows. The man's back was in Florence's direct eyeline making it impossible to read his face, but Rowena's agitated expression readily broadcast her feelings and the guy held up his hands in protest at something she said. Florence shifted over to the passenger window so she could hear. As much as she loved nature, she wished she could turn it down. The birds tweeting, gulls cawing and the wind rustling through the trees were muffling their words.

'I don't care about court, you'll have to fight for ever, I'm not letting you have access to the baby. I just won't turn up.'

'If you don't show up, the judge'll most likely rule in my favour.'

'You're not the baby's father!' Ro shouted. 'I'm not naming you on the birth certificate, you can't prove anything.'

'You told me I was, that's enough for me to fight for a DNA test.'

'This is so unfair, you didn't want to have anything to do with us. This makes no sense.'

He paused, Rowena caught her breath, Florence held hers.

'There is something you can do,' he said subtly, forcing Florence to stick her head out of the window in order to hear.

'Do what?' Rowena asked exasperated. 'I need to go.' He held her arm. 'Don't fucking touch me.'

'To get me out of your life. Promise I'll disappear.' Rowena cradled her bump with her hands, her face defiant. 'Pay me off.'

'What?!'

'Pay me to get out of your life.'

'You're joking!' She tried to move away from him but he grabbed her arm again.

'Pay me and you and the kid'll never hear from me again.'

'No!' She shrugged off his arm, pushing past him. 'I'll report you.'

'With what evidence? Your word against mine. Go right ahead; the police don't give a shit...'

'I'll tell your wife.'

'How? What wife?' He laughed. 'I'm not married, that was just to shut you up. I actually think we'd make a good team. You could be the serious one – homework, chores early to bed. I could do all the fun stuff for the next eighteen years. Unless of course you want to fly solo...'

Incensed, Florence jumped out of Nellie's door and rushed at them, tapping him on the shoulder, phone in hand, confrontational dread whisked away on the sea breeze. As soon as he turned round she started firing her phone at him, taking a million photos.

'What the fu—?' the guy cried, his face contorted, backing away.

'Leave her alone,' Florence hissed ominously.

'Who the hell are you?'

'Someone who witnessed you threatening to extort money from a pregnant woman. Quite happy to point you out in a line-up.'

'Yeah? The police haven't the time, too busy rooting out the bent coppers.' All at once intervening didn't feel such a good idea as he towered over Florence narrowing his eyes. 'I'll see you ladies later. Rowena, think about it...' The man strode purposefully to the end of the road and turned left.

'Florence?!' Rowena stared at her estranged best friend. 'What are *you* doing here?'

22

CATCH 22

'Look, Ms Beard, there's nothing we can really do. He's the baby's father, so you say. He hasn't been violent, but sent you a legal letter which is hardly threatening behaviour, asking for contact with your baby after birth. You had a relationship with him for...' the policewoman checked her notes, 'three months before you found out you were pregnant, upon which he disappeared, only to get back in touch again recently. You think he stalked you but you can't prove it because he never actually approached you, just supposedly drove past you in the street a few times.' Officer Gerrard couldn't have sounded more bored if she tried. 'Most romantic fraud cases involve the victim, that would be you, never having met the fraudster, being groomed remotely through email or phone contact before being asked to part with considerable amounts of money and never being heard of again. This doesn't fit that profile.'

Rowena glowered at the police officer, her partner standing behind her in the living room while she perched on the spare chair ready to spring into immediate action.

'I know what I heard,' Rowena defiantly insisted.

'Me too,' Florence piped up. 'He was pretty intimidating.' Florence studied PC Gerrard's youthful make-up free face. She wondered if it was a choice or were female police officers prohibited from wearing make-up or perfume. Florence's keen nose hadn't detected a cloud of fragrance either when both officers walked into Rowena's house. She'd never seen a fully made-up police officer in her life.

'Listen, d'you not think he's just angry you're shutting him out? Or that you decided to keep the baby after telling him you were having an abortion?' Rowena flinched. 'It's an empty threat to get you to comply, go through the courts and grant him access?'

'He can't do that!' Rowena protested. 'How do you even know it's an empty threat?'

'People do all sorts of things to keep hold of their children. Believe me, we've seen everything.' The officer's partner nodded in agreement. 'That bond is hard to ignore.'

'He has no bond, he's a devious wanker.'

'What can Rowena do in the meantime?' Florence asked attempting to be of assistance instead of feeling completely inept. It was a shame she hadn't filmed the whole thing.

'Well, she could keep a note of every time he makes contact. Keep all text messages or emails, also voicemails. Basically gather evidence should it ever be needed.'

'Evidence for what?' Rowena asked.

'In case anything happens...'

'That sounds ominous,' Florence said.

'It wasn't meant to,' Officer Gerrard said to Rowena. 'It's just that it might be good for your own peace of mind, see how often he contacts you, and notice how it tails off. In domestic disputes like this, unless the father has unlimited amounts of cash or is prepared to tunnel through the endless paperwork of legal aid, their requests often peter out. You might find that once the baby is here, you have a change of heart too. That extra help that seemed so intrusive may feel a bit more welcome...'

'So what you're saying is that he can continue to threaten me with extortion or he'll take me to court to get a DNA test in order to gain access to his child?' Rowena brutally summed up. 'What about social services?'

'I'm sure you can approach them through your midwife, they'll be able to advise you about access rights and what to expect. I'm not an expert.' Officer Gerrard shrugged her shoulders, her radio bobbing in time, its constant communications buzz accompanying their conversation. So far its perpetual patter had sent officers to incidents regarding shed break-ins, teenagers causing trouble at Morrisons, five bike thefts – all in one go, a domestic that had bled into the street... Rowena really was bottom of the pile with 'my ex-boyfriend was mean to me', which was how it was being handled.

'I would suggest keeping a record of everything, no matter how inconsequential you think it is, just in case,' the male police officer reiterated. Florence hadn't caught his name. 'Should you feel threatened, or *are* threatened, please contact us again, obviously dial 999 if it's an emergency, otherwise ring the station, here's the number.' He handed her a card. 'If you're able to ring while he's here if he's being aggressive that would be more helpful, then we can caution him. It's very difficult to do anything on hearsay.'

While Rowena walked them into the hallway and out the front door, Florence nosed round the snug living room painted a fashionable shade of dried plaster which complemented the rich blue camelback velvet sofa and a whimsical red leather antique cinema chair complete with drinks holder. The Diptyque candle on the coffee table infused the space with its rich musky aroma, even unlit. Family photos of Rowena's mum and dad were tactfully displayed at opposite ends of the wooden mantelpiece, a safe distance apart. Not for the first time Florence asked herself what it might be like to have stability, her own place, to build a life instead of incessantly jumping continents... When Rowena returned Florence had time to properly examine her. She hadn't aged at all in the intervening years, but that could have been pregnancy. Regardless of how exhausted she must be feeling, Rowena glowed from the inside out as if harbouring eternal life rather than another human being sucking the marrow from her bones.

'Heavens to Murgatroyd,' Rowena said unsmiling, attempting indifference, 'this is weird.'

'I know. Sorry.' Florence's lips twitched into a nervous smile. 'I haven't heard that saying for years...'

'Do you want another cup of tea?' Rowena flicked her eyes towards the living room door. The time for throwing insults, pies, or crockery had long passed, though nothing was ever a given with Rowena, her grudge holding notoriously outperforming the Gallagher brothers. The former friends were left politely dancing round what hindsight had transformed into petty grievances like British people are famed for. However, the question still remained: who would lay the first stone?

'I can make it, you sit down,' Florence said eagerly. 'You must be in shock.'

'What about? That idiot, or you?' Rowena comically raised her eyebrows.

'Both. Sit. Do you want anything?'

Earlier, Florence and Rowena had gawped at each other stranded in the sudden vacuum left by Jake the elephant between them tiptoeing into the laurel hedge of the adjoining property.

'Are you OK?' Florence had asked, concern dwarfing all other obvious factors. Like how to explain her timely presence.

'Yes, I think so. He literally came out of nowhere. He must have followed me from the high street.'

'Has he done it before?'

Rowena nodded. 'Do you want to come in?'

'Oh, where do you live?' Florence's innocent bystander schtick wouldn't win any Oscars. Rowena threw her the sagacious side-eye, instigating panic. 'Not that I'm stalking you, or anything.'

'What *were* you doing parked on my road then?'

'It's a cut through to South Hill Barn. I only stopped when I saw that bloke hassling you.' Plausible enough.

'I'm through here.' She keyed in some numbers on a touchpad next to the smaller side entrance attached to the large vehicular gate. Rowena's hands shook, meanwhile Florence made inane small talk into the void about the lovely housing development, how safe Rowena must feel, and how Seaford as a destination was very underrated.

'D'you think I should call the police?' Rowena asked uncertainly opening the front door. 'I mean, he was quite threatening.'

'Extortion's against the law. It's up to you. I'm not sure what they can do. If you've evidence he's using false names and stuff, then maybe. He could be one of those fraudsters who go around extracting money off women pretending it's for his mum's cancer treatment, then disappearing under another alias. How did you meet him?'

'Tinder.'

'Every chance he is a complete fraudster then. Isn't it teeming with total sharks?'

Rowena shrugged and sighed heavily before getting out her phone and ringing the police. With an indefinite wait time, Florence accepted a cup of tea, consequentially making a decision to leave after she'd finished it, Mr Harris's appointment for inspecting Nellie anchoring her return to Felworth. She'd be cutting it fine if she stayed for much longer. Meanwhile Rowena filled Flo in on the disastrous relationship, and Jake's phony identity with possibly fake family. Florence tried her best to listen but her mind kept screaming, IT'S ROWENA! *Tell her everything...*

'It's very opportunistic – the chances of getting pregnant are quite slim, I believe,' Florence said when Rowena eventually finished her tale.

'I know. That's what I felt as soon as he said it. It was such a long game and not a certain one either.'

'Ergo opportunistic.'

'Ergo... I forgot about you and the weird words.'

Rowena's lips twitched with a faint smile.

'Do you think something's happened to make him try and extract some cash?'

'Like what?'

'I don't know. Lost his job? Fathered another child with one of the other women he has possibly been shagging? It could literally be anything.'

'Maybe...' But before they could make headway into Florence's life, the exterior gate rang. The police had arrived, apparently they had been investigating a complaint from a nearby neighbour about a psychotic seagull attacking passers-by...

* * *

'Are the tea bags anywhere obvious?' Florence called from the kitchen, before spotting the retro orange and brown tea caddy alongside the matching sugar and coffee tins, hiding under the windowsill. 'It's OK, I've found them!'

'No need to shout!' Rowena stood in the doorway observing her, arms crossed across her chest, resting on her bump. 'I haven't thanked you for stepping in, with whatshisname.'

'Let's call him Jake, that's what the lawyer's letter said. I wonder how many names he has?'

'Seriously, thank you. I'm glad you're such a nosy parker otherwise I'd have had no witness. It'd have been his word against mine. Not that either way is going to help with the police, but you know what I mean.'

'That's OK.' Florence made her tea and topped up Rowena's hot water. Rowena sat down at the narrow kitchen table after ferreting some Jammy Dodgers from a pink and red striped tin on the side. The kitchen was as bijou and stylish as the living room, the main wall painted a gleeful buttercup yellow with a distinct absence of chaotic piles of papers eating up the worktops, or bags of bagels balancing on the already overcrowded bread bin. The spotless oiled wooden counters had not a crumb or misaligned chopping board in sight. Florence admired the flamingo pattern blind and the eclectic tin robots lined along the deep window ledge peeping out from in between the forest of succulents and billowing ferns.

'Sorry, I need to eat, feel a bit dizzy.' Rowena ripped open the packet and pulled out two in one go, offering the biscuits to Florence, who declined. Florence joined her at the table, her mind whooshing like a fairground waltzer. Her conflict-shy half wanted to leave, not deal with the inexorable conversation, but her inquisitive half wanted to stay. Rowena slowly ate her biscuits and when she had finished she made a meal out of dusting the crumbs from her fingers and blowing her nose on a crumpled tissue she found in her pocket. Florence sipped her tea, the liquid burning her tongue as usual. She stared at the table, inspecting her nails for imaginary dirt. *Who was going to speak first?*

'When are you due?' Florence asked staving off the inevitable.

'July 30th... Look, we need to talk... properly.' Rowena capsized the room.

'Yes. I don't really know where to start.' Florence placed her clammy hands on her lap, a strong pulse beating in her throat.

'I'm sorry I was such a dick about the whole Clinton thing I—' Rowena began.

'No, I'm sorry I didn't think—'

'Why don't I speak, then you go, or we'll be trapped arguing over who's the biggest twat, when we all know it's me for getting my knickers in a twist.' Flo smiled, shaking her head at the same time while Rowena inhaled a huge breath, holding it briefly before letting it go. 'I never opened your letters, but you knew that. I was so angry for quite a while, and they always seemed to arrive when I'd had a bad day at school...' Rowena cleared her throat. 'That first year learning on the job was like being in a nightmare some weeks, except one that I'd agreed to, yet I couldn't back out – too stubborn, as you know...' Florence grinned in agreement, 'but I didn't know what else to do after we fell out. Everything was such a mess in my head so in a way it was good because work took up all of my time and energy. I didn't have anything left to channel into what had happened. I don't know why I thought learning teaching on the job would be easier than marketing.' Rowena laughed hollowly. 'But it did get marginally better, and while it did, I realised my anger, rage, whatever else was eating me up, had worn off slightly. I didn't know what to do about it though, and couldn't face you and Clinton playing happy families. It felt like the worst break up in the world.'

'You and Clinton breaking up?'

'No! You and me. It was worse than any bloody bloke being a prick. Pricks come and go, friends are for ever. I know I instigated the whole split, overreacted, all my own fault "blah blah blah",' Rowena executed air quotes, 'but I just couldn't resolve it in my head. Like a whole arm or leg was missing, but still pulsing, reminding me every day that you weren't there, had chosen Clinton. *That* was the betrayal.'

'Oh, Rowena... I honestly thought it would blow over and you'd get back in touch.'

Rowena shrugged. 'I don't know what I was thinking. When Mum moved, I had no reason to visit Felworth any more. It was also a bit of a relief not bumping into your parents – I felt so dreadful for making you move out. Your dad's face...'

'Well, it had originally been *your* house share,' Florence said trying to alleviate any guilt. 'I crashed it when whatshername moved out.'

'Cindy?'

'Yeah.' A painful silence moved in like an unwelcome party guest. 'Why didn't you ever just ring me, text, smoke signal?' Florence bit her lip in anticipation.

Rowena searched the fruit bowl for a sufficient answer, choosing a banana. 'Pride, stupidity, also I was scared you'd be... I don't know. After a bit it felt like too much had happened, easier to pave over the whole situation and move on completely. I'd occasionally get angry thinking that you'd got what you wanted and just hadn't bothered trying to make amends, apart from letters.' Florence began to speak, but Rowena held up her hand. 'I know, I know, I didn't read them. I should have. Obviously I'd blocked you on everything. I didn't make it easy.' She stared at her silver bangle, twisting it round on her wrist. 'I think I was so terrified of being wrong, that not answering anything, cutting you off, meant that I would always be in the right because no one else was there to tell me otherwise... My back's also not been the same – you're the original Dr Pimple Popper. Terry-Anne was no good, not as thorough!' Florence burst out laughing prompting a rueful smile from Rowena. 'Even now, sitting here, I feel even more stupid than I thought I possibly could. Even more of a twat. I mean, who gets themselves wound up like that over a man they barely knew?'

'Someone who trusted their best friend in the whole world not to run off with the man they had considerable feelings for.' Florence smiled. 'It was always way more than what happened. It was your childhood returning to torment you. And for that I'm so utterly sorry. I tried everything, walking away, not engaging with him, but in the end, he was the only man I had ever felt like that for too. It wasn't a flash in the pan. It was the most honest love I have ever felt.' Florence's voice cracked, the words haunting her.

Rowena glanced at Florence's hands. 'Did you ever get married? You don't wear a ring...' Florence shook her head. 'Are you still together?'

Florence braced herself. 'Technically, yes.'

'What does that mean?'

'I don't know how to say this without upsetting you.' Florence restlessly gnawed her lip.

'What? Say what? He ran off with someone else?' Rowena clenched her fists.

Florence shook her head. The words rushing at her from across the room, the evisceration that had hollowed her out entirely, agony once more.

'Clinton... Clinton died in 2016.'

23

SNAP!

Rowena gaped uncomprehendingly at Florence, her eyes blank, the truth painfully downloading, hitting her consciousness, right... about... now.

'Florence! No! How? What happened?' Rowena promptly burst into tears. 'Why didn't you tell me? Oh my God. I need to sit down.'

'You already are.' Florence grabbed some kitchen roll from the counter and shoved it at Rowena, the response exactly as she had feared.

'Thanks. I mean sit somewhere comfy. I knew I should have got those seat pads for the kitchen chairs. Come on.' Rowena heaved herself up from the wooden highbacked Ercol chair, abandoning the Jammy Dodgers, and shuffled into the hallway towards the living room while Florence carried the drinks. She sank down into the sofa, wiping her eyes. 'I assumed you'd married, had kids. That's what Terry-Anne had said was on the cards, the few times we ever talked about you. Believe me, we didn't dissect your life, it was just, you know, if she'd seen you. But then you cut her off.'

Florence had such fond memories of Terry-Anne. Because she

dyed her hair monthly, the colour became a reliable marker of time when recounting past events, like Picasso's blue period. Florence had fallen for Clinton during the pink epoch.

'I couldn't cope with the fact that you were probably angry with her too for seeing me. I hoped we'd all reconnect once everything had blown over.'

'I wasn't cross, actually. I never made her choose. She said you dropped her. Then when I moved to Bexhill nearer school she moved in with someone called Rose.' Rowena took several deep breaths. 'I can't believe Clinton died. I thought I saw him in the supermarket the other week, followed the poor bugger round until I realised it wasn't him. I didn't know what I was going to say if it had been him – I hadn't thought that far ahead.'

'I'm sorry you had to find out this way.'

'Don't apologise, Jesus! You're the one who's suffered. I'm shocked, but I didn't know him – I was kidding myself. He was an illusion, someone to hang ideas on of who I thought he was, of who I'd wanted him to be. You were with the real person... How are you now?'

The taut barrel hoops squeezing Florence's chest yielded. 'The rawness has toned down, but there're still good days, bad days, fucking awful days where it feels like the sky's raining nails aimed at my heart.' Rowena winced. 'The best way to describe it is that someone ripped my skin off and stitched it back on inside out.'

'I'm not surprised. I'm so sorry you've had to go through this.' Rowena leaned over and grasped Florence's hand. 'Dare I ask, have you met anyone else since?'

'No... There was someone I was seeing on and off, remember Tariq from school?'

'Oh my God, yes! He was very quiet, wasn't he? Always sat at the back, seemed scared of everyone.'

'Scared of you, I think.' Florence smirked.

'So you're dating him?'

'Nah, he's getting married. I hooked up with him every time I was home, a friends with benefits kind of arrangement. But it didn't translate long distance while I was away.'

'Away? For work? I take it you left the council job?' Rowena sat back against the cushions trying to get comfortable.

'For sanity...' Florence sketched out her cross continent nomadic life, how dipping into different cultures and the distance from everything helped with the grief.

'Doesn't it feel a bit...' Rowena ruminated on the right word, 'disjointed, constantly packing up? What'll happen now your parents are moving?'

'I have a vague plan.' They sat in silence for a moment or two, both sipping their drinks, Florence's tea had tipped over the edge into insipidly warm territory. She placed it on the coffee table, unable to finish it.

'Can you... talk about what happened?' Rowena asked tentatively.

Florence hesitated before speaking. Of course she'd talked in therapy, but she'd had to dragoon herself, always grinding to halt, never quite managing to reach the conclusion. Leading herself gently by the hand she approached the facts from a different direction, like inching into unforgiving ice-cold seawater.

'Do you remember Mrs Higham from school, our old English teacher?'

'Yes?' Rowena seemed thrown by Flo's sudden switch in direction. 'As in she of the treasure hunts?'

'Yes! The very woman that made school OK. Well, she left me a camper van in her will.'

'Oh God, she's dead too? Please tell me Lennie's still alive?'

'She's fine. Anyway, this camper van...' Florence steered

Rowena down a more rambling route. She listened intently, until Florence reached the part about the Seven Sisters postcard.

'Sorry, you have a postcard with map coordinates on them?' Rowena's brows slid into each other.

'Yes.'

'Have you got it with you?'

Florence nodded and leaped up to retrieve her rucksack from the kitchen, thrusting the card in Rowena's face, making her jump.

'Wait there.' Rowena levered herself up from the sofa and disappeared to the hallway. The space under the stairs housed a narrow dark wooden desk and a slim rattan chair that slid directly beneath. She scrabbled around in one of the drawers. 'Ta-da, I knew it was there somewhere.' Waddling back to the living room she waved a similar-looking postcard in the air before handing it to Florence.

'What's this?' The identical painterly style instead showed the cliffs facing seawards from a northerly perspective, and the River Cuckmere meandering towards the beach along the flat plain. Florence turned it over to find another set of map coordinates, 50.77812, 0.15118, different to her ones, written in Cassie's handwriting, no postmark, no address. 'How?'

'It turned up on reception a while back, hand delivered in a wax-sealed envelope – I think I left that at school. Violet on reception thought it was from a bloke, but was so busy with latecomers she wasn't sure. Obviously there's CCTV at school, though there was no way Mrs Wilson was going to look through the day's footage. It wasn't threatening, but it gave me the creeps. I thought it was from Nate/Jake whoever, trying to get me to meet up; this was way before he started hassling me. Phil, the Geography teacher, decoded the map coordinates. I thought I better keep it in case, you know, it *was* Nate.'

'No it was Frank,' Florence said bluntly.

'Frank?'

'Cassie's son – he's her posthumous postman.'

'Wow, weird...'

Florence arranged the postcards next to each other on the coffee table, the same landscape from different directions. Friston Forest lay behind the artist's viewpoint on Ro's and Seaford on Florence's version.

'What was the destination?' Florence asked uneasily.

'A weird little lay-by next to Friston Forest in Exceat. Like I'm going to go and hang out there and get murdered waiting for the mysterious stranger—What? What's wrong?'

'A lay-by?' Florence whispered hoarsely. 'But *my* postcard was supposed to be the lay-by.'

'Didn't you check?' Florence shook her head violently. 'Flo, what is it? Tell me, please...'

Florence sucked in all the air her lungs could take. 'The lay-by was where C-Clinton and I used to camp, escape for the weekend... It was *our* place.'

'Why don't I put your coordinates into maps on my phone, might make sense of this?' Rowena kindly suggested. Florence nodded gratefully as Rowena typed them in. 'It's my road, just outside the gates! Not really a surprise, all things considered...'

Before Florence could agree her phone burst into life, startling them both.

'Hello?' Florence slapped her forehead, rolling her eyes. 'Oh God, I'm so sorry, Mr Harris. I really am. No, she's still for sale. A lot's going on and I'm a bit all over the place, no excuse though. Can you come tomorrow? Next week after work? Wednesday? Perfect. I promise I'll be at home, I won't leave the house at all. Thank you, bye.' Florence groaned.

'You're selling Nellie?' Rowena asked surprised.

'Yes. She's quite valuable; she'll pay for Costa Rica and beyond.'

'Oh.'

'What?' FloRo hadn't breathed the same air for eight years, yet their umbilical link still pulsed with familiarity, time and distance proving to be inconsequential.

'Nothing.' Rowena sighed and scratched her bump.

'I know it's something. What was the "oh" for?' Florence pressed.

'Don't you think you're meant to keep her?'

'Not you as well.' Rowena looked nonplussed. 'Everyone else thinks the same thing.'

'I have such a strong feeling about it. It's a sign that you forgot about that visit today.'

'I don't believe in signs. Though that's the second time I've sacked off Mr Harris,' Flo reluctantly admitted.

'There you go, your subconscious wants you to keep her.' Rowena's face lit up as an idea erupted behind her eyes. 'What if Nellie is haunted by Cassie's ghost!'

'Now you're being ridiculous or did the psychic finger just start burning?'

Rowena ignored the jibe and narrowed her eyes. 'Are you *sure* you didn't look at the map coordinates? They would have brought you straight here...'

'I swear on Lennie's life. I assumed they were for the lay-by, so didn't bother checking.'

'Poor Lennie, does she know you still do that? Remember that time she overheard you swearing on her life and put clingfilm over the toilet, except your dad went in before you. The splash-back got him in the eye!' Rowena burst out laughing. 'Oh Christ, if I wet myself, it's your fault.' Tears streamed down her face as she fought to control her cackling.

'Oh my God,' Florence squawked, 'we both got bollocked!' She giggled along until their mirth eventually petered out, leaving them wiping their eyes grinning like they were messing around in the lunch queue at Horsham High.

'I've missed this,' Rowena said quietly.

'Me too.'

'So how come you found me?' Rowena slipped in like a criminal lawyer.

'I didn't, I just happened to be driving down the road.'

'Don't give me that innocent look. Just like your act earlier, pretending you had no idea where I lived.' Florence blushed. 'This isn't a coincidence. If it wasn't the coordinates, then what?'

Florence understood the need for transparency this time round. 'OK, Lennie told my parents about the map coordinates…' Out spilled the mindless race towards the coast, spotting Rowena in Sainsbury's, the subsequent stalking, then the compulsion to repeat the entire journey again this weekend.

'So, to sum up, you refused to check the coordinates, but somehow found your way regardless. Cassie was whispering to your higher self!' Rowena was triumphant. 'Come on, Flo, admit it! That was the order you were supposed to follow. Find me first and then…' She left the dénouement dangling mid-air.

Below Florence's silence magma rumbled, then shifted; Rowena stepped into the ring. 'Come on then.' She stood up, obviously far too quickly because she wobbled, steadying herself on the sofa's arm.

'Yeah, I should go,' Florence mumbled, her voice as alien as a tape recording. 'I've taken up enough of your time.'

'Shut up! You're not going anywhere.' How easily they slipped back into lightly aimed insults. 'Apart from with me. We could take my car, but I reckon Cassie'd want us to drive Nellie.'

'What do you mean?'

'Oh, come on, you know where we're going.'

Flo's cheeks reddened. 'This isn't a good idea.'

'Which is why it's the only idea.' Florence feebly shook her head, but Rowena had already taken the reins. 'We don't have to stop. Just look then drive off. Like gradual immersion therapy. One day you'll be able to sit in the lay-by and have a whole picnic. Which reminds me, I need my snack bag or you'll be dealing with my hanger and possible prego-puke. Do you want anything?' Florence declined. Rowena nipped into the kitchen and snatched her Jammy Dodgers and banana from the table and filled a water bottle before heading to the front door, jingling her keys. 'Ready?'

'No.'

'How about we drive near the lay-by then go for a walk in the forest?'

Florence nodded, as if someone else was in charge of her responses.

It was one of those confidently hot early May days when memories of woolly hats, stiff wellies, cold city commutes and log-burning fires melted like snowmen under a blowtorch. Florence's cheap sunglasses kept sliding down, Sri Lankan knock-off aviators designed for someone with a meatier nose and bigger ears. The BFG came to mind. Florence had swiftly acclimatised to Rowena's unexpected presence in Nellie as they whistled along the A259 towards Cuckmere Haven. The last eight years unravelled as FloRo set off on one of their infamous adventures.

'I didn't actually know anything was seriously wrong for ages,' Florence fought to speak above the noise of the engine. Rowena turned her head away from the hypnotic trees zipping past the window. 'I knew something wasn't right because he would retreat into himself when he'd always been chatty and such a doer. We'd only been an item for a year when I started to notice he was different.'

'Were you living together?'

'Yes, we had this really cool flat in Brunswick Square. Right at the top of one of those old houses. We almost had a sea view.' Rowena smiled. In the past, FloRo had always harped on about finding the perfect flat with a sacrosanct sea view that was reasonable yet didn't sequester all your wages so the view was all you could afford to look at. 'His parents were funny about us moving in together. I'd only met them a few times. They thought it was all a bit quick – I mean it *was* quick, but we both wanted the same thing. Being settled, while not being boring, the possibility of a future together. I'd even talked about retraining as a teacher. There were a few schools in Brighton that offered on the job training. Anyway, his parents were OK, but I think they thought we wouldn't last... You know his real name wasn't actually Clinton? I did think it was a bit out there when I met his super straight parents. They occasionally called him Iggy, short for Ignatius.'

'What?! I've never heard that name in real life.'

'I know. His brother's called Luther, which is slightly less extra. He hated the pomposity of it so when he could he changed it, made them call him Clinton, after George Clinton, the musician.' Rowena shrugged nonplussed. 'He was a famous grandfather of funk, obviously Clinton made me listen to Parliament-Funkadelic on a loop.' She smiled at the memory of them dancing round the living room swaying Toffee and Bramble wrapped in their towels, all of them having a family boogie to 'Atomic Dog'... Guinea pigs' maximum lifespan reached eight years. Toffee and Bramble had surely died since. They'd been two when she'd met Clinton.

'His parents were disappointed he hadn't studied medicine like his brother. They thought a veterinary nurse wasn't worthy of his skills. Or so Clinton told me, I've no idea really and what does it matter anyway? I'm sure they wished he was still alive and well as a veterinary nurse rather than dead as a medic.'

'Exactly!' Rowena cried. 'Christ, if this one wants to go to clown school or be a member of the Monster Raving Loony Party, as long as she's happy and accepting of herself, I'll be OK with it. Might draw the line at a stripper unless she's the boss, but at the end of the day, it's her job, life, whatever. All you can do is guide your kids, you can't live their lives for them.'

'You're having a girl?'

Rowena shrugged. 'I don't know for sure. I just feel like she's a girl. Anyway, carry on, you were saying?'

'I got to know his friends, met his brother, and I made a few new friends, of sorts. People from work, no one I really see now. At the beginning it was just Clinton and me making a home together, in our cute flat with the pet seagulls pestering us for snacks. We were going to get a dog, but then...' Florence changed gear as they turned round a bend, traffic clustered up ahead at the bridge by the Cuckmere Inn. 'Anyway, that first year was exciting. I was happy, madly in love. Sorry.'

'Don't be sorry. It's right that you should have been madly in love. Don't ever be sorry for being in love. Please don't censor this for me. I want to hear about all of it, even the things you think I won't, I want to hear them too.'

'Thank you... About four months before Clinton's thirtieth things felt a bit... off. He kept having the odd sick day but saying it was nothing. I'd wanted to organise a party for him with his friends, maybe his parents and brother, but he refused. Gently at first, so I assumed he was just being bashful or whatever. I kind of ignored it, pushed away my misgivings about his grumpiness, lack of enthusiasm for everything, how exhausted he always seemed to be, how he wasn't interested in what was going on with anyone, not just us. He kept forgetting small things and protesting he hadn't, then biting my head off. He wasn't who I thought he was. I mean, he could barely you know, find energy for... sex. And that had *never* been a problem. Naturally I had this hideous sinking feeling he'd gone off me, hoped that he would miraculously realise we were crazy in love with a happy future together. But I couldn't talk to him about it. With my complete aversion to confrontation, and him hiding behind exhaustion, we were a walking problem page. I, of course, thought I'd caused whatever it was.' Florence exhaled, pressing her back into the seat, gripping the steering wheel as Nellie leisurely joined the slow-moving line of vehicles crossing the bridge over the River Cuckmere.

The open maw of greenery was a feast for even the most jaded eyes. The amplitude of the sweeping valley, scooped from the hills millenniums before by retreating melt water thrust all other concerns briefly out of the way, a worthy distraction from life. Florence surveyed the open road over the bridge, not long till they hit Exceat. She turned to Rowena. 'One day I burst into tears at work after Clinton cancelled plans yet again, saying he needed to go home early, I was a mess. My line manager asked what was going on, couldn't understand why I was upset about something so insignificant. I explained the last few months in a veiled manner, and she was so sweet. Suggested I went home early too, made sure he was OK, sort it out once and for all. But when I got home he wasn't there. He arrived just before six thirty when I would normally be home. Hang on, just need to concentrate...' Florence turned onto the bridge once there was a significant gap in the traffic and they drove across in silence, Nellie's engine propelling them towards the turn-off. Rowena stretched her neck to drink in the full view.

'I don't ever get tired of seeing this,' she said, a smile spreading across her face. 'I think the baby will like it too. I've already got one of those papoose things so I can go out walking with her, explore places a pushchair can't reach. She needs to see the Seven Sisters.'

'That sounds perfect,' Florence said, their destination fleetingly forgotten. But as the turning loomed into view opposite the paddle boarding hire on the banks of the river, the significance of Litlington Road burrowed into her chest.

'Are you OK?' Rowena asked, watching Florence like a hawk. 'This is it, isn't it?'

'Yep. God, I haven't been here since... well, a long time.' Florence's voice refracted, her throat somewhat dislocated. She steadied her breathing, pushing against the totemic power this location had over her. *It's just a road*, she silently breathed into her belly. *Just a road...*

'Why don't we park here, it's easier, go for a walk in the forest?'

Florence nodded while turning into the Seven Sisters car park, hectic with lunchtime families visiting the café, heading into the forest or along the meandering river path beyond. The hidden lay-by would have actually been a better choice instead of trying to squeeze Nellie into a tight spot. But a space suddenly appeared before them as a battered green army Land Rover splattered in mud reversed out from between a red and a silver car. It stopped midway, while the driver peered out of the window, winding it down.

'Florence?'

'That man knows you,' Rowena said when Florence missed his inverted greeting.

'What man?'

'Him,' Rowena murmured. 'The hot one reversing.' Rowena rolled down her window so the man could see in better. 'Hi,' she said and smiled, turning to Florence, giving her a death stare. 'Say hello,' she whispered. 'He seems... nice.'

'Hi!' he shouted from his window. 'I thought I recognised Nellie.'

'Don't say a word,' Florence hissed at Rowena out of the

corner of her mouth before leaning forward to speak. 'Hello, Frank.'

'How are you?' he asked, keen to catch up while Florence flicked her eyes to her rear-view mirror, longing for a line of disgruntled drivers to begin hitting their horns. Surprisingly there was no one there. Rowena poked her in the ribs, her eyes wide.

'Yeah, I'm good thank you. Things with you OK too?' she asked glaring at Rowena, who was trying not to laugh.

'Yeah, fine. How's Nellie? Is she running OK? No problems?'

'All good. Runs like a dream.' Florence was itching for him to finish talking and offer up the space so they could start their walk.

'How do you two know each other?' Rowena asked innocently when Florence was clearly not going to expand on her answer.

'My mum left her the camper van,' Frank answered good-naturedly. 'But I'm not bitter.'

'Oh, you're Mrs Higham's son!' Rowena acted along convincingly. 'Wow! She was our teacher at school.'

'You two were at school together?'

'Yes.' Rowena glanced at Florence, who returned the death stare. 'I'm Rowena. It was lovely meeting you, Mrs Higham's son.' If he knew who she was, he didn't let on.

'Frank. Yes, nice to see you. Hope Nellie continues to be reliable, Florence. You can always give me a ring or drop me an email if you need any help with her. I'll leave you ladies to get on with your lunchtime.' He shot them a vulpine grin while spinning the wheel anticlockwise and pulling off, throwing his hand out of the window in a faltering goodbye.

Florence stared at Rowena. 'You were flirting.'

'Someone had to.' Florence rolled her eyes. 'He fancies you.'

'Oh my God, Rowena, he does not!'

'Look, he does, and that's OK. He's allowed to fancy you, you're gorgeous and single, not pregnant, and you might need some fun.'

'I don't need any fun, especially with someone tied up in this... treasure hunt malarkey.'

'If anyone's in need of some fun, it's you...' Florence pulled into the space and switched off Nellie's engine. 'Don't you think it's weird that Frank just "happened" to be here, the exact same time we arrived, and it's his spot we're parked in?'

'No.' Florence refused to concede any ground.

'Yes it is! Admit it! It's like Cassie sent him there, as a sign to keep going on the treasure hunt, like she used to at school. She used to leave a Cadbury's Mini Roll poking out of somewhere or on a window ledge so we knew we were on the right track, meaning we were on a roll, remember?'

'Yes, I remember the mini rolls, like Hansel and Gretel breadcrumbs.'

'Exactly! Frank was a mini roll.'

'I'm sure he'd be chuffed to hear you call him that. Anyway, you're reading too much into this. He just happened to be here, that's all. Nothing supernatural about that.'

'I know I'm right!' Rowena clapped gleefully.

'Oh yes, forgot you can't ever be wrong,' Florence teased, sweeping her hair up into a high ponytail, securing it with the faithful band. 'Are you going to be OK walking?'

'I'm pregnant, not ill. I've got my snacks, I'll be OK.' To prove a point she unzipped her banana and bit into it. 'We can always go to the café after? I'll need a wee for sure. Do you want to do the river or the forest?'

'The forest, I think.' Florence checked outside the window, craning her neck. 'I feel OK, this is OK. Like when I walked over the cliffs. I managed fine.'

'You sound surprised.'

'I know. I don't know what I'm expecting. I came here with you a few times when we bought that weed from Jez Cartwright in sixth form. I couldn't drive home I was so spangled.'

Rowena started laughing, her belly shaking. 'Oh God, I'd forgotten about that. We had to ring Lennie to come and rescue us with that older boyfriend she was seeing. What was his name? Something weird.'

'Tizzo. Yeah, she blackmailed me for ages about that.'

The two women sat in the front of Nellie cushioned in companionable silence while Rowena scrabbled around for her bag in the footwell. She hooked her hand into one of its handles and sat back before hitting Florence with another question.

'So what happened when Clinton returned to the flat? You didn't finish the story.'

24

TICKING TIME BOMB

July 2016, Brighton

'*You're* back early,' Clinton over enunciated, eyes popping. 'I just nipped to the shop to get some bits.'

Florence spun her eyes over him for evidence of a shopping bag. 'Are you feeling better? What time did you go out?'

He chewed his lip before answering. 'Not long, about half an hour ago.'

'OK, what's going on?' Florence's voice shook. *Please be something banal, not someone else, a job interview, anything but splitting up.* Her university heartbreak crashed at her feet as she brought to mind how it had robbed all joy and the inability to function while torment incessantly writhed inside her.

'What do you mean?' Clinton asked shadily.

'I was here half an hour ago. Actually, an hour ago. You weren't. Where were you?'

Clinton's insouciance slipped, his shoulders sagging under his coat. He let his rucksack drop to the floor, the unmistakable clanking of tin cans inside. He had in fact been to the shop, just not half an hour ago, igniting a spark of hope in Florence's chest.

'I wasn't ready to tell you yet.'

'Tell me what...?'

'Sit down.' He shrugged off his denim jacket and hung it on one of the dining chairs.

Florence slumped on the sofa, her legs giving way beneath her. Nothing good ever followed someone suggesting sitting down before spilling their guts. Clinton perched on the occasional rattan chair opposite, a hand-me-down from his parents, one of their conservatory chairs that was, according to his mum, 'too threadbare for public use'. But OK for Clinton and his erstwhile girlfriend. Florence had been unable to find the worn patches on the pink and red striped seat, however the rattan was shedding in places, having been clawed by Clinton's parents' cat, Fuzzy. The guinea pigs rustled to the front of their cage, ringside seats on the unfolding drama.

'I have a suspected frontal lobe glioblastoma,' Clinton admitted.

'A what?'

'A brain tumour, but I don't know what type yet, we need—'

Florence's hands automatically pressed against her throat squashing down the scream winging its way out. 'I think I'm going to be sick.' She ran to the sink before Clinton could finish his sentence, dry heaving.

'Typical,' Clinton said wryly, rubbing her back. 'Making it about you...'

Florence whipped her head out of the sink flying into retaliation but his mirth-tinged eyes stopped her in her tracks.

'I'm sorry,' she said hoarsely. 'I couldn't help it.' He handed her a piece of kitchen towel to wipe her face, just like that morning they'd first met. Florence, dizzy with questions, folded herself into his arms and they stood by the sink in a comforting embrace neither of them wanted to leave. Too numb to cry, she stared dry-eyed across the kitchen towards the sofa and the mid-century teak coffee table they'd unearthed at a car boot sale and gleefully rammed into the back of Clinton's camper van. Would this mean they couldn't buy the matching sideboard they had their eye on eBay? *Oh...*

'You didn't let me finish,' Clinton said after a while, disengaging, smoothing down Florence's hair that had got caught in his necklace.

'Sorry.'

'Stop saying sorry, I should be apologising to you really. Acting all cloak and dagger.'

'Clinton, you... I don't know what to say. Are you going to...?' The word unforthcoming. 'How long have we got?'

'Let's sit on the sofa.' He led her by the hand and they sank into the cushions. 'I need a biopsy next, that's where I was today. Dad was with me, he knows the neurosurgeon. The scan determined where the tumour is.'

Despite the intense magnitude Florence hated herself for feeling stung that he'd told his dad first. 'So, what did they say at the scan?'

'It's in the frontal lobe, pressing on bits and bobs, but they're not sure how long it's been there or what it is yet, so it's a suspected glioblastoma. It's quite big, hence why I've been... you know...'

'Will they operate? How long have you felt... something... different?' Clinton stroked her hand. Florence suppressed a scream, wanted to beg him not to die.

'I'd been having those headaches, feeling I dunno, angry about everything for no reason, dropping instruments at work, snapping at you, realising I was being weird but not remembering why. Confusion about being confused. Marianna suggested an eye test cos my vision became blurry in one eye when I'd been feeling tired and nauseous. She said I might need to start wearing glasses now I'm almost thirty, started taking the piss out of me.' He smiled dolefully. 'But I'd been feeling shit for a while, thought it was too many club nights, burning the candle. God I wish it was.' He stopped, and wiped his face, tears slipping down his cheeks. 'This was why I didn't want to tell you.'

'Oh, Clinton, I'd have found out at some point, wouldn't I?' He nodded, wincing. 'What is it?'

'A brain tumour. It'll clear up.' She hit him playfully. 'Sorry, humour seems like the only medicine... Sometimes I feel OK – today not too bad, but then other days... Words disappear off my tongue, anxiety rolls in waves, and the exhaustion; I need to tell Marianna, take some proper sick leave. They said I can't drive any more either. In case...'

'In case of what?' Florence had alarming visions of him passing out at the wheel of the camper van and crashing into a lamppost, killed by its crushing blow rather than the tumour.

'Because of my patchy vision, and in case I have a seizure. So far I haven't, but because of where "it" is, I have to be prepared, especially when I can't remember where I'm going. That happened last week.'

Florence appraised him slowly shaking her head.

'What?'

'I'm just, I dunno, dumbfounded... How can you be so phlegmatic?'

Clinton laughed. 'Phlegmatic? Is that your word of the day, Flo and her fancy vocab. What does it even mean?'

'Unflappable, unemotional...'

'Oh, I see. Well, it's either that or I lose my shit entirely. Save the meltdown until we really know the overall outcome...'

Florence shook herself as if attempting to liberate them from this horrifically surreal situation. If only it were that simple...

'What happened at the optician's?' Lopsided and unstrung, Florence clawed back ground by firing questions. *Knowledge was power, right?*

'I expected to be told I was short-sighted or had a stigmatism and would need glasses, but she said she wanted me to go straight to the GP. I asked why, she said they needed to double check, maybe refer me to a specialist. Something was showing up at the back of my eye. I asked like what, she said she couldn't diagnose. She knew...'

'Why didn't you tell me?'

'I didn't want to worry you. Dad fast-tracked me, bypassed the GP. Perks of being a surgeon... Saw the neurologist then we just had the scan. Now I need to see the neurosurgeon for the biopsy.' How prosaic, avuncular meetings with Stephen's work colleagues.

'So the fact you were seen so quickly means they can start treatment. It's good, right? They caught it in time?' Florence wasn't even clear about what she meant. In time for what? In time before it greedily ate up Clinton's brain leaving him slurping soup through a straw? In time before it manifested its own spiky personality demanding a chat show and a cut of everything before commanding their lives entirely like a nebulous dictator? 'In time' appeared to be a query desperate people asked in TV hospital dramas when they were seeking some grave comfort.

'I don't really know. Dad thinks this neurosurgeon we're meeting next week is the best, so we'll see.'

'He's going to cut it out?' Florence shivered at the thought of Clinton subjected to such a hideous operation. Would he lose his beautiful hair?

'It's too big at the moment, touching too many vitals. They can do the biopsy to determine what type of tumour, what stage, find some biomarkers.'

The words were as unfamiliar to Florence as the off-side rule. 'When will that be? Biomarkers?'

'Next week, I think, depending on the surgeon.' Clinton shrugged, shifting on the sofa, rolling his neck. 'Biomarkers can help with diagnosis, define how tumours respond to treatment, determine how fast they grow, that kind of thing...'

'Can't they do it sooner? What if it gets worse?' Florence felt helpless against the churning surf of dread, the lack of control so all-consuming she feared being washed away. In dire need of anchoring she sought tasks, to make lists, to be busy, to organise. 'Can I do anything to speed it up? Ring people?'

'Dad's got it all under control. Just stay calm.'

'I am calm.' She wasn't. They sat in silence, bridled together in anguish, Florence pressing her fingers one by one against her thumb.

'I got some coconut milk and some lentils.' Clinton cracked the stillness. 'I was going to make that squash soup. Do you fancy it?' He massaged her hand between both of his.

'No!' she lashed out. 'How can you talk about soup? Fuck the soup. All I can think about is this!' She waved her hands in the air, desperate to grab the incumbent tumour and wrestle it into oblivion.

'Florence, I have to stop thinking about it. This is why I didn't want to tell you until I had to. Mum doesn't know for this exact reason, no one does, just you and Dad. If I obsess, it'll win. It *can't* win.' He ran his hands through his hair, his fingers catching on a knot. 'We had a dog in with a brain tumour a few months back. He didn't know he had a life-threatening disease. He still lived each day as best he could because that's what dogs do. They have no idea what's going on other than loving their people and enjoying walks. Life is good, until it isn't.'

'What happened to him?' Florence asked cautiously, holding out for a happy ever after.

'He was put down, because his life was untenable – he couldn't walk in the end. Maybe that's a bad example... But he wasn't consumed by his diagnosis, until the end he lived in blissful ignorance, occasionally fitting – but he didn't know he was, therefore he was happy. I want to be like the dog. I want to live my life, not spend every waking moment wondering what's going to happen until it does happen.'

'How are you able to do that? It's impossible. I could *never* do that.' Florence swayed tenuously between madness and violent anger.

'You don't know what you're capable of. Believe me, I was fucking freaked out, still am and I am scared, totally shitting myself. But if "it" takes over, I may as well jump off the pier now. This doesn't mean I'm OK with any of this. I promise you, I'm not. But as long as there's no news, there's hope. I'll probably feel completely different next week, but right now I need to feel like this, or pretend to at least.'

After dinner, in the end the soup made by Florence while Clinton dozed on the sofa, they chose a puerile film on Netflix in the hope it would hoodwink them for a few hours. Just before Florence woke him to let him know the soup was ready, she crouched next to his sleeping face. You wouldn't know there was anything wrong apart from two grey smudges beneath each eye. She couldn't believe he'd been hefting the bulk of this terrifying knowledge around with him for the last few weeks without unburdening himself. To think she had thought he'd met someone else. In essence, he had – the tumour was the third person in their relationship. From the second she'd been introduced to it, it became a consideration in everything, rather like the child they had still yet to conceive. Earlier, she'd asked him about chemotherapy causing infertility.

'Don't worry. Dad already has that box ticked. Guarding his future grandchildren. I can freeze healthy sperm before any treatment...' Florence was *so pleased* Mr Siems was in charge...

The night before the biopsy, Stephen Siems visited, staying for dinner before the nil by mouth deadline. He arrived straight from work in a well-cut charcoal grey suit, undoubtedly from a bespoke tailors. Clinton had hinted at Savile Row; people expect their surgeon to look well turned out, apparently. Gives them confidence in their abilities.

'I told your mother I was meeting a friend after work,' he explained, walking round the living area of the flat, idly picking up ornaments, inspecting them then immediately replacing them not having appreciated their charm at all. 'I'll tell her the prognosis when we have it post biopsy.'

He had insisted on collecting Clinton from the hospital and bringing him back to the flat, but Clinton had fought for Florence to do it. Florence had yet to tell her parents on the orders of Clinton and his dad. 'We need to focus on the results, not on drama,' Mr Siems had said. Florence wanted to slap him – he couldn't know how her parents would react. Her mother was a nurse! She wanted to tell him to work on his bedside manner, but kept her thoughts to herself as always. She allowed herself to miss Rowena, wishing she could call on her friendship in her hour of need, but hadn't the strength to open the door...

'Depending on the stage of the tumour, and side effects of treatment, I think it's best if you move back home for a while. We can get help, and set up a bedroom in the ground floor office so you don't have stairs to contend with.'

'Dad! I want to be here with Florence,' Clinton responded tetchily.

'She can visit.'

Florence wondered if she was invisible. Over dinner she closely observed Stephen. He didn't listen to people and she arrived at the conclusion he always thought he was right therefore no one else's opinion mattered. But she also noticed he appeared agitated, unable to express himself other than through control. She imagined herself as a parent watching her child battle something this insidious. It must be torture.

'Would you like some pudding, Stephen?' she asked scraping her chair back ready to bring her homemade banana cake to the table, Clinton's favourite. He glanced up, his eyes lingering on her face as if seeing her for the first time. His fiercely inquiring gaze softened.

'That would be lovely, Florence. Clinton says you're a prolific baker. You'll have to fatten him up after treatment.' That was the first time she felt accepted as Clinton's partner with a future, rather than a temporary fixture to be endured like a faddish hairstyle or soon to grow-over unsightly tongue piercing.

* * *

Florence lay stiffly next to Clinton in their bed. It had been two days since the biopsy and already there had been a shift. She didn't understand whether it was because she now knew everything, so was hyper alert, or having the biopsy had hoovered all his energy. He drifted in and out of sleep for the first few days, even though the procedure had been brief and he'd returned home immediately. She had taken a week off to care for him, spending time making healthy soups, googling everything she could about brain tumours, what vitamins to take, what foods to try, how to be the perfect support partner. Stephen had dropped in every day, his manner brusque and businesslike, only once did the façade crack. Clinton was asleep on the second evening and Stephen was about to leave, when he turned to Florence.

'I'm dreading telling his mother. She'll be so cross. Her youngest son suffering without her.'

'I'm sure she'll understand in the end, won't she?' However, Florence was quietly unconvinced – she thought it madness not telling Jen. Secrecy was poisonous as she knew only too well.

'You don't know Jen. She'll rip my head off.' Florence didn't know how to respond. 'How are you keeping, Florence? Are you making sure you're getting enough rest? This can be taxing. You just let me know if you need any extra help, please?'

When the results were due, Stephen accompanied his son to the appointment not Florence.

'Why can't I come?' she asked, wounded.

'Because if it's bad, I need to process, to be able to ask difficult questions without an audience. I'll call you as soon as I can.' Of course it made sense, but it didn't prevent her from feeling pushed outside the tent. Clinton didn't notice; he was in his own world, sometimes available, sometimes not. He could be terse without realising, morphing unintentionally into his father. Florence had researched every brain tumour charity website, discovering that personality changes were all part of the package, not to take it personally. Even though she was armed with all this new knowledge, she found it hard not to feel surplus to requirements. With no one to talk to apart from Clinton, she felt utterly alone, bobbing along on a sea of inadequacy. She longed for Rowena...

Florence was at work the day of Clinton's hospital visit, Stephen had suggested she keep back as many days as possible in case they were needed in the future. She checked her phone every ten minutes, unable to concentrate. Florence was woefully aware of her appearance having not slept for the best part of two nights as Phyliss repeatedly asked if she was OK. In the end, she missed the call because she was on the other line to a landlord. Stephen's number silently flashing across her phone screen but she was powerless to answer it. His number signified a fiery beacon: prepare for an oncoming armada. As soon as the landlord rung off, Florence grabbed her phone and ran out into the echoing corridor away from eavesdroppers.

'Florence. Thanks for ringing back.' Stephen's neutral tone distracted from the incoming update. 'Not good news I'm afraid. Clinton wanted me to ring instead.' He took rather a large breath, Florence held hers, her heart trying its hardest to hammer through her sternum.

'Stage four glioblastoma. Quite advanced, been building for a while, and they're not sure how it will respond to treatment, but we're willing to try and slow the growth. The biomarkers were inconclusive.' Florence wished she'd been obsessed with *Grey's Anatomy* like Terry-Anne instead of always burying her nose in a book. She had triumphantly named many medical conditions in the Tuesday night pub quiz, winning them numerous bottles of Prosecco. Terry-Anne could certainly have held her own in a conversation with Stephen.

'Sorry, Stephen. I... I need you to explain for me, pretend I'm ten and know nothing.'

'Of course. Yes, yes, right... we could go down a road of extensive research trials that may or may not work, but even they are not guaranteed to permanently stop the advance of the tumour. Just buy some time, as it were. Some of the more recent trials are closed now, so that avenue is even narrower. The tumour is embedded in some pretty tricky tissue so that cutting it away and shrinking the last few cells with radiotherapy is not possible – it's too big. We discussed radiotherapy to try and reduce its mass, make things a bit more comfortable...' He cleared his throat. 'In other words, Clinton has terminal cancer.'

Sliding to the floor, her back against the wall, Flo squatted under the weight of the diagnosis, her mind throwing up visions of whispering in dark rooms, funerals, weeping, basically her university heartbreak pumped up on steroids. She gazed between the black metal balustrades and through the impressive picture windows stretching down the hollow stairwell. Gulls hovered in the thin ribbon of sky above the tumbling chimney pots and hulking air conditioning units studded along her immediate eyeline. People were getting ready to leave work, meet friends for drinks, living their ordinary monotonous lives while she was unable to navigate back to her desk in case her skin unzipped and she crumpled to the floor like a smashed piñata.

'Florence, are you there?' Stephen asked, showing her concern.

'Yes.'

'I know it's a lot to absorb. But there are options. We've discussed radiotherapy to reduce the tumour, and if it's successful, reassess.'

'Reassess?'

'Yes, stop the growth and live with the diagnosis.'

'Like a ticking time bomb.'

'Well, not quite. Anyway, I'll bring him back now and stay until you get home.'

'How's Clinton doing?'

'In shock, as you can imagine.'

Florence wasn't sure how long she'd been sitting on the floor by the time Phyliss found her. She was past caring about keeping this secret and divulged the whole sorry tale. Phyliss packed her off in a taxi. 'I'll tell them you're ill,' she said after gathering Flo's things for her so she didn't have to re-enter the office.

Clinton was in bed when she reached home, while Stephen waited on the sofa. Florence lost her composure the minute she saw him and burst into tears, Stephen leaping over to hug her awkwardly.

'Don't let him hear, Florence, he needs you to be strong.' He patted her back before releasing her. She decided to sleep out here tonight so Clinton could get some unbroken rest. But the truth was, she was terrified to even look at him. Maybe she should start retreating, prepare for the worst, act as if he was already dead, like she had with Toby.

25

LAST CHANCE SALOON

May 2023, Friston Forest

'Bloody hell, Flo, why on earth didn't you reach out?' Rowena cried from Nellie's passenger seat. 'I would have been there in a shot, put all that pathetic shit behind me.'

'It wasn't pathetic, it was how you felt.'

'It's pathetic compared to that. You should have rung Terry-Anne, she'd have put me straight.'

'When you're in the middle of something as stressful as that, you literally can't think about anything else other than breathing. People just have to turn up unbidden because it uses too much brain power to ask for help. Obviously I considered trying you, but felt like I'd left it too long, and then when I started travelling I was beyond talking so thought what was the point...?' Florence leaned into the back and grabbed her bag from the floor behind. 'Shall we go a for a bit of a walk?'

The two women headed into the forest, mostly populated by

stately beech trees. Despite the number of vehicles in the car park, the woods were peaceful, absorbing intrusive traffic noise from the nearby A259. A red kite soared above the treeline, scavenging for carrion below; it was lunchtime after all. They passed a few people, families mostly, small kids in wellies even though it hadn't rained for some time. Rowena's face lit up at the cutest ones running past, chubby knees and round faces red from the exertion. Florence watched with interest. She didn't have an apparent biological clock, if she did, she couldn't hear the ticking. When she'd been in the throes of romance, she'd anticipated children in her future. But not now.

'We've missed such big chunks of each other's lives,' Rowena lamented. 'It feels so stupid now. I should have made an effort, looked you up. I was the one who caused this.'

'Rowena, I hurt you. Why should you be the one to feel bad? We both made mistakes.'

'I know, but I can't help feeling you might have coped better had I been there. I didn't know though.'

'No, you didn't, and I hadn't the energy to reconnect. I spiralled, things got very dark.'

Rowena grabbed Flo's hand. 'What *did* happen?' Florence didn't answer for a while, just looked skywards at the newly unfurled leaves wafting on gusts, bows supplely bending towards each other, touching briefly before breaking free.

'Clinton sunk into a depression, which was totally expected. He didn't get out of bed for a week apart from to go to the loo. Not even the guinea pigs cheered him up. He couldn't sleep because of the steroids, but refused to engage in any talk of the future, of further treatment. By this time his mum knew – she was a force to be reckoned with. Jen took some time off work and came over every day. She made me keep my routine of going to work, and she was there making us dinner when I got in, but he barely ate.

Apparently she had gone mental that Stephen hadn't told her so felt like she was making up for that lost time. She told me Clinton had reacted like this when they'd made him move schools at ten. Wouldn't talk for a week; she said he'd cave in eventually, we just had to not get involved, let him feel his feelings. I obviously had to sleep in the same bed as Clinton but he wouldn't touch me, not even by accident. My parents were worried sick about it all. Even Lennie would drop in unannounced with food and wine, just sit with me while he stayed in our room watching films or staring into space. No one knew what to do. At the beginning of the second week I took a few days off and I made him his favourite breakfast, and willed him to get out of bed. He actually did. I'd begged his mum not to come, to give him some space. I needed the bloody space too!'

'I don't know how you coped with her up in your grille the whole time.'

'Her son was dying, the poor woman was heartbroken. But no one would talk about the fact he *was* dying. Every conversation focused around when he would start more treatment... Anyway, that morning, we chatted and things felt less scary...'

The two women reached the duck pond on the outskirts of West Dean, a Hollywood director's mood board of an archetypal English hamlet. Florence had last visited with Clinton on one of their camping trips. West Dean had always felt magical, steeped in history stretching as far back as the Normans, the crooked houses and ancient flint cottages enhancing the ambrosial vibe. The village remained reassuringly unchanged.

'Do you mind talking to me about this?' Rowena checked. 'If it's too much, stop.'

'I only ever really talked around this in therapy,' Florence admitted. 'It was too soon for me to access it I think, too raw. The idea had been I would continue with therapy and reach that point, but I left the country instead. That had felt like a better option at the time. Safer.'

'You know what, doing what I do, I've realised there's no one correct way to deal with trauma. There are set guidelines that can result in a full circle moment of healing and recovery, but these guidelines don't take into account the human condition or diverse human personalities. We're not robots and not everyone responds to treatment in the same way. You did what was essential for you at the time. Maybe *now* is the time for you to reflect, to face whatever "this" is. Take it as a nudge from the universe, or coincidence as you believe it is – you found me whether you meant to or not, guided by Cassie or by your own third eye. The stars are in alignment for the full circle moment at the right time for you.'

'I love that,' Florence said as a shaft of sunshine spilled through overhead branches and feathery leaves showering them in dappled light, the luxuriant woody scent of ferns filling the air. They stopped by the duck pond, watching dragonflies flicker over the oily surface, their wings catching sunbeams sparkling off the water while a cloud of gnats swarmed over the far side, seeking fresh blood to suck. Along with Rowena's presence bolstering her, nature tenderly held Florence's hand; no wonder GPs prescribed nature walks to alleviate depression.

Florence picked up her story. 'Clinton was exhausted thinking about everything, but one thing he wanted above all was to try and extend his life. If they told him three years, he wanted to strive for five, beat the odds. And who knew, a miracle might happen, they weren't unheard of. He reasoned that none of us knew how long we had and that he wanted to fill the time with living, not merely existing. So after that awful week of depression, he managed to switch it around. The steroids had initially made him feel sick and the insomnia was bad, but he gradually got used to the dose and was able to eat more and more. He remained positive, well, as positive as you could be knowing it could go either way. We restarted our lives in our new normal, Macmillan support were amazing, they helped with paperwork, work stuff, there was a group I could talk to if I needed anything. Everything now revolved around the hospital appointments. We still saw friends on weekends for brief meetups at the flat if Clinton was well enough or maybe on the prom, get out of the flat. My parents were amazing, they would leave us alone, but ring, ask what treats we wanted, if they could come and clean, change the bed, etc. Really useful help. I mean, Clinton's parents were great, they did loads too, but it was all mostly centred around hospital visits so I could still work.

'After six weeks the tumour had barely shrunk and Clinton was starting to lose sight in one eye. He felt dreadful a lot of the time and suffered two seizures – Jesus that was scary. I thought he'd died on the kitchen floor, called an ambulance, his parents came too. I spent the following week awake every night to make sure he was still breathing. The radiotherapy made him sick too – the whole thing was such a nightmare. Not everyone responds the same, just like you said earlier, he was having adverse reactions to everything. The steroids had reduced the swelling in the beginning but then the tumour suddenly accelerated, growing aggressively. The next option was chemo, but that wasn't guaranteed either. He was utterly miserable. One of his friends had suggested seeing a healer, and at this point, he was desperate. His parents were trying to tell him chemo might be the answer, to leave the healer to the hippies, but he wanted to give it a try. I drove him there, to a little house in Kemptown where this woman lived. She was lovely, very kind, but she took one look at him and started talking about blocked chakras and dirty auras, childhood stuff he'd not thought about for years. He didn't have time to unpick his upbringing – he didn't want to know. He thought he was going to sit on a bed and have some magic wand waved over him, a quick fix. I think that was what broke his resolve. And you know my feelings on esoteric claptrap...' Florence wrinkled her nose. 'Chemo was going to have to be super harsh to fight this thing and his body was already severely compromised.'

The concurrence of sombre conversation amid such a beautiful spring afternoon had drawn Florence to All Saints, the twelfth century church nestled in the heart of the village. During its inordinate lifespan it must have encountered every kind of death, assuaged all manner of grief, celebrated many different lives. It felt like a fitting place to discuss Clinton's final weeks. Florence found a shady spot underneath a sprawling hornbeam presiding over wonky gravestones. The ground was dry, valiant dandelions sprouting amongst the sprinkling of crunchy leaves. She spread out her cardigan for Rowena to sit upon.

'A few days after the healer, Clinton asked me what I thought about assisted dying. I screamed I wasn't going to kill him, and he couldn't do it either. That he had to try chemo, couldn't give up. We had a terrible row, culminating with him smashing a utensil jar; we'd never had that kind of ugly fight before. He yelled that he was trying to stay alive for me, not for himself, that I was selfish. The worst thing was, I think he was right.'

'No, he was just rightly angry. He had no control over his own life, or his death. For someone who loved life, he probably felt like he wasn't even living. So he threw that onto you.'

'I did the worst thing, I didn't know what else to do. I rang his parents and told them what he'd said. That I was worried he was going to end it all before trying chemo. They of course flew round to the flat; oh my God, that evening was awful. He was furious with me, with them, he walked out. His dad tried to follow him, but Jen stopped him. I didn't recognise Clinton at all now. While he was gone, they said they'd make the room up at home for him, get it ready for chemo. The side effects were going to be worse than the radiotherapy. They were basically absolving me of any duty of care whether I wanted it or not. And this is the horrific, most terrible thing: I was glad.' Tears spilled down Florence's cheeks as Rowena scrabbled around in her bag for some tissues. 'I'm a bad person.'

'No, you're not! You're human. Bloody hell, Flo, the man you loved more than anything in the world had given up and was taking it out on you. You hadn't slept for days whilst he was so ill and never going to get better. Who wouldn't want a break from that?' She proffered a pristine packet of tissues. 'See, I've been practising; mums always have tissues.'

Florence smiled through her tears. 'Thanks.'

'Did he succumb to the chemo? I'm gathering not.'

'He came home after an hour; his parents were still there. They told him what they'd planned, that his dad would talk to the hospital about starting chemo and if that wasn't something that he wanted, they would get things in place for palliative care.'

'He cried, I held him in my arms on the sofa, his mum and dad either side, and he said he didn't want to die, but he didn't want to live like this. He didn't know who he was, and the longer it went on, he felt less and less himself. Animals didn't have to go through this. They didn't lose their dignity, didn't end up having their bums wiped by their dog parents. We agreed, you couldn't not. However, he was willing to give chemo one last stab. If it made no difference he would live with whatever followed. His mum was beside herself, hugging him, I just felt numb. I knew it meant more months of physical torture, and this time he didn't feel strong enough. He was in pain, he'd lost himself, it felt cruel to prolong it if the result was going to be the same, but that was the one thing the doctors couldn't guarantee. It was fifty-fifty for a two-year extension. He'd gone downhill in such a spectacular fashion from diagnosis to last-ditch chemo, three months felt like a year.'

'Fucking hell, Flo. I'm in awe of what you've been through. Every emotion has literally torn through me and I know it's not over yet. Sorry, I need a Jammy Dodger, don't take this as I'm sitting at the cinema having a jolly, this one inside is holding me to ransom for biscuits. It's the Dodgers or me puking in that bush.'

'Eat the Dodgers!' Florence watched Rowena crunch down a biscuit in two bites, ready with the second one. 'We had just over a week before the chemo began, I'd taken some leave and that was the best week of all. I drove us over here, we couldn't stay the night because it was so cold and I was terrified of him having a seizure and an ambulance not finding us. But he managed a walk on the river path and we brought a picnic. He wanted friends round, so we had a dinner party, his brother came, it was like having the old Clinton back. He made so much effort to engage. I felt, not hopeful, but less anxious. Hopeful seemed decidedly optimistic, I'd been burned by hopeful before. I'd learned to live each day fully. We even planned his birthday for the following month, something to aim for. I bought some presents online in case I got swamped with caring for him. On his birthday he wanted just me and him in the van for the day, maybe have a bonfire on the beach, and if he did go into remission, the chance of the rescue dog we'd always wanted...'

Florence recalled the morning of the first round of chemo as if it had happened last week, not seven years ago...

26

I'LL SEE YOU ON THE OTHER SIDE

November 2016, Brighton

'I can sit with you, Macmillan said I could.' Florence beseeched Clinton who insisted on sticking to the plan he and his parents had cooked up.

'It'll be so boring. Mum's already taken the day off. You've had so much time off recently, I need you for after, when the side effects hit.'

'*If* your mum lets you stay here...'

'I've said I'm staying here and that's that – I'm a bloody grown-up!'

'OK, OK, I give up. Don't blame me if she does your head in. I was going to tap dance and do magic tricks, I've been practising my spoon bending...'

'You can wow me with them when I get home.' Clinton stood in the kitchen, sipping a strong coffee, not his usual warm lemon water post diagnosis. Florence would subsequently forensically comb over every single sign, and that one had felt glaring. But in that moment, her spidey senses had been dulled by an entire week of Clinton and Florence reliving their best bits. The rest of their morning chat was scattered with inconsequential small talk encircling the hospital visit as the clock ticked towards Florence running for the bus. The substantial weight of meatier conversations lay heavy in the air, but neither of them were in the mood. *One day at a time...*

'I have to go, or I'll miss the bus. Like it matters. I could just stay here, come with you...' Florence flung down one last attempt.

'Go! I'll be OK. Mum will do my head in, but I have you to look forward to later.' He pulled her into a hug, smelling her hair. 'I've always loved your shampoo. I used to sniff different bottles in Boots to try and work out which one it was after you said you didn't want to see me again.'

'You never told me that!' Florence pulled away to look at him, his mouth set in a despondent smile.

'I also never mentioned that you're the love of my life.' Florence looked into his brown eyes, tears forming at the edges. 'And you've had to go through a lot these last few months. I'm sorry.'

'Clinton! Don't. You're the love of my life too. I'll never love anyone like I love you. I'd do anything for you.'

'Anything?' She nodded enthusiastically and his eyes clouded over, brows bunched together in thought. 'I want you to be happy.'

'I am happy. I know that's a weird thing to say when you're about to have chemo. I wish I could do it for you. But the last week has been lovely. We can have future weeks to look forward to like that. And we've got your birthday, no party, I promise!'

He hugged her hard, almost cracking a rib, burying his head in her neck. When he tenderly kissed her on the lips, it roused memories of their first ever kiss in the Bath Arms the year before, the gateway to Florence's actual sexual awakening. She wanted him so badly, but she was about to miss the bus, not that it was the end of the world, that had already been actioned. She was equally terrified of causing a seizure...

'I love you, Bidet Girl. Don't forget, hey?' He kissed her forehead.

'I won't. I've got to go. I hope it's OK later. Think positive thoughts, the drip is sending your soldiers into battle, reclaiming ground.' She pecked him on the lips, he dropped his hands, setting her free to walk towards the door by the front bay window, light streaming in transforming the ends of her hair into an auburn halo. 'I'll see you this evening. Phyliss said I could leave early.' He smiled, but she chose not to acknowledge that it never touched his eyes. Down on the street she glanced up to their window. He stood behind the glass, already a ghost, waving until she reached the end of the road. Before she turned the corner, she blew him a kiss and he caught it, pressing it into his heart.

When she arrived at work, Phyliss had left a squidgy almond croissant in a white paper bag on her desk and a little pink Post-it note saying she was here if she needed to talk. She texted Clinton twice, but didn't get a reply for an hour, she assumed he was sleeping before his mum arrived to drive him to hospital. She had a busy morning with meetings and a report she had been putting off, but the words swam in front of her eyes. Why hadn't she caused a fuss and insisted on accompanying him? Her parents texted, Lennie asked if she wanted to meet for lunch but Flo just wanted to sit alone at her desk. At two her phone rang.

'Hi, Jen, is everything OK? Are you at the hospital?'

'We're not at the hospital. I don't have a key.'

'A key? For our flat?'

'Yes, Clinton isn't answering the bell or his phone.' The croissant tickled the base of Flo's throat. 'I'm outside in the street. I can't see his van anywhere. Can you remember where you last parked it?'

'On the other side of the square.'

'OK. Stephen's on his way, he'll be here in five minutes.'

'Maybe he's fallen asleep and didn't set an alarm?'

'When did he last text you?' Jen asked. Her breathing sounded forced, like she was holding back tears.

'A few hours ago, said he was good.'

'I texted him an hour ago, asking if he was ready, no reply, but wasn't worried, he can be rubbish at texting.'

'I'm coming now, I'll get a cab.'

After a sketchy explanation to Phyliss, Florence ran from the building, her coat flapping in her hand, her bag digging into her shoulder, dread lodged in her chest. He *could* have just fallen asleep. Or maybe he'd had a seizure and had passed out, lying on the floor in a coma, barely alive. Why hadn't she given his parents a set of keys? It had been on the to-do list. She repeatedly called Clinton's phone all the way but it rang out each time. She arrived to the sight of Stephen pressing all the bells outside the building, to no avail. The couple downstairs were either away or she just hadn't seen them for two weeks, and the basement people were at work. One of the women, Esme (was that her name?), was manager at Aldi. Florence had seen her sorting out a mess at the checkout once. They'd nodded hello and had exchanged harried smiles.

'Florence, thank God!' She'd never witnessed Stephen in a flap before. She sprung up the steps and let them into the shabby yellow communal hallway, then tackled the stairs two at a time, no mean feat, until she reached their landing.

'Stop!' Stephen called behind her. 'I should go first, just in case. Don't switch on any lights.'

'We have an induction hob and electric oven!' Florence cried, reading his mind. He let her open the door. The flat felt empty, she knew Clinton wasn't there. She walked over to the window while Jen and Stephen checked the bedroom and bathroom, opening cupboards, the wardrobe. Nothing. She looked over the square.

'He's taken the van.'

'How do you know? I didn't look earlier, Stephen arrived before I had a chance,' Jen said, joining her at the window. Florence pointed to where she had parked it at the weekend.

'He could be anywhere,' Stephen said grimly. 'Think, Stephen, think!'

'There's one place he might be,' Florence said, her fist covering her mouth. 'But it's a bit of a drive. I'm not sure he's up to managing that far on his own, he forgets where he's going sometimes.' She recalled the coffee earlier and checked the cupboard – his thermos cup was also missing and the plunger sat on the side, warmth clinging to the base where dregs of the grounds swam in brown soupy water. Florence rang Clinton's number, but it went straight to voicemail this time. She couldn't bear to listen to him asking her to leave a message. An idea niggled and she hastily swiped to the Find My app on her phone. There he was, still in her contacts as Common Dog, eighteen miles away, but that had been twenty minutes ago when he'd switched off his phone. With her heart galloping in her ears, throat, chest, she faced his parents. 'He's in Litlington, near Seaford, I found him on Find My Friends. That's his last port of call, he may have since moved. His phone's been switched off for twenty minutes.'

No one spoke as they hurtled towards Litlington along the A27, Stephen flooring it, smashing all speed limits. Florence stared out of the back passenger window, scenery shooting past her face, a blur of greenery and concrete, silently chanting in her head: *please be in time, please be in time…* Bolting through the

picturesque village of Alfriston, they got stuck behind a blue tractor. Florence stared at the back of the driver's neck, at his red and
blue checked shirt underneath his body warmer as Stephen
uncharacteristically beeped the horn, swearing, edging round,
being forced back by oncoming cars. As soon as they hit the A259,
it was a matter of ten minutes before the left-hand turn down
Litlington Road.

'Keep going past the car park. It's on the right in a bit,' Flo
instructed, her chest taut, her belly swilling with dread. How was
she able to speak levelly when all she could hear was screaming
between her ears?

They met no one coming in the opposite direction as Stephen
slowed the pace, taking into account the single-track road skirting
the edge of the forest.

'Here, there he is.' Their lay-by loomed into view. Florence
could barely see the van, Clinton had manoeuvred it into the
secluded space behind the trees. There was an unofficial opening
if you moved the bank of bushes by hand, but he must have
driven right through them. From her view in the rear of car, it
looked like he'd repositioned the broken branches, camouflaging
his forced entry.

Florence's legs refused to cooperate. Jen had already unclicked
her seat belt and was running towards the van, the engine
humming, that much Florence could hear over the pounding in
her head. Stephen switched his engine off and jumped out.
Florence knew Clinton was dead before Jen's full-throated scream
cemented the fact. In a daze, she unclipped her seat belt, opened
the door and walked towards the van, her feet sinking into the
mud from the recent rainfall. A buzzard circled above screeching
loudly before swooping into the field opposite. Stephen opened
the van's driver door and reached in to switch the engine off

before feeling Clinton's pulse. He had to hold Jen back who was clawing to join her son in his van.

'The fumes! Wait for them to disperse, there's nothing we can do now.' Jen howled in his arms, Stephen clasping her tightly as Florence approached them in a fugue state. She stood a metre away, not wanting to peer inside the van, but knowing she had to or would spend the rest of her days on this earth searching for him. The exhaust fumes were overpowering, but she imagined the trees in their sacred little hollow collectively bowing down to absorb the poison.

'How could he? How could he?' Jen wailed, her glasses skew-whiff, her thick woollen scarf trailing in a puddle. 'Iggy! Iggy!' In a sudden call to arms, Florence strode round to the passenger side and flung open the door, a cloud of fumes flooding out into the crisp forest air. Clinton sat in the driving seat wearing his favourite Route One khaki fleece and skater jeans, his head lolling forward onto his chest like a rag doll, clipped into his seat to prevent him slumping forward and hitting the horn. He looked peaceful, asleep. The hosepipe had been rigorously gaffer taped into place through the wound-up window, cream bathroom towels stuffed in the slender gap. He'd even taped up the inside of the passenger window in case a sneaky draught confounded his carefully laid out plan. Florence wafted away the last of fumes, picked up the two white envelopes on the passenger seat and climbed in next to him, grabbing his hand. Jen clamoured to join her, but Stephen gripped her, pinning her to his chest.

'Give her a minute, Jennifer.' Florence would for ever love Stephen for that gesture.

'Hello, Common Dog. B-Bidet Girl here. I... I hope... you're OK now. I love you so much.' Her heart broke, shattering into a million shards, lacerating her throat as guttural sobs wracked her body. How anyone endured such pain was an experiment she

wanted no part of. This was her life now, she had no compass and
no map to guide her elsewhere. She wanted to remain in the van
for the rest of time, holding his hand, even though he was cold
and had slipped off somewhere she couldn't follow. The next step
was too much to bear. She glanced up through the windscreen
and an Admiral butterfly settled on the left wiper. She'd never
seen a butterfly in November before.

27

THE LAY-BY

May 2023, West Dean

Florence shivered despite the sun scorching the leafy canopy above, silently weeping while Rowena blew her nose on an endless supply of tissues secreted away in her mum-in-waiting bag, her face blotchy from crying.

'Oh, Flo...' was all she could mumble. 'Hideous.' She shuffled over on her bum and cradled Florence in her arms as best she could, the bump hindering her efforts, thrusting tissues in her friend's face.

'Thank you,' Florence gasped, wiping her cheeks. 'It *was* hideous.'

'No wonder.' Rowena dropped her arms from Flo's shoulders, the angle ungainly.

'No wonder what?' Florence balled the used tissues into one giant blob.

'No wonder you don't want to visit the lay-by. I can't imagine what it must have been like for you and his parents. So utterly tragic...'

'I know. I've never allowed myself to think about it, until now. That's the first time I've acknowledged it out loud.'

'Not even to your parents?'

'No one.' Florence twisted a rogue tissue into a spiral, ramming it into the centre of the pile. 'In therapy I couldn't mention the lay-by without having a complete out-of-body experience. The therapist was great, but I escaped abroad before I could unpick it, thought being somewhere else would help. And it did. But it's meant that Clinton's... ending is still very much there.' She tapped her forehead. 'I need to absorb it, I guess.'

'How do you feel now?' Rowena sipped from her water bottle, offering some to Florence who gratefully took a swig.

'Spent. Hollow. Sad. But I'm alive. I think being here with you in Friston Forest while I offloaded was probably why I was able to do it. You're part of it.'

Rowena nodded. 'I think I know what you mean... It feels obvious now, but I reckon I felt so strongly about Clinton, apart from him being a total babe, because of his fierce connection to you. My spidey senses got confused; I thought he *was* you...'

'That sounds about right.' Florence looked tentatively around the graveyard, as if road-testing her new-found freedom. She'd managed to spit out what had been driven into her heart for seven years, and survived. She'd not been slammed out of her body, she had been present the entire time, and Rowena had remained her faithful friend, not morphed into a hallucinogenic grotesque monster or a futuristic robot which had been past experiences whenever seriously triggered. Maybe she was finally ready...

Florence jumped up and extended her hand down to Rowena.

'Where we off to?' she asked, allowing Flo to hoist her to her feet.

'Finishing the treasure hunt.'

Rowena raised her eyebrows then smiled. 'You sure?'

'Yes. No. Maybe a ninety-five per cent yes. You're here, it'll be OK. You up for a bit more walking? It's almost a full circle back to the road where the car park is.'

'Full circle is good with me.'

Wandering along behind All Saints church they circumnavigated the back of the village towards the aptly named The Lane, this time sauntering past the opposite end of the duckpond, under the weeping willow languidly draped over the water before re-joining Litlington Road, marshalled either side by towering clouds of cow parsley.

'Are you sure you're up for this. It's a bit of a trek?'

'Listen, I would say. How is this going to be any worse than squeezing a watermelon out of my mum hole?'

'Touché.' Florence laughed, same old Rowena, always over-stepping the mark. Strolling in companionable silence amidst melodious birdsong, several red kites soaring overhead, stonechats and other thrushes dive-bombing hedges beside them, Florence marvelled at how the mere thought of the lay-by usually spun her into a horror-steeped vortex. Her gut felt unsettled, like she'd eaten something unpalatable, yet her feet carried on striding. Reaching the second bend with the sun directly in their eyes, Rowena slowing slightly, out of breath, Florence steeled herself. 'It's down here on the left.'

'You OK?' Rowena checked.

'I'm not sure what I am. It's just a place.'

'No, it's not just a place,' Rowena reminded her. 'You're allowed to feel whatever you feel. But I agree letting something have a hold over you is giving it all the power. You need to take it back. Maybe step out of the trauma and look at it objectively – time allows that.'

They reached the tip of the lay-by where the hedge bled back into the untamed woodland, allowing cars to pass on the single-track road. But behind the manmade lay-by a hollow space was concealed by easily parted hawthorn bushes. A bunch of flowers had been tied to a branch with a single red ribbon, a note protected by a see-through plastic bag. It had been almost six months since the anniversary of Clinton's death on 17 November. Florence had consistently made sure to be abroad when it swung around. She moved towards the flowers, now fossilised and rotten, pink carnations the hardiest of the funeral bunch. The note was legible through the plastic, written in sloping black script on a plain card, edged in gold. She ran her fingers over it.

Darling Iggy

We miss you more than life itself. We think about you every day. You will always be in our hearts. Forever yours until we meet again.

All our love Mum and Dad xxxx

'They must come every year.' Rowena stated the obvious. 'Do you keep in touch?'

'No. The last time I saw them was at the funeral. They were his next of kin, so they organised it all. I was in no fit state to do anything though they did ask me. I just about turned up. I can't remember anything about it, other than Mum and Dad had to hold me up between them. They called him Ignatius throughout the whole thing; it felt like they weren't even talking about him. They rang me for a few months after, but I never rang back. They might have sent some letters too, I can't really remember, blocked it out. I think it was best for everyone we just, you know, didn't bother pretending...'

Rowena frowned as Florence tugged at the bushes, pushing

past the sharp twigs and foliage, anticipating a flashback, so one obliged: the van's engine running, Clinton asleep in the front, Jen screaming. Standing in the clearing, Florence breathed deep, allowing it all, combing the trees for solace, her feet rooted in the earth, in reality, facing the truth. The sycamore sentries shielded the tiny woodland dell from hikers and fellow wild campers. Clinton had pulled in there once to let someone pass the van on the way back from West Dean and Florence had noticed a shaft of sunlight flooding the glade just before he drove off. She had been enchanted by it and it quickly became their hideaway, their Narnia, where time stood still allowing them to jam so much life into their days.

'What's that?' Rowena asked. She'd squeezed through the hedge, scraping her arm on twigs. She pointed deeper into the treeline to a barely visible black bin bag stashed beneath a layer of purposely laid branches. Florence stepped over low-lying saplings urgently stretching towards the light in an endless battle to reach the sun. 'Flo! It might be a murder victim.' Florence shot her a look. 'Sorry. Just be careful.'

'I am being.' She gingerly lifted the damp twigs and moss-covered branches disturbing a pungent smell of rotting leaves uncovering a bin bag, a recent addition to the forest floor. The bag was carefully folded, about the size of an A4 envelope, and gaffer taped all around keeping it watertight. Florence delicately picked it up, weighing it in one hand then the other, before splitting the bin bag apart like skin. She drew out a brown A4 envelope containing *The Collected Poems, Vintage Frost*. Holding it up to Rowena she picked her way back to the clearing.

'A book? Who's that?'

'Robert Frost. Remember when we hated everything Mrs Higham was throwing at us in English? One day she pulled out *The Outsiders*, that American teen novel. We all became obsessed with the poem central to the story, "Nothing Gold Can Stay" by Robert Frost.'

Rowena sighed fondly. 'I used to love that poem. There was a really old eighties film too? We watched it, Tom Cruise was in it when he had wonky teeth! Before he went all Hollywood.'

'That poem changed things for me, that book too. I realised reading could inspire people, like the poem had for the characters in the story.' Florence brought the book up to her face and sniffed the edge of the pages, the evocative smell of books and bookshops vying for space amongst freshly cut grass and Christmas trees. The papery aroma held endless possibilities stashed between the covers, rather like a forest from whence they came. 'I haven't read a book since Clinton died...'

'You used to read all the time.'

Florence nodded. There was a smaller familiar cream envelope place-marking page 222, where the exact poem was printed, a red wax seal embossed on the flap. Even though she could recite the poem word for word, reading it on a crisp page brought tears to her eyes. Rowena grasped her arm and squeezed it.

'It was in his note, this poem. Bloody hell. How did she know?'

'Because she told you about the poem. She's the reason the poem exists in your brain, why you love reading... She *was* also clairvoyant.'

Florence furrowed her brow incredulously as she ripped open the cream envelope, retrieving a sheet of thick writing paper, Cassie's now recognisable writing scribbled across the page, a final benediction.

Dear Florence

Congratulations on completing the treasure hunt. Forgive the melodramatic methods, I blame Leo, my guide, he loves to be theatrical! Like at school, this convoluted and engaging route was sometimes the only way to get you children to take on board the business of learning, the answer being hidden in plain sight all along. I trust Nellie is behaving herself and that this letter finds you well and hopefully reconnected with an important part of yourself. Friendship is the bread of life. By the way, you gave me this book, look in the front.

With fondest love
Cassie

Florence flicked to the title page seeking her jejune inscription.

Dear Mrs Higham, thank you for being such an inspiration. I think I want to be a teacher like you when I leave school. I hope you like the book. Best wishes for the future Florence

She turned the pages to read their poem again, but something else caught her finger, a slip of paper jammed into page 105, marking the poem 'The Road Not Taken'. Florence unfolded it.

'Jesus.'

'What?' Rowena cried.

'Look!' Flo shoved the piece of paper at her friend.

'Wow, when's this from?'

'No idea, there's no date on it.'

Florence motioned for her to hand it back and scrutinised the printout from the *Guardian* Education Jobs. Circled amongst various positions was a learn on the job English teacher at a school in Hailsham not too far from Lewes.

'Do you think it's still available?' Rowena asked uncertainly.

'I doubt it – who knows how long ago Cassie or Frank planted this here.'

'You could type in the link, have a look on your phone?'

Florence shrugged, the idea of permanency digging into her embryonic composure. 'Is it time to stop running?'

Florence deeply breathed in the smell of musky woodland, a floral note carried lightly on the breeze from the nearby hedgerow reminding her of walks she and Clinton took from the glade towards the sea.

'Hmmm, maybe...' Florence muttered unconvinced, shoving the printout back inside the book.

'Do you mind taking me home?' Rowena asked leaning against a tree. 'My ankles are starting to swell and I'm worried I won't be able to get my trainers off.'

'Oh God, yes of course. Let's go.'

* * *

Florence ordered Rowena to sit barefoot on the sofa, her ankles expanding like bread dough, while she ran around getting drinks and making pesto pasta. She rather enjoyed being needed.

'The fucker!' Rowena suddenly shouted startling Florence who dropped the sieved pasta into the sink. She found her gaping at her phone in horror. 'He's sent me another text. Said he's going to contest me unless I succumb to our agreed terms. This'll drag on for years. Where does he keep getting new numbers from?'

'He'll have bought a shedload of sim cards probably.' Florence tapped her fingers along the back of the cinema chair, thinking. 'He's clever, not mentioning what the "terms" are. No proof of extortion or real threat. He's a sneaky little bugger. He needs teaching a lesson. Oh shit, your pasta, hang on...'

As she rescued the pasta, pouring boiling water over it blasting away any germs, an idea popped into her head.

You able to chat this evening? Nothing's wrong, just want to pick your brains.

She didn't have to wait long. A meme preceded a reply. A skeleton slumped on a park bench: *When you're waiting for a text back.*

Hey, long time no hear. Hope you're OK. Yeah, ring at nine. Should be able to escape for ten minutes then. X

28

THE BAND'S BACK TOGETHER

Subscribers to complementary therapies and esoteric healing believe that the human body miraculously renews its cells every seven years. Rowena knew this not to be medically correct (some organs *could* regenerate, others took a tad longer than seven years, a whole skeleton took ten years to restore itself, for example). But she was tickled by the idea she and Flo had shed their lost eight years and been reborn anew.

Whilst they made up for time wasted, Rowena noticed how Flo tended to retreat if they spent quite a few days together. In three weeks they had already developed a friendship where they read each other's mind, or spoke in unison, similar to FloRo of old. Meanwhile, Rowena had unearthed a resonating passage about soulmates in one of her spiritual books: Florence was her twin flame, they had been separated during creation in a former life and were now reunited. She ignored the inference that twin flames were usually romantic, because Rowena had yet to meet a man who could shoulder such responsibility.

Rowena had been religiously attending her single parent birthing classes in Brighton, run by a woman who used to be single, but didn't everybody? No one was born coupled up. So far, Rowena hadn't brought a birth partner along and while everyone else seemed to be palling up, Rowena couldn't bring herself to force friendship just because they were in the same boat. Even though that had been the entire point of the group in the first place.

'Will you bring a birth partner on the big day?' Petra had asked at the end of last week's class. 'I highly recommend you do, obviously it's your choice, but it's nice to have someone there for you, as a support.'

'I want to, but I haven't got round to asking. My mum offered, but she's... not right for the job.'

'You have to be comfortable with whoever you ask, that's an absolute must. Any more family members that would be any good?' She unequivocally understood that by asking her dad, she was in danger of reviving the parental cold war when things had just started to thaw. Also her dad witnessing her give birth – way too Freudian for her liking.

'I'll have a think. I've looked at doulas...'

'I'm a doula, here take my card, prices are on my website. And if you feel I'm not the one, no offence taken, I can recommend some people for you.'

* * *

Still McJobbing at Si's recruitment firm, time was careering into mid-June and Florence was, as yet, without a solid plan, having only just pinned down potential flights to Costa Rica. Things kept stalling her, primarily, Rowena. She had temporarily removed Nellie from the specialist VW website (poor Mr Harris!). It didn't mean she wasn't selling her or going travelling, she just required her services until Squodge was born, which was fairly soon.

Florence felt slightly hesitant about FloRo's reconnection. Rowena was still Rowena, the intervening years not having dulled her vibrancy and there was certainly no bitterness, how could there be? But Florence had changed considerably in the last eight years. She had turned in on herself, a kangaroo diving into its own pouch, wary of people and their motives, retreating whenever her social battery felt flat. She had learned to rely only on herself (plus her parents if she was being truthful). She'd survived the hardest seven years of her life without a best friend, surviving being the optimal word. Having refrained from extending the arm of friendship towards anyone, excluding Tariq and some women at her transient places of work, Flo had built her walls thick and high, oil poured from the battlements on those who crept too close. Until Rowena approached with her battering ram of easy presence.

She'd been out with Ro to the cinema twice and to collect a cot in Hailsham bought from Facebook Marketplace, the only way Rowena could transport it was in the back of Nellie. Helping out was a practical way of rewiring their friendship without forcing staged get-togethers or dinner where neither of them could rely on alcohol's social lubricant. Rather like lovers rekindling a romantic affair without the familiar sex and texting anxiety. After a few weeks they found themselves not where they had abruptly left off, but somewhere else. Rowena was the first person Florence texted as soon as she awoke each day.

How are you feeling? How's Squodge?

Then there was her other new friend, Mr Ogby... She'd caught him in the front garden without his toupee for the first time last week. He was wearing his uniform of perfectly pressed trousers and short-sleeved chequered shirt to scatter seeds all over his front lawn. Florence was walking back from the station after work and stopped to watch.

'Not mowing, Bob?' She tried not to stare at his shiny bald pate.

'No, Sarah suggested I turn the lawn into a wildflower meadow, better for the environment and biodiversity.'

'Wow, what a good idea. I didn't have you down as an eco-warrior.'

'It's never too late to try something new. Got me refilling the washing-up liquid and shampoo at one of those refill stations on a day trip to Brighton.' Florence bit her lips so she wouldn't laugh. *Shampoo?* She'd never seen him look so happy.

'So it's going well then? You and Sarah?' Florence was certain she detected a sudden reddening across his cheeks. She had hovered behind her bedroom blind to inspect Bob's object of affection, very different to Judy whom she remembered as being rather insipid if not kind. Sarah, in contrast, was cool and hippy-ish. Long floaty skirts and scarves, her hair scooped into a loose grey and blonde bun. Mr Ogby had fallen for someone 'alternative', his polar opposite; a woman like Cassie. Maybe she was also a psychic and she and Mr Ogby were going to run mediumship retreats from a yurt in his back garden. *Florence!*

'It is yes. I didn't think... someone like me would ever meet anyone again. Had resigned myself to the single life. She's... so much freer that I am. She suggested I got rid of Fred, be myself.'

'Fred?'

'My little hairpiece.' Now he was undeniably embarrassed. She wondered what had become of Fred, if he'd been repurposed...? Tea cosy?

'It suits you, being yourself.'

'Thank you. How about you? You've been off gallivanting in Nellie I see. Met someone special?'

'No, just a friend from way back. We've been hanging out more.' Flo had yet to tell anyone about Rowena's reappearance, wanting to keep her all to herself for a while longer.

'When are you off again on one of your big trips?'

'I don't know, Bob.'

'Thinking of staying put for a bit? You'll be wanting your stuff then?' He looked unexpectedly stricken. 'That wasn't a hint by the way – it can stay in the garage as long as you want.'

Florence sighed. 'I'll eventually have to find somewhere to live when I'm not travelling, unless I don't return, make a life abroad... But everywhere's so expensive – I'll definitely have to sell Nellie to afford a place. I don't know what to do, to be honest. Life's very much up in the air.'

'You'll work it out. Dogs of any age can learn new tricks, you know. Maybe find a permanent job?'

She'd already typed in the teaching link Cassie had earmarked, just to see, not because she wanted it. Naturally it was no longer available, however, other similar jobs were. She'd spotted one post teaching adults with learning difficulties to read, but her daily newsfeed was regularly flooded with teaching horror stories about wages, strikes, lack of funding, stress-related illness, she'd be mad to consider it. She tried to ignore the omnipotent voice that whispered *you might actually love it...*

As she walked towards her parents' front gate, her phone pinged.

How's your week? Would you be able to come round at all? I need help with something.

* * *

Florence arrived with two Co-op pizzas, one pepperoni, the other topped with mushroom. Rowena had been pacing, aware she was probably about to breach the boundaries of their incipient friendship.

'Hiya. What's wrong?' Florence asked immediately. That was the trouble with a twin flame, they *always* knew...

'Nothing, I'm fine, fine. You OK?'

Florence eyed her suspiciously. 'I'm good thanks, been busy with work, they keep making noises about me permanently climbing the greasy pole...' She shook her shoulders, rejecting the idea. 'I brought you something, wondered if you wanted it. Mum and Dad are still throwing out anything that isn't stapled to the floor. Here take these, I'll get it.' She handed over the pizzas and nipped back to Nellie, slid her door wide and picked up a tiny red wooden Windsor chair. The linseed oil stain had rubbed away on the bottom of each leg, exposing the bare wood beneath, the same wear and tear had affected the seat. She shut the front door and placed it in the hallway.

'The step from the café!' Rowena cried delighted.

'Yes, Carol's Café. I could never reach the hatch to pass you the food, so used this. It's been under the stairs for donkey's years. Mum's clearing everything out in preparation for the move. I think my aunty gave it to me for my third birthday. Best present ever!'

'Carol's Café! I was wondering about it a while back and couldn't remember what we'd called it.'

'We named it after one of the dinner ladies at Green Lane school, remember? She always used to give us extra mashed potato if you smiled nicely.'

'Yes, she had those massive glasses and wrapped tinsel round them at Christmas, like Elton John. Do you remember that year she had lights? I still don't know how she did it.' Florence nodded fondly while Rowena crouched down to inspect the chair. It was so dinky; she'd wanted her mum to get her an exact model, but she couldn't find one anywhere. She and Florence had loved it because it was a precise mini replica of a grown-up chair, like the wooden Ercol ones now sitting round Rowena's kitchen table. 'Are you sure you don't want to keep it?'

'No. I haven't got anywhere to put it. You should have it, for Squodge. She might want to play cafés one day...'

'Thank you. That means a lot...' Rowena could feel tears brewing in the corner of her eyes. 'I'll take it up to her room later.'

'You shouldn't be carrying anything.' Florence scooped it up and climbed the stairs. While she was gone, Rowena took the pizzas through to the kitchen and switched on the oven. *Just get this over with...*

'So what was the thing you needed help with?' Florence asked as she breezed into the kitchen, pulling a bag of salad out of her rucksack.

'I need to ask you something. You can say no, I won't be offended in the slightest, especially after everything, and the fact you're so squeamish.' Rowena paused. Florence glanced up from tipping the salad bag into a bowl. 'What would you think about being my birth partner?'

Florence's phone started ringing before she could formulate an answer. She looked wide-eyed from Rowena to the phone. 'I kind of want to take it, I think it's important. Sorry!'

'Get it, this can wait.'

Florence gratefully answered and walked into the living room, the low hum of chatter wound its way back into the kitchen. Rowena wrung her hands. It had been too soon, she'd been right about that. The look on Flo's face had said it all. She busied herself making a salad dressing while Florence reappeared in the doorway.

'Look, I'm sorry about asking you such an enormous thing, just say no, it's fine. We've only just started being friends again. It might be a bit much witnessing me birth a—'

'Stop! Will you let me speak?' Rowena nodded obediently. 'Before we discuss birth partners, I've got some news. I know where Jake lives.' Now it was Rowena's turn to be speechless. 'Jake – Squodge's father.'

'I know who Jake is. How do you know where he lives?'

'I asked Tariq. He used to be a private investigator.'

'What? Tariq? Quiet as a mouse, Tariq?' She raised her eyebrows and started nodding. 'Yeah, I guess I can imagine that, sneaking around spying on people.'

'Oi! It's not like that. It was his job and they were mostly people pulling a fast one.'

'Why did you do that?'

'Cos Jake needs frightening off so he'll leave you and Squodge alone. If you're up for it, that is...'

'As long as it isn't illegal...' Rowena's already compromised tummy turned at the thought of her future dealings with him.

'He's tried to extort money out of you, he hasn't got a leg to stand on.'

'OK. I can't be seen to be mixed up in anything dodgy, the school might fire me.' Rowena squeezed her hands into fists. 'But I need him *gone*...'

'I've a plan, and it doesn't involve you in any way. Tariq said he'd meet me just before closing time, hand over some info.'

'Thank you, I think.' They sat awkwardly at the table, the salad bowl between them.

'Are you sure you want me at the birth?' Florence eventually asked. 'We've only just, you know... after so long. You're not just asking me because your mum would be a right mare? You must have other friends more qualified than me to be a birth partner.'

Rowena briefly compressed her lips. 'I do have other friends, but I don't want them there. Just because you've had kids doesn't mean you'd be any good as a support. Mum did ask me if I wanted her but all I could think of was in an ideal world I'd prefer you. Anyway, she'd just boast how easy her birth was or tell me off for having an epidural and not white knuckling like she did.'

'What if there's loads of blood? You know what I'm like...' She shivered illustrating the point.

'There might be blood, but you don't have to look at any of it. Stay up by my head, giving me a pep talk. Or let me bite your hand, whatever. I can reap revenge for you crushing my fingers when we got our tattoos...'

Florence picked up her phone, looked at the screen and started typing. Rowena wasn't sure what else to say. Flo eventually stopped scrolling and glanced back up, offering her phone for Rowena to see: Florence's email inbox. She'd just opened a message from Amazon, they'd received her order of *The Modern Midwife's Guide to Pregnancy Birth and Beyond*.

'So, that's a yes?' Rowena asked, her heart tap dancing in her concertinaed ribcage.

'Yes! I need to play catch up.'

Rowena attempted to stand and hug her but Florence intercepted. 'Sit down.' Rowena air-kissed her from across the table. 'Don't worry, I'm honoured you asked me. I just needed to make sure you were doing it for the right reasons.'

'So, now you've said yes, I need you to come with me on Wednesdays after work to a birthing course. Is that OK?'

'That wasn't in the small print!'

* * *

'Don't ask me where I got this from,' Tariq said, sliding a brown A4 envelope across the table towards Florence. He picked up his lime and soda and sipped it, clearly disappointed it wasn't an ice-cold pint of IPA.

'OK, I won't...' Florence smiled appreciatively. 'Thank you. How have you been? How's wedding planning?'

'It's... interesting.' Tariq glanced round the pub, before spilling the truth. 'I literally have no say. Everything's blown up into this traditional monstrosity like something from a Bollywood extravaganza. Every person that's ever seen a photo of me or Shani has been invited; I'm not like that, was hoping for something intimate.' He cracked his knuckles. 'Anyway, I want to invite you... You could bring Rowena, now you're talking again. She'll have had the baby by then.'

'Look, I'd love to come to your wedding, and I'm sure Rowena would too, but only if it's OK.' Tariq nodded. 'Can I open it?' She tapped the envelope. They sat in the far corner of the Hope, Florence drinking a red wine, her head spinning that she'd agreed to be Rowena's birth partner. What if she fainted?

'Yes, but keep everything under the table, I can't have anyone seeing it. Uncle doesn't know I used the company name to acquire stuff. To be fair, it was my own contacts, but still, he'd go nuts. I'm doing a boiler overhaul for free for this info.'

'Thank you, Tariq.' Florence slipped a load of photos out of the envelope and flicked through them on her lap. There were pictures of Jake playing with his family in a park, two small girls about eight and four. He just looked like a normal dad who adored his kids, maybe he was. His blonde wife was smartly dressed, an expensive handbag slung over her shoulder, pregnant by the looks of it with kid number three. Further photos pictured them climbing out of a massive black Porsche SUV walking into a new-build McMansion. Additional prints of him leaving a flat on four different occasions, once with another woman, then grainy pictures of him kissing her in a restaurant.

'What an absolute sleaze,' Florence hissed under her breath. 'He's still seeing someone else *and* he's married, or partnered up.'

'That's not all,' Tariq said. 'He was sacked three months ago from his job in London. He's never worked in France – all lies. And he's not a banker. He works in sales for online security. He was fired after being caught out using his company credit card to pay for a hotel stay, possibly with Rowena, trying to pass her off as a client. Not the first time either, but he'd blagged his way out of previous accusations. This was instant dismissal. I got hold of his records, some hotel in the Cotswolds. He's currently without a job, can't find any evidence of him in employment anywhere. He's registered with some recruitment agencies – his LinkedIn profile still says he's employed by his last company, and he's seemingly lying to his wife about where he's going every day. A lot of the time he heads to that flat where the other woman presumably lives, and sometimes he gets the train to Brighton. He's a man without purpose, and a growing family. His wife doesn't work and the mortgage on that house in Steyning is massive. He's overdrawn in the joint account and the secret account he hides from his wife only has a hundred odd quid left in it. Both credit cards are maxed and the family car payments are about to default. The company repossessed his Audi when they sacked him, who knows how he explained that to his wife. He's screwed.'

Florence absorbed the shopping list of disasters. 'So, knowing what we know, he's a desperate man out to find a buffer before he defaults on literally everything in his life. Ergo, Rowena's an easy target... Tariq, I could kiss you, but I won't, just in case Shani has a private dick onto you too and we're being staked out right this second.' Tariq laughed nervously eyeing the two newcomers at the bar. 'He can't afford to live let alone take her to court! The last thing he wants is a baby, it's all empty threats. Rowena can ignore him, tell him to fuck off.'

'He's a bully, though, isn't he?' Tariq cautioned. 'He won't take the proof from her, plus it's a scary amount of stress for Rowena to deal with. He needs the evidence delivered by a figure of authority. Someone that he won't question so he'll leave her alone for good.'

'You don't think he'll just leave her alone if she tells him all this?'

'Put it this way, he's ticking all the misogynistic narcissist boxes. Say it all goes tits up and his wife leaves him takes the kids, etc., he's still got Rowena and her baby as some kind of backup family. I don't trust him not to pester her.'

'How come you're an expert on narcissists? Come across them regularly fitting boilers?'

'After a while of working for Uncle I really started noticing behavioural patterns, so read up on loads of stuff. Honestly, I came across all sorts of people like Jake; they believe their own lies and don't give a shit who they trample over to get what they want. They can't lose face and would argue the toss for eternity, rarely taking no for an answer, even when they're in the wrong, *especially* when they're wrong.'

'Wow, you've witnessed the real underbelly of life then.'

'Yeah, it wasn't all benefit fraud, there're some really shitty people out there.' He took a sip of his water, grimaced and swallowed.

'Do you want me to get you a real beer?' Florence offered.

'Nope, I'm being good, gonna stick to this no drinking until at least after the wedding.'

'Tariq! You're giving Shani the wrong impression!'

'Nah, Shani knows I drink, she does too! It's her parents.' Florence laughed. 'So, you up for being the nasty cop to my good cop with this bloke? Serve him a taste of his own medicine?'

'I can't, he's already seen me.'

'I *could* do it on my own.' Tariq cracked his knuckles thoughtfully. 'It's always better to have two of you though...'

Florence drummed her fingers on the table as someone barged their way into her subconscious. 'Hang on, I have a pretty good idea of who'd make a great bad cop... She'll have to rein herself in – she gets carried away sometimes... Could be a bit of a wild card?'

29

THE STING

'You're all set with what you have to say?' Florence instructed her sister in a low voice as they sat in Lennie's flash red Alfa Romeo opposite Jake's girlfriend's characterless eighties apartment building in Shoreham. The engine wasn't running and Florence had opened the window seeking some air.

'Yes, all good. Can you believe he's shagging this bird practically in his front garden?' Lennie said in disbelief. 'At least Rowena was a bit of a distance away.'

'I *am* here,' Rowena said darkly from her seat next to Florence. She was spending the first official day of her maternity leave on a stakeout squashed like an overloaded shopping bag in the back of Lennie's car. Of course she didn't have to come, but she'd insisted on witnessing Jake being handed his marching orders first hand. Lennie and Florence had taken annual leave for the sting, while Tariq had to reach a boiler service in Lancing by four thirty. It was two twenty-five. According to the intel, Jake usually left the flat between two thirty and three before walking to a greasy spoon – he had three alternate cafés on rotation.

'Sorry, Ro. But you know what I mean,' Lennie said, turning round. 'I guess he hides in greasy spoons because his wife wouldn't set foot in one. Bloody walking a tightrope though!'

'It's the thrill,' Rowena spat sarcastically, 'he lives for it.'

'Can we test the set-up again?' Florence requested, her palms sweating. 'But turn the volume down in case of feedback?'

Lennie switched on the tiny camera secreted inside the lid of a portable coffee cup and faced Tariq who talked in her direction while the footage streamed live on his phone in Florence's hand, recording it at the same time.

'Genius,' Rowena admired. 'No secret bitchfest is safe with that around.'

'What if he realises?' Florence mildly panicked, the weight of responsibility resting heavily. 'Calls the police?' What if Rowena got into massive trouble, if they all lost their jobs, just because she wanted to blast away the last bastion of guilt for choosing Clinton? She'd hoped that by fixing this she'd wipe out her final sliver of debt for the last eight years; FloRo would have a clean slate. The niggly worm of shame should have disintegrated on agreeing to be Ro's birth partner, yet it hadn't. It continued to thrive, only now it had been given the oxygen of attention after years of being squashed under distraction. What else did she have to do?

'He won't realise,' Tariq reassured her. 'He's the one in the wrong, not us – he wouldn't dare call the police. We're just delivering a few home truths like we're doing a GCSE Drama project. As long as we play our parts, he'll never be any the wiser. Right?' He looked round the car, gathering supporters. Florence marvelled at her friend – always the quiet ones...

'He deserves what we're dishing out,' Lennie drawled menacingly, already in character.

'Flo, I want him wiped off the face of the earth, but that *is* illegal, so this is the next best thing. I wouldn't have agreed if I thought it would backfire,' Rowena said calmly.

'Hey, look, he's leaving. Let's go,' Lennie cried excitedly. Dressed the part in one of her tailored grey trouser suits, a sober tie round her collar, auburn hair slicked back into a neat ponytail with minimal make-up bar fire-engine red lips, she made an imposing sight, pitched somewhere between Netflix ball buster cop and an underworld boss. Conversely, Tariq wore a tired suit he'd borrowed from his dad, slightly on the baggy side. Florence had suggested something a bit smarter, but Tariq had disagreed. 'It's good to look down at heel, like a proper gumshoe!'

Lennie started the engine and they followed Jake at a snail's pace. He only walked for about a hundred metres before diving into Beach Café. With the car parked discreetly on a side street, everyone tumbled out. Florence and Rowena slipped in their earpods and hid round a nearby corner within the livestream radius, while Tariq and Lennie marched purposely towards the café.

'Get some popcorn, the first act's about to begin.' Rowena clapped her hands gleefully, parking her bum on a low garden wall. Florence's armpits were drenched with foreboding; it was too late now. The screen burst into life transmitting jerky footage of the café interior as they scanned it for Jake. Once spotted, Lennie walked in front of Tariq and sat down opposite him.

'Mind if we sit here?' Lennie carefully placed the camera coffee cup in front of him on the table, cutting off the top of his head, but it didn't matter, his face was clearly in focus.

'I do mind actually, someone's meeting me.'

Tariq scraped out a chair and joined them, shoving the manila folder on the table. 'Jake Bellfield, we've got to deliver some news, so I'd keep listening if I were you.'

Jake took out his earpods and slipped them in his pocket. 'Who are you? Why are you harassing me? I don't have to take this.' He pushed back his chair and began to stand up.

'Sir, I'd sit down if I were you, or the contents of this envelope will follow you out into the street. Believe me, you don't want that,' Lennie drawled intimidatingly.

'Oh my God,' Rowena gasped. 'She's terrifying!' Florence nodded, every muscle in her body tensed.

Jake sat down slowly. 'Who are you?' he repeated, his voice tinged with bravado.

'We're from Chatti's Angels Detective Agency,' Lennie said firmly, flashing a card at him, too quickly for him to grab it.

'Oh my God, I can't believe Tariq's uncle called his agency that – why didn't we make one up?' Rowena hissed.

'He'll check it out – it needs to be real!'

Jake had the audacity to smirk, but he'd underestimated Lennie.

'What's so funny? I don't think anything about this is funny.'

She opened the folder and slid all the photos over the table.

'You can keep these, we have copies. I believe you've been telling a lot of different women a lot of different lies,' Lennie continued. 'Does your wife know about your girlfriend?'

Jake sucked in a sizeable breath.

'I believe you've been trying to extort money out of a Miss Rowena Beard with regards to the paternity of her baby. We're here to tell you, this stops now.'

'I've been doing no such thing,' Jake bluffed.

'Does your wife also know that you've been unemployed for three months and that you've not managed to find another job? That you were sacked for expenses fraud?'

'What? The fraud was unproven!' His audacity was astounding.

'We have the records, your bank account details, the name of the hotel, the straw that broke the camel's back.'

Within his silence clanging kitchen sounds competed against a crying baby and the low hum of indiscriminate chatter.

'You little bitch,' he finally said quite clearly, the quiet venom unnerving Florence. The voice of someone capable of anything.

'Please don't talk to my colleague like that.' Tariq could muster up menacing under pressure.

'So, what do you want? I haven't got any money, I can't pay you off for not telling Emma.'

'You know what we want.' Tariq took his turn. 'Leave Ms Beard alone. If you *ever* contact her again, try to gain any kind of access to her baby, we'll forward all this information to your wife. I suggest you leave that other woman you've been lying to as well, save her any further heartache. I believe you have many profiles on Tinder and across all the apps, why not delete them too? Your poor wife wouldn't want to find them, would she?'

'Are you threatening me?'

'Not at all, sir.' Tariq's obsequious tone set Flo's teeth on edge. She imagined him cracking his knuckles to hammer home the point. 'Just offering some friendly advice.'

'As an insurance policy, if you *do* happen to think it's a good idea to pester Ms Beard at any time down the line, we will send any future organisation who is stupid enough to employ you a copy of everything *and* this video footage,' Lennie snarled, rapping her blood red nails on the tabletop.

'What video footage?' Jake glanced round as if looking for a camera.

'From this meeting.' Lennie cleared her throat.

'Look, Emma's no idea we're about to go down the shitter.' Jake's tune changed, he attempted a winning smile. 'Baby number three's on the way, I don't know how I'll pay for everything. I love my wife, the girls *are* my life, I just need to find another job, that's all. We're one wage packet away from homelessness. Please don't show this to anyone. I'll never bother Rowena again. It was never meant to get this far, just a bit of a joke. You're not completely heartless, are you?'

'It's all an act,' Rowena hissed. 'Fucker.'

'A bit of a joke? You sicko,' Lennie snapped at him. 'Stick to your word, and we'll stick to ours. Make your life easier and ditch the mistress, yeah? Have a good day.' Lennie picked up the coffee camera and stood up in time with Tariq, their chairs grating against the floor.

'Hang on,' Jake said before they walked off. 'How do I know you're going to stick to this and won't try and extort money from me at a later date?'

'We're the messengers. I can't vouch for the morals of our clients and what they ultimately do with the information we dig out for them, but I can assure you, Ms Beard wants nothing from you in the future as long as you obey the rules. But if you *do* harass her, she's willing to go the whole hog and drag you through the gutter. So I would stay in your lane from now on, sir. Be on your best behaviour, you never know who's watching...' The screen turned black.

* * *

'Oh my God, you were both amazing!' Rowena practically screamed as they careered towards the huge roundabout on the outskirts of town, picking up the A27. No one had dared utter a word until they were clear of Shoreham in case Jake, or anyone else, heard or recognised them.

'I thought I was going to punch him,' Lennie said laughing

with relief. 'He's such a cock! The way he called me a bitch. I mean, I am a bitch, but only *I* can say that!'

'Thank you both so much, such a massive weight lifted off my shoulders,' Rowena said gladly. 'I'm exhausted, just watching was so stressful. I can't imagine what it was like having to engage with him.'

'I sweated through Dad's suit; I'm going to have to get it dry-cleaned.' Tariq lifted up his arms circulating air into the pits. 'I went a bit too deep fake, like someone took charge of my mouth.'

'You were so bloody cold,' Florence cried. 'Never seen that side of you before.'

'Yeah, I did get a buzz I'm ashamed to say.'

'Oh my God, me too!' Lennie fervently agreed. 'I love being a badass.'

Florence decided it was much less of a leap for her sister.

'I want to do it again. It was better than five hundred likes on the Gram.'

'You ever thought of amateur dramatics?' Tariq suggested. 'One of my cousins is into it. You get to play all sorts of characters in front of an audience. Might be right up your street?'

'Really? You don't need to have gone to drama school?' Lennie asked, her interest piqued. Florence could totally see her on stage, acting her socks off, getting her kicks in a more meaningful way.

'The clue is in the name. Amateur...' Tariq laughed.

As they left the A27 behind, Rowena silently stared out of the window.

'You OK, Ro? Glad it's over?' Florence asked.

'Yes, I'm just so utterly knackered. I think I need to have a lie down when I get home.'

'You can do whatever you want for the next month!'

After everyone had climbed out of the car on Lennie's drive, Rowena started prodding her clothes, perplexed.

'What's up?' Flo checked. 'You lost something?'

'No, my dress is a bit damp, like I've sat in a puddle. Did you spill some water in the back seat? The lid's on mine; I didn't drink any in case I needed the loo on the stakeout.'

'Where's the wet patch?'

'I think it's all on my bum. Can you see?' She twisted her head over her shoulder but her bump constricted her movement.

'Yes. Shit.' Florence's heart pressed against her ribs.

'What? It's OK, it's just water, it'll dry.'

'I think your waters have broken.'

'No! I've a whole month left,' Rowena protested. 'There's hardly anything there.' She picked at her dress, feeling the fabric.

'Your waters broke in my car?' Lennie almost screeched. 'I just had it valeted!'

'Lennie!' Florence cautioned.

'Sorry,' Lennie mumbled. 'Do you need to call an ambulance?'

'No! Christ, it'll be something else,' Rowena said irritated. 'Honestly, I probably wet myself after all the excitement.' Lennie's face paled. 'I'm kidding!'

'You need to go to the loo and see if the plug's fallen out,' Florence said calmly, while her head set adrift at the improbable thought of a futile dash in Nellie to Eastbourne hospital instead having to deliver Squodge on the hard shoulder of the A27.

'The what?' Tariq asked, a look of faint disgust on his face. 'There's a plug?'

'Yes, over the cervix, keeping everything in. It falls out before or during labour, a bloody show, like a period. It's a sign labour's about to start.'

'Ewwww, TMI!' Tariq cried, dramatically cupping his hands over his ears.

'You wait till it's your turn, you'll have to read about it *and* be there!' Florence chastised him.

'Bloody hell, Flo, you've been doing your research!' Rowena said impressed as she shuffled towards the house.

'Loo's under the stairs,' Lennie said showing Rowena where to go. 'Jesus, do you think she's in labour?'

'I don't know, I'm no expert.'

'You've read a book and been to some classes.'

'Read *half* a book,' she admitted. 'I missed the beginning part of the course so I'm cramming.'

'Flo, can you come here?' Ro called from the tiny loo. Florence hurried inside the hallway. 'I think the mucus plug's fallen out. Fuck. I'm not ready for this. We've not had a tour of the labour ward yet. I haven't even packed a bag.' Rowena sat on the toilet, head in hands. 'The house is a tip, I haven't waxed, and you've not done my back; I've a massive zit brewing.'

'It's going to be fine, I'll ring the midwife, see what she says. Come on, get your pants on!' This was exactly how not to start a labour, miles from home with waters having already broken. It was half an hour to Seaford without school traffic, even further to the Eastbourne hospital. Florence got through to a messaging service where she left a rambling voicemail only just remembering to give Rowena's number at the end. But she'd also read in the book that waters breaking can happen twenty-four hours before, so really, there was no panic...

Tariq, now in his British Gas uniform, hovered next to his van uncertain how to help while they all waited for Rowena to exit the loo. Lennie was manically spraying the back seat of the car with stain remover and soaking up the excess with a hay bale of paper towels. She hastily closed the car door on the evidence when Rowena walked onto the driveway.

'You're going to have a baby,' Tariq said, awestruck. 'Bloody hell, hope it goes OK.'

'Yes, good luck, Rowena,' Lennie said, hiding the spray bottle behind her back. 'It's been fab seeing you again. I'd love to visit once Squodge arrives.'

* * *

By the time Beach View was in sight, Rowena, now sitting on a giant TK Maxx plastic bag, was in a fair bit of discomfort, the psychic finger almost bursting in its eagerness to sound the alarm. She'd texted her parents. Obviously her mum was desperate to be involved, possibly the one and only time she volunteered to leave work, but Rowena banned her, said she would keep her updated. Dad had just asked if she was OK, and did she need anything. He couldn't wait to meet Squodge. The midwife rang as soon as they hit the A27.

'And you've no contractions yet? You're almost thirty-seven weeks, aren't you?' They agreed to swing by the house, throw things into a bag, and head to the hospital just to be safe. 'You'll probably be sent home because you're almost term, but someone will check you over.'

'Do you want a cup of tea or anything while we do the bag?' Florence asked as they pulled in behind Rowena's Polo on the driveway.

'No thanks.' Rowena wasn't mentally prepared. How had she thought she was going to cope with a baby? What if Squodge looked exactly like Jake? Why hadn't she read any of those books properly? Every time she'd sat down with the *What to Expect When You're Expecting*, she more often than not found something more interesting to do. One time she'd painted the bathroom in Aquatic Life green rather than face her rapidly incoming future. In the few weeks since Florence had been attending the group, she'd taken on board more knowledge than Rowena. Why had she chosen to have a baby on her own? Why had this seemed like such a good idea? Why Why WHY????? Her chest tightened, her belly hardened, griping pain ripped through her groin, tearing up her back like a zip, slamming into the base of her skull.

'Fucking hell.' She gripped Nellie's dashboard, her knuckles straining against her skin.

'Ro? Oh shit. OK, breathe, breathe.'

'I... can't. No breath...' Rowena's face turned puce.

She was sitting in a pond of amniotic fluid, a whole paddling pool leaking out of her. All those rosy silver-screened depictions were clearly bullshit; so far labour was a visceral feast and it hadn't even reared its ugly head, that much she was certain. As the pain receded, Rowena's chest softened and she was able to take in a lungful of air.

'If that's pre labour, then we're screwed. I want all the drugs.'

Florence helped her into the house where she waddled up the stairs and into the bathroom.

'I'm timing them,' Florence called efficiently. 'We have to get in Nellie as soon as I've got the bag ready.'

Rowena lay on the bathroom floor issuing instructions about where all required articles were stashed. The impossibly small white sleepsuits she'd found in a bulk buy on eBay, the nappies that looked more like hulking sanitary pads, her paper knickers, currently as much use as a chocolate teapot. Packing the bag had been tomorrow's job. All this prevaricating pointed to the obvious fear she'd refused to address. For months now, she'd almost pretended birth wasn't an actual event. That Squodge would miraculously materialise, announced by the Angel Gabriel, with no actual struggle into the world, but delivered from the heavens by two rosy-cheeked cherubs wrapped in muslin cloths. Or another fantasy along those lines. There would be no leaking bodily fluids, no pain, no grossness, just a sanitised bloodless burp. Two more contractions tore through her, rendering her mute, unable to catch her breath. She'd meant to practise that golden thread breathing technique when she'd been watching Netflix, but she always fell asleep, proof she wasn't qualified for this...

'I can't breathe through them,' she told Florence, panic broiling in her chest.

'Petra said to take a massive breath at the beginning of each one, use the breath to let go of the contraction, imagine it spooling out in front of you like a gold thread.' Florence made it sound so easy.

'Fuck Petra.' But she gave it a stab when the next contraction hit sooner than she'd anticipated. Annoyingly Petra was right, of course she was!

'I'm going to ring Mum, it's her day off, she might have some suggestions, and then we're going to leave.'

'I can't go anywhere.'

'We have to, the hospital's expecting us, I rang them too. Hang on...' She dialled her mum.

'Mum, yes, hi. No, no, listen, Rowena's in labour. Yes, *that* Rowena. Sorry, I meant to tell you... I know, I know. She's OK... Established? Five to three minutes.' Rowena could hear Edie's tinny voice firing off probing questions. 'She said she can't go anywhere. Ring the midwife? OK. Yes, it's number 6 Beach View Seaford. Thanks, Mum.'

As Rowena inhaled against another slaughterous contraction, Florence rang the midwife.

'She's heading right over, said most first labours last for ten hours if it's straightforward, longer if it drags out or gets complicated. So we should be OK.' Another contraction smacked into Rowena just as the previous one receded, forcing her breath out in a guttural mooing sound, her entire body rupturing simultaneously.

'There was no break with that one,' Rowena panted as it waned.

'Do you feel like pushing?' Florence asked, biting her lip, sweat glistening along it. With the hospital bag filled she was about to nip downstairs and grab some snacks to ram in there. Rowena was on all fours, a bathroom towel beneath, still in her stretchy summer dress.

'No. Where's the pre labour? It's gone from nothing to full speed in an hour and a half.'

Florence was still timing them. 'Well, we're now at five minutes since the last one. Maybe that was just some mad practice run? Like I have any idea?' She laughed nervously. 'This is the blind leading the blind. I'm going to google.' She scrolled and started reading.

'Ah, it says on the NHS website that labour can stop and start. It's probably early labour. Midwife will be here soon.'

'Bloody hell, I'm deffo having all the drugs in that case.' After half an hour of relative calm, just a few terse rumblings, Flo offered to get Rowena a Coke from the fridge.

'You're going to need some energy. Maybe think about getting trackies on for the hospital?'

As Flo went downstairs, Rowena crawled into the bedroom. Her tracksuit bottoms were in the chest of drawers. Speaking had been reduced to an out-of-body experience, Rowena just wanted to draw the curtains and climb into bed. But the idea of her amniotic fluid seeping into the mattress turned her stomach. She had fitted a protector for that exact reason, but she wasn't having a home birth. For all her fascination with alternative therapies and the spiritual world, when it came to pain, she wanted every drug they could throw at her.

Just as the gate buzzer sounded in the hallway, a tidal wave of agony unexpectedly crashed over Rowena, who barely found a second to breathe in. The birthing illuminati had the secrecy thing well and truly sewn up.

'Flo!!!!!' Rowena screamed from the bedroom floor on all fours. She missed Flo dropping her tea, the mug smashing on the kitchen floor. All she could hear was her own yelling at the impertinence of the contraction hitting without warning.

'The midwife's here. She'll be up in a sec. I left the door open.' Florence rubbed her lower back. But it wasn't the midwife...

'Get her in the bathroom,' Edie instructed once she'd run to the top of the stairs, snapping on some latex gloves. 'I'm no midwife, but I think the baby's coming sooner rather than later. Hello, Rowena, nice to see you again – you need to take your knickers off! Here, Flo, help me pull her dress up. Then ring an ambulance – have to have all bases covered.'

Rowena looked up into Edie's composed and reassuring face and did as she was told. With Rowena stationed on her hands and knees in the bathroom, Edie started running a bath. 'Let's be prepared for anything. Towels, Ro, where are they?' Rowena pointed to the airing cupboard on the landing as another gruelling contraction battered her entire body. Even her feet throbbed.

'Ambulance will be here as soon as they can, they're on the line, do you want guidance, Mum?' Florence's voice wavered.

'Yes, put them on speaker.'

'Hello, I hear you're a nurse,' the man's mollifying voice seeped out of the phone. 'Is the head crowning yet?'

'Gonna puke!' Rowena cried. Edie pulled down the hand towel and Rowena hurled into it. 'I need a poo.'

'Baby's here, bloody hell!' Edie cried. 'I can see its head. Yes, it's crowning!'

Florence knelt by Rowena's head. 'You're doing so well, Ro, Squodge is almost here. I think you have to pant – when, Mum?'

'No panting yet,' the male voice instructed. 'On the next contraction Mum needs to push.'

'Did you hear that, Ro?' Edie asked. Rowena barely nodded, sweat blinding her, Flo wiped as fast as she could. When the next one rolled over her, Ro pushed, positive a vein was going to pop somewhere. *How did women survive this? Death would be a breeze...*

'Need to be careful of tearing when the head crowns,' the voice ordered. 'Time for panting then. Nurse, you're going to have to deliver the head slowly. Check for the cord. Is she ready?'

'Next push should do it,' Edie confirmed as the gate buzzer sounded again. Flo ran downstairs to let the midwife in and scarpered back up.

Her insides were falling out, Rowena was sure of it as she juddered to a cresting standstill uncertain whether she was going to do a poo or vomit all over the floor.

'Now pant,' Edie urged.

'Helloooo?' a voice called up the stairwell.

'She's about to birth!' Florence yelled.

The thumping of feet sounded on the stairs as the midwife appeared in the bathroom doorway.

'Wow! Have you called an ambulance?'

'Yes, the handler is on the line. My mum's a nurse.'

The midwife ripped her plastic apron out of her bag and yanked on her latex gloves, stepping over Florence. Sirens echoed outside over the sound of Rowena's panting-mooing hybrid. Florence jumped up to open the gate.

'Well done, Nurse. Shall I take it from here?'

Rowena's face was buried in a clean towel, her dress bunched up over her boobs. Florence returned in no time.

'Push with the next one, I've got the head, they're almost here. And head's out! Well done, Rowena! Shoulders next.' With the final contraction, Squodge swam into the midwife's waiting hands a slippery purple seal. 'A girl!'

Florence burst into tears. 'Oh, Ro!' Rowena just sank her head further into the towel. The lunchtime excitement felt like a lifetime ago. She just wanted to sleep.

'Congratulations, everyone,' the call handler announced cheerily. 'I'll leave you to it now.'

30

ONE LAST THING

'You only have to stay another night. I'll collect you tomorrow,' Rowena's dad reassured her, sitting at the opposite side of the bed to her mum, avoiding all eye contact Just In Case. Florence must have been about twelve the last time she'd seen them in the same room. Denise oozed her usual glamour, rake thin, fully made-up, rings on all her manicured fingers (and bells on her toes), whereas Andy now resembled a yoga teacher gone to seed, the prayer beads completely at odds with the man she recognised as Rowena's incorrigible dad.

Elissa was perfect, but because she'd arrived virtually a month early, she and Ro had to remain in for a few days. It would give everyone time to stock the fridge and clean the house after the birthing bombshell.

'You were amazing, Ro,' Florence said again, leaning over to kiss her goodbye.

'Thank you for keeping me calm.' Elissa lay sleeping in her arms, a flawlessly formed cutie with rosebud lips and a head of thick dark hair, startlingly similar to Mr Ogby's retired toupee.

Florence mercifully failed to find Jake in amongst her nascent features. She hoped it remained so.

'Let me know when you're taking visitors. I can help out with anything you need, food, bedtime, whatever...' Tears overwhelmed Florence once more. How midwives didn't spend their entire lives weeping was a mystery. 'Call me!'

'I will, I promise!' Florence waved and found her way to the lifts. Lost in her own world, she stepped out from underneath the brutalist royal blue portico of the main entrance into the glaring evening sun, blinded after the low lighting in the post-natal ward, accidentally clipping someone's shoulders as she strode past.

'Sorry! I don't know what I'm doing,' she flustered.

'That's OK, Florence...'

She shaded her eyes to look at the man. Frank.

'What are *you* doing here?' she asked indignantly. 'Jesus, that came out wrong.'

'No worries.' He smiled, obviously amused.

'My friend just gave birth and my brain's shot to pieces.'

'Your friend I saw you with last month?'

'Yes! Baby came early while I was with her. She had one of those super-fast labours, I had to call an ambulance...' She became aware she was gabbling. 'Sorry... I hope everything's OK?'

'Yes, I'm just visiting Dad. He had a hernia operation yesterday. Not surprised with all the rugby and sports he's done over the years. Anyway, nothing serious, not as exciting as *Call the Midwife*!' Florence smiled. 'How have you been?'

'Surely you have inside track on that...?' Florence unconsciously dabbled with a new concept: low-level flirting.

'I don't know what you mean!' Frank laughed before glancing at his watch – an old-fashioned Timex with a worn black leather strap. Something about the classic timepiece inexplicably moved her; maybe its stalwart reliability in a continually changing world offered some comfort after such a frenetic day.

'Look, I have to go, I'm already late for visiting hour...' Frank paused. 'I don't suppose you'd like to have a catch up some time? You could tell me all about Mum when you were at school...'

What was the worst that could happen? The worst already had yet Flo was still living her life, scars and all.

'Yeah, I'd like that.'

* * *

Florence was late for work the second day in a row. She'd pretty much stopped caring, instead wishing she could spend all her free time with Rowena and Elissa. She'd ignored all the emails cluttering up her inbox, reminding her about flights to Costa Rica, about surfing hostels, about rainforest tours, sloth sanctuaries... She'd stayed over two evenings that week already, assisting with night feeds like an old pro. Unperturbed by Elissa screaming, she just cradled her, rocking her till she stopped, then dream-fed her with a bottle of Rowena's expressed breast milk. That tiny little girl had already muscled her way into her heart, yet the almost intangible sliver of shame remained clinging to the pit of her stomach, grumbling every morning on waking. *What had she missed?* Something wasn't right. She wondered if it was because she'd still not booked her ticket to Costa Rica and thus not offered Nellie to Mr Harris, who still texted every now and then for a progress report, ever hopeful. Going away would mean leaving Rowena and Elissa... and there was still the small concern of somewhere to live on her return.

'I don't know what I'd do without you, Flo,' Rowena iterated on a weekly basis. 'You're such a good aunty. Elissa loves you already. So do I. I wish we could take back the wilderness years.'

'We are exactly where we are meant to be,' Florence sagely replied.

'Are you saying you believe in fate and the universe?' Rowena gasped in ersatz shock. 'Everything happens for a reason?'

'No, I'm just saying maybe we were supposed to take a break so we could experience all the other stuff. Maybe if I'd been in your life you wouldn't have met Jake the snake ergo no Elissa.'

'Ergo!' Rowena had laughed. 'That should be Elissa's middle name!'

Dashing for the train, her bag banging against her leg, Mr Ogby called Flo from his front garden. 'Florence! Florence! Have you a minute?'

She was about to shout no, but he appeared to be genuinely thrilled about something. Sod work, she was going to leave at some point...

'Yes, Bob, what is it?' She ground to halt just after his gate.

'Just wanted to run something by you.' He paused dramatically. 'Sarah and I are moving in together.'

'Oh, congratulations!' She wanted to hug him.

'Thank you. She's moving in with me because she's no garden in her little flat in Lewes. Loves the idea of getting stuck in here. We're going to get a pagoda in the back. Anyway, she had a thought. She's going to let out her flat but doesn't want to go through an agent. Wondered if you would take it on a peppercorn rent, just pay the bills and a bit extra, keep it in tip-top condition?' Florence pinched her hand. 'You could even go travelling, as long as you came back every now and then. What do you think?'

That Rowena would start banging on about the universe was her first consideration. This was NOT a sign to take stock, grow roots, no matter Ro's reaction; it was pure coincidence. Wasn't it?

Mr Ogby stared at her expectantly.

* * *

The mass exodus from under the stairs had ended, however the attic was currently being stripped of all impediments, some of which had not seen the light of day for decades.

'Your mother insisted on keeping the cot for some unknown reason!' Florence's dad said when she walked in the front door after work to find it flat packed against the wall in the hallway. 'Will Rowena need it?'

'She has one, Dad. Give it to charity...' But as she walked towards the bottom of the stairs she retraced her steps. Maybe it would come in useful? 'Actually, Dad, leave it there, I might have a home for it.'

'Love, can you come in here?' her mum called from the kitchen. She sat at the small table a dark grey box file in front of her. 'I've got something you might want to keep.' Her name was printed in Sharpie upon the white label stuck to the thick spine. She'd never seen the box before.

'What is it?'

Her mum hesitated, closing her eyes whilst taking a breath. 'Clinton's parents' letters.'

'I threw them in the bin. Why did you keep them?'

'Because I thought you might need them one day.' She tentatively pushed the box towards Florence as if it were a bomb. 'It's up to you what you do with them, but there's other things in there that they wanted you to have, but again, we couldn't get you to look at anything, let alone talk about it...'

'Why now?' The unshakable shame unstrung itself from its ballast.

'It feels like the right time. And we're moving soon, it's your box. It was in the attic with a whole load of stuff we're getting rid of. No idea why any of it's up there. Old kettles, a broken iron and a record player with no arm – your dad and his dreams of fixing everything. Pointless.'

Memories Florence had obscured with indifference, with exotic destinations and elated anticipation of outrunning her pain came crashing down while her mum carefully monitored her reaction from her seat at the table. At the time, she'd screamed at Edie for opening one of the letters she'd angrily discarded in the recycling. 'I'll never read them, they never liked me anyway!' That outburst had slipped from her mind, like a needless lie. But as she flipped open the box file, it was like witnessing the memory for the first time. Inside were eight envelopes, all unopened some clearly holding photographs, others a uniform letter size. There were several Jiffy bags, none of which had her address on. She lifted one up and looked at her mum.

'Jen hand delivered them. You threw that one across your bedroom. I never looked to see what it was, but I'm sure it wasn't breakable.'

Florence was sideswiped by a memory of hanging at the top of the stairs like a small child, too scared to see who was at the front door. She couldn't bear other people while she was subsumed with intractable grief. Her mum had tiptoed into her room to let her know Jen was downstairs, with something for her, but Florence had refused to take the parcel, let alone see her. Anger had been a common denominator in most interactions whenever Clinton's parents were mentioned. She felt ostracised by her own misery, how was she able to witness another's? And how were his parents able to live life like he was still alive? Her whole word had ended...

Florence sank into a chair at the kitchen table, tears streaming down her face.

'I was awful...' Edie pushed back her chair and sat next to her daughter. 'I didn't care they'd lost a son, I was so self-absorbed, everything was about my pain, my loss.'

'You weren't awful, love, you were just grieving. Anger's one of the stages. And boy were you angry!' Florence smiled weakly. 'Do you want me to stay while you open anything, or you'll do that on your own?'

'I'll open this... See how it goes.' She slipped her finger under the flap and tipped out the contents. A pink coral beaded bracelet slid onto the table – she had given it to Clinton, it had been one of hers. He never took it off. A T-shirt that he slept in got trapped in the flap. He'd kept it under the pillow in their bedroom. Florence brought it up to her nose and sniffed it. Any trace of his scent had been usurped by the Jiffy bag, but perhaps an underlying impression remained of the bedclothes. The letter was brief, asking her if she was coping, if she would like to come round for tea some time, have a look through Clinton's belongings, take anything she wanted. Kind, and yet she'd spurned them, many times. She spotted a New Home card loose among the letters and the Jiffy bags. She picked it up, flicking it open.

Dear Clinton and Florence,

We hope you're very happy in your new flat.

Don't forget to come and visit us any time you want. Have fun, never go to bed on an argument and always be kind to each other.

With love Mum and Dad xx

How had she thought they didn't like her? Or was it afterwards she'd thought that?

'I never told you, Flo, but me and your dad met with Stephen and Jen for tea once you disappeared abroad. They were desperate to know how you were. I don't think you ever realised how fond of you they were. It never felt like the right time to mention it because, well, you know... We couldn't utter his name, could we?' Florence shook her head sadly. 'What's changed? Rowena?'

'Maybe. I don't know. Time?' Florence ran her fingers round the edge of the grey box, feeling her way. She should disclose Mr Ogby's proposal, but remained quiet on the matter; she'd still to accept the kind offer. Something else felt more pressing, a bridge that needed crossing before considering any more best laid plans of mice and men...

* * *

Florence hovered in the road once she'd shut Nellie's door, checking her face in the wing mirror. Butterflies, wasps, peregrine falcons, in fact critters of all species currently circled in her belly. The red-bricked semi was more modest than she'd expected, but how else did downsizing work? Her parents were about to do the same. She pushed the stiff black wrought-iron gate, the loud squeaking horror film comical. She'd spray some WD40 on it before leaving. She didn't even have to ring the bell, Jen opened the door while she was halfway up the path, presumably alerted by the murderous gate hinges.

'Florence, how lovely to see you, do come in.' On the phone, Jen had briefly explained they'd moved to Littlehampton, further down the coast towards West Sussex, where Stephen was now a consultant. She had retired as exams officer and instead volunteered at the Brain Tumour Charity based in nearby Fleet.

Florence followed her into a light-filled living room where pictures of Luther and his kids decorated every available surface. Clinton was also represented, as was Florence in a gold frame with her arm round Clinton's waist, but the grandchildren stole a larger slice of the pie. Stephen stood up and enveloped Florence in a hug.

'What brings you here? You look very well, not aged at all.'

'Thank you. It's been too long and I've been doing a lot of thinking recently.' Before Florence could recite her semi-rehearsed mea culpa, Jen offered tea and a specially made banana cake.

'Clinton's favourite ever since you made it for him. Now it's our favourite.'

Florence took a slice even though she hadn't baked or eaten banana cake since Clinton's death. Sat in the Siems' living room, eating was the furthest thing from her mind, but when the caramelised wafer-thin crust yielded in one bite unveiling the softest, sweetest, buttery crumb tickled with a pinch of cinnamon, her eyes filled with tears.

'I made this for him every week until... he died.'

'Oh, Florence, I'm so sorry, I wouldn't have—'

'No, it's OK. I need to feel it, I need to talk about him, tell our story, how we were. I blocked everything out until very recently. No one was allowed to mention his name in case I freaked out. I couldn't cope, refused to cope. Refused to believe he was even dead. It wasn't healthy... This is delicious by the way!'

'Thank you, that means a lot.' Jen took a sip of tea. 'Everyone deals with death in their own way. You did what you had to...'

'I was rude and never contacted you. I'm so sorry,' she said, hands knotted on her lap. 'I didn't consider how it was for you, losing a son. I mean I did, I just couldn't hold it along with my own grief which felt so hideous. You were there when we found him; I wasn't on my own, the trauma was shared, and I acted like I had borne it all alone. But you had both shouldered it in equal measure.'

'If you've come here to ask forgiveness, there's nothing to

forgive.' Jen reached across the sofa and squeezed her hand. 'You did nothing wrong. Your reaction was your reaction. I had to throw myself into charity work, and Stephen, well, he went to a dark place.' Stephen nodded in agreement. 'As did Luther...'

'We've all had our struggles, no one comes out of something as harrowing as that without scars.' Stephen cleared his throat. 'You endured a huge amount. You were there for him twenty-four hours a day. You loved him even though he railed at you, when he was so utterly bereft with his lack of choice, with the unfairness, the side effects – I didn't have to deal with a lot of it, you did. You didn't walk away. You should be proud of that. I don't think you ever gave yourself credit for that. We will never be able to thank you enough for loving our son the way you did. You deserve all the happiness in the world, Florence. I mean that from the bottom of my heart.'

Florence's eyes spilled over and Jen hugged her shoulders.

'You're a special woman, Flo,' Stephen concluded, his voice thick with emotion. 'All those letters would have told you at the time if you'd read them. But it doesn't matter, you're hearing it now.'

After Florence spoke about reconnecting with Rowena, Elissa's dramatic birth, and Cassie's treasure hunt, and they shared their own news of becoming grandparents, moving house, life without Clinton, they took her upstairs to the back office where a few rows of shelves were solely dedicated to him. His photos were dotted all over the house, but this was just for his belongings. Not quite a shrine, but books and odd curiosities from the flat that had been his. The canvas he had made for her when they moved in together held court in the centre, surrounded by a cortege of small pottery animals that she'd bought him.

'Take anything you want, I think the canvas belongs to you. Your mum said it might be too much at the time...'

A framed photo of her and Clinton on Brighton seafront also caught her eye. She touched it. There were similar photos boxed up in Mr Ogby's garage, this should remain there. But she reclaimed the canvas and a small dog figurine. *One day...*

As they both walked her to the gate, Stephen spoke. 'Please don't leave it so long next time. It's been wonderful to see you.'

'And don't ever think we won't want to hear about a new love,' Jen assured her. 'That would be the best news of all. Clinton would want it. You know that.'

'Wow, this is Nellie?' Stephen whistled in admiration. 'She's a beaut. I hope you're keeping her.'

'I am actually.' The decision felt right. She wondered what other concrete conclusions she would come to. One thing that was certain, saying Clinton's name out loud and talking about his absence no longer crippled her, it validated his existence and her love for him which no longer felt like a tragic secret.

'Good. We sold Clinton's van, donated the profits to the Brain Tumour Charity. I think he would love that you own one, keep that free spirit alive, go on an adventure.'

Florence opened the door and scrabbled around in the glove box, withdrawing a can of WD40. 'I just need to do something before I leave...'

* * *

Nellie bombed down the A259 from Littlehampton towards Seaford in time for dinner at Rowena's as an improbable idea bubbled in the back of Florence's head. Ignoring it just fed its credibility until it formulated into a crystal-clear plan without her permission. By the time she reached Beach View, it had spawned a mind of its own and had talked her round. She hoped Rowena would like the sound of it. Elissa would have to come too of course...

As she switched off Nellie's engine on Ro's driveway, an email pinged.

So, I'm setting the ball in motion. I'm free tomorrow or the next day, or the next day, the whole time really. I believe you're very busy thinking of moving house and maybe sorting a new job. Don't ask me how I know! If you don't want to get in touch, I totally understand, but I think we might have a laugh. At the very least we can talk about Mum and her mad notions. Did you ever hear about Leo? Now there's a story.
Best wishes Frank
PS Do you like castles?

Florence smiled to herself. And clicked reply.

Dear Frank,
As it happens, I do like castles. Where did you have in mind to meet?

The front door of 6 Beach View opened and Rowena stood on the front doorstep with Elissa in her arms.

'What you grinning about?'

EPILOGUE
NOTHING GOLD CAN STAY

September 2023, Hastings

It was windy at the top of the funicular railway; Florence pushed
Elissa's buggy into a gust. It had been a week since Tariq's glamorous wedding which had turned into a riotous affair at the Grand
Hotel, a mainstay of Brighton's Victorian seafront. Florence had
felt safely hidden among the thousand or so guests, Rowena and
Elissa (in an adorable lemon-yellow tulle dress) faithfully by her
side. She'd shaken hands with a surprisingly puckish Shani in the
official line-up pre-empting the incredible wedding feast in the
main ballroom, her golden embellished eyes glazed over from the
effort of remembering so many names.

'Wow, Tariq's married Audrey Hepburn, look at her!' Rowena
whispered in Flo's ear before they shuffled up to meet her. 'You
never stood a chance.' Florence elbowed her in the ribs, giggles
ricocheting into a more acceptable coughing fit.

'Well done, Tariq, she's a real a catch. I hope you're both really happy,' Florence had said snatching a moment with him at the buffet as they reached for the jewel in the wedding banquet's crown – the lamb biryani.

'Thanks, Flo,' he whispered. 'She's actually already pregnant, so fingers crossed it all goes well.' Flo had joyfully squeezed his hand, wishing she could hug him instead. There would be time for that once the baby arrived.

Rowena lifted Elissa out of her pushchair once they reached the café. She smiled at her mum as the warm breeze lifted her tufty hair in one solid flap. Rowena laughed.

'She definitely needs a nappy change,' Rowena sighed, sniffing her bum through the sleepsuit.

'Do you want me to do it?' Florence offered.

'No, it's OK, you go and find your spot, we'll come and join you.'

Florence ambled towards the top of the cliffs away from the castle ruins. The buggy bounced over the tufty grass, the bottle of fizz taking a battering in the net carrier below. She had thought about doing this on top of the Seven Sisters, but that was near where Clinton had died. It needed to be a place that pertained to a new beginning as well as remembrance. Also a location that knitted together her and Rowena's Great British Castle Tour. Hastings had been where Clinton had told her he loved her for the first time. Perfect.

'Mum had wanted to drive Nellie to all the castles in the British Isles; it was going to be her grand tour,' Frank explained when he and Florence initially met up. 'She'd never really visited any apart from locally; Sussex does have its fair share. She loved the idea of the detailed history, all those untapped ghosts!' They had met at Lewes Castle on an overcast Saturday, the first Motte and Bailey fort built after the invasion of William the Conqueror in 1066. Florence had visited on a school trip once, though not with Mrs Higham. Frank had bought them fish and chips from a shop further down the hill and they ate them in the walled garden, formerly the Bailey, where the animals would have roamed, the sharp vinegar stinging Florence's nose. The spectacular views over Lewes from the top of the first tower reminded her of a camera obscura, the entire town laid out before them like a model village.

'You must really miss her...' Frank nodded, stoically pursing his lips. 'You may find this weird, though maybe not all things considered, Rowena and I are undertaking a bit of a grand tour ourselves. Though we haven't planned it yet. We're starting in September once Elissa's had all her jabs. Driving Nellie around I realised I've never been a tourist in my own country. There's so much to look at here if you have the time. And time is what I do have. We're just going to go for six weeks before it gets too cold.'

'And work don't mind?'

'I'm temping, but I have ideas for when I get back, your mum helped with that...'

'Where are you going?' Frank shaded his eyes as the sun finally showed its face from behind a grey cloud, blue sky beckoning beyond.

'Well, I'm liking the idea of using the castles as pinpoints.' Florence screwed up her greasy fish paper, gathering Frank's too and ramming it all into the white plastic bag.

'See, Mum's got in your head! I told you, she's here, there and everywhere. Just like Leo...'

'Tell me about Leo. Not that I believe in ANY of that ghostly gaseous exchange!'

'I will, as long as you promise to send me postcards from every castle you visit.'

'It's a deal.'

'This looks a good spot,' Rowena agreed when she found Flo

gazing down from the cliffs onto Hastings town, past the amuse-
ments and mini railway, out across the patchy sea. No pencil line
of France visible that afternoon, the haze blurring the horizon like
an artist's eraser.

'Do you think anyone will stop me from lighting this?'
Florence asked, concerned by the threat of numerous No Barbe-
cues signs pinned on trees and by the small café.

'If we sit down and do it quickly no one will notice.' Elissa
sucked her entire hand as if it were the tastiest of morsels. 'I think
she's teething.'

Florence kissed her head and whipped her hair away before
Elissa grabbed it (she'd been caught out before) and tried to shove
that in her mouth too.

Flo had actually rung Tracey and asked if they could stop by
on their trip. She had been delighted, and promised to show them
round Berkhamsted Castle, another Norman construct, and said
they could park up on her drive and have use of hot water, toilets,
whatever they needed. 'I love that you're finishing what Cassie
started, on so many levels,' she'd said down the phone. 'I'm also
greatly looking forward to meeting Rowena and Elissa. It sounds
like you're going to have a wonderful adventure, just like Cassie
wanted to.'

Florence slipped her hand inside her rucksack and drew out
the dog-eared envelope.

'You're sure about this?' Rowena asked for the millionth time.

'Yes. Never been more sure. I don't think it's healthy to keep
your boyfriend's suicide note. I'm not going to use it as a book-
mark, or put it in a frame. I don't need his last words to be the
only thing I remember about him. He was a bright, caring, beautiful man who loved me and we had so much fun. He is not his
final words, as lovely as they are. I choose to remember him in
other ways...'

Florence unfolded the letter and read it one more time, silently telling Clinton that she would always love him, no matter what, even if she fell in love with another, he was the one who had opened her eyes to the beauty of romantic love. And for that, she would be forever grateful. Florence now believed she had not been running away at all, but in fact running towards life, by a more convoluted route. Full circle once more. Rowena handed her the lighter and she lit a corner, holding on to the paper for as long as she could before letting go, the flames fanned by the breeze, carried up into the air like a feather, the last burst of heat charring the words, grey ash falling like snow until only a slither remained. It fluttered onto grass in front of Rowena, its scorched edges still glowing.

'Oh my God, look!' Rowena pointed at the seven words still visible on the scrap of paper. 'If you don't believe in signs now, I'm going to punch you.'

Florence gingerly picked it up and smiled at Rowena's astonished face. 'We'll see...'

Dear Bidet Girl

This is one of the hardest letters I have ever had to write. There's too much to say and not enough time to tell you every single thing going round my head, so forgive my rambling. I feel so lucky to have met you because you are the kindest, most amazing person. The way you have dealt with the last few months has been so selfless and full of love for me. I need you to know that I am madly in love with you, in case you hadn't realised! You overtook Jessica Taylor from Year Six as the love of my life pretty much straight away. You beat everyone. I wanted to grow old with you, have children with you, build a life, adopt our dog, explore the world, but instead the world has become small and life short. Since we met, the time we have spent together has been the happiest I can remember. You've even made this whole hideous experience bearable, especially the last week, but I'm afraid I just can't carry on any more. Euthanasia should be legal and it's a crime that it isn't. Dogs are put out of their misery – no creature should have to endure the humiliation and torture of a long and painful drawn-out death. This is why I chose to slip quietly away, fall asleep in our spot among the trees where we've had some special nights star gazing and drinking wine. This feels the least traumatic way I could think of that was a guaranteed success. I'm so sorry if you find me, but as far as I can tell, it won't be grisly, so your squeamishness shouldn't get all fired up. See – I've thought of everything. I realise I'm being selfish, but life's become intolerable – chemo was never a guarantee. I want to live, not just exist in constant pain, drugged into oblivion. I hope you understand one day. I've eaten a Cadbury's Wholenut bar, had three cups of coffee. Right now, I'm OK, ready for what happens next. I'm too exhausted to be frightened but if I believed in the afterlife, I know I'd miss you there. Any kind of life without you just feels wrong. Hopefully all the talk of ghosts is true and I can haunt you, be so annoying that you get over this a bit quicker! Kiss Toffee and Bramble for me, tell them I'm sorry. But most of all I'm sorry to you, the beautiful person who when I first met them recited poetry even though she couldn't see straight. That poem is why I'm here now, 'Nothing Gold Can Stay'. That night is burned into my brain for ever. How could I forget the romantic morning after in the bathroom? Even now, your antics make me smile. You might hate me right this second because everything is shit, but I wish you a life of happiness and I want you to find another love. As well as being impossibly gorgeous, you have a big heart, even if it bruises easily. I love you to the moon and back, but someone else will too. This won't define *you, you're stronger than you think, Bidet Girl, I have faith in you. One last thing, ring Rowena, please.*

All my love, forever

Common Dog

Nothing Gold Can Stay

Nature's first green is gold,
Her hardest hue to hold.
Her early leaf's a flower;
But only so an hour.
Then leaf subsides to leaf.
So Eden sank to grief,
So dawn goes down to day
Nothing gold can stay.

ACKNOWLEDGMENTS

Thank you to my agent, Charlie Viney, for the constant encouragement and to Sarah Ritherdon at Boldwood for being the best editor and understanding the inside of my head. Thanks to the whole team at Boldwood who work tirelessly at magically getting our books traction and out to readers. Shout out to Sue Lamprell for keeping us on track, to Shirley Khan for her beady eyed copy-editing and to Sandra Ferguson for her proof-reading skills.

Thank you to my dad, Paul, for the flying false teeth story from a 1987 WH Smith Travel Senior Management trip to Tunisia and the subsequent visit to the hotel disco. I'm also very grateful to Kate Sansom for letting me steal her Gordon's gin production line accident as a plot device. Sadly, unlike Rowena, Kate didn't benefit from a psychic finger as a result of her injury.

Thanks to Sarah Hoggarth for filling in the gaps of my knowledge about Seaford, Brighton and the surrounding area.

Finally, thank you to Andrea Patel, who is my longest standing friend (I won't say how long, but it is decades). Your child protection and maternal rights knowledge was extremely helpful. It doesn't matter if we don't see each other for ages, when we meet up it's still the same as if you were knocking on my back door in West Kirby aged two asking if I could come out to play. Friends for ever.

MORE FROM JANET HOGGARTH

We hope you enjoyed reading *Us Two*. If you did, please leave a review.

If you'd like to gift a copy, this book is also available as an ebook, large print, hardback, digital audio download and audiobook CD.

Sign up to Janet Hoggarth's mailing list for news, competitions and updates on future books.

https://bit.ly/JanetHoggarthnews

Who Do You Think You Are Maggie Pink?, another unforgettable, life-affirming novel from Janet Hoggarth, is available to buy now:

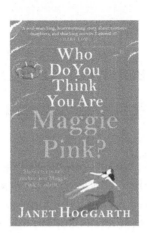

A soul-searching, heartwarming story about mothers, daughters, and shocking secrets I adored it!
HILARY LOW

Who
Do You
Think
You Are
Maggie
Pink?

She's just about to find out who Maggie Pink is afraid of...

JANET HOGGARTH

ABOUT THE AUTHOR

Janet Hoggarth is the number one bestselling author of *The Single Mums' Mansion* and the highly successful *Single Mums'* subsequent series. She has worked on a chicken farm, as a bookseller, a children's book editor, a children's author, and as a DJ (under the name of Whitney and Britney!). She lives with her family in East Dulwich, London.

Follow Janet on social media:

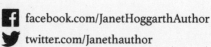

facebook.com/JanetHoggarthAuthor

twitter.com/Janethauthor

instagram.com/janet_hoggarth_author

Boldwood

Boldwood Books is an award-winning fiction publishing company seeking out the best stories from around the world.

Find out more at www.boldwoodbooks.com

Join our reader community for brilliant books, competitions and offers!

Follow us
@BoldwoodBooks
@BookandTonic

Sign up to our weekly deals newsletter

https://bit.ly/BoldwoodBNewsletter